MW01254873

To Catch a Magic Thief

A Magic Collectors Novel

E.J. Kitchens

Catherine,
Enjoy the adventure!
E.J. Kitchens

Brier Road Press

Cover Design by Levierre at 99designs
Magic Collectors Logo by Ammonia Book Covers
Edited by Janeen Ippolito

To Catch a Magic Thief / E.J. Kitchens — 1st ed.
ISBN-13: 978-0-9993509-2-8

To Forest Lake Baptist Church, my other family,
And especially to Kyle and Debbie,
For all your love, your kindness,
And your example of the Christian life

But thou, O LORD, art a shield for me; my glory, and the lifter up of mine head.

Psalm 3:3

For God hath not given us the spirit of fear; but of power, and of love, and of a sound mind.

2 Timothy 1:7

Prologue

In a time when the world was quiet and magic was little more than the pride and amusement of enchanters, when half-magics were hidden in legend and sorcerers were banished, rumors arose of a Magic Thief.

The Magic Thief, a fairy tale, by Charlotte James

ASHTBUL, THE EMPIRE OF CEUR, IN THE YEAR OF OUR LORD 1826
MARCEL ELLSWORTH, BARON OF CARRINGTON

OWNING ANYTHING MAGICAL *would* be illegal in this wretched country." I rubbed my hands together and blew a silver breath into the night air, then pounded on the door again. Emil Farro never left his home unattended. Yet tonight, his four-story town house appeared as uninhabited as the moon. My carriage was long out of sight, not to return for hours. I cast a glance at my traveling ring, then up the empty street, lit more by the moon's glow on the snowbanks than by inviting lamps at the neighbors' doors.

Be careful of that ring of yours, Marcel, Emil had warned. *It's illegal for a non-magic to possess anything magical in Ceur. They'd confiscate it though you are a Sonserian. And there are plenty who'd turn you in if they even suspected magic, hoping they could lay claim to the ring.*

Or profit by selling it to an unscrupulous enchanter or a sorcerer. Probably the latter, knowing the Ceurians. They'd steal anything magical from a non-magic yet give shelter to the sorcerers. Did they not know or not care that the sorcerers used the dark arts to increase their magic? Or was "the dark arts" merely a phrase to them, something from an old fairy tale detached over time from the horror the phrase should conjure?

Be that as it may, a traveling ring held this beauty: I could make it—and me—hard to catch. A glance up showed a cloud about to pass over the moon. The street-facing windows, crusted with ice, revealed no silhouettes of nosy neighbors. It was freeze or travel.

I took a step toward the door, as if someone had opened it, and twisted the ring a quarter turn about my finger. *Beside that comfy chair by the fireplace in the drawing room.* And there I stood. In the semi-dark. The chair was there, but not the cheerful blaze I'd hoped for, or the negligent host I wanted a word with.

Making use of the little glow coming through the window, I lit a candle and stoked the fire. Thankfully, my inventor-enchanter cousin kept this particular room clear of his inventions. My sudden arrival wouldn't trigger any magical protections.

Was Emil absorbed in some experiment in his laboratory and oblivious to my attempts to announce myself? Or had some incident drawn him away? For all his eccentricities, Emil was conscientious about welcoming visitors, especially those he invited. He'd learned I was traveling through Ceur on business for my estate and asked me to call on him.

A crash sounded above me, coming from the direction of Emil's laboratory. So he was home.

I hissed through my teeth. *Marcel, you've done it again. Will you never remember to slow down and read carefully?* Emil wrote his nines in a peculiar way that, at first glance, resembled eights. Today was the eighth, but the invitation must have been for the ninth. He wasn't expecting me until tomorrow.

Another crash sounded, accompanied by a muffled howl of pain. Alarmed, I snatched up the candle and hurried to Emil's workspace on the top floor.

"Emil, it's Marcel. May I come in?" I rapped on the door. It swung silently open on its own. "Hello?" I walked inside, my skin prickling at the sudden quiet.

Pale slivers of moonlight streamed through gaps in the curtains. A yellow glow radiated low over the floor some paces away. A covered lantern? Why not light the whole room?

A thief. I reached for the knife in my boot, but then stopped. A thief in a dark room full of magically protected, volatile items. Not good odds. Emil always said his inventions could take care of themselves, that he pitied the fool who tried to steal them.

Prudence won. I backed toward the door, drawing up short as my candle's light hit on a long, prone form beside a trunk I knew to be both valuable and protected by magic.

When the figure didn't move, unease and curiosity drove me closer. As I drew opposite the trunk, the man shifted onto his knees. He was too slim in the shoulders to be Emil. He raised his fist to the trunk's lock.

"No!" I pivoted toward the doorway.

A blast shook the room. The window behind me shattered. A wave of air crashed into me and swept me through the billowing curtains. As I shot out over the courtyard, a man shorter and stouter in silhouette than the long form I'd seen lumbered past the window.

A half-magic! The Magic Thief, my mind screamed as I fell.

For only a half-magic could hit the lock and not be blown away. He could manipulate the magic of the trunk's protective spell to blast me and spare himself.

I slammed into the bank, puffing up snow around me.

"Thief! Thief! There in the snow!" someone cried.

My mind went as dark as the spaces between the stars above.

Chapter 1

In conclusion, there are but two types of people in this world: those who possess the gift of magic and those who do not. The so-called half-magics are but a legend created to scare children. It is inconceivable that there should exist a people who can feel the presence of an enchanter or a sorcerer. Or any who can control and collect a spell simply by touching it. This would almost give them abilities beyond those of an enchanter or a sorcerer! It is not so. The nobleness of magic is preserved in the enchanters, the defenders of the non-magics and the vanquishers of the sorcerers. Half-magics are a legend.

Half-Magics: Only a Legend by Charles Floraison, 10th Duke of Henly

A VILLAGE INN NEAR FLORENBURG, KINGDOM OF SONSER
TWO MONTHS LATER
MARCEL ELLSWORTH, BARON OF CARRINGTON

THE INSPECTOR IN Ceur wants to question me again." I folded the letter and tapped it against the scarred wooden table of the village inn. Much of the dining room's firelight disappeared into the darkly stained wainscoting, and our candlelight into the heavy beams of the low ceiling, but there was enough light to know I wasn't misreading the missive. Much as I wished I were.

"Will we go now, my lord?" Henry's mouth pinched into its familiar line of displeasure. "You requested permission to join the Duke of Henly's mentoring season three

years ago. Backing out so late, and to visit the constabulary—"

I slapped the letter flat on the table. "No, we're not going. Now or ever. I'm not at the beck and call of a Ceurian
inspector." Nor would I give my great-uncle ammunition
to strip me of my estate and take it for himself. Being accused of the theft in Ceur had nearly done me in in that
regard—it didn't matter I'd been acquitted. Great-Uncle
Mauldin would twist a failure to attend the Duke of Henly's mentoring season into proof of my incompetence,
disinterest in the affairs of my estate, general depravity,
and whatever else he could come up with.

"Yes, my lord." Henry smiled appreciatively and returned his focus to his food.

I envied my manservant's appetite. I'd lost mine
somewhere in the course of reading the letter. If Emil
hadn't vouched for me, Inspector Olan would have
locked me up for the attempted theft even though I'd
been thrown out into the snow by the Thief. By magic.
But there were too many ears in the inn to mention that.

Magic wasn't a secret, but the affairs of enchanters and
sorcerers were, to the general populace at least. Since I
was neither an enchanter nor a wicked sorcerer, my opinion on the matter had been ignored. I was no fool when it
came to magic, but I couldn't convince them of that. Not
without revealing proof.

"I should never have risked using the ring, Henry. I
should have sought refuge with one of Emil's neighbors."

"I agree," he answered between bites. "So would your
grandfather."

Trust Henry to agree with a guilty conscience.

I slid Inspector Olan's letter back and forth across the
tabletop as the innkeeper led a tall, silver-haired man our
way, presumably showing him to the empty table behind

us. What did Olan really want from me? Other than a fake confession.

"The inspector says there's been another attempted theft," I said. "Emil set a trap for this Magic Thief but didn't catch him. What does Inspector Olan expect me to know about it? I was abed with pneumonia at Silvestris then. I'll reply and tell him he may send his questions to me, but I am continuing to Henly Manor."

The silver-haired gentleman paused abreast of our table, his keen gaze taking in the both of us.

The innkeeper hurried back to his side and looked up deferentially at the taller man. "Does Your Grace know these gentlemen? Would you prefer to eat with them?" The inquiry was accompanied by a questioning glance at me and my servant, which wasn't surprising considering Henry was a beefy fellow and I resembled a wraith, thanks to my recent, extended illness. An illness likely brought on by the time I spent unconscious in the snow and then in wet clothes answering the good inspector's questions.

"I haven't had the pleasure," the man replied. "But it would seem we are destined for the same place: Henly Manor."

I nodded.

"I hope you will forgive the liberty," he continued, "but I prefer learning names one at a time instead of three dozen at once, as will be the case at Henly." He held out his hand. I rose to shake it, surprised by the unstuffy friendliness of the high-ranking man. "Jonathan Lofton, Duke of Lofton."

His name rang a bell. Though I couldn't remember where I'd heard it, the name of Lofton was connected with admiration, and not solely honor for his rank.

"Marcel Ellsworth, Baron of Carrington." I matched his firm grasp.

He repeated my name with the air of a man committing something to memory. "I should very much like to hear something besides the rumbling of carriage wheels," he said. "Might I be so bold as to invite myself to join you? I'm an old man and can no longer bear the solitude of travel."

"It would be our pleasure."

"Your food and drink will be brought out immediately." The innkeeper glanced from the duke to our table. He startled as he noted my untouched plate of food. "Is the food not to your liking, my lord? Shall I get you something else?"

His mortified expression promptly resurrected my appetite. "No, thank you. I wanted to read my letters first. I shall commence enjoying the meal as soon as you have brought the duke his." I gave my servant a significant look.

"It's the best meal I've eaten on this trip." Henry obligingly put in with an expressive gesture at his near-empty plate. "As I've been telling Lord Ellsworth this whole time."

"Thank you, sir." The innkeeper's shoulders relaxed, and he scurried off.

"Have you been traveling long?" the Duke of Lofton asked as he sat.

"Yes, from my maternal grandfather's estate at Silvestris. I grew up there and return as often as I can."

"No wonder you're late." He smiled lazily. "I've only traveled from Gersemere and so haven't your excuse."

"Illness prevented me from leaving earlier." I had hoped my cousin Giles, who'd caught my illness, would recover in time to join me as planned, but it was not to be.

I sighed contentedly as I slipped the inspector's letter into my jacket pocket. On this trip, I'd traveled from one part of the peaceful Sonserian countryside to another. Nothing like what had happened at Emil's house in Ceur would happen here. *Stay away from enchanters*, Inspector Olan had ordered, as if I was in the habit of fleecing them of spells and magical items. Staying away shouldn't be a problem as enchanters rarely announced themselves. Yes, for the next month, I could relax and focus on the Duke of Henly's lectures.

Upon coming of age last year, I had become responsible for my late father's estate. It had potential to grow tremendously in good hands, and my father always said that if the estate flourished, the whole region would. I intended to make certain I had good hands, because Carrington desperately needed some flourishing. For too long it had withered under my great-uncle's stranglehold, his influence being strong with my paternal grandmother, who ran the estate until I became of age. Carrington was fully mine now, and he wasn't touching it again.

HENLY MANOR, ESTATE OF ALFRED FLORAISON, DUKE OF HENLY, LOCATED NEAR FLORENBURG
LADY GABRIELLA FLORAISON

The thief! If ever there was a man who tempted me to turn him into a frog, it was my brother, but we Floraisons never engage in revenge, especially not with magic. We are known for many things—beauty, wealth, wit, and poise, among others—but not revenge. Still, it was fortunate for Fred he'd made his escape to the university before we discovered the extent of this year's game.

"Fred's gone too far this time," I whispered to my younger sister as we made our way to the window in the corner of the drawing room, an empty nook in a crowded room.

"What did he take, Gabriella?" Eva smiled politely in response to a greeting from one of Papa's guests.

I nodded to the man and was relieved when he walked on by. Papa's guests fell into two categories: those who came to better themselves and their estates, and those who came for the prestige and the connections to be formed. Something about the self-satisfied way this man looked about him irked me. I decided he fell into the latter category, which, sadly, promised to be larger than usual this year.

"The scoundrel took the guide to birds I was writing and illustrating for Papa's birthday," I answered Eva.

"He what! Will you be able to finish it in time?"

"If I find it soon. I still have half a dozen sketches to paint and their information to copy." At least I'd had the forethought to hide my other manuscript. If he'd taken that ... I resisted the urge to touch the wand concealed in my skirt's pocket ... definitely a frog. And then I'd set the cats on him.

"When I find it, you mean, Gabriella?" Alexandria, my older sister, joined Eva and me beside the window.

"Don't be so cocky," I said.

Alexandria laughed and leaned against the windowsill. We turned from the crowded drawing room to look out across the gardens, hidden in darkness except for a few patches that caught the glow of the candles lighting our lower rooms.

"What did Fred take from you this year as your incentive to play his game?" I asked.

"My lute." Alexandria shrugged. "I'm not too concerned, but I'll get it back, nonetheless."

"Well," Eva whispered. "'Night with its velvet coverlet hath claimed the manor garden for its repose, spreading its blanket so none may see it in its hours of slumber.'"

She gestured toward the windowpane, rimmed in an intricate lace of frost, and continued the poem from Fred's first clue, left in place of our purloined belongings. "'And who would dare look on it? Who could catch it unawares? It flees stealthily before the lantern's light to another, more sheltered, sanctuary for its dark bower. Will no one catch it, and by slaying it, secure day's eternal reign?'"

"That would be a pity, for night has its own beauties," I said.

"Not the least of which is concealment." Eva tapped the pane, pointing to an unlit garden path, and gave Alexandria a significant look.

"Nay, little sister," Alexandria said, "for all his impishness, Fred is a protective older brother. Thus, I can safely say he did not mean for us to wander the gardens at night, especially not with all the guests here. It would hardly be proper. Didn't he warn us of a thief stealing magical items, wands even, to smuggle to the sorcerers of Ceur? Not that anyone would dare rob us, but doubtless, Fred would have taken that into account when crafting his clues."

"'Would it have taken lessons from the stars instead of the moon—'"

"'How brilliant the day would be, though clouds the sky doth conceal,'" Alexandria finished the clue. "We don't have enough information to decipher his meaning. We should wait until his next clue arrives."

Eva huffed and leaned against the windowsill, resting her chin on her palm. She gave me a sidelong glance. "What say you, Gabriella? It's Fred's last year at the university. I fear he's done something challenging to commemorate it, not to mention purloining actual valuables to stash in the tresor box."

"More likely, he's done something mischievous, like the time he hid the spell that made us speak backward in Ceurian until we found the counterspell." I could have banished him to a snowcapped peak for a year for that.

"The tresor box in the Dreydon Caves," Alexandria said. "He's not hidden anything there yet."

"He wouldn't put it there." I fingered the pendant of my necklace, my scarred index finger rubbing against the cameo. Realizing what I was doing, I flexed my fingers and laid them flat on the windowsill. *It was only a nightmare.* "The caves have been locked up since the earthquake." *It was only a nightmare caused by the trauma of the earthquake.*

"That wouldn't stop Fred," Alexandria replied. "Besides, I heard the housekeeper mention they pulled a few casks of wine from the caves last month. The main chamber appears stable, so they may start using it again. And that *is* where Fred hid it. His expression went quite calculating when the housekeeper spoke of the caves. But it would spoil the fun to simply go there. I'll solve the clues *first.*"

"His expression is always calculating. And just because you were right last year—" Eva stopped as a dance of lights reflected off the windowpane. The four corner lamps of a coach rocked on their hooks as the coach slowed to a stop in front of the house. "Not another one?"

"Two," I added drily as a second carriage bounced up the drive.

The pianoforte flared to life with the introductory strains of a popular aria, drawing our attention across the room to Aunt Helene. My father's sister and one of our nearest neighbors, she played well, impressively so, but preferred others to sing.

Uncle Bertram waited beside her to turn pages. Mama beckoned me from her station in front of the pianoforte. Her voice rang clear through the room with the opening lyrics, and I joined in as I made my way to her. The music wrapped around us, and for a time, I was lost to the beauty of it. Then shrill laughter shattered the moment.

A brief glance in the direction of the rude noise showed the reddish hair and gaunt figure of an unfamiliar young man. A latecomer—otherwise, we would have been introduced—and unmannered.

After a few songs, Mama took over as page-turner for Uncle Bertram. He and Alexandria sang a duet, and I made my way back to Eva.

"We simply must discover the tresor box," Eva whispered as the music began again. "Though Alexandria's not concerned about her lute, you want your book back and I my box of shells—before Fred returns to gloat over our failure."

"If there's any gloating this year, it will be done by me."

"Gabriella," she cajoled, "Alexandria's being a stick-in-the-mud. Papa's taken precautions against the thief, and as she says, no one would dare accost us to take our wands. It would hardly be sensible of them considering we're enchantresses. No, I'm certain Fred has hidden something in the gardens and intends for it to be seen at night. I told him we'd have it figured out by Papa's birthday celebration."

That gave us a month. How many clues would it be this time? "All right."

"What?"

Laughing at her surprise, I took her hand. "All right, I'll go on your crazy hunt tonight. These days of rain and snow and being cooped up inside with strangers make my chest tight. Besides, Fred's always hearing rumors."

Eva's eyes crinkled as she grinned. "An hour after everyone retires for the night?"

"If only we had the powers of a half-magic, we'd know exactly where the enchantment was," Eva said as we inched along the dimly lit garden lane. The moonlight, when it escaped the clouds, was not terribly helpful.

"Yes, but half-magics couldn't do this." Even if they existed. Pulling my wand from its hidden pocket in my skirt's folds, I lit the path with pale light from the wand's tip.

"Put that out."

Eva and I jumped at the gravelly voice.

A tall, thickly built man tromped up behind us, a lantern in his hand. "Do you want all the guests to know you're enchantresses?" His scowl barely showed amid the deep lines of his weather-beaten face.

Of all the impudent servants ...

"I thought you had more sense, Lady Gabriella." His reprimanding glare shifted to my younger sister. "You too, Lady Eva."

... Harvey was my favorite. Fortunately for him.

Eva huffed, but I snuffed out the wand.

"Who would be out on a cold night like this anyway?" she said.

"Other than the three of us?" Bringing his lantern closer, the middle-aged stable master inspected us both and then gave a satisfied grunt.

"We're quite warm enough, Harvey," I said with a smile at his concern.

"So I see."

"And the wand's light would look like a lantern's glow from the windows of the house."

He merely narrowed his eyes.

I changed tactics. "What brings you out tonight?"

"Your horse. Some fool put Sterling in the wrong stall. He let himself out as quietly as you please some time ago. We just noticed."

"Not again." There were drawbacks to having a brilliant horse. A twinge of panic overshadowed my annoyance, but I shook myself of the feeling. Sterling never went far.

"That horse of yours is a pooka, Gabbie Marie."

"Don't be superstitious, Harvey. I'll help you find him. When are we leaving?"

Eva gasped, but Harvey smiled smugly.

"As soon as I've saddled the horses. I expected you'd need time to bundle up for the ride."

"Well then"—my wand lit up again, the exact brightness as Harvey's lantern—"Eva and I have a few minutes to continue our own search."

Harvey looked at my wand as if tempted to hang his lantern on it. He grunted and then turned back onto the path from which he'd come.

"Really, Gabriella?" Eva said. "Let the servants find the horse."

"You know I'm the only one Sterling tolerates when he's in one of his moods, and it's too cold for him to spend the night outside."

"You and that horse. Now"—she clasped my hand and motioned for me to lead on—"what exactly are *we* looking for?"

"I thought you knew."

"Fred mentioned something about slaying the dark. No, the dark fleeing before us."

Laughing softly, I squeezed her hand. "Let us chase it then." I broke into a run.

The darkness fled before us, ever the same distance from my wand's light. Then, the darkness halted, arrested as we were by men's voices. We stood on the main path, a broad, open way paved with stone and divided into two lanes by square pools of water spaced twenty feet apart along its length. Hedges bordered the path, opening even with the pools to allow passage to the more winding trails leading farther into the gardens, out to the grounds, and to the river.

"Are you sure about this?" The baritone voice carried through the hedge from one of the paths that would intersect ours.

"Of course. My manservant saw the ladies leave."

My wand warmed with magic in my hand, but Papa would hardly approve of me bespelling the men for their insolence in following us. There were disadvantages to being considered among the most desirable women of Sonser.

I let the warmth build in the wand even as an old question assailed me: What defensive or offensive spells did I know? I could make Henly beautiful with blooming flowers in the midst of winter and light the night with my wand, but teach impudent suitors a lesson? Protect us from thieves stealing for the sorcerers?

I snuffed out my wand. Henly was perfectly safe. My family's reputation had seen to that. Some of the guests might be nuisances, but none would dare harm us. In case of emergency, I could come up with something.

"Which way?" Eva whispered. The wind toyed with the men's footsteps, sometimes bringing them from before us, sometimes from behind.

"Toward the stable," I said. "Harvey can give them a good dressing-down."

"I mean," the accomplice asked, "about what you're going to tell her?"

"Of course. Such a fervent love as mine must be expressed, and what more romantic setting than a garden at night?"

Of all the arrogant, ridiculous ...

"But you've only known her a few days."

"That makes it all the more romantic, don't you think?" responded the moonstruck suitor.

Arrogant and ridiculous were too mild for this man.

"Are you sure you want to marry the middle one?"

I gasped, but Eva giggled. Why did one's companions find unrequited love so amusing?

"The older," Moonstruck Suitor continued, "is so tall, and the younger is so, well, young." His voice was clearer now, as if coming from our path.

"I see."

"How? It's so blasted dark out here."

"It adds to the romance," Accomplice said drily.

Moonstruck heaved a sigh. "Yes, no one could equal her beauty. It was 'love at first sight.'" He chuckled. "I'm certain she'll be pleased by the reference. Females generally are. It's highly flattering to them."

Pompous, preposterous nincompoop. The man must have been too much into the wine. No one could be that foolish sober. To think I should be charmed by his professed affection!

Gripping my wand tighter, I twisted around to make certain we hadn't missed the adjoining walkway. The moon broke free from the clouds, lighting our path. A patch of inky air, like the night sky without stars, remained unlit, hovering like a suspended box in a gap between the shrubs lining the path. *Who could catch the darkness and slay it?*

Good heavens. Fred *had* hidden something in the garden. What a time to find it. I glanced at Eva, but she was focused on the cedar beyond the unnatural blackness, away from where the two men were.

"Yes, to be chosen based on beauty, height, and age, that's certainly an honor." The bite of sarcasm laced Accomplice's voice.

From the shadows ahead, beside the cedar, came a soft snort of disgust. "For a show horse."

Not another would-be suitor?

"Eek." Eva jumped, bumping into me. My foot slipped off the paving stones into the soft mulch. My wand slipped from my hand.

"Wait," I hissed as Eva tugged me forward. Wrenching my hand from her grip, I spun around, my boot slipping on the uneven stones. Unheeding, Eva ran, and I tumbled headlong, but I was snatched from my descent as if by a guardian angel. Or by a tall man with a firm grip.

"Shh," he said as he righted me, but my pounding heart refused to obey.

"She's around the corner. I'm certain I heard my fair one," exclaimed Moonstruck in a whisper that failed to be quiet. "You go around to the other side of this path and head her off."

Head her off! Was I a sheep that I should be herded? At the very least, my pursuers deserved a headache from a blinding flash of light. Straining to catch sight of my wand, I pushed away from the man who'd interrupted my fall.

He released my shoulders and twisted away for a moment, returning to my side to press the wand into my hand. Then he slipped a bulky ring onto my finger and twisted the ring a quarter turn.

"To the hidden bench beyond the cedar," he whispered.

Chapter 2

How quickly we forget! Would that it were only the non-magics who forget the horrors of the Caffin Wars and the evil of sorcery, but many among our own people, enchanters from low to high, no longer call it to mind. Is it the comfort of ease or the wish to never recall days dark with evil works: men tortured and cursed into forms neither fully animal nor fully human; families enslaved, controlled through magic, made to murder one another for the amusement of the sorcerers and for the blood needed for their heinous rituals; children tricked and bound to sorcery before they knew the truth of it. Heaven spare us should the sorcerers ever rise again, should they ever gain the wands and magical weapons needed to fight us— enchanters as weak and soft in magic as noblemen are of hand.

Editorial by the Duke of Lofton in *The Gersemere Times*, secret newspaper of the enchanters

MARCEL ELLSWORTH

W HAT LADIES?" STUFFING my hands into my pockets, I tried to make out the faces of the two men before me. *Head her off*, the shorter had said. He deserved to have his head knocked off for attempting to corner a woman.

"The ones who just passed," the shorter answered.

"Oh, the fleeing maidens. I thought by '*my lady* and her sister' you had a previously arranged meeting."

The man bristled, making his sturdy figure appear somewhat rounded. "It wasn't previously arranged, but it wouldn't have been unwelcome. They ran away because *you* startled them."

That I certainly did. "I'm terribly sorry. Shall I help you find them? This way perhaps?" I gestured to the path opposite the one by which the younger woman had fled. The two men glanced at each other.

"No. We'll retire for the night," the taller said. "Come along." He took the suitor's elbow and steered him toward the house.

"Good night, sir," the amorous fool said stiffly as they departed.

"Good night," I replied, uncertain whether to laugh or to return his scowl. But his impudence did provide one benefit: an excuse to talk with Lady Gabriella. During the duchess and Lady Gabriella's stunning performance, a little peacock of an earl had laughed loudly enough to draw attention to himself and, unfortunately, to me. He'd stood so closely and was so short that I'd been the one noticed and given disapproving looks. But fate had seen fit to give me a chance to apologize to one of the affronted singers.

Judging that the men were out of range of my voice, I walked around the cedar to the hidden bench. "Lady Gabriella?"

The bench was empty save for my ring. I stifled a sense of disappointment with a firm "Good." After slipping on my ring, I picked up the covered lantern I'd left beside the bench and returned to the path. A hovering patch of air, a cube about a foot tall, refused to be illuminated by the lantern's light. Curious. Squatting before it, I removed my gloves and felt the ground under the floating box. Muddy, unlike the mulch beside it. Light sparkled in the box, winking like moonlight on water. I stuck my hand in it. A wind, wet and bitter, whipped over my fingers, and I yanked my hand to my chest.

"Aha! I knew it. Where is she?"

I jumped up and spun around. The suitor stood before me, leaning to the left and then to the right as he peered around me. What an insufferable man. Stepping toward him in hopes he wouldn't spot the wavering thing, I crossed my arms. "Where is who?"

"The Lady Gabriella."

He was bolder than I expected, admitting to following the daughter of our host outside, and at night. He was at least fifteen or twenty years her senior. No wonder she'd been distressed. "Why ask me? You were the one stalking her."

"Stalking her?" His reply was half-angry, half-alarmed.

"You hadn't an appointment with her." I stepped forward. "Had you?"

"No ..."

"Yet you followed her here."

"It was purely a personal matter." He puffed out his chest. "What were you doing?"

"Enjoying the night air."

"Do you want pneumonia, man?"

"No." Not again. My dear aunt would be furious if she knew I was out in the damp air.

He drew up to his full height and bulk. "Well, I think it's time *you* were inside."

"I think it's time we were *both* inside." I gestured to the path back to the house, and stared at him until he started along it. I fell into step beside him.

My stomach rumbled as we walked. Perhaps what I needed, after getting this fool inside, was another meal.

The village inn was remarkably good, I'd heard, and kept late hours. With my ring, I could be there in a twist.

GABRIELLA FLORAISON

"Do you think Sterling went to the meadow outside the village?" I asked Harvey as we rode down the village lane. We'd escorted Eva back to the house without running into the suitor, or the stranger with the ring, and were now chasing after my horse.

"Yep. At least that's my first guess."

It was some minutes before he spoke again. "Are you sure you don't want me to clobber the fool who followed you into the gardens?" he asked for the third time, each time with more hope in his gruff voice.

"It's not a matter of what I want," I said with a significant smile.

He answered with a guffaw. "If you'd finish that book of yours, maybe the duke would quit these mentoring seasons."

"That will never happen. Papa loves his month of teaching, and the information's too valuable not to share—in lecture and in print. His talk on—"

"I know, lass. You've told me." A fond smile crinkled Harvey's face, and I pressed my lips together. He did know. He'd been the one to suggest I write the book covering what Papa taught during his month-long mentoring season, since Papa felt no need to write it himself. I had often transcribed Papa's lecture notes for him. I knew the material and its worth aside from familial partiality.

"Sometimes I wish he would quit it," I said. "The guests are worse than usual this year. One *laughed* during

Mama's and my duet tonight, during a stirringly beautiful aria from a tragic opera! From *La Baguette Magique Cassée*, no less! Sometimes it seems few are truly interested in what Papa has to say. Yet, interested or not, they should all have manners."

Harvey made a noise I suspected was suppressed laughter, then coughed. "The duke's no fool, lass. He wouldn't continue if not convinced even the disinterested picked up something useful whether or not they intended to. It's the gentlemen fluttering around you and your sisters that are no good—unless I say so, that is."

"I doubt you'll have anything positive to say this year."

We rode on in silence, the air invigorating in its pristine coldness but burning bitterly all the same. I was grateful for the windbreak of the woods rising on either side of the lane. The night was quiet except for the occasional hoot of an owl and the steady clop of our horses' hooves. And another horse's?

We spurred our mounts and hurried around a bend in the lane, but instead of spying Sterling, we found ourselves some fifty feet behind a small party of travelers. Harvey slowed his pace, and I reined in my borrowed horse.

"Did you send anyone else after Sterling?" I asked.

"No, and no one lives on this side of the village." He grinned a wide, wicked grin, and pulled a revolver from his belt. "Maybe I'll finally get to use this—or at least scare some miscreants with it."

"Harvey," I whispered fiercely, pulling closer to him. "You know no one has been robbed or assaulted on Henly Estate, or in the village, for three hundred years. No one would dare."

Snorting, he cocked the revolver. "Yeah, well, maybe someone forgot they were on holy Floraison ground. I, however, would be happy to remind them. Stay back in the shadows and be prepared to use that wand of yours to zap them if they prove a tougher lot than I expect. Actually, gallop away if I say *zap*. Your father would have my hide if I got you involved in anything unseemly."

"The Floraisons do *not* zap people, despite what Fred says. Or run away. This is nothing more than a group of farmers looking for a lost sheep."

He snorted again and turned his back on me. "Oi. You up there!" He rode forward, murmuring under his breath.

I guided my mount off the road onto a strip of grass. A bush snagged my skirt, and I tugged it free even as I squinted to make out the men in the moonlight. The night had swallowed me without Harvey's lantern to keep it at bay. If I was quiet, they'd never know I was there.

The men jerked around at Harvey's hail, their horses neighing in protest. Four men. One on foot and three slouching in the saddles of a couple of horses that looked like old nags compared to any Floraison mount. "Oi, you back there."

One of the riders, the one not riding double, rocked in the saddle as if struggling to sit upright. His hands were tied in front of him, and the bridle of his horse was firmly in the command of the man walking beside him.

"What have we here?" Harvey eyed the bound man.

"It's none of your concern," the walker answered.

They were a surly lot. Harvey would enjoy this.

"Anything that concerns Henly concerns me," Harvey said.

"We caught this man stealing. We're taking him to the village."

"Stealing what? You're on the Duke of Henly's lands, and I'm his man."

"The duke's land, you say?" The walker looked Harvey up and down, his gaze lingering on Harvey's revolver. "I guess we got a little lost looking for the sheep." He jerked his chin toward the bound man. "Didn't see the sheep but caught him trying to steal a fine horse wandering free in a meadow. Knew it couldn't belong to him."

"Perhaps not, but that doesn't mean he was stealing it," Harvey said. "The people hereabouts know the duke's horses and would return them."

The bound man gave his head a shake and leaned forward as if to get a better look at Harvey. A thick wool scarf encircled his mouth, whether his choice for warmth or theirs for silence, I couldn't say. His heavy, tailored coat and polished boots weren't that of a farmer or common criminal. Had one of the guests been assaulted by these doltish vigilantes?

I started forward to assert his innocence, but stopped as the unusually tall man riding double spoke. His voice was rough and its accent Ceurian. No Ceurians lived in the village or the nearby farms. "He had no intention of returning the horse. Did he boys?"

"Nope. He told us to keep away, claiming he'd found him first."

Harvey's attention followed the man's gesture to the prisoner, the uncovered moon throwing its light on the latter. Harvey's posture stiffened. "Where's the horse now?" The strain in his voice magnified my growing unease. I reached for my wand.

"Still in the meadow. Couldn't catch him."

"Yep, that horse is something else." Harvey backed his horse a step. "A real *zapper* that one." He continued to retreat, but the men were focused beyond him—on me.

They'd not caught a thief. They'd caught a ransom. And now they were looking at another. Cursed moonlight. Raising my wand, I took a fortifying breath and met the men's stares. But nothing happened. No spells of defense or offense rushed to my mind. How did one handle a situation like this?

The men crept forward, but I sat dumbfounded, my heartbeat pounding in my ears, overshadowing all useful thought. *Do something, Gabriella.*

Then something brushed against my skirts, and twigs snapped on the bush beside me. My heart jumped back into rhythm, and only the mumbled cry sounding very much like an apology kept me in place.

A man with bound hands knelt on the ground, half in the bush and half out. He raked his cheek against the bush's sharp twigs until they snagged his scarf and dragged it to his chin. I looked from him to the rider-less horse where he'd sat a moment ago. How?

"Yep, he's a real *zapper.*" Harvey gripped the lantern like a weapon in one hand, his revolver in the other.

"Is that so?" The bandit nudged his horse, and the group moved toward me.

"He might be hinting at something," the bound man said as he struggled to rise.

Of course he was. *Think, Gabriella. What to do?*

Leaning over, I grabbed his sleeve and dragged him upright. "The Floraisons do not zap people." For the first time in my life, I wished we were more like the fairytale witches of the non-magics' stories, ever ready with a curse. Cataloguing what I had to work with, I spotted the coiled rope we'd brought to help catch Sterling.

"You might want to reconsider that policy, unless you're particularly anxious to be held for ransom." He pulled a knife from his boot and sawed awkwardly at the rope around his wrists.

"I will not." The warmth of magic stole into my arm and out to my fingertips, but my wand was oddly slow to heat. Was it true what Aunt Helene always said, that a Floraison could handle any situation with confidence and poise? It would have to be.

"A Floraison can handle any situation with confidence and poise," I murmured with a firm nod.

"I hope so," the man said.

"We most certainly can." I released the reins and grabbed the coiled rope.

"Hey! Where'd he go?" A ruffian jabbed furiously at the empty saddle.

"Never mind him for now. Grab the horse and get her."

"Ride, girl!" Harvey roared, spurring his horse toward us. The commotion agitated my mount, and she reared. The stranger grabbed the reins with one hand and pressed the other against my side, steadying me.

Whispering the appropriate spell, I slung the rope with all my strength of arm and magic, and directed my wand to a sturdy tree near the men. The rope snatched up each of the scattering bandits, wrapped around their ankles and wrists, and flung itself across an overhanging limb. The ruffians flew up, feet first, toward the thick limb, spewing profanities like a bad lunch.

The man beside me sucked in a breath. "That wasn't done by magic at all," he said, his words a blend of awe and sarcasm.

"It's a favorite spell among gardeners and is quite useful for the climbing roses." In fact, that's all I'd ever used it for. Was that why my palm was painfully hot?

He dropped his hand from my back and stepped away. The hard feel of a ring against my side faded, as did the sensation of magic from my hands, which burned. An unusual pain, except when practicing the more difficult spells.

Knife in one hand and rope still clinging to his wrists, the stranger gaped at my prisoners. "I thought the Floraisons wouldn't flaunt their magic." He added softly, "*I didn't know they were a family of enchanters before I came.*"

"I think it was neatly done." Pointing to the ruffians dangling over the road like icicles over a doorway, I called out, "That's only temporary, Harvey, though the rope may hold when they fall."

"Pity." Harvey dumped the men's weapons into a pile and then cracked a couple of heads together. "Teach you to ruin Henly's reputation for peacefulness."

"My wrist is bleeding." The shocked statement came from beside me. The way the stranger stared at his wrists, one would think he'd lost both his hands.

"I've never cut myself doing that before," he said slowly, "but my cousins never tied the knots so tightly for our games either."

Surely he didn't get sick so easily? A coppery whiff assaulted my senses. A line of blood oozed along his sleeve. "Give it here."

"What?" He stared at his exposed wrist like it was in danger of falling off.

I held my hand out in front of him. "Your wrist. Hold it up."

"Oh." He shook himself and laid his wrist in my open palm.

"Not such a bad wound for a brush with bandits," I said lightly as I examined the cut in the moonlight. It wasn't a gushing wound but certainly one requiring attention.

"I suppose not," he said flatly.

Needing both hands free, I gently gripped my wand between my teeth, then fumbled for my handkerchief. Wincing on his behalf, I wrapped my handkerchief around the wound and secured it tightly.

He hissed and spat out some nonsensical phrase under his breath. "Thank you."

"You're welcome," I said around the wand.

The man flashed a half-smile before returning to his frown of concentration, as if determined to think of something other than the blood.

"I think you'll survive." I released his hand, then slipped my wand back into its pocket. "You won't even need to see the physician. The housekeeper will be happy to sew it up for you."

"Sew?" He groaned, then jumped at Harvey's booming voice.

"What's your association with those men?" Harvey led his horse, carrying a bulging bag of weapons, over to stand in front of my companion. "Do you owe them money?" he bellowed, glaring at the stranger, who'd taken a step back in alarm, nearly falling into the bush. "If you've brought your sordid dealings to Henly, I'll have the duke toss you out this night."

"Really, Harvey," I began, but I could tell by the men's facial expressions that any interruption from me would be ignored. In truth, such an explanation as Harvey's would be more agreeable—more in keeping with the tenor of Henly and its village—than bandits abducting travelers for ransom. But it wasn't polite to accuse the man so readily and so loudly.

The accused set his jaw, his injured arm falling forgotten to his side. "My association is the same you would have had in a few moments if not for the lady's intervention."

Harvey crossed his arms. "Is that so?"

They took one another's measure, and the accused's shoulders sagged. He hugged his wrist to his chest. "It was a long carriage ride to get here." His was the blank voice of a man repeating an answer voiced a hundred times before and never believed. "I wanted a long walk to make up for it. The inn serves meals until midnight, and since I've missed a lot of those in the past few months, I wanted to make up for that too. I wasn't intending on being struck on the head and abducted on my way back."

"You're staying at Henly, then?" I asked, suddenly wondering if I should have examined his head as well as his wrist.

"Yes," he and Harvey answered together.

"I visited the inn before this happened. The innkeeper can confirm my story."

"I'll have a chat with him." Harvey nodded twice, then grinned. "And get some of Anna's pie while I'm at it." Laughing, he uncrossed his arms and clapped the guest on the shoulder. The less brawny man stumbled forward, his face registering shock.

"I remember you, Marcel Ellsworth," Harvey continued. "You thanked the stableboy for taking care of your horses. I wanted to make sure my first impression of you was right."

Marcel Ellsworth? I didn't remember being introduced to an Ellsworth.

Harvey blew out a breath and slapped his hands together. "Those men had me worried for a bit, but I knew Lady Gabriella could take care of them, though I'd told her to flee." He glanced at me. "Remember that if the duke asks."

"Thank you, Harvey. I appreciate your confidence."

"I was a mite concerned myself." With a laugh, Lord Ellsworth tugged off his scarf and rubbed a hand over his face. "For a moment there, I thought I was about to be hauled back to Ceur." He glanced at me before loosely wrapping his scarf around his neck. "I can see why now," he said softly to himself.

He stepped under the light of Harvey's lantern and took off his hat, brushing a hand over his reddish hair—hair I remembered.

You. It was the Laugher. The plain, rude, late, barely-in-the-nobility Baron of Carrington. No wonder I hadn't recognized his proper name. He'd arrived during our duet and laughed so obscenely during it someone mentioned it later, saying his manners matched his rank.

Lord Ellsworth was afraid he was about to be "hauled back to Ceur," was he? That settled it. The trouble was obviously his, and Harvey and I had nearly been dragged into it.

"What did you mean someone wished to return you to Ceur?"

He quit eying his bandage and gave me a sideways glance, whether at the question or my sharp tone, I couldn't say. "Nothing."

"This sort of thing doesn't happen at Henly, you know." Neither did laughing during a performance.

He turned away to collect a lantern from the bandits' fallen items. "Which," he said as he adjusted the lantern's flame, "is exactly why it's the perfect place for enterprising young bandits to come. Lots of wealthy men known to be on their way, thinking all is peaceful." He held my gaze, which I must confess was highly critical. "May I ask what brought you and your escort out on this cold night, other than to provide timely assistance to this humble guest?"

"You may not." How dare he insinuate misconduct on my part.

"We're looking for her pooka of a horse," Harvey said with an appropriate warning edge to his voice, which the baron ignored.

"I had wondered at the magnificent creature galloping across the meadow—a creature I neither approached nor claimed as my own. Do you require help collecting him or in alerting the local authorities about these men?"

"No," I said.

"In that case, if you'll excuse me, I'll return to the manor and get this seen to." He held up his wrist, then returned his hat to his head, wincing as he did so.

"Good night, sir." *Good riddance, rude, weak-kneed, trouble-bringing baron.*

He bowed, wished us a good evening, and walked away, refusing the use of the bandit's horse.

"Don't forget to see the housekeeper about your wrist *and* your head," I dutifully called after him. He waved an acknowledgment and walked on.

My mount whinnied as I turned her head toward the village. I wouldn't be one whit surprised if Marcel Ellsworth was one of those "enterprising young bandits" himself, only of a less violent sort, come to exploit the relationships to be formed among Papa's wealthy, influential guests.

That night, I dreamed a familiar dream of an opening in the riverbank. Woodland shrubs and vines strove to conceal it, even twining around an ancient door's metal hinges with their clinging splinters of rotten wood. Still, the hint of black behind the greenery could not be hidden from me. The very air revealed the cave's gate with that peculiar odor of damp coolness belonging only to a cave. The limbs and vines lashed out, clawing at me, as if to keep me from that place. I pushed past them. Somewhere down the long, black path was a rock with jagged teeth. In a lightless chamber, the rock gleamed red. Everything in me wanted to touch it, to feel its sharp edge. To run from it. But the gleam was so inviting. Was the rock cool as cave rocks often are, or warm like the blood of a living thing? If I could but touch it … I reached for it, then awakened.

The dream always left me with a feeling of unease, but it rarely made my heart race as it did this morning. I sat up and pressed back against the headboard, willing my heart to slow. Still, the blood pounded through me, flushing my fingertips to mark each wild beat of my heart. With a sense of foreboding, I searched for the scar on the tip of my index finger. It didn't redden with the pulse of blood under my skin, nor did it stay white.

It was black.

Biting back a scream, I scrambled from my bed, holding my hand out like a bug I wanted to dispatch. I hurriedly dressed, snatched up my gloves to hide the scar, and rushed downstairs. I needed air. A long walk.

Before I realized it, I'd passed halfway through the gardens, making for the river and the old, overgrown path along it, though I couldn't say how I knew my feet would take me there. A small, persistent voice niggled at me, telling me I needed Sterling, that I shouldn't go anywhere without Sterling. Heedless, I walked on.

A stableboy came running, the din rising from the stable announcing the message he bore.

"Sterling's going berserk, my lady." He stopped before me, forcing me to halt likewise.

I stared at him, wanting to ask "What's that to me?" but knowing better. I looked toward the river path, then stepped around the boy. "Thank you for letting me know. I'm sure—"

He blocked my way. "Harvey said to fetch you. To drag you back, if need be."

"How dare—"

"Please, my lady." He held out his hand, both his fear and his determination to follow Harvey's order evident.

Something in my head cleared, and the niggling voice grew louder. "I'll come." Mustering my strength, I turned away from the river path and ran after the boy, calling to Sterling as I entered the stable. "Sterling! Be still!"

He quieted. Only the frightened whinnies of the other horses and the barks of the dogs remained.

"Get back to work," Harvey roared to the grooms. They scurried past me as I ran between the rows of stalls. He unhooked the special latch on Sterling's stall, and the giant beast shouldered his way around Harvey to face me. Sterling's eyes flashed, and he snapped at me. I jerked back, fumbling for a stall door. He lunged, snapping at my right hand.

"Sterling!" I staggered back, gasping as I hit Harvey's solid form. Sterling pressed forward, careful not to step on me but still biting at my hand.

"Be still, child." Harvey gripped my wrist and pulled off my glove. "You know you must let him."

Sterling's teeth found my scarred finger, and the pain from the bite stole away my scream. He lowered his head and nudged my hip apologetically. The haze—that drive for air and a walk to the river—dwindled to nothing but memory. I sagged against Harvey.

Even as the blood sped down my palm, Harvey let out a heavy breath and patted my shoulder. He wrapped his

handkerchief around my finger and pressed. I hissed.
How many would this make? Three rings of horse's teeth
marks and the nick at the top?

Harvey didn't say anything. I wanted him to, but at
the same time, I didn't. Turning my face away from him, I
rubbed Sterling's muzzle until he raised his head, once
more looking like the proud Pyren stallion he was.

With Sterling trotting behind, Harvey led me to a basin of water. The blood seeped away, leaving a red ring of
raw flesh around my finger and a white scar on top.
Teeth-gritted, I tugged on my gloves.

I was the only Floraison with a Pyren.

Chapter 3

There are three rules to remember when using the traveling rings: one, the ring carries but one person and no baggage; two, long trips must be broken into multiple jumps; and three, you must know where you are and where you are going. Even with these limitations, the rings are powerful and dangerous on the wrong hands. Guard them with your life.

Prince Gérard Bête of Silvestris Castle to his grandsons
Prince Giles Bête and Lord Marcel Ellsworth

MARCEL ELLSWORTH

THE PINK OF dawn was fresh in the sky and the garden path empty. The only disturbance to the morning's quiet charm was the inspector's admonition ringing in my head: *stay away from magic and those who wield it.*

I hadn't known the Floraisons were enchanters until last night, and I couldn't leave now. Great-Uncle Mauldin would use it against me. No, I was staying. And praying the inspector didn't know about the Floraisons' abilities. Besides, unless I was called on to answer questions about the attempted abduction, I wouldn't have a reason to interact with the Floraisons on a personal level, which would be a relief on both sides. Lady Gabriella's scornful look as we parted assured me of that. What was she doing in the garden and then traveling to the village at night? Going to meet someone she couldn't meet publically? A stab of pain made me grimace, but it wasn't from my cut wrist, now sewed and bandaged, or even the goose egg on the back of my head. Of all the sisters, it would have to be her.

Snagging a tiny leaf from a shrub, I redirected my thoughts. This early morning jaunt wasn't about the Floraisons. My godfather, a talented half-magic who'd often let me watch him train young enchanters, would never forgive me if I didn't investigate any unusual magic I ran across. Like that box.

I found the cedar concealing the wrought iron bench and worked backward, scanning the shrubbery. I saw no darkness, but ... there ... over the mulch between shrubs, the air shimmered. Last night the box had been dark, but today, it matched the greenery behind it. Clever. Only those looking for it would notice it.

Once again, I squatted in front of it and reached my hand into the *something*. The air in it was cool and moist, similar to that in the garden. The paving stones bordering the walk teetered. I adjusted my footing and reached further in, noting with alarm that my hand wasn't visible on the other side. Nonetheless, I scooted forward until my shoulder was inside. I felt nothing. I inched closer. The stones rocked, and I lurched forward. A tug far stronger than that of my traveling ring drew me, and I fell headlong into the shimmering box.

The mulch-covered garden disappeared, only to be replaced by a large stump, which I crashed into, landing precariously on its edge. The roar of a river echoed in my ears as I scrambled for a handhold on the stump, but my fingers closed only around a slender stick, which I dragged along with me as I tumbled off. I skidded downhill headfirst, foamy water slurping against the bank below in anticipation. I caught one of the many roots worming its way from the bank long enough to get my feet underneath me, but then I lost my grip and skidded the rest of the way down.

With a bone-chilling splash, I found myself standing in the river. I tipped forward, water pounding the back of my legs with the same force with which my heart hammered against my ribs, but the water only reached to my knees. I was in a floodplain. The main channel of the bloated river was somewhere off to my left.

A clump of dislodged grass sailed swiftly downstream, and I let out a breath, grateful not to be going the way of the grass. The winter wind slicked my wet trousers to my legs. I pulled my jacket closer about me, poking myself with the stick I'd grabbed on the stump. I threw it away and slogged through the water to the bank. The discarded stick hit a rock in the incline with an odd clink and slid toward the water, the pale, early sun making its movement a radiant silver line.

I sprang to the bank, catching the slender object before it sank into the murky depths. Heedless of the chill wind and pounding water, I stared at the wand in my hand, my surprise eclipsing even what I'd felt at my journey to wherever I was. What would my godfather say if I'd lost a wand, a rare and precious object, both treasure and weapon? What would its owner say? I stowed the wand in my inside jacket pocket and scrambled up to the stump.

"I'm sorry about that," I began as I cleared the bank, but no angry enchanter awaited me there. Where had the wand come from?

The wavering box I'd fallen through was barely visible three feet above the stump. Sitting carefully on the stump's edge, I dumped the water from my boots and surveyed my position. I was at a river's ford. A dirt road and barren trees were all that was visible between me and a line of snow-draped mountains. It was a beautiful sight, charming in the way of winter landscapes, but it gave no hint of its whereabouts with regard to the duke's manor. My traveling ring, the confounded thing, wouldn't take me anywhere if I didn't know where I was.

"Hello?" I yelled several times into the morning silence but received no answer. I might be somewhere along the river that cut through the duke's estate, or I might not. Who knew where the road led?

"Do you work both ways?" I mused at the box. Then I pulled out the wand to examine it. I'd never held one quite like it. The sunlight played on the wand's silver shaft, giving it its own brilliance. Engravings of roses twirled up it, and I followed them with my fingertip before closing my fist around the shaft. It was cold in my hand, for I had no power of enchantment nor even a speck of a half-magic's ability.

Was the wand lost, or its owner lost? Good heavens. The owner may have been sucked through the box in exchange for me! But, to my relief, when I considered what I knew of magic, a swap seemed doubtful.

I replaced the wand on the stump—its owner would return for it sometime—then faced the shimmering box. Yet I hesitated.

The rumors I'd heard while traveling through Ceur and Tormir came back to me: *The sorcerers of Ceur are buying magical items smuggled from other kingdoms as well as stolen from their own. Magic thieves know no boundaries.* The rumors had been confirmed at Emil's and my expense. I couldn't leave something as valuable as a wand unattended.

Have no dealings with the enchanters, Olan had warned. I'd give the wand to the Duke of Henly. He'd know to whom it belonged. What could possibly happen?

I collected the wand, stepped to the box, and let the tug pull me through. The Floraisons' garden appeared.

Brushing off my muddied clothing as best I could, I hurried to the house. I stopped outside to scrape the mud from my boots, then cracked open the side door and peered inside. An empty hallway. It wouldn't be long before the guests and family filled it, however. They would be looking fresh and clean, unlike me.

Judging by their stern expressions and usual self-possession, the Floraisons were strictly no-nonsense. No humor. No tolerance for a stutter or a stammer or a tendency to meet the ground headfirst. No imperfections tolerated. No imperfects loved. So like my late paternal grandmother, or Lady Ellsworth as she preferred I address her, who never scrupled to conceal her dislike of me during my time with her at Carrington.

I passed quickly up the stairs and along the corridor to reach the staircase leading to my room, my boots squishing with every step. The library door swung open, and the beautiful Lady Alexandria wafted out. Book tucked under her arm, she paused, disdain clear in her blue-green eyes. As lovely and cold as a statue, she was.

Adjusting my collar, I stumbled to a halt, keenly aware of my ridiculous appearance and of the wand in my pocket, which weighed on me like a stolen toy. Would I be able to meet privately with the duke and pass it on this morning, or should I relinquish it to his daughter now? "It's a nice book for a morning, isn't it?"

"Or for falling into a mud puddle." Her lips curled in a derisive smirk, like Lady Ellsworth's. That look had always tripped up my tongue.

"Yes, a nice morning for that too," I answered absent-ly, considering again giving her the wand. I'd rather give it to the duke myself, but he was going to be inundated with demands for his attention.

Wait. Mud puddle?

Cheeks afire, I brushed at my trousers. "N-n-no, it's-it's not a morning. Th-th-that is, I mean, it's ..." My words faded as she raised her critical brow higher. "I ... um um ... Good night—morning. Forgive me for intruding."

Cursing my feeble tongue, I continued to my room. What did I care for the opinion of the snooty Floraison daughters? Training in estate management was what I'd come for.

My manservant was doing something or other in his typical busy manner as I burst into my room.

"Have a pleasant walk?" Henry asked before he looked up. When he did, he raised his eyebrows, a frown twisting his mouth as he scanned my appearance.

"I survived it." I flopped on the edge of the bed. He fetched a towel as I tugged off my soaked boots.

"Snowbanks and mud puddles," he muttered, "and bloody handkerchiefs. We haven't been here seventy-two hours, and already I've had to clean a bloodstained *woman's* handkerchief and now soaked boots. If I have to pre-pare your body for a funeral before the month is up, I'll quit."

"I wouldn't blame you."

"You're not going to get us arrested again, are you?"

"Not if I can help it." I put my jacket aside. "Lay out another suit and pair of boots. Quick. I can't be tardy to the first lesson of the day, especially not after arriving two days late."

Squatting, Henry rocked back on his heels, holding the boots out like they were contagious. "Are you sure we should stay? The Floraisons are enchanters. I'd thought I'd heard as much but was hoping I was wrong. Remember what the inspector said."

"Devil take the inspector. He said a lot of things he had no authority to say. This is Sonser, not Ceur. I will not be bullied by him here. And I fully intend to keep out of any magic business." I laid the wand carefully on the bed.

Henry rose slowly, eyeing the wand. "Do you?"

"Yes. I found it. I'm returning it to the duke. This morning. End of adventure."

"I promised your aunt to keep you out of trouble."

"You work for me, not my aunt."

"Yes, but my mother works for your aunt."

"Just get me the suit."

He didn't move. "What of Lord Mauldin?"

"What about him?" Thank heavens the relationship was by marriage. I'd hate to share blood with that man.

"He's after your estate. One misstep and he'll have you declared incompetent and take it. The terms of the will allow it."

"Believe me, Henry, I know. That's why I've got to stay. I need the Duke of Henly's approval in case of emergency as much as I need his wisdom on estate management."

Henry's eyes narrowed, and he considered for a moment. "We'll stay."

"I'm relieved you agree. My suit?"

After exchanging my muddied articles for clean ones, Henry collected my boots and walked to the door. "Anything else, sir, before I erase the evidence of your morning's escapade?"

Glancing at the clock on the mantle, I fumbled with my cravat. I could still make it, but I wouldn't have time to talk with the duke about the wand beforehand. A clean pair of boots stood at my feet. I peered into the empty shaft of each. "Give me a lift, will you?"

"Are you going somewhere, sir?"

"No, no. A lift." I raised my right boot.

"Ah. Your third foot."

"Don't call it that. It's a *lift*, an insert."

"A lift is something that moves something, like a dumbwaiter."

"And a third foot is a third foot, complete with ankle and toes," I ground out. "Just get another *thing-that-goes-in-my-shoe-and-makes-my-legs-even-so-I-can-walk-without-limping*." I didn't need to give the Floraisons another reason to scorn me.

He's weak, Lady Ellsworth had proclaimed more than once to my great-aunt and great-uncle. *It's been a year, and he still limps, still stutters, still cries himself to sleep. How did he survive the crash when my son did not? My son, whom neither illness nor harm ever touched until he married* that *woman? The boy will always be weak.*

"I'm not sure we have another," Henry said, rescuing me from memories of the two years I spent with my paternal grandmother after my parents died in a carriage crash.

"Don't tell me that. You always pack spares of everything. I carry around more luggage than a duchess on holiday."

Henry sniffed as if offended. "I'll see what I can find, though it may take a while to locate the object you desire in your overabundance of luggage."

By the morning break, I'd confirmed the rumors that Alfred Floraison, Duke of Henly, was a genius. He thought himself and his family above the rest of the world—in truth, I could scarcely blame him—but he was fair and treated his servants and tenants wisely and generously. I had come to the right place to learn.

However, many of his guests thought themselves above barons. I left them to themselves and found a bench in the maze of the gardens, a comfortable seat on which to review Alfred Floraison's lectures. So engrossed was I in my studies that I didn't hear the Duke of Lofton approach, nor realize I was absentmindedly using the wand like a pencil to guide my eye along the page.

"Where did you get that? And stop using it like a stick."

I jumped like a frog from a sinking lily pad at the duke's voice.

"I repeat, where did you get that?" The silver-haired duke stared at me with those piercing blue eyes of his. There was a hard set to his jaw, which was alarming considering what I'd finally remembered about him: he was a powerful enchanter and, purportedly, knew more magical warfare techniques than anyone alive.

As an enchanter, he could be the answer to my wand troubles or the cause of a whole lot more. He could turn me in as a thief, and I'd be imprisoned. I'd lose my estate for good. Actually, wand stealing was probably a capital offense.

"Ah, the river." Standing, I reprimanded myself for not having left the confounded wand where I'd found it. "That is," I corrected at the duke's startled look, "on the stump of an old tree beside a river. It was underneath the magical transportation box I fell through, straight from a similar box here in the gardens."

"So you took it?" With an accusatory look, he motioned for me to sit.

Sinking back onto my seat, I laid the wand beside me, but not too close, rather like a pistol I wanted my companions to know I wasn't going to use. "There was no one to claim it, and since there are rumors of a magic thief, I decided it would be best to give it to the Duke of Henly as soon as I could meet with him privately. He can figure out to whom it belongs."

With only a slight nod of approval, Lofton joined me on the bench. "You're not an enchanter, Ellsworth. How did you know that was a wand and not a child's toy?"

"How do you know I'm not an enchanter?"

"Because you're not." His tone suggested no patience for vague answers, or even for genuine questions.

I paused, choosing my words carefully. Mentioning my godfather was a half-magic who'd trained many enchanters and other half-magics would likely get me laughed at, especially here at Henly, ancestral home of the author of the renowned and utterly false *Half-Magics: Only a Legend.* What's more, if the Duke of Lofton did believe in half-magics, he might fear I'd give the wand to my godfather.

"I'm not an enchanter, but I've always enjoyed tales of magic and so assumed it was a wand. And," I added for good measure, "it doesn't have the markings of the toy wands I played with as a child. Real wands, or at least those not of ancient make, are never marked by the wand maker to safeguard—" *the few remaining wand makers.* I stopped short at the warning flash of surprise in Lofton's eyes. *Marcel, you fool. Are you trying to make him think you're a magic thief? Non-magics aren't supposed to know such things.*

"What of the pattern on this one? Is it not the maker's mark?" he asked in that tone which cautioned against anything but the truth.

Next time you find a wand or a magical box or anything magical, leave it alone, Marcel. "This one identifies the family or individual to whom it belongs."

Behind his hard gaze, I saw myself, the accused, undergoing trial as a magic thief, an all-too-common accusation of late. I had the feeling the prosecution was winning.

Much as I hated bringing up my illustrious relatives to further my causes, there was nothing else for it. "My distant cousin Emil Farro is an enchanter. I've seen his wand."

"Farro? The inventor-enchanter of Ceur?" the duke repeated in surprise, sitting up. "Wasn't he recently robbed?"

"Yes," I said curtly. "An attempted theft, that is."

He settled back against the bench and continued his trial of me. "They said," he began at last, "the Ceurian inspector tried to pin the crime on one of Farro's friends, a Sonserian, nearly causing an international incident. Farro himself had to intervene on the man's behalf." He laughed, his eyes showing relief as well as humor.

I found no cause for mirth in any of it, but did it mean I was acquitted?

"Forgive me," he said, sobering up somewhat. "Being in the middle of the tale, I don't suppose you would find it amusing. That was you, I presume?" He continued after I nodded, "I remember hearing you spoken of now and am glad to find you innocent of this"—he picked up the wand and examined it as I had, running his fingers along the pattern of roses—"perceived theft. You did right in collecting this to give to Alfred—much better than the fool who lost it. I will discover the owner. Until then"—he held the wand out to me—"you will keep it with you at all times. Do not mention it. If anything happens to it, I will hold you responsible. The lack of wands is one of the few things keeping the number of truly dangerous sorcerers low. They mustn't get any more."

The thing looked as inviting as a soldier's pike. Holding my hands up, I scooted away. "Forgive me, but I am not getting caught up in anything remotely involving enchantment. I came here to learn, and that's what I shall focus on. Things magical have tended to get me into trouble of late, as you apparently know."

"You would refuse a duke?"

"It's a nice title you have, Your Grace, but titles hold little authority in Sonser, and you know it."

I'll be darned but he didn't crack a smile. He lowered the wand to his lap and requested I tell him about the incident at Emil's. I began with my arrival at my cousin's.

"A neighbor saw me flying off the balcony of Emil's locked house," I said as I wrapped up the tale. "Emil was forced to admit some of his enchanted items could have sent me soaring if I'd tried to steal them. It was only his adamant assertion of my innocence and refusal to press charges that saved me." Judging by the inspector's letter, however, he didn't believe Emil or me.

"I heard there were two thieves," the Duke of Lofton said softly. "A tall man and a short man."

With a snort, I leaned back and crossed my arms. "The inspector doesn't know how to listen. I said there was one tall man, but after he tossed me through a window, there was only a short man."

"Only one?"

"I wouldn't swear either way."

The Duke of Lofton stilled. His right wrist twitched as if he wanted to roll it but decided not to. He held up the wand again, his hand wrapped around it as if he were about to use it. I braced myself.

"Nonetheless, Marcel Ellsworth," he said, his tone as commanding as a king's, "you will keep this wand until I tell you whom to give it to. If I should leave before the end of the month, give it to the Duke of Henly at his birthday celebration." He lowered the wand, and I finally breathed. It appeared I had little choice in the matter. "If you interrupt another theft," he continued as I reluctantly took the wand, "don't hesitate to use it."

With a laugh, I searched my jacket for a proper place to keep the long thing. I'd have to get Henry to make a wand clasp for my arm. "I can always threaten them with it. They wouldn't know I couldn't give it any power. It's no better than a stick in my hands." I gave up and stuck it in the short pocket I'd had it in earlier.

He rose and motioned for me to follow. "You never know. Come. We must return before we're late again. Alfred will think I'm a bad influence on you."

Chapter 4

*There is no one more suited to steal the ancient treasures
and weapons of the enchanters than a half-magic, and
there is no house more open and inviting than that of an
enchanter who does not believe in a half-magic magic thief.
A successful magic thief is patient, biding his time. He
learns his way around, worms out the secrets of the very
building until he has planned the exit of every item he desires. His antagonists may know he is there, but they do
not know who he is or when he will act.*

"The Half-Magic Magic Thief," a controversial, anony-
mous essay in *The Gersemere Times*

GABRIELLA FLORAISON

H E LOOKED AS if he'd joined the pigs wallowing in
the mud." Alexandria smirked as she selected a
pastry from the breakfast spread.

"Where did he find the mud?" Eva scoffed as she
joined Alexandria at the sideboard. "Perhaps he's a
sleepwalker and can't control his feet any better than his
tongue. He stuttered so during the introductions last
night that I could hardly keep my countenance."

"Who?" Stifling a yawn, I settled into my place at the
table. Thanks to the delay caused by that insinuating
baron getting himself kidnapped—it was highly unfair
that his indiscretions should follow him to Henly—it had
been the wee hours of the morning before Harvey and I
returned with Sterling. Then the nightmare. Fortunately,

Sterling's bite wounds hurt worse than they looked. If I was careful, no one would notice the blemish. Or ask how I came by it.

"Lord Ellsworth," Alexandria answered. "The young man with strawberry blond hair who tried to upstage your and Mama's duet last night with a chorus of off-key laughter."

The baron. Of course. What was the man up to now?

Eva laughed, her expression warning me of approaching embarrassment. "Upstage? He was trying to make it a trio." My cheeks burned. Was there no end to this man's mischief? She continued, "You should have seen the way he looked at you when he walked into the room and saw you singing. Positively smitten, he was. 'Love at first sight,' he might even say."

Was it possible? No. The voices had been different. Lord Ellsworth was neither Moonstruck Suitor nor Accomplice. Nor could he have been the one who sent me away, for Lord Ellsworth must have been on his way to the village inn by the time we were in the garden.

"I'm glad I didn't see it," I said. "I might have missed a note in my revulsion."

"I wouldn't blame you. He's as plain as a pumpkin. There's not more than half a dozen among the lot of Papa's guests worthy of sketching," said Eva, ever the artist.

Lord Ellsworth's plain face was the least of his faults.

"Or worth talking to," Alexandria said. "I dare say good subjects will be scarce in conversation as well. At least we have Fred's riddles."

Yes, about those. What *was* that thing in the shrubbery? If it was a clue, Fred would have mentioned it casually while he was visiting, for he thought himself clever at foreshadowing.

The ham on my plate smelled appealing, yet I pushed it around absently. I half listened to my sisters critique the guests and half wondered about the incident in the garden. I didn't care to be pursued by any of Papa's guests or be treated as a damsel in distress. I could have handled the situation myself with a few choice words to the love-struck nincompoop.

"Gabriella?" Alexandria rested her fork, with its piece of bacon, on her plate. "Whatever is the matter? You've hardly eaten a bite, despite the occasional vicious stab at the ham."

Scolding myself for my absentmindedness, I relaxed the grip on my fork and glanced from her to the Duke of Lofton, newly arrived to the room, who was also watching me. "I was puzzling over Fred's riddles."

"Why don't you share them with us so you may eat your breakfast in peace?" The duke's expression was inviting as he settled his plate on the table. The old enchanter once hosted us at his country estate and had long been a favorite of mine.

I recapped the riddles. "Eva and I searched the gardens late last night, and we discovered something—that is, I did. It was like a cube of un-illuminable darkness suspended between the shrubs, but right as I noticed it, some men startled us, and we left."

"It seems I spoke hastily about Fred hiding something there," Alexandria admitted. "Have you searched for it this morning? I know you were outside for a time."

"Not yet. I was checking on Sterling." I refused a self-conscious desire to look at my finger. "I'll search for it later."

"Mama and I are engaged for the day at Lady Tannon's house. The midwife assures us the baby will come today, and Mama promised our attendance, else I'd join you."

"Good." I smiled mischievously. "This is a competition after all. You shan't win this year."

"We'll see about that."

"You will be on your guard during your searches, won't you?" the duke said with a serious look at me. "You've no doubt heard of the Magic Thief prowling the treasure troves of the enchanters?"

"Yes, to both," I said.

"The Magic Thief would be foolish to come here," Alexandria said. "Our ancestors took long-lasting precautions to keep our treasures safe." We shared a smile. I almost wished the Thief would come so we could see the precautions in action.

"Have you tested them to ensure they still function?"

"They are tested every six months, as is customary," Alexandria said as Papa and Mama entered the room. Mama kissed my cheek and Papa patted my shoulder as they passed behind me.

"Lofton and I disagree on the type of thief and thus whether or not the precautions would be effective." Papa smiled at the Duke of Lofton, a smile the duke didn't return.

"I sincerely hope we don't have to find out," the duke replied.

Soon, I left the aroma of sausages and pastries behind for the library's equally enticing fragrance of paper and bindings. After selecting a few books on enchantments, I settled into my favorite chair to search for information on Fred's box.

Overstuffed and large enough for me to curl up in, the chair angled away from the fireplace, affording a view of the length of the library. The towering shelves replete with books never failed to inspire me whenever I wanted to consider what I'd read.

Yet this morning, I stared more at the suit of armor opposite me. It stood guard in front of a broad, bare wooden beam like a knight of old defending the king's doorway. Was the box protecting the next clue? Would I have to force it open? No, it had appeared more ethereal than solid.

A knock roused me from thought, and the housekeeper peeked around the open door. "Forgive me for intruding, my lady," she said.

"It's no intrusion, Mrs. Baxter. Can I help you?"

She wrung her slender hands around a rolled sheet of paper as she joined me beside the fireplace. "If it please, my lady, might I have a glance in the Mirror of Memory?"

My gaze flicked from her to the locked drawers under a particular section of shelves. "You know we aren't allowed to use the mirrors lightly."

"Oh yes. It's just that, well, you see"—her words came out in a rush—"I lost the menu the duchess and I made. I've searched everywhere for it and can't find it. I must start preparing, but your mother's been away at Lady Tannon's so much ... or the Countess has been with her."

"I see."

The Countess, my Aunt Helene, had dismissed her housekeeper for occasional forgetfulness. We had high expectations of our servants, but we weren't so unforgiving and exacting. Still, Aunt Helene would make an unpleasant fuss if she found out. I laid the books aside and met Mrs. Baxter at the section of drawers.

"Oh, thank you, my lady."

"There's no sense in disturbing Mama when you can use the mirror to review the memory." Several keys hung from my chatelaine—a decorative belt clasp that had belonged to my mother's mother—and hid themselves in the folds of my skirt. I drew out an ancient key, ornate and long, and unlocked the second drawer from the top. I handed Mrs. Baxter the ebony hand mirror and directed her to the small writing desk nestled between two sections of floor-to-ceiling shelves.

The bottom drawer and its mirror beckoned me. Tempted me. Ignoring them, I firmly shoved the second drawer shut and returned to my seat. Of the three mirrors in the three drawers, the one in the bottom drawer was the one not to be tampered with. It had the power to reveal whatever or whomever was requested, including the tresor box.

Papa's warning rang in my head. *The mirror is powerful and dangerous*, he'd said. The time Fred disappeared he'd let the search go on for two hours before he finally called upon the mirror. I picked up my books again, smiling at Mrs. Baxter's muttered comments as she reviewed her meeting with Mama.

"I thought she'd changed her mind about the custard," she said as she scribbled away.

Changed ... Changer ... Place Changer. Fred had talked about learning how to create a Place Changer, a small area of space stolen from one place and temporarily situated at another for the purpose of connecting the two locations. A pair of Changers would allow objects to pass between them. *That's* what the cube was. Smiling smugly, I flipped to the index of a book on advanced enchantments.

Sometime later, after the Mirror of Memory had been put away, I collected my cloak and made my way to the gardens. I greeted several of Papa's guests out walking during the afternoon break. Jonathan Lofton, one arm folded across his chest and the other forming a support for his chin, stood on the garden walk considering the Place Changer.

"Well met, Lady Gabriella," he said as I drew near. "Have you come to see the Place Changer?"

When I replied in the affirmative, he continued, "I suspected that's what your brother had created. Very clever of him. He's a talented enchanter. However, this"—he gestured to the transparent cube barely visible as a waver in the air—"is still the work of a novice. May I tell you a secret?"

The teasing glint in his eyes brought a smile to my face. "A truth potion couldn't drag it from me."

He snorted as if to say "don't be too sure."

"Traveling through a Place Changer is possible"—he cocked a silver brow—"but not recommended. Place Changers, especially, if you'll forgive me, amateur ones, are easily destabilized, in which state they are prone to connect to the wrong places." He paused until I nodded my understanding. "Your brother doubtless intended for you to use a reveal spell to determine the Changer's home, which is likely somewhere on your estate that you'll easily recognize and can, more safely, walk to."

"I read about the reveal spell and came prepared to perform one." I drew my wand from its hidden pocket. The length of it was oddly dull in the cloud-filtered light.

The duke's eyes flashed with surprise, and he said quickly, "Would you humor an old man and let me do the spell?"

"Gladly." Putting away my wand, I stepped aside.

He knelt in front of the shimmering cube and ran his finger along its edges. "It was well done. Give my compliments to your brother." After ascertaining that we were alone, he flicked his wrist, and a wand shot into his hand. The hidden pocket in my skirt suddenly seemed clunky and amateurish.

He gave the reveal spell, and the shimmering stilled. A dull gray overtook the box, then brightened into earth tones that drew together into shapes, finally resolving into a riverbank with a large stump at its edge.

"Judging by my lady's furrowed brow, she recognizes the spot and is wondering, why there?"

"It's the river's ford." I pulled my cloak closer about me. Though winter hung in the air, a walk would be welcome.

"You're certain?"

When I nodded, he touched his wand to the Changer. The river and trees dissolved back into earth tones, then blended into background. He flicked his wrist again, and his wand disappeared. "Should I inform your sisters as to the location of the next clue?"

"No. This is a competition after all."

He returned my grin. "May you be the first to find the treasure."

I thanked him and took my leave.

"Lady Gabriella," he called as I walked away.

"Yes?"

He joined me on my path, his brows drawn together as if in concern. "Did you recognize the men in the garden last night?"

"No. I only heard their voices."

"It was a cold night to be out," he said, a subtle question in his tone.

"I'm afraid I was the cause, moonlight being so romantic and all—and apparently disposed to make suitors of two-day acquaintances. And one a nincompoop, at that," I said, muttering the last phrase.

The duke's laugh was cut short, and he looked at me earnestly. "Did he actually say this to you—that he wanted to court you?"

"No, to his companion. They were discussing it as they walked an adjoining path." That was their reason. What was the other man's?

"You heard no one else? No one *alone*?" He stressed the last word, as if there was culpability in walking alone.

"There was another. He was sitting there." I pointed toward the bench hidden behind the cedar as we approached it.

"And he was ...?"

"Tall. Your height or a few inches taller, I should say. To my surprise, he possessed a magical ring. He used it to hide me behind the cedar before the others turned the corner. He had startled Eva and me as we were walking by the Place Changer. Eva ran on, but I stayed to pick up my dropped wand. I suppose," I said icily, "he presumed I needed rescuing, but I was in no danger beyond that of being embarrassed."

"You've heard the rumors of the Thief. A crowded guest list is a perfect place for him to hide."

"For an ordinary thief, yes, but a magic thief at Henly? Nothing more exciting or bothersome than an occasional earthquake has happened here since the Caffin Wars." Nothing until last night. But that was minor and hardly counted. It was the baron's affair and was now over with, the perpetrators locked away in the village.

Papa always asserted that our reputation as powerful and skilled enchanters had guarded us for years, until people forgot the magic and remembered only the warning. I resisted the urge to rub my raw finger. If anything of a serious nature had occurred, my parents would have told me. Henly was as safe as a child's nursery.

"Not even the Floraisons will be above trouble forever, Lady Gabriella," the duke said.

An unruly eyebrow shot up, but I quickly regained my composure. "Thank you for the warning. I hope that time shall not be for many years yet."

"As do I, but I would not count on it if I were you."

After parting from the duke, I returned to my room for a sturdier pair of boots. As I sat at my desk to change, its bottom drawer caught my eye, and a familiar fear gnawed my insides.

Not even the Floraisons will be above trouble forever.

I shook my head. Much as I respected the Duke of Lofton, he enjoyed being a herald of doom. I yanked up my remaining boot and jammed my foot inside. If anything of a serious nature had occurred, my parents would have told me.

My gaze returned to the third drawer. Wouldn't they have?

Stamping my foot to get my heel into position, I opened the drawer and pulled a folded, yellowed set of papers from its back corner, a copy of a passage that had made Mama pale during a lesson on the history of magic. She'd paused mid-sentence, turned a ghostly white, and looked at me as if I were a ghoul. I asked what was wrong. She claimed her throat was bothering her. I offered to read. She gave the book to Alexandria and moved to sit beside me, wrapping her arm protectively around my shoulders. I'd later returned to the schoolroom and copied the passage, though I couldn't say why.

I smoothed the wrinkled sheets and scanned the familiar lines from Bachman's *Sorcerers: Their Various Kinds and Their Slaves.*

Those whose blood has been offered on the black altar always know when a sorcerer has reopened a lair. They feel the call to return even stronger then. ... In the

E.J. Kitchens

Caffin Wars, the sorcerers often stole the children of the enchanters and spread their blood on the altar, intending that the children should join their number, sooner or later. Even the children who were rescued and returned to the enchanters often succumbed to the lure of sorcery, or returned under the power of some curse, and became their will-less slaves. Only those under the protection of the ancient animals from the White Mountain, such as the Pyren horse and the Beanan goat, could be saved, if they stayed near their animals and escaped capture and a forced return. ... Few of those called survived past their seventeenth year, a period known as "The Year of the Called" to this day in Tormir.

I folded the sheets along their well-worn creases. *A Pyren horse ...* Why shouldn't I have one? Sterling was magnificent, beautiful, clever, loyal. A horse fit for the daughter of a duke. But he resembled a workhorse more than my sisters' sleek mares or my brother's stallion. Yet what did I care about that? He was admired by all who saw him.

I thrust the sheets back in the drawer, shuffling other papers on top of them, and shoved the drawer shut. Scrunching moist eyes, I gripped the edge of the desk. *You're nineteen, Gabriella—nineteen. It's time to stop this foolish worry. It was a nightmare.*

"Only a nightmare." Taking a shaky breath, I opened my eyes and scanned the stack of story-filled leather journals weighting the bottom of the short bookcase beside my desk. I'd been an imaginative child. Aunt Helene was right about that. I was always making up stories, and several featured a girl who escaped being a Sorcerer's Called. Yet I'd never shared those particular stories with my family. They'd always seemed too far-fetched. A Sorcerer's Called in peaceful Sonser? Where sorcerers were banished, and their lairs destroyed? Where the disappearance of any child, especially the child of a nobleman, would cause too great a stir for any sorcerer to dare the attempt? No, Sonser was too safe for such tales.

Soon, I was on my way to the spot from which the air of the Place Changer had been stolen, my thoughts switching between the chapter I was working on for my book on estate management and suppositions about Fred's next clue. Why would he send us to the ford? Were we to dig for buried treasure as in a children's pirate tale?

The roar of the swollen river greeted me even before I neared the ford, a section of the river shallow enough for carts to cross. The odor of debris-filled water tainted the air as I left the walking path for the wagon road that led down to and across the river to fields and farmland.

Not far ahead, the stump of an old oak clutched the edge of the bank above the deluged flood plain. A tall man in a chocolate-brown suit and heavy coat stood by the stump. His clothes were too rich for a peasant. Surely none of Papa's guests had walked this far from the house. A bandit with stolen clothes? This man's hung loosely on him. *Please, no more bandits.*

I retreated behind a holly. The man's lanky form stirred a memory, but his face was averted and his hair covered by a hat.

He contemplated the stump much as the Duke of Lofton had the Place Changer. His focus shifted above the stump to the view of the countryside. No, to the shimmering box floating above the stump. The connecting Changer.

He removed a wand from his jacket and positioned it on the stump under the Changer. Where had he gotten a wand? It was silver as were my family's. What if the duke was right and this man was a magic thief, or *the* Magic Thief?

Tossing aside my horror, I considered how best to tackle the man—not physically of course, or by shouting. The Floraison dignity must be preserved. But no one was making a souvenir of a Floraison wand.

But he was putting it down, not snatching it up. Maybe he was leaving it for the Thief. Or emptying his pockets of all his stolen items to package them. Or ...

Whatever he was doing, he had no business doing it. The Duke of Lofton was the only enchanter staying on the estate, and no one else had any right to handle a wand.

My own wand out, and with a number of useful spells in the forefront of my mind, I left the shelter of the holly. "Perhaps you should return that to whomever it belongs. Better yet, leave it, and I will return it."

The man spun around, his face plain, angular, and registering surprise, his hair strawberry blond.

Marcel Ellsworth.

Again.

"L-l-lady Gabriella." He bowed in greeting. "I-I-I will gladly leave it now that I-I-I know a Floraison is h-here to claim it." Flinching as if ashamed of his stuttering, he moved aside, allowing room for me to collect the wand.

I put my wand away, for he raised no sense of personal danger, but I watched him as I picked up the lost wand. Papa said the Duke of Lofton was the only enchanter here this season, but there was something about Lord Ellsworth that suggested otherwise.

The warming sensation which accompanied an enchanter's touch to a wand stole the bite of the winter's day from my hands. Was that an image of a rose vine encircling the wand?

"I-I-I would like to apologize for last night," he said.

I glanced up from my inspection of the wand's design, which matched the Floraison's mark. Who could be so irresponsible as to lose a wand or let one be stolen? "The Floraisons do not take kindly to having personal quarrels brought to our land, Lord Ellsworth. Let us drop the matter, and in future, please settle your differences elsewhere."

He stiffened, his eyes hardening with a look of contempt. "Your father spoke only this morning on the danger of making assumptions, Lady Gabriella. Perhaps you should ask for his lecture notes." He paused long enough to tempt me to fill the space with an insult in return, but I held my tongue. "I meant," he continued, holding up his hand, on which sat a thick gold ring, "for startling you and Lady Eva in the garden."

I blinked, my anger momentarily forgotten. The man with the ring. Good heavens. *Him?* The plain baron who tripped over his words—when he wasn't angry, that is— possessed the magic needed to send me away? It would explain how he got himself off the horse and away from the bandits. He hadn't needed our help after all, only time for his head to clear from the blow he'd received. Yet, because of him, I'd revealed to half a dozen bandits my power of enchantment, and they would surely tell everyone who asked exactly how a woman captured them.

"And for giving you the wrong wand," he continued.

My breath caught in my throat. *The wrong ...* The one in my hand was assuredly a Floraison wand. I snatched mine from its pocket. It was a dull silver with a carefully penciled sketch of rose vines running up it. It didn't grow warm at my touch. *A toy!* I'd carried around a toy and almost used it in front of the Duke of Lofton. Anger and shame slapped color onto my face.

"How—How—" How could anyone be so despicable as to play such a trick? How could I, a Floraison, a family praised for its intelligence and wisdom, not have realized the trade? To lose a wand was the ultimate disgrace.

To return one was the ultimate mark of good character. Or cunning.

I sought Lord Ellsworth's eyes. They were wide and green and expressive. Gone was the hard look. His eyes spoke of embarrassment and apology. Why could he not give me reason to bespell him and have him locked away! *Plain, rude, frustrating baron.*

"I do apologize," he continued. "The toy was under the bush beside the Place Changer. I assumed it was what you dropped, but now I realize your wand fell *through* the Changer, which was why it was here on the stump, and why I am returning it here."

Mortification. It was not a state of mind a Floraison should ever find herself in, much less dwell in, but I felt myself a sojourner there. *Think, Gabriella, think. Say something.* The man was either a supreme actor or genuine, if his manner was to be believed. I didn't want to jump to conclusions about him again.

"My brother, Frederick ..." I barely stopped an undignified *uh* from escaping, "... made the Changer as part of a game, a treasure hunt, he always leaves for my sisters and me." *Slow breaths. Enunciate. A Floraison can handle any situation with confidence and poise.* "It must be part of that. Yes, he left the toy as a clue for us to use a reveal spell on the Changer instead of traveling through it." *Yes, that makes sense. Good work.* I swallowed hard. "Thank you for looking after my true wand until I could collect it. How did you know I would come for it now?"

To Catch a Magic Thief

A weight seemed to drop from his shoulders as I spoke. "The Duke of Lofton. I found the wand this morning and talked with him about it. He said you'd be along to look at the Changer soon."

"The duke?" My knees went weak. No wonder he'd insisted on doing the reveal spell himself. He'd recognized the toy for what it was when I hadn't.

"Yes." Lord Ellsworth's expression was one of studied blankness. Was he pitying my embarrassment or laughing at me? He was probably laughing.

Piqued, I scolded my knees, stiffened my spine, and slipped my true wand into its pocket. There. I felt myself again. *A Floraison can handle any situation with confidence and poise.* We could. If only the heat of a blush would leave my cheeks. "I just left the duke in the garden. How did you make it here before I did?"

My ring finger remembered the weight of the ring slipped on it last night. Another finger recalled the pain of Sterling's bite. *No true Floraison needs a Pyren horse,* Aunt Helene had declared to Harvey when she first met Sterling. No true Floraison would lose a wand either. I shoved the thoughts aside. *A Floraison never lets her mind wander during a conversation.* "Your ring. How silly of me. It was astute of the duke to recognize the problem. In future, I shall be more attentive."

"I'm glad to hear it. There are many who'd give a life for what you have."

"The sorcerers, you mean?" I replied sharply, stung by his tacit accusation of dangerous irresponsibility. Originally enchanters, the sorcerers sold themselves to evil and called on the dark powers to increase their magic. The king of Sonser had banished them at the end of the Caffin Wars.

• 71 •

"Yes, but enchantment is also the desire of many others. There's so much good that could be done with it." He grinned as he shrugged. "It would also be entertaining and a challenge to master."

"Yes. Very entertaining," I said icily. As amusing as tricking young women and laughing at their embarrassment. "You're not an enchanter then?"

"No. A non-magic." He examined his pocket watch. "If you'll excuse me, Lady Gabriella. I must return before the break ends, and I wouldn't want to delay you in your pursuit of your brother's clues."

"Nor I to detain you. Good day, sir."

"Good day, Lady Gabriella."

He bowed, twisted his ring, and vanished. Though I should have expected it, I drew back in surprise, bumping into the stump. Remembering the Changer above it, I threw myself forward and barely managed to right myself before falling. Confounded man. How had he, a non-magic, come by that ring? Not that it mattered. I would have no reason to speak with him again.

A loose curl tickled my forehead as a sharp breeze blew across the river, and I recalled Fred's riddles. Pulling the hood of my cloak further down, I searched the stump for a clue.

Nothing seemed out of place or unusual, except for depressions in the grass around the stump leading down the steep bank. A young shrub's roots were exposed as if something had used it as a hold to pull itself up the bank. Or someone. The disturbance in the wet ground began at the stump's base, close to the Place Changer, as if someone had fallen from the Changer onto the ground and then down the bank.

Frowning, I turned away from the river, remembering the laughter Eva and I had shared with Alexandria at her description of Lord Ellsworth's muddied clothing and disheveled state this morning. Guilt stabbed my conscience, but the blade didn't catch. He had no right to be poking around in the affairs of enchanters. I should ask the duke to confirm the baron's story before pronouncing him as "the misjudged man who had gone through much to retrieve my wand." After all, if he hadn't startled me, I wouldn't have dropped it in the first place.

The familiar twittering of a cardinal drew my attention to the limbs of the old beech across the wagon road. Not far from an old nest, the bird sang its song, hopping around a brown string that didn't belong at all.

"Oh, Fred," I groused as I studied the hanging pouch, memorizing its location and calculating how much additional height I would need to reach it.

Pinning a scented handkerchief to the collar of my jacket, I stepped into the stable, the latest chapter of my manuscript tucked under my arm. "Good morning, Harvey."

"Morning, Gabbie Marie." Harvey pushed his cap back as he greeted me by the nickname only he used. He eyed me narrowly, focusing on my hand. I tucked it behind my back.

"The pups will be happy to see you, especially Bitsy," he said. "Or do you fancy taking Sterling for a ride?"

The tiny yips of the wolfhounds decided my course. "A ride, but in a few minutes." I'd waited a day to return to the ford because of bad weather. A few minutes more wouldn't hurt. Eva was still trying to figure out what the Changer was.

Harvey fetched a blanket and led the way to the stall Nympha, our wolfhound, insisted on using as her kennel.

He laid the blanket on the straw beside Nympha and her six pups. Bitsy, so called because she was the runt, tottered over to me as I set my papers in a safe corner. My heart ached for the little girl. We never kept the runts— only the best of the litter for the Floraisons. She was Harvey's to do with as he pleased, and he usually sold the runts to less fastidious buyers.

The other puppies clambered over one another in their attempt to get to me. Hardly had I greeted them all before Harvey's booming voice stole my attention from my delightful furry companions.

"Cox, what the devil are you doing?" Harvey's bellow was followed by a muted reply from a nearby stall. "I didn't ask you to rub down Lord Tyndale's horse. You're terrible at it anyway. Muck out the stalls like I told you." Harvey huffed, and his boots clapped against the stone floor. "Temporary servants," he muttered as he approached my refuge.

"Pleasant morning, Harvey?" I asked as he stuck his head in the doorway.

"Always is when you're here, even if there's a few nincompoops here as well." With a heavy sigh, he lifted his cap to brush his hand over his sandy blond hair. "Sterling's antsy to get out, if you're ready."

I scooped up my papers and moved to the far corner of the stall, brushing away straw to uncover a leather satchel. "Let me put this chapter away, and then I'll—" I sucked in a breath. The satchel was too light. *No. Please, no.* I only had three months to complete and polish the manuscript to make the deadline the publisher and Papa had given in their reluctant acceptance of my proposal. I threw back the leather flap, my stomach twisting like the knotted string holding my papers together. A scrap of stationery and a stack of sheets too thin to be more than one chapter were all that remained. I snatched up the scrap written across in Fred's handwriting.

Dearest sister,

I sincerely hope this was your first draft. While I can't complain about the grammar, the prose is dull indeed, even ignoring the subject matter. Where's your style? Your passion? Your voice? You can do better. In fact, you must, as I've hidden all but your first chapter (I thought you'd like something to practice the rewriting on).

Your loving and wise brother,

Fred

P.S. You'll thank me for this one day.

P.P.S. I agree—Papa

Chapter 5

Fools! Romantic fools! They've made a roguish hero of this uncatchable Magic Thief as they did of the witty highwaymen of yore. Tall and handsome, a man of noble birth, they say he is. May it not be so! Would to heaven this is not true. In place of each treasure of enchantment he steals is left a flower, a silk blossom, as repayment. The ladies wear them in their hair or hat. The men are scarcely better. It's almost a matter of pride to be a victim of this Thief, though he sells our treasures to the sorcerers of Ceur.

The Duke of Lofton to the Council of Enchanters

MARCEL ELLSWORTH

BEYOND THE MEADOW'S billowing grass, the forest and mountains rose up under a scattering of clouds. Book in one hand and mat in the other, I paused to enjoy the scene and was surprised by a sudden pang of homesickness for Carrington. When had I felt more than a sense of responsibility and concern for the place and people now in my charge? That had driven me to Henly. As desperate as I was to keep Uncle Mauldin from it, I'd never yearned for the cold house where Lady Ellsworth once lived.

"Are you all right, Ellsworth? You look as though you've seen a ghost." The Duke of Lofton, an easel tucked under his arm, looked from me to the scenery at which I was staring. "Bit early in the day for those, I should think." He jutted his chin toward my book. "Or was it inspired by your reading choice?"

With a shake of my head, I held out the book. "Nothing like that. A thought caught me unaware, that's all." I'd heard feelings sometimes followed actions. Perhaps if I did my all to secure its future, Carrington would one day feel like home and its bitter associations would be put aside for good.

"An adventure. Well chosen," he said as we resumed our walk to the ford. "I remember the year Brammar's first novel was published. One of my nephews carried it about with him all summer and talked of nothing save 'going on adventures.'" He smiled as if in bittersweet memory.

"My cousins and I did the same thing when we first read them. Did your nephew go on any adventures?"

His smile vanished. "That's debatable. A more talented, soft-hearted man you never met. After his wife died, he fell apart and then disappeared, about the same time as his worthless brother-in-law. He was presumed dead, but let us not speak of the past."

"Your Grace," a familiar, petulant voice interrupted. I spun around, then forced a polite nod of greeting to the broad-shouldered man before me. The unlucky suitor who'd followed Lady Gabriella into the gardens gave me an icy stare before bowing to Lofton. "May I have a word with you?"

"Of course, Lord Mavern." Lofton cast an apologetic look my way.

"Allow me to take the easel for you." I relieved him of his burden, then continued on alone.

When I reached the ford, I set up his easel on the bank where the wagon road dipped to cross the river. The afternoon sunlight highlighted the rounded edges of the bluish-gray storm clouds sitting high above the fields beyond the river. Only a stone's throw down the bank, a charismatically gnarled oak scratched the air around it with its long, gray branches as if determined to climb to the sky.

I tweaked the angle of the easel to include the old oak. Then, choosing a sizeable birch for a backrest, I settled down on the mat with my book. A few pages later, a blend of voices drew me from the story world. Surely Lofton hadn't invited Mavern to join us. The man regarded me with all the friendliness of a vulture. No, that was definitely a woman's voice. Jumping up, I laid the book aside and straightened my jacket.

"Fate has shined on us, Ellsworth," Lofton said with a sweeping gesture toward Lady Gabriella. She sat astride one of the most magnificent horses I'd ever seen—a well-muscled stallion that would dwarf the typical noblewoman's horse. A wolfhound the size of a small pony lumbered beside them.

Had it? I acknowledged Lady Gabriella's cool nod with a bow, then held out my hand in invitation to the wolfhound, who quickly came my way.

"Lady Gabriella has promised to show us the best places for painting in exchange for a small favor"—he removed a canvas from his satchel and set it on the easel, with barely a nudge to the easel's position—"from you."

My mouth fell open, which unfortunately allowed sounds to escape. "Huh?"

The tilt of the lady's head as she swung her gaze from Lofton to me and back plainly announced Lofton's speech had been solely his idea.

"I would be honored to assist."

"You have my thanks, Lord Ellsworth." She swung out of the saddle, landing on the ground with practiced ease.

I couldn't help but note the Floraisons' sense and independence: Fashion dictated women ride sidesaddle. The Floraison ladies rode astride, yet maintained an appearance of elegance and propriety while doing so.

Eying the wolfhound at my side as if the dog were a traitor for allowing me to pet it, Lady Gabriella handed me her horse's reins, then joined Lofton as I anchored the horse to a sturdy branch.

"You'll need that creature, Ellsworth." Lofton didn't even turn as he mixed paints.

"The horse?" The giant beast eyed me suspiciously.

"Yes. See that oilskin pouch swinging from the beech's limb?"

I searched out the indicated object some fifty feet away. "Yes."

"You ought to be able to reach it standing on the horse."

"Standing?" Put the clumsy oaf on a horse in front of a woman? The beautiful, scornful type of woman at that?

Lady Gabriella's eyes clouded with concern or, more likely, doubt.

I tugged my hat down as a stiff breeze threatened to carry it away. "N-n-no t-t-trouble at all." *Fool tongue. You're an adult, not a cowering boy. Speak like it.*

I maneuvered the beast under the tree and handed the reins to Lady Gabriella, fervently hoping she would put a stationary spell on the horse. If she knew one, she didn't offer it. Why couldn't she have brought a ladder instead?

Taking a deep breath, I reminded myself to speak deliberately and confidently. "I'm trusting you to keep this creature still," I said lightly. "What's his name?"

"Sterling, and he will behave." She ran a soothing hand along the horse's neck, then took a firm hold of the bridle. "Be still, Sterling. You too, Nympha," she added to the dog.

The horse obeyed. I climbed aboard, standing slowly, my feet at odd angles on the curved saddle. I grabbed the lower branch, and we both swayed.

"Are you feeling secure, Lord Ellsworth?"

"As a willow in the wind." Easing up on tiptoe, I stretched toward the pouch and caught the tip of it between my fingers.

Nympha growled, and Sterling twitched at the loud creaking of a tree. The hair on the back of my neck stood up, and I scanned the forest beyond Lofton. The old spreading oak leaned forward, looking as if it wanted to reach down and crush the duke in its embrace.

"Lofton! Look out!"

The earth groaned as the old oak ripped up from the ground and crashed through the bare branches of its neighbors.

GABRIELLA FLORAISON

"Sterling!" With a shrill neigh, my horse tossed me aside and reared, sending Lord Ellsworth flying. The baron's cry was cut short, and he vanished mid-fall, mere feet above me. Sterling bolted.

A burst of light flared to my left, in front of the duke. He jumped back as the canopy of the falling oak blackened and hung in the air, separated from its base. The trunk hit the forest floor with a vibration that knocked us to the ground. The canopy crashed, dusting up around the duke like ash and stinging my eyes as I regained my footing and sprinted toward him.

A figure, indistinct through the blur of protective tears, raced through the trees beyond the fallen oak. The dark figure halted, turned solid and gray like roughly hewn stone, then burst forward, dark as ever, but shorter and thicker. I blinked, and it was gone. Lost in the trees, if it had ever been at all.

Coughing, I covered my mouth with my handkerchief and sank to my knees beside the duke. "Are you all right?"

He sat on the ground, wand in hand, one leg stretched out, the other pulled up, an arm resting on his knee. He nodded between heaving breaths and coughed into his handkerchief, his searching gaze never leaving the forest. "Perfectly all right." Coughing again, he continued to stare without attempting to get up.

"Are you certain you're all right?"

He smiled faintly at my tone. "A little winded, that's all." He gave me a sideways glance. "My dear, you'll ruin your dress kneeling in this mess."

As if that mattered. With a scathing glance, I hopped up and called for Sterling and Nympha. My faithful horse trotted over, and I retrieved a water canteen from the saddlebag.

Recalling Lord Ellsworth's mid-air disappearance, I glanced around for him, half-expecting him to appear out of nowhere. Concern nagged me, but I dismissed it. He'd been singularly ungrateful after Harvey and I helped him with the bandits. He had his ring. It took him away; it could return him here if he chose.

I gave the duke the canteen, and he drank heartily before handing it back.

"My lady is most obliging." He pushed to his feet, then draped an arm over Sterling.

I shook the ash—all that remained of the picturesque tree canopy—from my dress, and marveled. There was no smoke, had been no fire, but there was a spread of ash and a tree missing a canopy. Next to a man known to be a powerful enchanter. One who had studied the magical warfare techniques from the Caffin Wars.

"Was that a ... a power burst?" A strike of pure magic, highly dangerous and taboo to practice, much less use. It was for destruction, not for any useful purpose like the spells we usually cast. Yet I shuddered to think what would have happened had he not employed it.

Looking more himself, though still pale, the duke began to dust off his clothes. "Very astute of you, Lady Gabriella." A touch of approval blended with his condescending tone. "Power bursts, especially sudden ones, are challenging even for the young, and I am not young." He gave me a pointed look, as if to assure me nothing save a temporary shortness of breath, as if from overexertion, was wrong with him. If rumors were true, he was well acquainted with adventures and dangers of all kinds, which made his calmness somewhat less annoying.

"I'm glad to hear I may put away my nurse's cap."

He patted my shoulder and looked about. The oak's long trunk settled precariously on the bank and ended abruptly in a black scar.

"I admire your skill," I said.

"Years of difficult training." He added in a murmur, "For which I am grateful."

Nympha sniffed around the oak's exposed roots. We joined her there, my heart sinking. What had happened to peaceful Henly? Were all our guests to be accosted by something, be it bandits or falling trees?

The duke held up his hand to stop my stammered apology. "Your family is not to blame." He swiped his thumb over his jaw in a thoughtful manner as he strode around the tree's base, examining the roots and the surrounding earth. "I noticed this tree myself but didn't anticipate it trying to come down on me." He toed a shallow trough ending abruptly in the new hole left by the upended roots. "Soft, wet ground and windy weather—we'll give them the blame."

"What is it?"

"Hmmm?"

"You're examining the ground as if something's amiss." How could someone uproot a tree without us knowing it?

"Whatever gives you that idea? I didn't take you as the kind to spook easily."

"I don't. Did you see the man, or beast, running through the forest after the tree fell? It appeared as if he were trapped in stone, then burst out and kept going."

"What a fanciful idea."

"So says the man who disintegrated half a two-hundred-year-old tree." But he was right. It was a ridiculous notion.

"Likely a deer running by and the effect of ash in your eyes." He slapped the oak's base, getting a solid thump in return, and strolled to his fallen easel. "Pity about the tree. There's good wood in there. Your father will want it collected, I'm sure, but the missing canopy would lead to questions. Don't suppose we could convince anyone it was a lightning strike, could we?" I shook my head. "Oh well." He righted his easel and nonchalantly gathered his scattered supplies.

Dismissing my wild speculations, I picked up Lord Ellsworth's book, its title a familiar one, and dusted it off.

The soggy ground sank beneath my feet. A combination of rain-softened earth and high wind. That's all it was.

"If you wish to be helpful to your father's guests, Lady Gabriella"—he glanced at the book in my hand as he wiped ash off a paintbrush—"I recommend you give assistance to Lord Ellsworth."

"Lord Ellsworth?" I dropped the book onto his empty mat. He might have been the one running through the forest. No. He'd use his ring. "His traveling ring allowed him a convenient escape."

"An escape from falling on you." The duke waved toward the old stump marking the Changer's location. "He appeared there, then fell through the Changer, which is no doubt destabilized by this time. I noticed a dullness about its fringes earlier. You might use the reveal spell to ensure it's working properly."

"He landed in the garden then and is safely back at the house changing his muddied clothes," I said, trying not to think about Lord Ellsworth's fall being my fault. "I'll send a servant after him."

He didn't respond but, with a critical expression I didn't care for, silently moved to Sterling and brought him to me. I drummed my fingers against my crossed arms as the duke approached. To be respectful, I kept my thoughts to myself and allowed him to boost me onto Sterling.

"Please do me the favor of ensuring Lord Ellsworth's safety yourself, discreetly," he said as I settled into the saddle. "This old man needs a few minutes of painting to relax, and you wouldn't want to have to explain to a servant why he needed to search for Lord Ellsworth, would you?"

I stiffened. Of all the underhanded ... But what else could I do? I turned Sterling's head toward home. "I will ask about the house and grounds for him."

"Lady Gabriella." The duke's tone prepared me for a lecture. I was tempted to touch my heel to Sterling's side and speed away as if I hadn't heard, but I didn't. I faced him, and his intense gaze locked me in place.

"Marcel Ellsworth returned a wand to you—you should know the value of that. Give him a chance."

"A chance for what?" I scoffed, remembering Eva's comment. "To be a suitor? I hardly know the man."

The duke's look was rebuke enough, but he continued in words. "No. Give him a chance to show you that respect should come not from inherited rank or personal beauty but from other qualities—integrity and kindness, for instance."

"The Floraisons value virtue and integrity as well as beauty."

"Do you? Tell me, in practice, which do you value more? Would you have forgotten me—the duke and enchanter—until it was convenient? Or only the 'plain, bumbling baron' as your sisters call Ellsworth?"

My cheeks burned, but I held his gaze for a moment before turning away. Nympha still sniffed around the tree. "Nympha"—I directed her to the duke's side—"I will leave with you."

"Your concern does you credit." The duke bowed, a humoring lilt to his voice.

Self-righteous busybody. I pursed my lips and then touched my heel to Sterling's side.

A delayed reaction to the shock of the near-tragedy left me trembling in the saddle for part of the ride, but before Sterling's hooves clapped against the stable drive, I'd regained my composure. I'd need it for questioning the servants and guests. I couldn't help but wonder if I had seen one of them running near the river. The illusion was the man turning to stone.

Has a man in a dark suit come from the direction of the river? Anyone strangely out of breath? Nympha startled a stranger, and I wish to assure him she is not as dangerous as her size suggests.

But my investigation was fruitless. "Man in a dark suit" matched the description of several guests, and none had appeared out of breath or hurried. Moonstruck Suitor and Accomplice, Lord Mavern and Lord Tyndale, respectively, as I'd since discovered, had been out as well, but I doubted Moonstruck could move as quickly as that figure had.

Having failed to see Lord Ellsworth as I returned to the house, I was forced to inquire after him. One servant thought he'd seen a lanky man like him but wasn't certain. Another said he hadn't seen him and he had just come from the wing where the guests were housed.

Eva met me at the door to the conservatory as I dismissed the latter servant. Aunt Helene, whom I sometimes wished was not our closest neighbor, was with her.

"Why are you asking after that scarecrow?" Eva gave a derisive snort as she took her muff from her lady's maid.

Because he disappeared before the duke was nearly crushed! I tugged at the clasp of my cloak, conscious of the servants around. "The ... Duke of Lofton asked that I let Lord Ellsworth know of a change in plans for their afternoon outing."

"My dear Gabriella," Aunt Helene sang in her clear voice, lovely in tone but so often harsh in its words. "It's unseemly of you to act as a messenger, even for the esteemed Duke of Lofton, especially to such a low-ranking young man. You must think of your reputation." She looked down her perfect nose at her white kid gloves as if they were the offensive Lord Ellsworth.

"I agree, Aunt, but the duke isn't one to be refused."

Eva laughed gleefully and took Aunt Helene's arm. "Did Alexandria tell you, Aunt, of Lord Ellsworth showing up covered in mud yesterday? How he stammers through every sentence?"

I yanked off my gloves. "Yes and is very plain." And honest enough to return a wand. But what did that matter? "Not to mention falls into everything—rivers and Place Changers," I muttered under my breath. Why had he not returned?

"Gabriella, wherever are you going? You just came inside," Aunt Helene called after me as I marched through the doorway, ramming my fingers back into my gloves as I went.

"Back out," I called over my shoulder.

I made my way to the garden Place Changer. No fresh footprints marred the earth or muddied the path near it. As the duke said, it was fuzzy about the edges, a dark fuzzy that made it easier to see than usual. I touched my wand to it. The tree stump at the river appeared, but then faded to blackness and back again. With a sinking feeling, I touched it when next it was black and whispered an illumination spell. It was still dark—dark walls, dark floor, dark ceiling.

I stilled. Though voices warned of others approaching, I couldn't move, my legs as cold and useless as fear itself. The Changer shimmered as normal again, and I clutched my fisted hand to my chest.

If Lord Ellsworth had any sense, he'd go back through the Changer or use his traveling ring. He could take care of himself. There was no need for me to follow.

No need at all.

Chapter 6

Brown tinted the petals, blending the tips of the red roses
into the freshly turned earth.
Brown and Red.
Death and dying.
There are no other colors.

Diary of a magic thief

Marcel Ellsworth

IT WASN'T A pillow my cheek was resting on. Groaning, I raised my head, but the sudden pain pulsing through it encouraged me to ease it down again. When the pain dulled, I pushed into a sitting position, my hands sliding over cool rock as I raised myself. How long had I been unconscious?

Dampness seeped into my clothes, and aches from my falls made themselves known. It was completely black and completely silent around me. I gingerly rubbed a sizable knot on the side of my head. What had happened to get me wherever I was? Bandits? No, that had already happened this trip. A quick check confirmed I still had my ring and money bag. What then?

Fear knotted my stomach as the memory of the falling tree and Sterling's neighs filled my mind. I'd used my ring to keep from falling on Lady Gabriella, but instead of landing by the stump and then going to help Lofton, I'd tripped and fallen into the Place Changer. If I didn't know my tendency for falling, I'd say I'd been drawn into the thing. How could I have been so clumsy at such a moment? Yet what could I have done for the old enchanter? Even as I fell I noted the wand already in his hand. My rush to help would have aided him nothing and had landed me who knows where. Actually, it had probably landed me in the garden as it had the previous time.

Groaning again, I started to rise, but the groan dissolved in the silence. Curious. I would have expected some rustling of stirring creatures, some lights from the stars. I also would have expected the Floraisons, or at least Lofton, to have found me by now. I was sitting on the flagstones of the garden walk, wasn't I?

My fingers skimmed over the ground and then out around me. Rock. Solid, water-worn rock, below me and rising like a wall behind me. *A Place Changer can easily become destabilized,* Lofton had said.

Heaven help me. I was in a cave. Without a light. And no one knew where I was. And if I didn't know where I was, I couldn't use my traveling ring.

Making use of the wall behind me, I scrambled up. No shimmering box disturbed the darkness, and I felt no tug as I waved my arms about and shuffled around where I'd fallen. *Destabilized.* It must have reconnected with the garden after dumping me.

A sudden desire to write my last will and testament overtook me, but considering I had no light, no quill, and no one would ever find my body, there didn't seem to be much point. *Get ahold of yourself, Marcel.*

I felt my way back to the wall, gritting my teeth against a headache and the discomfort of my cut wrist. "That's right, get ahold of yourself. The air's not stale. There must be a way out."

I was *not* going to die so easily. I didn't survive a carriage wreck at six and a month-long battle with influenza and then pneumonia—ending only a few weeks ago—to die alone in a dismal cave.

Praying for help and running my fingers along the wall as a guide, I inched in the direction I decided to call *forward*. It ran slightly uphill, which was hopeful.

Counting my steps, I kept flush to the wall. Then my fingers hit a rough projection. It stretched into the tunnel in a pattern of long rectangles with a crumbling substance surrounding each unit. One rectangle shifted and crashed beside my foot.

"Are these ... bricks?" Moving faster, I tracked the man-made barrier. It spanned the tunnel but was mostly collapsed at the other end. Had I found a cellar under the duke's manor?

I climbed over the rubble, but my chest tightened as I crossed the partition. I crouched at the bottom of the rubble pile and sniffed. Nothing. The air *felt* foul, filled with something that had no outright odor. Had this part of the cave been blocked off because of toxic mold or fumes rising from a subterranean vent?

Dismissing the feeling as a figment of my imagination, I worked my way over to the wall. My fingers recoiled from the rock though it was the same ragged cave wall as on the other side of the bricks. I flexed my fingers, then lightly touched the wall again, cringing as I moved along the chamber. "Anyone would think you were a half-magic in a den of sorcerers, as jumpy as you are."

The words echoed and lost themselves, giving me the impression of being in a domed chamber. My fingers dipped as the wall receded and changed texture as if hewn. A trough? I couldn't stop myself from jerking away, and in my retreat, I lost touch with the wall and my hip collided with a rounded stone disc. A table. Dust, a stone knife, a small cauldron, but no lantern. I wiped my hands on my trousers, unable to stop the gooseflesh rising on my arms. I felt my way back to the wall and over the fallen bricks. Whatever that room had been, it was not the way out.

My chest released, and I sucked in the cool air of the tunnel. Obviously, I needed to choose another direction as forward. Like back to where I'd fallen from the Changer.

Soon, the shuffling of my shoes over the stone grated almost as much as the darkness.

"Yes," I said aloud to break the eerie silence, "this is likely a smugglers' cave. There'll be torches hanging on the walls and treasure lining the path a little ways ahead. As well as surly smugglers with bloodstained swords, to make things interesting. You don't have enough adventure in your life as it is, Marcel. It'd be a good experience for you to escape their clutches." I gingerly touched my aching head. "Then again, I'll save that adventure for another day. It's too far from the coast for smugglers anyway. Catacombs? There might be an empty burial slot to take a nap in."

The path began to descend. I reached out for the wall again, but touched only air. I froze. Was that also what was before me? Air?

I inched one foot forward. Solid. I let out a breath, then realized I must have wandered to the middle of the tunnel. Closing my eyes to better feel my way, I shuffled to the left until reaching the wall again, then continued on, following its curve around a bend.

"Or maybe it's where they make the local cheese—not that nasty blue kind, I hope—or store the wine. Yes, this is probably the outer chamber of the wine cellar under Henly Manor. At least I'm out of the wind here. It's always the same temperature in caves, they say. That's what makes them so useful for making and storing cheese and wine."

"Are you a ghost?" a voice, like that of an older child, spoke out of the darkness ahead.

I drew up short. Dare I hope a young servant at Henly? "Not unless you are."

Rejoicing at the rays of light angling up to me from farther down the path, I continued on. The tunnel must take a sharp decline.

"That makes the two of us human. In which case, you'd better stop before you fall in that pit."

I skidded to a stop. A mixture of fear, relief, and a sense of adventuring excitement coursed through me. "Thank you, my friend. Since you're not a ghost, are you an angel who could lift me across? I only see your bright light." In the pit, it seemed.

A laugh echoed around me. The light began to rise, accompanied by an alarming scraping of metal against rock. Then a boy's face appeared some twenty feet ahead, made ghastly by the light of the lantern in his hand. Between us was the utter blackness of a chasm.

"The name's Ryn," he said. "I lowered the lantern to see how deep the pit was and if anything was in it."

I liked the kid already—curious in nature and with a tendency to save lives, chief among them mine.

"Marcel Ellsworth. Pleased to make your acquaintance, Ryn. Did you find anything of interest?"

He shrugged. "Only the bones of some animal, a wolf or dog of some kind."

"I'm grateful you kept mine from being added to them."

"We explorers have to look out for one another. Where's your lantern? Don't you know to always carry a spare? How long have you been in here? You didn't pass me earlier, and I've been here over two hours. Is there another way in?"

I chuckled at his enthusiasm, remembering mine and my cousins' as children. "I do know to always carry a spare and have made use of my spare on more than one occasion while out exploring with my cousins. But I came here quite by accident from another route and am thus unprepared and unequipped for such a venture as this. I trust you'll help me?"

The boy, about eleven or so, stood straighter. "Of course. Lucky for you, I brought a lot of rope. My father makes me tie a length about my waist so I can find my way back to the storeroom, and I have the rope for the lantern."

"Very wise of him. We're under Henly Manor then?"

"No, in a cave on the estate they used to use for making wine. This tunnel leads to their main storeroom."

"You don't know the name of the cave, do you?"

"Nope. Begins with a *D* though." Ryn untied the rope from around the lantern's handle and coiled it for better throwing. "Catch." He swung the coil back, then tossed it across to me.

"What exactly is the plan? Nice throw, Ryn." Catching the rope, I studied the pit that was too wide for me to jump. It would be run, jump, swing, and get hauled up, and I suddenly felt like I weighed a thousand pounds. "Not to insult your strength, my young friend, but I'm too heavy for you to pull out."

"I know."

"Is there something sturdy over there to tie this to so I can pull myself up?"

"Nope."

"Now, Ryn—"

"Ryn?" The call echoed up the tunnel.

I had no idea caves in this part of Sonser were so popular, but I wasn't complaining.

"Here, Papa. *We're* here," Ryn yelled over his shoulder, then faced me again. "He's my plan. I knew he'd be along soon. Like Uncle Damien says, Papa can get a man out of any scrape."

"Does he do it often?"

"For Uncle, yes," Ryn said, his voice lowered and laced with censure. Reverting to his usual cheerful tone, he continued, "Don't go anywhere, especially not forward. I'll be right back." He laid his end of my rope down and scampered off, returning a few minutes later with a man about my height. The man dropped his arm from around Ryn's shoulders, set his lantern on the floor, and picked up the rope.

"Tie your end of the rope securely around your waist," he said as he began to tie his end onto Ryn's rope, and thus to something in the storeroom. "You have an odd tendency to show up in the most unexpected, dark places, Lord Ellsworth. Do you know how to tie a good knot?"

I knew the explorer's father? "Yes, I do—I mean I'm well versed in knot-tying. You'll have to enlighten me as to what dark place we've met, however."

"A few nights ago I was passing through the gardens on my way to the stable—to fetch my horse and return to the village, where my son and I are staying for the month—when Lord Mavern accosted me with his plans for wooing the Lady Gabriella. I deemed it best for the lady's sake that I accompany the man on his fool's errand, if I couldn't persuade him to change his mind before we found her. You, however, more expediently saw to the lady's wish for privacy. I congratulate you, sir."

"Lord Tyndale?" The quiet man who'd encouraged Mavern to return to the house? Tall and lithe, handsome with that slight air of melancholy about him that women tended to consider romantic, Tyndale was a contrast to the blustering Lord Mavern in more ways than one.

"You pick up names quickly, Ellsworth. Let's see if I can pick you up as quickly." Tyndale tested the slickness of the tunnel floor as he spoke. "Take a running leap—do step lightly as you are standing on a shelf, not a solid floor—and arch your body. We'll try to swing you up onto this side, since its lower here. If we can't, prepare to be bruised when you slam into it."

"We'll haul you up, though. Don't worry," Ryn added cheerfully as he and his father took their positions.

"That we will, my boy. Ready, Ellsworth?"

Backing up to a good running distance, I steeled my body for more aches. "Ready."

I ran, jumped, dropped, arced, swung, slammed, and slid up the opposite wall. A section of the shelf I'd been standing on collapsed the moment my feet left it.

"Sorry about that," Tyndale commented as he hoisted me over the rim with a grunt. "The pit wasn't wide enough to get a good swing going. We almost made it, though."

"I'm not complaining." I rolled over and accepted Ryn's hand and tug to my feet. I untied the rope from my waist, trying to ignore the pain shooting through me and the wet warmth at my wrist. Ryn picked up the two lanterns, and we began following his rope tail toward the storeroom.

"What exactly brings you here?" Tyndale coiled the rope as we walked. He didn't waste time or words, this man.

"I fell through a ... a hole and landed in the cave." I self-consciously straightened my jacket and reached for my hat, which wasn't there.

"Uh huh. Well, in that case, you must be tired. I was about to have a drink at the village inn while my son ate dinner. Would you care to join us? We'd make it back in time for dinner at Henly."

The jolt of every fall and crash of the day pulsed through me, and every muscle and limb remembered the weakness of my month abed. "What's the dessert of the day?" Aunt Coraline made me promise to eat hearty and fatten myself back up.

"It's gooseberry pie night."

"I feel revived already. Lead on." Steeling my heart against bad news, I posed a question that wouldn't necessitate mention of the Place Changer. "Have you seen the Duke of Lofton this afternoon? I was supposed to meet him but lost my way."

"I saw him at the house before I left."

I let out a long breath. He was alive. Now I could enjoy that pie.

We came to an open chamber with a high ceiling and torches in holders on the wall. Only a couple of the torches were lit, and those, I suspected, were for Ryn's use.

Casks of wine lay in racks stretching across the broad chamber. Each cask was stamped with the crest of the Floraison family. Behind one row, against the wall near our tunnel, was a long, low box, like a pirate's chest, rather out of place amidst the rounded barrels. Two large barrels lacking the duke's crest stood beside it, to one of which was tied Ryn's rope.

"Hello? Is anyone there?" The timid, feminine call brought us all to a halt in the middle of the chamber, and we cast curious glances at one another. It sounded like Lady Gabriella, but I'd never heard a Floraison so lacking in confidence before. Concern put speed in my steps.

"Here, Lady Gabriella."

"I repeat, Lord Ellsworth," Tyndale whispered. "You have an odd tendency to show up in the most unexpected, dark places—with the beautiful Lady Gabriella. Perhaps it was you and not Lord Mavern I should've been watching that night."

I gave a quiet scoff. "You couldn't be more surprised than I, but I have no intentions toward the young woman, honorable or not, so you needn't worry." I knew better than to care for anyone who valued perfection in beauty and social graces above all else. If I learned anything from my two years with Lady Ellsworth, it was that I didn't fit that crowd, and frankly, I didn't care to.

"I'll see you at dinner then." Tyndale's mouth curved in an annoyingly knowing smile. I bid him and Ryn farewell, then hurried past them to meet Lady Gabriella.

She hesitated just inside the cave entrance, in front of a gate resembling a portcullis, and leaned to the left to look around a row of barrels, her hand cradled to her chest. Her gaze caught mine, and her shoulders sank in a relieved sigh that stopped me in my tracks. "Lord Ellsworth, thank goodness." Then she spun on her heel and marched out, her head as high and proud as any queen newly risen to the throne.

What had I done now? Grandfather Gérard was right: women were an unfathomable mystery.

I caught up with her at a tree not far from the entrance, where she worked to untie Sterling's reins. "Did you come here seeking me?" If so, why dismiss me as soon as finding me?

She didn't look my way, simply kept fumbling with the reins. "You're the one who disappeared, aren't you?" she snapped. "To this of all places." She cast a nervous glance over her shoulder at the cave.

I stiffened. I deserved that, I supposed. "I didn't mean to. How is the Duke of Lofton?"

"Fine."

"I'm glad to hear it."

"I'm sure you are, and in future, Lord Ellsworth, have the kindness to stay away from Place Changers as well as any part of the estate where you have no business."

I should have landed on her earlier. "I'd be happy to oblige. If you will kindly tell me where I am, I'll use my traveling ring to return to the manor. I'm sorry to have caused you the inconvenience of a search."

She glanced at the cave entrance, then quickly turned back to Sterling, jerking on the reins more than pulling them loose. "You're at the Dreydon Caves, about two miles southeast of the house." Sterling tossed his head, then nuzzled his mistress, but she scooted away. "Be still, Sterling."

She was even mad at the horse; it was definitely time to leave. I touched my fingers to my ring, preparing to turn it, but then stilled.

To this of all places.

It wasn't me, or even Sterling. It was the cave. She was terrified of it, and from the way she bit her lip, angry with herself for being so. I had my doubts as to how well the Perfect Floraisons could handle any faults they happened to recognize.

The anger tightening my chest loosened, and I slipped my ring into my pocket. I gently caught Lady Gabriella's trembling hands and tugged them free of the reins. "Please, allow me."

She didn't say a word as I boosted her onto Sterling and then untied the horse's reins and handed them to her, making mundane comments on the weather and the possibility of another snow all the while to allow her time to regain her composure.

"Shall I accompany you home?" I asked.

"If you wish."

It wasn't exactly an invitation, but it would do.

Sterling plodded forward, and I walked beside him, discreetly studying his mistress. It wasn't as sweet as gooseberry pie, but there was some satisfaction in Lady Gabriella's stiff posture. The Perfect Floraison had a weakness after all. And she knew it. She tried to hide it in pride and disdain of me, which was hardly a promising way to deal with one's faults. But despite her fears, she had come for me.

A muscle ticked in my jaw. I wished she hadn't, for I had something in common with Mavern: Of the three beautiful daughters of the Duke of Henly, it had been Gabriella who stirred more than an admiration for beauty. Fair-haired while her sisters were dark, with more sweetness in her face and gentleness in her manner, and a voice like a songbird, she alone had captivated me. But she was still a proud, elite Floraison. Too good for the likes of me. No different than Lady Ellsworth, a woman ashamed and harshly critical of her orphaned, limping, stuttering grandson.

"Lord Ellsworth?"

"Yes?"

She glanced at me, her eyes shaded by the hood of her cloak. "I shouldn't have been cross with you. Please forgive me. I ... The Dreydon Caves are dangerous. I do not like anyone to get near them."

I forced down a smile at her euphemism for "terrified stiff of the caves."

"Don't trouble yourself, Lady Gabriella. I suspected fear for the safety of your father's guest was the cause. I can't blame you for disliking the caves. I nearly fell into a pit there myself, and I heard tell of some poor wolf not so lucky as I."

Her face, suffused with a blush, paled. I wanted to kick myself for upsetting her.

"Y-you nearly fell into the pit?" Her voice was barely a whisper.

"I stopped a foot or so from it. I was in no real danger. You are always coming to my rescue it seems," I added lightly.

"A Floraison never abandons a guest," she said quietly. She turned her gaze to the road ahead, though I doubted she noticed the snowcapped mountains in the distance, or how the forest was thinning as we approached the vineyards. Shortly, however, she once more rode with her head held high. I could almost feel her mask slipping into place.

I retreated into my own thoughts. What had I missed in the afternoon lecture? I'd have to look for Tyndale after dinner and see if he took notes.

"This is yours, I believe."

My eyes registered the brown hat Lady Gabriella held out to me. I managed to grab it before I walked into it face-first. Apparently, I needed *An Ellsworth never ...* statement: *An Ellsworth never neglects to pay attention to his surroundings.* "Thank you. Where did I lose it?"

"It was beside the Changer."

"Ah." I blew out a relieved breath. "I thought the duke was finished when that tree fell." One should never underestimate an enchanter.

"He used a power burst." A radiant smile lit her face. "It was amazing. The top half of the tree turned to ash mid-air and settled around him with nothing more violent than a *poof.*"

"I wish I could have seen it." Anything that could make her smile like that must have been incredible.

A wistful look in her eyes, she touched her skirt near where I'd seen her slip her wand into a hidden pocket. Summoning my best imitation of a scolding music instructor, I shook my finger at her, "If you practiced more, Lady Gabriella, you could be as good."

"I'm sure of it. Are you volunteering to be a test subject?"

"Not for a power burst." Though it'd be tempting if it'd draw another of those dazzling smiles from her.

Stumbling over a rut, I laid a steadying hand on Sterling. I was beginning to favor my weak leg, and it was growing difficult to ignore the messages of pain and exhaustion my body was sending me. My whole body was stiffening up. Whoever first said "walk it off" needed a kick in the shin—from Sterling. There were days when I would give almost anything to be of sound body, or at least have the power of enchantment so I could use a doppelganger spell to make me into someone without a bum leg. Someone without verbal glitches.

"Lord Ellsworth," she said in a contemplative manner. "Have you ever had the feeling something wasn't right, but you couldn't prove it?"

"On occasion. Have you had such an experience recently?"

"This afternoon, when Sterling reared and sent you flying—I am sorry about that—he knocked me over. As I fell, I thought I saw a man racing through the forest. He was suddenly encased by stone, but then he burst out and ran away, appearing shorter."

Tall, then short. My heart took a blow like the one that sent me sprawling into the snowbank in Ceur. The Thief. I should have left as soon as I'd realized I was in a den of enchanters. What better place for the Magic Thief than in a crowd at the house of enchanters famous for believing half-magics were nothing more than legends?

"But such a thing isn't possible," she continued, "unless it was you using your ring combined with a trick of the light. Or two men." Her face lit with a faulty conclusion. "Poachers. Why didn't I think of that before? It was only poachers running away, thinking the gamekeeper was after them."

"It was not I. But why is it impossible he was encased in stone? The Duke of Lofton could have bespelled him."

"If he were turned to, or covered by, stone," she said, "it would be because of a spell, and no man, not even an enchanter, could break free of another's spell so quickly. It's not likely he'd have a reversal spell stored in his memory. Unless he turned himself to stone and burst out immediately, which doesn't make sense. It would be a waste of magic."

I hesitated, but spoke against my better judgment. "A half-magic could. He could absorb the power of the spell and break free."

"A Magic Collector?" Laughter rang in her words. "You believe in legends?"

"Some would call an enchantress a thing of legend."

"We are firmly rooted in history, sir. Half-magics are not."

"Depends on which history you read." On whom you knew. But the half-magics didn't want to be known, in general, so I contented myself with making my rebuttals mentally.

"I'm afraid my stone man was merely a figment of my imagination, perhaps a gray wolf my mind misinterpreted in my alarm. The duke himself told me what I saw was unlikely."

"Did you look for bits of stone?"

"No. I didn't think to. The duke sent me to look for you."

"You've heard the rumors of the Magic Thief, haven't you?"

"Yes, yes, and we've taken precautions." There was an unmistakable irritation mixed with smugness in her tone.

The battle in me ceased. They'd taken precautions; there was nothing I could do. No one would believe me if I said anything anyway, being a mere baron and a non-magic. Enchanters with their Place Changers and magical toys. I scoffed. They could keep their powers and their troubles. Let the proud Floraisons continue in the ignorance made popular by their ancestor. It would be no loss for me to stay away from them and out of trouble with the Ceurian inspector and his Sonserian associates.

We continued in silence, me wondering what was for dinner, when Gabriella surprised me by speaking.

"By the way, you were wrong the other day," she said.

"About what?"

"I have listened to my father's lectures. I often serve as his scribe as he prepares them."

"Have you?" I responded without really thinking. "Then perhaps you could summarize what he covered the first two days. I was late because of illness and poor travel conditions."

Again surprising me, she laughed. "'Would I?' you mean?" Her gaze turned searching, as if she were trying to delve my heart. "Do you truly wish to know?"

"Of course. If you would be so kind?"

She smiled, but it didn't reach her eyes. "Happily. I am glad you came to learn and not to try to persuade my father to invest in some scheme or other, or to make acquaintances who would increase your influence."

I bristled at the thought and at her look, which suggested she wasn't entirely positive what she said was the truth.

"I want to improve my estate and help the villages around it."

"Very noble of you." The mocking tone I expected was there, but mild. She focused forward as if gathering her thoughts. "He begins with this story ..."

I glanced up in wonder as she spoke, for she mimicked her father's intonation as well as fully recited his lecture. My mouth, only too apt to give voice to my thoughts, exclaimed after a few minutes, "That's incredible. You sound exactly like your father. It's as if I'm listening to him, only in a different—"

Gabriella gasped, and I shut my mouth. There were times I wished I was mute.

"I-I-I ... I meant your voice—no, no, no, not your voice. You have a lovely feminine voice. I mean you don't sound like your father at all, but your—"

Gabriella held up her hand, her expression grim but not offended. "You mean I have the same *voice* in the sense of a *writing voice:* the same tone, diction, and style as my father." She said it with an air of weary admission.

"Yes. Please forgive me. I did not intend any slur. I-I-I was merely surprised at the unexpected similarity." I flinched and sighed. "Sometimes words escape me."

"And sometimes they fail me." She echoed my sigh and smiled ruefully. "At least words of my own. Thank you for pointing out the similarity. There is no offense to be taken in your honesty. Shall I continue?"

"Please," I said, grateful I hadn't been (figuratively speaking) made into a toad for my rudeness, not that I would have blamed her.

She continued, a bit haltingly, but sounding less and less like her father. More than once I patted my pockets, searching and wishing in vain for my notepad. When I asked questions, she was patient and answered as one who understood and did not simply repeat. After the third question, she gave me an odd look, and her manner relaxed, as if she finally believed my interest was genuine.

"Would you," she began in a surprisingly hesitant manner some minutes later, "ever read a book based on my father's material?"

"Would I? I'd be hounding the bookseller's until it arrived."

She nodded in an appreciative way. "In what style would you expect the book to be written?"

"Style?" I shrugged. "A comprehensible one. I'd appreciate it if it wasn't the literary equivalent of a monotone lecture. A little humor is always good, as are personal stories and examples."

"A good voice, in other words, and humor and examples." She chewed her cheek, reminding me very much of Aunt Coraline when she's contemplating the dinner menu.

"Exactly. Is your father writing a book to go with his lectures?"

"No," she answered quickly.

"Are you—"

"Shall we continue the lecture? Where was I? Oh yes."

A becoming blush colored her cheeks, urging me to question her more. But remembering the purpose of my visit, I fell back into the place of attentive listener.

A few minutes later, she suddenly quieted. The feeling of an intense glare drew my attention to a man walking on the opposite side of the road. His dark look took me aback. He didn't say a word as he passed us at a brisk pace. He was short, a bit on the heavy side, somewhere around forty years old, and sported a disgracefully patchy brown beard.

"Do you know him?" Gabriella asked when we were a suitable distance from the man.

"No."

"He looked distinctly as if he doesn't like you." There was amusement in her tone.

"I'm at a loss to know why." Unless it was jealousy of my companion. "Do you know him?"

"No. His attire indicates he may be one of the temporary servants hired for the month, though he'd never be allowed to serve in the house with *that* beard."

She caught me snickering and cocked her head.

"I couldn't agree more, Lady Gabriella. No man worth his salt would suffer such a monstrous thing on his face. Only bandits and other unsavory characters would refuse to shave a scraggly beard like that. No, I would certainly never trust him in my house."

She smirked as if she wanted to laugh.

"Do you have something against a preference for well-groomed servants?" I asked in mock censure.

She finally, genuinely, laughed. "Not at all, Lord Ellsworth. I much prefer them." She paused, and I followed her gaze to another passerby, this one also fixing a dark look on me.

Lord Mavern. Going to the village inn to change for dinner? I thought he was housed at the manor.

I nodded to him, then stepped closer to Sterling and Gabriella. To my immense satisfaction, Mavern's scowl deepened, but it instantly disappeared as he greeted Lady Gabriella. She wished him a pleasant walk, and we continued in our separate directions.

"He also looks distinctly as if he doesn't like you." Gabriella's lips quirked into a smile. "I can't imagine why."

Oh, but I could. "It must be the company I keep."

Chapter 7

Many have tried to find and destroy the lairs, but only those the sorcerers will to do so can find them. Or those who have already seen them.

Sorcerers: Their Various Kinds and Their Slaves by historian Lionel Bachman

.

These enchanters thought themselves so clever, protecting their treasures against the thief yet leaving them accessible to the family. Fools. All the thief required was one among them to be his willing helper. To gain that, all he had to do was Call.

The Fall of Bevvelian, a fictionalized story from the Caffin Wars, by Edgar Frock

GABRIELLA FLORAISON

MY PARENTS WERE greatly distressed when I told them of the fallen tree. The next day, they visited the site and ordered the remaining timber checked for stability. Aunt Helene, Alexandria, Eva, and I accompanied them to the ford.

After examining the tree's exposed roots, Papa told me he'd spoken with Lord Ellsworth about the kidnapping incident and had turned the matter over to the village constabulary.

He glanced at Mama, then gave me a serious look. "The constable has promised discretion, but I must warn you that you, Harvey, and Lord Ellsworth might be called on to testify."

"I expected as much." How could my voice remain calm when my stomach twisted in revulsion?

Aunt Helene sputtered, her face stained with color to match the supposed stain to the Floraison honor at my needing to attend a trial. I braced myself as she opened her mouth, but Mama's tsk-tsk forced a temporary lock on Aunt's thoughts.

Mama took my arm and pulled me to her side. "I never thought a daughter of mine would ever be called on to participate in a trial. Nonetheless, your father and I are proud of you for capturing the bandits and preventing further harm to Lord Ellsworth." She gave Aunt Helene a significant look, at which Aunt set her jaw. The subject had been sealed. Whispering my thanks, I hugged her.

"That we are," Papa added as he took Mama's hand. "Speaking of guests, I must return to my lectures."

"And I to Lord and Lady Tannon's," Mama said. "She and the baby are doing better, but I would like to keep an eye on them. We'll leave you to your tresor box hunt." Mama kissed my cheek and then released me.

After they left, I recounted my finding of the pouch. It was weak of me, and a sure forfeit of my boast of finding the tresor box first, but after what happened yesterday, I was leery of pursuing Fred's clues all over the estate by myself.

"How on earth did Fred get it up there?" Alexandria asked when I led them to the tree where the pouch had hung. The limb was empty now.

"I haven't the faintest idea, but it appears to have fall-en."

"Here it is." Eva picked up the oilskin pouch from the edge of the path. "Judging by the hoofprints, a horse nearly crushed it."

"Sterling spooked while Lord Ellsworth was reaching for it."

"I don't understand why the Duke of Lofton associates with that dreadfully plain man. His clothes don't even fit properly." Aunt Helene sniffed as she lifted her skirts and crossed a muddy patch to Eva. "Even if he weren't so plain, he's only the son of a baron. Completely undistinguished family, no significant accomplishments."

Alexandria and Eva voiced their agreement, but I couldn't. I saw Lord Ellsworth before me once again: thick reddish hair, green eyes so expressive I could feel his empathy even before he spoke, the dark circles under his eyes, the bony cheekbones. So ... pale and thin. For the first time, the sharp angles of his face became gauntness, an unhealthy thinness. Had he recently suffered a severe illness? Or did he normally look as he did now?

Whatever might be the faults of his appearance, however, his passion for serving his estate had become obvious during our conversation. That was something to admire, something he had in common with the head of the Floraison family.

I joined Aunt Helene and Alexandria in crowding around Eva and the pouch. "Remember the time Fred—" I began.

"Yes," Alexandria said. We backed away from Eva.

Eva held the pouch out from her, loosened the drawstring, and cautiously peeped inside. She gave a puzzled frown. "A note and a chip of rock?"

Aunt Helene risked a closer look. "Marble. I hope he didn't smash a statue or tabletop to get that and expect us to piece it back together. I've always told your father

Frederick was too fond of jokes." She picked the chip out, looked at it briefly, then passed it off to Alexandria.

"Fred would never destroy anything for the tresor box hunt." Alexandria examined the chip. It wasn't smooth, but I wasn't certain what design had been worked on it.

I fished out the square slip of paper and unfolded it. "'The warrior stands alert, ever on his guard. The battleground has changed, but still he stands, watching for his foes. Watching, waiting, this century long. The beast of ivy green, the beast of feathered wing assail him even now, but these he doth ignore in favor of the ones viler still. Chisel and hammer he doth fear, but nothing can he do but stand in watch and silent plea throughout eternity.'"

"It's one of the statues commemorating the Caffin Wars. He mentions ivy so it must be in the pleasure gardens." Alexandria slipped the chip into Eva's hand. "I would've expected something more challenging from Fred."

"Oh!" Eva shifted the chip so only its edges touched her fingertips. A slip of paper materialized around it with a sound somewhere between the crinkle of paper and a sizzle.

Alexandria's eyes sparkled. "Perhaps there is a challenge to this after all."

"Some word you spoke must have triggered a spell." Aunt Helene took the chip and the paper from Eva, who seemed glad to be rid of them. "'It's not as easy as you may think.'" She gave Alexandria a look. "'To one alone does this piece belong. If you place it wrong, to the wrong you shall belong.'"

"Ominous sounding, I must say," Alexandria said.

"Whatever does he mean?" Eva asked.

"I don't know, but I don't want to find out." I gathered the items and returned them to the pouch. "To the library, ladies. Let's look up the date of completion for the statues."

"Your great-grandfather commissioned a number of statues a century ago. We can begin with those," Aunt Helene said as we departed for the house.

The sweet song of a redstart arrested me, and I searched for its source, finally spotting the male with its white-banded forehead near the fallen oak. My fingers twitched. My painting of this species was hidden away in the tresor box.

The redstart sailed away as a strip of blue emerged out of nowhere beyond it, where the Duke of Lofton had set up his easel the previous day.

Dressed in a loose-fitting blue suit, Marcel Ellsworth stood covering one hand with the other as if he'd just twisted that ring of his. Come to see what he'd missed by falling into the Changer?

He startled when he saw me but quickly tipped his hat in greeting, an apologetic smile on his face. He gestured to my companions, who were walking on oblivious to his arrival, and pressed his finger to his lips.

I nodded, returning his smile of thanks before rejoining my companions. It occurred to me then to wonder if he'd suffered any injuries during his falls and journey through the Changer. He had been limping by the time we reached the stable yesterday. I hadn't noticed until Harvey mentioned it with a frown at me. *For shame, Gabriella. A Floraison does not neglect her guests.* I hadn't meant to. We'd been engaged in conversation, and I simply hadn't noticed.

When we got to the library, Aunt Helene pointed out the books and documents likely to provide information on the statues, then left us to our work.

As I replaced a volume on the history of our estate, a book poking out from among the others caught my eye— a biography of one of the sculptors employed by my great-grandfather. The artisan, also an enchanter, was said to have turned his models to stone, temporarily of course, to get a better idea of how his statues would look. Some said it was my great-grandfather who gave him the idea. I added the book to our pile.

A howling wind kept me awake that night, prompting me to get up and write notes on the conversation Lord Ellsworth, Lord Tyndale, and I had at dinner. Lord Ellsworth hadn't said it outright, but I suspected his relative and nearest neighbor had sabotaged Carrington with the hopes of acquiring it, which wasn't a new tactic. The investigation he and his new estate manager had undertaken to determine how the old estate manager did it, and how to fix it, would be a valuable addition to my new, thoroughly restyled manuscript. Lord Ellsworth had graciously given me permission to use his material.

Sleep was still as far beneath the horizon as the sun when I finished my notes, inducing me to return to the library and our research. Using my keys, I unlocked the door, heavy and forbidding in the candlelit hallway with its relief of battle scenes from the Caffin Wars, and shut it behind me, but didn't lock it. I selected the sculptor's biography, poked the fire back to life, and curled up under a thick blanket in my chair by the fireplace.

The firelight glowed cheerfully but not enough to read by, not even with the help of its reflection in the burnished metal of the old suit of armor standing guard in front of the massive wooden beam opposite me. The beam, broad as a man's shoulders, was almost the only place in the library not covered in books, scrolls, or maps.

Fred had begged and begged to be allowed to wear the armor beside the beam. Alexandria and I even joined in, but always we were refused. Then one stormy afternoon while everyone else was engaged, Fred dismantled the empty knight and struggled into the armor. That was the day he disappeared and Papa was forced to use the mirror to find him. Our intrepid knight was soundly spanked and wouldn't even enter the library for a month.

Laughing at the memory, I laid my wand in the groove between the open pages of the biography. *Dilucesco.* My wand now glowing, I held the book close and snuggled deeper into the chair. Did the sculptor really turn people to stone for his art? It appears he did, and he had worked out the perfect spell for it with the help of one of his patrons, who "shall remain nameless."

Skimming the text, I hunted for more information on the stone spell. "The spell was built so that the time of transformation was limited to twenty minutes for the sake of the models." I ran my finger under the words, tapping on the period. "Thank goodness for that," I murmured. "It was likely my great-grandfather's contribution. He never suffered mistreatment to his family or to the servants belonging to his house."

It would be useful not to have your subject move or flit away as my birds did. Nevertheless, it would be unthinkable for me to engage in such a practice. Not to mention turning a bird to gray stone would hide its coloration and therefore half the reason for sketching it.

Yawning, I nestled deeper under the blanket and read over the spell itself. It seemed simple enough. I yawned again but was too comfortable and snug to return to my room.

A vase of hothouse flowers sat invitingly on the table near me. Should I try the spell? Why not? Both the Duke of Lofton and Papa intimated that we youngsters didn't practice magic enough. I read over the spell again, then readied my wand. Choosing a peony as my subject, I performed the spell.

The pink of the petals faded to light gray. Perfect. Well, almost. The stem was still green and the tips of the petals soft pink. I found the reversal spell at the bottom of the entry and restored the flower. I repeated the spell and reversal until the peony appeared as a lovely stone replica.

Very nice. Now, how was my aim? Choosing other flowers, I created a lovely mixed bouquet. With a sleepy smile, I admired the arrangement. The gray blended so well with the soft pinks and ... My head nodded to my chest.

A bony hand grabbed my wrists. I cried out as the jagged nails dug into my arm, deeper with each desperate tug of mine to get away.

"Where is it, child?" hissed the creature. It might have been a woman once, but only a monster could live in the depths of the cave beyond the broken wall. Her other hand with its abnormally long and strong fingers groped blindly over me. "Where is it?"

"Let me go. Fred! Fred! I'm back here!" I kicked and pulled, but she was too strong for me. My heartbeat thumped in my ears and the darkness blurred, leaving nothing but two eyes and a broken row of bared teeth in front of me. The pain of her grasp and the cut on my finger,

gashed earlier against a trough in the rock wall, faded underneath the fear. "Let me go! My father's the duke. He'll throw you in prison. He'll—"

The woman stilled, then sniffed.

One drop of blood slipped from my finger to splatter on the floor, echoing through the chamber like a pebble tossed into a well.

The crone cackled and jerked my face to hers. "Welcome, little one. You spilt your blood in a sorcerer's lair—on our altar! You belong to us now." She cackled again, then shook me. "Give it to me. Give me the wand! I'll show you the power of the sorcerers!"

"No! Dilucesco." My hidden wand flared bright as the sun. The woman screamed. I shoved her back, wrenching my wrists free as we tumbled. I jumped up and ran back to the broken wall, back to the long, dark tunnel that had promised the best place for a game of hide-and-seek with my brother and favorite dog.

"You will come back!" She crawled over the rubble of the ancient room, knocking rock and pottery together as she moved. "The Call will find you. You will be ours!"

I leapt over the broken wall, then screamed as I crashed into Fred and the wolfhound around the first curve of the tunnel. Shoving Fred's hand away, I shot up and ran, yelling for him to follow, calling Roma away from the dreadful room and the hag. Growling, Roma loped behind us. The ground began to tremble.

I startled awake, my heart racing, expecting the floor to open beneath me. Expecting to hear once again Roma's yelp as she fell into the forming chasm, to hear Fred's cry as he grabbed a jutting rock with one hand and my arm with the other. But all was silent except the ticktock of the mantel clock.

It was only a nightmare. A nightmare caused by the fright of the earthquake and the shock of Roma's death. That's what everyone said. *You've let your fear run away with you,* Aunt Helene said. *Your fear and your imagination. No true Floraison does that. No such place as a sorcerer's lair could exist on Floraison land.*

Though Papa didn't contradict her, his pallor suggested a fear of his own. He closed the Dreydon Caves, claiming the earthquake had made them unstable. And he bought me Sterling to help me get over Roma's death.

You belong to us now. I shivered but forced myself to ease back in the chair and tuck the blanket beneath my chin. I rubbed my fingers against my palm. *A Floraison is always courageous.* Even after nightmares of nightmares. That's all it was.

My legs tingled as I uncurled and stood. The floor squeaked, and I bolted upright, my heart pounding. The noise hadn't come from beneath my feet.

Another squeak sounded near the door. My wand flared to brightness, but it revealed no other insomniac in search of relief.

The squeaking stopped. I crept along the hallways to my room.

"Which of the Five Warriors?" I glanced about the square garden chamber, the junction of two paths. A statue guarded each of the four corners. One took his stand in the center. A dusting of snow crunched softly under our feet and changed the normally opaque off-white of the marble statues to a crisp, bright white in the mid-morning sun peeking momentarily through the low clouds.

"The middle one, I think." Eva pointed to the archer in full armor poised as if ready to shoot his arrow into a canyon below. "He looks alert for battle, and it's the same color and pattern of marble."

"I'm not risking belonging to any of these based on your hunch, Eva." Alexandria walked around one of the corner statues, trailing her fingers along its base. "I don't see any missing pieces for this one."

I examined another corner statue. "None here."

"Nor here," Alexandria said at another.

"Here's a spot." Standing on tiptoe, Eva pointed to an apparent depression in the center archer statue until we came to look. The archer rose to a height of eight feet, two feet of which was pedestal.

Uncertainty weighed heavily on me as I considered the dark spot at the archer's hairline. We hadn't checked the fifth statue, the tallest one, standing straight and staring ahead. He looked more like a watcher to me, but Eva would never let us go to it without thoroughly crossing this one off.

One arm on the archer, Alexandria stood on tiptoe to get a better look at his hairline. "Surely one of the gardeners would have noticed damage in such a prominent place. What could have caused it? Fred knows better than to damage a statue."

I dusted the snow from the top of the pedestal and then hoisted my skirt.

"What are you doing, Gabriella?" Eva looked askance at me.

"Getting a better look. We'd have to climb up to replace the chip anyway, if it belongs."

With a boost from Alexandria, I climbed onto the pedestal and ducked into the open space between the warrior's chest and the arm that drew back the arrow.

The marble was polished slick and, with the additional help of a light snow, quite treacherous. Carefully positioning my feet, I scooted around. "Hand me the chip, and I'll see if it's a match."

I leaned over the arm to reach Alexandria's outstretched hand. My foot slipped, and I bruised my ribs against the archer's arm protector.

"Are you okay?" Alexandria drew the chip back to her chest.

Wincing, I straightened. "Yes."

"Do be careful. If you touch the chip to anywhere other than the right location—the wrong statue or the wrong place on the right one ..." She held out the chip again.

"I'll be careful. Why don't you and Eva put a steadying hand on my legs?" After accepting the chip, I eased around until I was leaning into the archer's shoulder.

They pressed against my legs as I peered up at his hairline. There was something odd about the spot Eva had taken for a hole. It was dark but not hollow. Using the marble shoulder for support, I stretched up and ran a finger over it. As I suspected, black grease smeared my fingertip. "It's only grease."

"It's that one then," Alexandria said of the last corner guard.

"Let go of my legs; I'm coming down."

Eva released me and backed away. "We'd best hurry. Papa and his guests are doing a walking tour of the estate today. They might pass this way."

"Now you tell me." My feet twisted in the cramped, uneven space as I turned. I sought a hold on the archer's chest but remembered the grease on my finger and stopped myself. "Hand me a handkerchief, would you?"

Alexandria stretched to hand me the white cloth over the archer's elbow. As I scooted forward to receive it, my boots skidded on the snow. I stumbled into the statue's arm. The chip fell from my grip and glanced off the pedestal.

The statue flared red, and with a crack, straightened. He grabbed me around the waist and tossed me over his shoulder like some wench about to be carried off by a barbarian invader.

With a cry, I grabbed the quiver on his back to steady myself. A chill swept through me, and I tried to pull my hand back, but it wouldn't budge. It was as cold as the marble it touched. So were my chest and stomach. I tried to shove off his shoulder but couldn't. *To the wrong you shall belong.* Oh no. No no no!

I stilled, one arm of stone stuck to the quiver and one of flesh extended. Seething, I looked down at Alexandria below me. "I'll get Fred for this if it's the last thing I do."

She stared at me wide-eyed, her hands hiding her mouth.

"Don't you dare laugh, Alexandria Floraison."

She shook her head, then lowered her hands. She was biting her lip. I clenched my jaw as her laughter burst forth in gleeful melody.

"Oh, Gabriella"—she waved toward my posterior—"you look like you're about to get the spanking of your life."

"What?" The statue's large hand came into view as I twisted around. His other hand, complete with bow and arrow, pressed me to his shoulder. My gasp was followed by a growl. *Frederick Alfred Floraison, you had better not come home for a long time.* "What are we going to do? You and Eva have got to get me out of this before someone sees me."

Alexandria coughed but couldn't douse her smirk. "Well, I did tell you I thought it was the other one."

"Don't be such a know-it-all."

She laughed again and motioned to Eva, who was still trying to get her laughter under control. "Let's find Mama. She's the best of us at spell reversal."

Eva winked at me. "Don't go anywhere, Gabriella."

They hurried off, and I craned my neck to watch them go. *Please no one walk this way.*

Relaxing my neck, I stared at the pedestal's edge and the gravel path below me. Minutes ticked by. I was certain the birds flittering over the walk, grating the rocks together as they hopped about, had lived a lifetime before I heard someone approaching. No, not someone, but *someones.* The rumble of their voices was too deep for women—Papa and his guests.

Panic sped my heart faster than any arrow shot by the archer on whose shoulder I indecorously hung. I could *not* let this happen. A Floraison was not the type to be carried off on a barbarian's shoulder. *Think, Gabriella, think.*

The sculptor's stone spell reversal? I whispered it and tugged against the statue, but to no avail. *Come on, Gabriella.* I couldn't leave. Therefore, I'd have to hide. With my cloak blue as a song bird? But many birds' coloration faded in the winter. Faded like the color of hothouse flowers graying into stone.

Fumbling awkwardly with my free hand, I grasped the tip of my wand in its pocket. The wand warmed in response to my touch, and I pictured the lifeless gray of the peonies in the vase in the library. How much did I value my dignity?

The crunching of gravel grew nearer.

A Floraison does not embarrass herself or her family. Turning my face toward the archer's back, I whispered the spell. A chill overtook me as a marble-white haze dimmed my vision.

Papa's rich voice found my ears as he discussed leadership principles to those nearest him. It passed by, and other softer-spoken conversations followed.

Walk on. No one notices the statues after the first visit. Just keep walking.

My ears picked out another familiar voice. It was unlike Papa's orotund voice, but good in its own way. It had an energy and good humor to it. The speaker swapped the order of two words, corrected himself, and kept going. Marcel?

"I don't recall that archer having a ... um ... companion before."

I take it back. Lord Ellsworth's voice was despicable.

"You must not have been paying attention. Come along."

Thank you, whoever you are.

They marched away through the garden, but I couldn't relax. How much longer until help arrived?

What was that?

The gravel stirred in a soft scraping, as if in light footsteps, but from which path, I couldn't tell. A shiver ran through me, emanating from my shoulder, and left a coldness well beyond the earlier chill in its wake. The soft footsteps circled me, paused as another shiver raced through me, and hurried away as gravel crunched in a normal step from the direction by which the men had left.

"There you are, Tyndale."

"I was wrong, Ellsworth. I don't remember this," Tyndale said, drawing near. "I would have expected better taste from the Floraisons. That's no way to treat a woman and certainly nothing to glorify in art."

There was amusement in Tyndale's voice, but I found little comfort in it, yet not much concern either. I was so cold. Who would have thought stone could get so cold? The book hadn't warned of the cold.

"There's a good story behind it, no doubt," he continued.

A pair of polished shoes stepped into my vision. The trousers above them were the exact shade of Marcel's at breakfast, a rich chestnut brown. Not that I was in the habit of noticing his clothes, but that particular shade worked well with the red of his hair. It was something the artist in me appreciated.

"The woman has a remarkable resemblance to—"

Please don't say it. Please don't say it.

"Well, that is ... she doesn't fit the archer's time. Her dress is too modern. Don't you agree, Tyndale?"

"Quite so."

Thank you.

A slight pressure lingered over my fingers stuck to the quiver, sending an odd feeling through me. The white haze that had come over my vision when I implemented the stone spell left in a rush, leaving only the icy chill. Beneath me, the archer shuddered. He popped me on the rear like a mother does a disobedient child, shrugged his shoulder, and sent me flying.

My cry caught in my throat as I hit Marcel's chest. He staggered back, and his arms tightened about me, cradling me to him.

"Gabriella!" he cried.

"By heaven, where did she come from?" Tyndale helped Marcel shift me from my lopsided position to fit securely in Marcel's arms.

"Lady Gabriella, are you all right?" Marcel asked.

Gasping for air like a drowning man newly surfaced, I couldn't do more than nod. My head flopped against his chest. Though limp as a rag doll, I felt as heavy as stone.

"Stay with us, Lady Gabriella. Don't faint."

Faint! A Floraison does not faint.

"Lay her on the bench," Tyndale said.

"I ... I'm fine." I forced the words out.

Marcel arched an eyebrow as he settled me on the wrought iron bench, propping me up in the corner, then stretching my legs along the seat. "Your Floraison spirit seems unharmed anyway." Kneeling in front of me, he took one of my hands and began to rub it. "Your hands are like ice. Who did this to you? Was it the man you saw at the river?"

Tyndale shot him a glance, then nudged my feet away from the seat's edge.

I shuddered, and the warmth of embarrassment replaced the heaviness and chill. I pulled my hand away from Marcel, grabbed the ornate bench arm, and tried to straighten, but my head swam, and I sank back against the bench.

"Take it easy, child." Tyndale's tone reminded me of the parental one the Duke of Lofton sometimes used. "Tell us what happened. Or would you prefer we fetched your father?"

I cracked one eye open. Interrupt Papa's lessons? Have all the guests chattering about his daughter's *incident*? It was bad enough these two should know.

Slowly this time, I pushed myself into a sitting position and clasped my hands in my lap. *A Floraison is always dignified.* Even when she's never wanted to disappear so badly in her life.

"It's nothing like that. There's no need for alarm." With a self-conscious laugh, I drew my cloak over my lap as a cold wind blew through the garden. "I almost wish it were. You see, I turned myself to stone. I had hoped to avoid being seen in the undignified position in which I was stuck due to a trick of my brother's—a spell on the archer and on a marble chip we thought belonged to it."

"You ..." Marcel rose and crossed his arms, a hard look on his face that didn't suit him at all. "You turned yourself to stone to save your precious Floraison pride?"

If his tone hadn't rankled, his expression of contempt would have. How dare he lecture me! "Yes, I did, and I am perfectly capable of performing such a simple spell. My great-grandfather helped invent it."

He rolled his eyes. "So capable of performing it that you fell like a lump of lead—excuse me, marble—as soon as it ended."

"That had nothing to do with the stone spell." Working hard to keep the edge out of my voice, I motioned for him to stand aside. "I refuse to be seen tossed over a man's, even a statue's, shoulder like a tavern wench."

"She has a point, Ellsworth," Tyndale said quietly. "It was rather an awkward position for a lady to find herself in, especially with all the men who were about to pass by."

Arms still crossed tightly over his chest, Marcel glanced from Tyndale to me, his lips pursed as if considering. Tyndale and I watched him expectantly.

I gave myself a mental shake. This was ridiculous. I was not waiting for that man to pass judgment on my actions. "I—"

"I suppose you're right." He moved aside. "But I still don't like it."

"Your opinion is duly noted, sir. We Floraisons always take the opinions of near strangers into consideration when deciding on a course of action."

"Somebody has to be the voice of reason." A hint of chagrin crept into his tone.

"But the Floraisons are never lacking in reason." Tyndale was charm itself compared to his companion. "Isn't that so, Lady Gabriella?"

I glared at Marcel before turning back to Tyndale and accepting his proffered arm. "Neither are the Tyndales, I'm sure." He led me to the statue. Then, releasing me, he picked up the chip from the gravel walk.

He looked beyond me to the path from the house. "If you'll excuse us, Lady Gabriella, we won't detain you any longer. We must catch up with your father." He placed the chip in my hand, tipped his hat, and walked briskly away.

Marcel took his friend's place beside me. "I meant you could've found another way. You're clever enough. Spells worked on yourself can be more dangerous than those worked by or on others." He bowed stiffly, then followed Tyndale.

I ground the gravel under my heel. That man had no right to look at me so disdainfully. He was only another ignorant non-magic with no understanding of enchantments or respect for our abilities.

But what he said about casting spells did ring true. I shook my head. What could he possibly know about it?

No sooner had they left than my sisters, Mama, and the Duke of Lofton hurried up the opposite path.

Tamping down my frustration, I tucked away loose hair, then smoothed my skirts. Something about my dress felt odd, lighter than usual. I brushed my hands over the fabric again, a sinking sensation sucking the breath out of me.

My wand was gone.

Chapter 8

The night was black and grief yet dulls my mind. What did he trick me into doing? I feel I should care. I know I should. Yet his treachery only reminds me of my promise to look after him. If we disappear, he says, they'll think I was a victim. My family wouldn't be disgraced. But I would lose them. My family, my home, even my name would be lost to me. What choice do I have? I've already failed them. They don't want me to grieve. I don't want to be joyful. They don't want me to be alone. I don't want to be in company. They warned me against my brother-in-law. I promised to look after him. He says if I help him now and train him properly in the ways of the half-magics, he'll find suitable work and never again do anything that would've distressed his sister. His is a silver tongue, moldable to what the listener wants to hear. But he may be in earnest. What might I make of him if I help him? Why do I fear what he might make of me?

Diary of a magic thief

MARCEL ELLSWORTH

T HE WOMAN OBVIOUSLY needed looking after. But I wasn't offering myself for the position.

Some feet away, my host and Jonathan Lofton examined the base of the fallen, half-disintegrated tree and argued over the possible causes of its upheaval. Stuffing my hands in my pockets, I kicked a snow-dusted pile of dead leaves, scattering them into a more natural look over the forest floor. A pile of leaves in the middle of a bare patch of forest floor, a withered heap where Gabriella's mystery man would've broken from his encasement of stone.

After the incident at the statue, I'd realized I couldn't leave the Floraisons to their fate. I told Lofton, and together we tackled the Duke of Henly. He didn't believe us, merely thought us an entertaining distraction from the other guests and their endless questions.

I continued to spread the leaves with the toe of my boot. Lofton had admitted using a stone spell on someone running away through the forest. If I were a clever, talented enchanter like Lofton, and unlike some I could name, I'd use leaves to create a stone encasement instead of turning the body to stone. This encasement would turn into a pile of leaves if the spell were collected by the half-magic Thief. But the Perfect Floraison thought half-magics, with their ability to control cast spells, didn't exist. And Gabriella always knew best. So did her father.

"You turned something running through the forest to stone, Lofton," the Duke of Henly said. "I believe that, but I don't believe it burst out on its own"—he gestured to the leaves I'd redistributed—"turning the stone back to leaves. There were two creatures. Your spell simply wore off before you were able to examine what you caught."

"Two is correct." Lofton held up two fingers, looking ready to poke his friend in the chest. "The stories are always the same with the Thief—two forms. But I'm not convinced it's two people." There was an almost desperate yearning undergirding this statement.

"One story, Lofton. One story." The Duke of Henly glanced over his shoulder at me. "Lord Ellsworth is the only one who has claimed to see the Thief in these two forms, isn't that correct?"

Lofton confirmed the assertion with defeat in his voice. Gabriella must not have told her father what she saw. And what good was the word of a baron accused of theft in Ceur and of bringing kidnappers—bounty hunters essentially—to Henly?

Turning away, I brushed snow from my collar and stuffed my hands back in my pockets, which were already bulging with a packet of letters from my family at Silvestris Castle. I was rarely envious of my cousin Giles's rank of prince—a hereditary title only but still impressive—yet I did envy the respect it gained him, however foolish it was for people to give respect to an inherited title. If I were a prince, the Floraisons might listen to me.

My companions continued talking, Lofton in earnest and the Duke of Henly batting away his arguments with the flair of a man who enjoys a good debate.

"Lord Ellsworth."

"Yes, Your Grace?" I jerked around at the Duke of Henly's voice—the patient tone indicating I'd missed an earlier hail.

Alfred Floraison, Duke of Henly, was an intimidating figure of a man. Tall, handsome, well-spoken, and well-respected. He never stuttered. Probably never got angry. And certainly was never accused of anything criminal. It was little wonder his daughters rebuffed every advance from the unmarried among the guests. No one could compare to their father.

"Have you heard anything more from Emil Farro?" he asked. "There are rumors of another attempted theft. What is it this Thief is trying so desperately to obtain?"

My thoughts shot to the letters in my pocket. I felt a shameful satisfaction that I possessed something the duke did not, even if it was only the confidence of an eccentric inventor-enchanter. "Forgive me, but what reason would an enchanter of Farro's rank have to tell a non-magic such things?"

The Duke of Henly arched an eyebrow. "You have nothing to tell of what the Thief desires?"

"I can tell you nothing."

Something of an amused smile settled on his face as he regarded me.

"That is a matter Lord Ellsworth should stay out of," Lofton said. "As he should stay out of matters here."

I startled at the command in his tone. Hadn't we agreed to talk to the Duke of Henly together? He'd seemed glad enough of my information and help then. Why was I now being cast aside?

The Duke of Henly laughed and clapped Lofton on the shoulder. "I agree. You've both done your duty in alerting me to the threat of a thief on my property. Now, it's time to return to the purpose of your visit to Henly." He nodded toward the path back to the house, and we started down it.

"Ellsworth," he began, turning to me, "I read your plans for your estate. I must confess to being impressed. The plans are sound, and if you achieve them, you'll deserve the acclaim you'll receive. I do have a few questions and comments, nevertheless."

He proceeded to elaborate, and I gratefully took note of everything he said. If the Duke of Henly believed in me, then I could make something of Carrington after all.

If I could keep the Ceurian inspector at bay. And Uncle Mauldin.

The Duke of Henly left us as we neared the house. With a hand at my elbow, Lofton steered me down one of the garden paths, reiterating his earlier warning about staying out of the affairs of Henly Manor. He held out that ridiculous toy wand I'd accidently given Gabriella and instructed me to keep it with me always.

"You want me to keep *that* on hand?" I protested.

"Yes." There was no humor in his expression.

I took the toy wand as reluctantly as I had the real. "It's useless, you know."

"No more so than a non-magic in a hunt for the Magic Thief."

"I—" I started to retort but stopped. There was a double negative in that exchange. Did he mean that I was useful but should stay away anyway, or that I was useless?

Before I could figure it out, he continued, "I meant what I said. Leave this to the enchanters."

"How can I when you're constantly handing me wands? Even a toy one could get me into trouble with Inspector Olan. But if you make me a full partner in this hunt for the Magic Thief, Olan can't harass me, not when I was invited by an enchanter. Besides, I'm sure I can help."

"No. You're—"

"A non-magic, I know. But I'm not ignorant in the ways of magic. And this isn't merely a matter of personal curiosity. Since I've come to Henly, I've been snubbed, scorned, and accused of one thing after another. If the Thief is caught, my name is cleared. I can go back to being only snubbed and scorned. I can handle that—a baron expects it in such a crowd—but I won't suffer my name blackened with false accusations any longer."

He only smiled mildly. "Your best chance of impressing Alfred, and a certain daughter of his, is by making a success of your estate. Or by proving you truly are a trusted confidant of an enchanter as well-respected as Emil Farro."

"I'm not seeking to impress anyone," I growled. "And what the Thief wanted in Ceur is Emil Farro's business *alone*."

"I agree, and I commend you for keeping the contents of your recent letter to yourself."

I froze mid-stride. "How did you know I had a letter about Emil?"

"When Alfred mentioned him you touched your pocket, as you are doing now."

Chagrinned, I pulled my treacherous appendage away from said pocket.

"You must be careful of more than what your mouth says," he continued.

I cleared my throat and began walking again. "You've heard of the repeated theft attempts as well, I suppose?"

"Yes, though I don't think the latest was by our Thief. It wasn't his style, was it?"

There was something of a test in his manner. I searched his face. Was the question genuine or was he baiting me for information? But Giles's letter had answered any questions I might have about Jonathan Lofton's trustworthiness. Giles, sick in bed with little to do but write letters, had learned from reliable sources that the silver-haired duke was integrity itself and had likely come to Henly on behalf of the Council of Enchanters and of the king himself for the express purpose of catching the Magic Thief.

"No, murdering Emil's guard doesn't fit the Thief's typical pattern," I said. But if not the Magic Thief, then who made the last attempt? "The Thief is here, and someone else—sorcerers perhaps given it's Ceur—have taken over where the Thief failed."

"I fear so," Lofton said, sinking into an air of melancholy. A moment passed before he shook himself and spoke again. "I hope your relative takes care and hides well"—he smiled wryly—"himself and whatever he has. Tell me, what reason would any have to believe you could find the inventor?"

"I've been wondering that myself."

"Really?" he replied with equal insincerity.

"We were childhood friends, like brothers," I answered after a moment's consideration, recalling my cousin's defense of me to the inspector, "and since I am a non-magic with little or no use for the majority of his inventions, I'm not a threat." That was true, but ... I resisted the urge to touch my ring. Some secrets were better left untold.

He regarded me thoughtfully. "I suppose an old friend with no use for your treasures would be safe to confide in."

"I wish more thought as you do."

He soon returned to the house, but I continued to wander the gardens, considering the matter of the Magic Thief and his intended prize. *Whatever he has.* Lofton had said it knowingly, and the Duke of Henly had asked. But that was Emil's business alone. And he was missing.

With a troubled mind, I retreated to the bench behind the cedar and pulled out the packet of letters. In addition to the one from Giles, the packet held a forwarded message from the inspector and a short letter from Emil, which was dated some time back. The inspector practically roared his displeasure at my refusal to return to Ceur and informed me, with the insinuation I somehow already knew, that Emil Farro had disappeared. I'd told Emil to get away from town, not to disappear completely. But if the sorcerers were the ones now after his work, disappearing had been wise. I could think of only one place that would allow him to seemingly vanish.

The inspector confided that the guard at Emil's house had been killed with a knife poisoned through sorcery. Those could be bought in Ceur and didn't necessarily indicate the presence of a sorcerer. Emil couldn't be reached about the incident, having left secretly two days before. That was all the inspector could discover.

I skimmed the letter from Emil to me the inspector claimed to have found open on Emil's desk. There was nothing to it really, some vague references as to how his research was coming and how he intended to leave town. It was his handwriting and even had some of his usual doodles, including a variety of flowers, a child's rocking horse, and geometric patterns. Why hadn't he sent it?

I puffed out a white breath into the silent garden. It had snowed all afternoon without managing to create a winter wonderland, only a thin dusting of white over brown earth that was sure to melt and make a mess on the morrow. Is that what I'd create if I tried to find out anything about the Thief? A mess? It wasn't as if I had the half-magic's ability to locate the objects of enchantment and somehow protect them. Still, I wasn't as incompetent as they thought or as lacking in character as Gabriella assumed. Even the duke had asked me for information. I tapped the letters against my palm. Even a non-magic could collect information.

I pocketed the letters and returned to my room in a twist. Henry sat with his feet propped up, reading.

"I hope that book's on the best way to iron shirts," I said as I crossed the room behind him.

He bolted to his feet as if suddenly realizing he was sitting on a hot iron. "I wish you'd use the door."

"I don't have time." I pulled a chair up to the writing desk and spread out the three letters. "Why, Henry, did the inspector tell me the guard was killed with a knife poisoned by sorcery when before he refused to mention anything magic-related to me since I was neither an enchanter nor a Ceurian?"

"I've wondered that too." Henry settled back in his chair and stretched out his legs, the picture of concern. One reason I bothered him with my troubles was that he only pretended to listen and didn't try to fix anything.

"Nevertheless, he wants me to return to Ceur for questioning," I continued. "I wasn't even in his bloody country during the last two attempts. I have no knowledge to offer."

"The inspector will be disappointed."

"That would break my heart." My mind returned to the falling tree incident. Had the Thief, suspecting Lofton's mission here, felled the tree as a way of testing him? Of letting him know the game was on? Thief versus enchanter? That sounded more like the Thief than attempted murder. "Henry, the Magic Thief is here."

His feet hit the floor with a thud as he sat up. "Shall I start packing?"

"No."

He clapped his book shut.

"Henry, who knows the most about what goes on at an estate?"

"The servants, of course."

"Exactly. Go make friends. I'll go and do likewise."

After eying me a moment, he folded his hands over the book in his lap. "I thought we were going to stay out of the enchanters' business."

"That was before."

"Before what?"

"Never you mind. This is for our reputation. The inspector thinks me culpable. I will prove him wrong." I scribbled notes on what I knew so far over a sheet of stationary.

"Well, it could be worse, I suppose," Henry said with dramatic woe a moment later. "You could be distracted by the duke's daughters."

"I wouldn't be a man if I didn't notice her, but that doesn't mean I'll let her distract me."

"You've narrowed it down to one already, sir? It's worse than I feared."

My reply stuck in my throat and my quill on the letter *e*, flooding it. With a cough, I resumed writing. "Don't be ridiculous."

"I never am."

"Let's get back to the matter at hand, shall we? I want a list of all the servants hired for this mentoring season, especially any new this year or new last year. The Thief may have come last year to determine the lay of the land and the goods, so to speak."

"Must it be a servant?" There was as much stuffy disdain in his voice as in any newly made lord's.

"No, but it's a good disguise. Also, I want you to find out anything you can about the guests' servants and what the servants say about their masters. Be on the lookout for a combination of a tall, trim servant and a short, stocky master, or vice versa. I'll see what I can discover about the guests, and I'll talk with some of the servants myself. The trouble is, most of the guests are prominent men or the sons of prominent men. The Duke of Henly will have thoroughly vetted them. If suspicion falls on one of them, he'll be even less likely to believe me than if it falls on a servant."

Not that he was likely to believe me at all. When he questioned me about the abduction, he gave the impression he shared Gabriella's opinion of the incident being my fault.

"The trouble is," Henry said, still in that sullen tone, "we've less than three weeks to complete the questioning, sort the responses, convince the duke, and catch the Thief."

"Why is that? Oh, of course. Everyone will be leaving after the duke's birthday celebration at the end of the month. The chaos would be a good time for the Thief to leave, wouldn't it?"

"Yes. The night before or the day of would be the perfect time for the theft." He brought his book to eye level. "In that case, come to think of it, we've plenty of time. It won't take the full three weeks to question everyone. We know he's here. All we have to do is set a trap for that night." He said it as if setting a trap for one of the cleverest thieves in a century would be as easy as lighting a candle.

Laying aside my quill, I twisted around to give my servant the look meant to remind him who paid his wages. "I'm not a demanding master, Henry. You work a little and spend most of your time reading. If you'll help with this—if we prevent the theft and any harm to the family—then when Carrington is running smoothly and has extra money, I'll let you bring the library up to scratch."

He lowered the book to his lap.

"I'll even let you borrow books from it for the 'roving village library' you've been talking about for years."

"Your grandmother would roll over in her grave."

"Good. It'll keep her from getting coffin sores. I intend to do a lot of things differently than Lady Ellsworth."

The next day, I made the stable my first investigative stop. By the time I'd chatted with several stable hands, including the temporary one with the disgraceful beard, my friendliness reserves were drained, and I had too many names running around in my head to think straight. I also had notes to jot down and a new puppy to get acquainted with—Bitsy, the runt unfit for the Floraison family. Bitsy and I had a lot in common.

After settling matters concerning the purchase of the puppy with Harvey, I let myself into Nympha's stall and settled onto the hay beside her and her pups. According to my pocket watch, twenty minutes remained of the afternoon break. I might as well write my notes with the most companionable souls around for company.

"Sun's out," Harvey stated matter-of-factly a quarter of an hour later.

"Will it be out for long do you think?"

"Still here, Lord Ellsworth?" Harvey's footsteps changed direction, clapping against the straw-dusted floor.

"Yes." Rising, I brushed hay from my trousers. The disturbed puppies whined. Nympha stretched her long body and yawned.

Harvey leaned on the stall door, a smile softening his weather-beaten face. "Aye, it's nap time for the little ones and their mama, is it?"

"And time for me to return to the duke's lectures."

"Didn't you hear the special messenger thunder into the yard earlier?" Harvey thumped me good-naturedly on the shoulder. "Were you napping too? The messenger requires a response, and my master never rushes a response. It'll be an hour at least."

"Well then ..." I started to sit but Harvey caught my elbow.

"Nay, 'tis time for sunshine for you, my lord." He winked and released my arm. "My Lady Gabriella is due to come, and I must clean up after the little ones."

"*My* Lady Gabriella? So that's how it is." With a wry grin, I stepped out of the stall. At least I wasn't the only one besotted with her.

"Aye, if the physician had been half an hour later, the master would've had me deliver her, though I told him babies were a bit different than horses. She's a fine lass. Don't let her fool you. She's not so proud as the rest but every bit as lovely."

Too late.

That soft-hearted smile cracked his weather-beaten façade again. "She's a mite attached to that runt Bitsy. She'd be real disappointed to find her missing." He scooped up Bitsy, plopped her into my hands, and nodded to a chair in front of the opposite row of stalls. "And right glad to find her in good hands."

As I sat, sunlight streaming through a window over the stalls hit me in the face. Tipping my hat to gain its shade, I slouched comfortably in the chair and laid Bitsy on my chest. She made quite a game of scrambling up my shirt to lick at my chin only to slide back down to my lap. It wasn't long before a chorus of feminine voices sounded from the stable entrance.

"Pity's sake. Not the old girl," Harvey muttered. "I thought we were done with her when she married twenty-five years ago." Nympha's stall shut with a soft bang, and Harvey's footsteps trudged away from me.

"Harvey?" Gabriella's sweet voice was overshadowed by the fearsome Aunt Helene's.

"There you are, Harold."

Aunt Helene, Gabriella, and Eva met him several stalls from me. Pulling my hat further down, I rested my chin on my chest and tried not to smile at Harvey's grousing.

"It's *Harvey*, my lady."

"Your mother christened you *Harold*, and that's what I shall call you despite your father's choice of appellation for you. Now, fetch your hat. I have something for you to do."

The swish of skirts accompanied slow steps in my direction. They hesitated near me, then crossed to Nympha's stall, setting the puppies to yipping.

"But I need you to carry a crate of equipment to the glen," Aunt Helene continued.

"Get whoever brought it this far to keep going with it," Harvey said. "The duchess and Lady Alexandria will be along soon, and I must have the carriage ready."

"The regular servants are busy, and I'm not trusting one of the temporary servants with it. Furthermore, you're one of the few who know where and what the glen is."

"Yep, Lady Tannon and her new babe can't seem to do without the duchess. Every day, sometimes twice, the duchess has me hitch up those horses. Now Larry, he says going the same road all the time is about to run him and the horses mad. If this goes on any longer, I might have to drive her ladyship myself."

The dignified Aunt Helene stomped her foot. "The coachman's name is *Lawrence*."

"You could've fooled me. He's always answered to *Larry*."

The squeaking of puppies escalated to a sorrowful pitch. The soft steps brushed across the floor in my direction and once again hesitated. I held my breath, then scolded myself for caring. The footsteps started quietly forward, and the hem of Gabriella's blue cloak edged into view, her perfume heaven in the pungent stable. Landing with a plop in my lap, Bitsy yipped in excitement. A shadow fell over me, and I tilted my hat back.

"You're not trying to kidnap my hound, are you?" I teased.

"Your ...?" Gabriella backed away, shock in her voice, and something other than incredulity in her face.

Apparently, I wasn't even worthy of the Floraison's runt. "If you don't believe me, you can ask Harvey. She's his, isn't she, to do with as he pleases?" I said, half in jest, half in anger, furious at myself for having let a few conversations delude me into thinking a Floraison and I could at least be friends.

"I didn't say I didn't believe you," she said.

"You implied it."

"I didn't know she had been sold."

"She has. You're welcome to continue visiting her if you like since she'll be here until she's weaned."

"Aren't you the magnanimous one?"

I shrugged.

Gabriella spun on her heel, and I watched her go with a sigh. *That's right, Marcel. Give her a legitimate reason to dislike you.* But better her mad at me than ever smile at me again. After all, I was no better than a runt in her and her family's eyes. Still, I shifted uncomfortably. *You're all too apt to assume people are judging you harshly,* Aunt Coraline had scolded me growing up. *Most aren't, and even if they are, it doesn't give you leave to disdain them or behave rudely.* Be that as it may, I was definitely not assuming the Floraisons' critical attitude.

"I'll tell you what," Harvey said, "I've got to see to the carriage horses, but there's a lad here who's been underfoot all day; I'll send him. He's no temporary servant and hasn't the sense to know what the glen is, so sending him along would help us both."

I pitied the poor blighter Harvey was sacrificing up.

"Are you sure he's trustworthy?" Aunt Helene asked after a moment.

"As sure as spring follows winter." Harvey's steps pounded over the stone floor, vibrating my chair as he drew even with me.

The air around me felt crowded. I glanced up as Harvey scooped up Bitsy and then hauled me up by the collar. As soon as I'd gained my feet, he shoved me forward.

"Lord Ellsworth here would consider it a great honor to assist. Why, he was saying to me earlier how he needed a bit of sunshine and exercise."

Aunt Helene eyed me skeptically. With a glare at Harvey, I stooped to retrieve my fallen hat. He flashed a grin before reinstating his stoic expression.

"I—" I began.

"Shouldn't Lord Ellsworth be returning to the house for Papa's lectures? That's why he came to Henly," Gabriella said quickly.

"I—"

"The duke delayed the session to answer a message," Harvey answered as quickly.

"I—"

"Isn't there a cart and horse available?" Gabriella asked. "We shouldn't trouble him with family business."

"You are not driving a cart, Gabriella," Aunt Helene said. "It's unseemly, and Harold already said no one is available to handle it."

Sighing, I dusted off my hat and put it on. I raised my hand, palm out. "Ladies. *Harold.*"

They snapped around to stare at me as if surprised the topic of their conversation had a voice of his own.

"I would be more than happy to assist the family of my kind and generous host." Especially since, if I read Aunt Helene's hesitancy correctly, I might have the opportunity to learn something about the Floraisons' magical treasures and thus where the Thief might strike.

With a wave at Harvey, I strode toward the stable door in my most imperious manner. "Hitch up the cart, Harold. This way, ladies."

As I reached the doorway, I glanced over my shoulder. Gabriella, arms crossed, eyed me narrowly but then followed. The other ladies looked from me to Harvey and fell into line behind Gabriella.

A smug smile tugged at my lips. The crate's contents weren't breakable, I hope? It was likely to be a bumpy ride to the gle—

My boot cracked against the crate, and I tumbled forward. I threw myself to the side and landed to the right of the crate. *Breakable* stared at me from the wooden slats in big, black letters.

"You all right, Ellsworth?" Harvey boomed from somewhere in the stable.

"I've made worse landings."

Grandfather Gérard's words rang through my head as I stood and dusted myself off: *Pride's always been a failing in this family. Careful it's not your downfall.* Nice choice of words, Grandfather.

Strangled snickering sounded behind me, but Gabriella, my hat in her hand, stood silently beside me. She picked a piece of straw off the hat brim and tossed it aside with flourish. The arch of her eyebrow as she held out the hat said it all.

With a sheepish grin, I took it. "Yes, I deserved it. And I apologize for being rude earlier."

She huffed in acknowledgment, then pointed to the crate. "That's breakable. Try not to smash it." She leaned toward me, eyes blazing, and I was reminded of stories of angry enchantresses and the unfortunate things that happened to those around them. "If you ever mistreat or neglect Bitsy, I *will* turn you into something *worse* than stone." She glared home her point, then marched off into the stable calling for Harvey.

We were soon on our way to the glen, and it was a slow, smooth ride.

Chapter 9

It's dangerous to be a man with no name and no home. The matters of life are gray and indistinct. Such a man is invisible to the world and may even be glad of it. Unless he carries in him a fear of the all-knowing One, there would be no darkness of iniquity he would not enter.

Diary of a magic thief

GABRIELLA FLORAISON

STERLING DIDN'T LIKE to be hitched to a cart, but he was a tough horse and could take it. There was no other animal I felt as comfortable with hauling us around. If Marcel Ellsworth couldn't handle a cart, with Sterling under harness, I could. But he and Sterling were working well together thus far.

Secured behind me in the cart was the crate of potion-making equipment. Fred's next clue, found on the corner statue, involved making a potion. I still couldn't believe he set up a spell to send my wand to the tresor box when the archer released me, but there was no other explanation, unless one believed in legends, which the Floraisons did not. My some-odd great-grandfather had thoroughly investigated the matter of half-magics and published the definitive volume on them: *Half-Magics: Only a Legend.* They were easily explained as weak enchanters captured and stretched in folklore.

The rutted dirt road passed slowly under my dangling feet. Holding to the edge of the floorboard, I squinted against the sunlight glaring off the snow remaining on the fields and mountains.

Aunt Helene, seated with Marcel up front, interrogated him on his family history and then sought to inspire him with our illustrious heritage. Had anyone else in our family done something as ignominious as lose a wand?

Beside me, Eva snickered. "Son of a baron and a nobody," she whispered. "Did you notice how he avoided all mention of his mother's family? I wonder how he even qualified for Papa's training."

I started to respond but found I wasn't sure what I wanted to say. Agree or rebut? I couldn't give a rebuttal of a heritage he gave himself, but what did it matter anyway? It wasn't as if his honor had been attacked, only his heritage demeaned. As the Duke of Lofton pointed out, they weren't one and the same, though we often acted as if they were. After all, Marcel returned my wand. But he laughed during my duet and possibly drew the ruffians to Henly.

Shaking my head, I clutched the side of the cart as the wheels slipped into a rut. Following the rut, we turned onto the road leading to the clearing before the forest.

"Sorry about that," Marcel said. "It's a rough road ahead too. Hold on."

Aunt Helene admonished him to be more careful, and I barely kept myself from turning around to glare at her. Poor man. Yanked from his break to act as a servant for us, and she derides him.

"What's the matter, Gabriella?" Eva asked. "You look almost as angry as when the statue grabbed you."

"Nothing ... I am simply anxious about my wand." I rubbed my forehead, hoping my cheeks weren't as red as they felt. What was the matter with me? Aunt Helene's arrogance and Floraisons-above-all attitude had never bothered me so much before. Harvey must be wearing off on me.

Eva snickered. "Fred's going to be in so much trouble for that trick when he gets home."

"Serves him right." The too familiar tightening of my stomach returned. My wand had to be in the tresor chest. It had to be.

We stopped at the forest's edge a few minutes later. After helping us from the cart, Marcel hoisted the crate to his shoulder, then followed Aunt Helene down a narrow woodland trail. He walked slowly, carefully avoiding the snake-like laurel roots poking out of the dirt path, and soon fell behind. I slowed my pace until he caught up with me.

"Would it be inquisitive of me to ask what's in this?" he asked, his face hidden by the large crate. "I feel like a pirate hauling a treasure chest into the jungle to bury it."

The amusement in his tone made me smile. "Be at ease, sir. We won't bury you with it to hide the location. It's potion-making equipment."

He swiveled to look at me, which took some effort considering the size of the crate. His brows knit together in a stern expression. He was unnecessarily critical when it came to my abilities.

"We know what we're doing."

"I didn't say you didn't."

"You implied it." I mimicked his earlier statement.

He opened his mouth, then shut it, his lips quirking into an abashed grin. He cleared his throat and turned back to the path. "Does this glen have a hidden entrance? I shall be disappointed if it's marked by an *X*."

"No, no *X*. Not even a revolving wall like in the book you abandoned at the ford."

"You've read it?" He and the crate turned again, and he stumbled. Righting himself, he heaved the crate back into position on his shoulder.

"I've read all of Brammar's books."

"You have?" He started to turn again, pleasant surprise in his voice.

One corner of my mouth curved. "Stay there." I moved to the other side of him, within his view. "All right, continue on, and yes, I have."

"May I compliment your taste in books?"

"You may," I said with a laugh. "And I compliment you on yours, since ours seems to be similar."

"Well, you know, great minds and all that." He took one hand from the crate and flexed his bandaged wrist.

"How is your wrist?"

"Hmm? Oh, it's healing nicely. Thank you again for your ministrations that night."

"You're welcome. It was far from the worst I've seen. Once, when out riding, my sisters and I came across a man who'd been thrown by his horse and trampled. Alexandria and I tended him as best we could while Eva fetched the physician, who was, thankfully, able to save him. After that, Sir Guy gave us instruction on handling such situations."

"Lord Ellsworth?" I said when he didn't reply. He stared straight ahead as if having forgotten my presence, his red hair a stark contrast to his bloodless face. "Are you unwell?"

"I'm fine," he said sharply.

I recoiled at his tone. He certainly wasn't about to keel over in a faint. "I'm relieved to hear it." *Irritable, weak-stomached baron.*

He rubbed a hand over his face, then looked at me with an apologetic smile. "Forgive me. My leg was badly broken in the carriage crash that killed my parents. The physician feared I would lose it to infection." A shadow passed over his face, and his voice hitched at "lose," as if considering what all he had lost. "I've been squeamish around blood ever since, despite my efforts to overcome it. My weakness and the fight against it make me short-tempered."

Squeamish, or terrorized by memory? What images might he be trying to keep buried? I shuddered to think of it. "I'm sorry."

He shrugged as if to say "That's life," and adjusted the position of the crate. "Which of Brammar's books is your favorite?"

With the thought of losing my own parents in such a horrific way fresh in my mind, I had difficultly summoning an answer, but I managed. Several minutes later, when we were in the middle of a disagreement on whether or not Brammar's most intriguing mystery had a plot hole in it, Aunt Helene interrupted.

"Lord Ellsworth, you're lagging behind." Her voice carried from the glen our path was sloping to meet.

Though the descent was gentle and Aunt Helene impatient, we slowed our pace to enjoy the view. Dark-barked laurel and bushy azaleas wove a tangled pattern along the banks, breaking here and there to reveal patches of gray stone frosted with lichen and moss.

Two large boulders as alike as mirror images dug into each of the glen's banks, one to the right on our side, the other across. Between them, a stream dropped into a deeply shadowed pool. The water played lazily amid the forest's reflection before remembering the force that dropped it there. It hurried off into the woods, rushing underneath a simple stone bridge that lay flat above the watercourse.

Aunt Helene, with Eva standing beside her, tapped her foot on a square of bare earth a few feet from where the bridge met the bank. "You may leave the crate here, Lord Ellsworth. Thank you for your assistance. Take the cart back with you, if you would."

"You're very welcome," he replied with admirable politeness.

"You should be in time for the recommencing of my brother's lectures," Aunt continued. "That is why you came after all."

I blushed at Aunt's dismissal of him, but Marcel gave me a faint smile and veered off to the indicated spot, leaving me at the foot of the bridge. He deserved a better thanks than that.

I touched the long chain around my neck and ran my fingers down to its thumb-sized pendant, a miniature blue amphora. I tapped the Amphora, considering. Aunt would be furious.

Marcel lowered the crate to the ground. His brows furrowed as he looked around, no doubt wondering why we wanted the crate deposited in the middle of a forest. He straightened and brushed off his jacket as if glad to be relieved of the crate's weight, then looked toward the path to the cart.

"Lord Ellsworth, please, wait a moment." Stepping onto the bridge, I lifted the necklace over my head.

"Gabriella, what are you doing?" Aunt Helene demanded. "Don't be in such a hurry, child."

"Surely, after his great kindness, you wouldn't deny Lord Ellsworth the privilege of seeing a Floraison secret passage?"

She pressed her lips together, her expression snootier than usual. "I don't see that it's necessary."

"Lord Ellsworth's opinion of the Floraisons' skills needs improving, Aunt."

Marcel's gaze swept over Aunt and me, an odd mix of expressions flitting over his face.

Halfway across the bridge, I brushed aside a light litter of snow and leaves and knelt at the upstream edge. The Amphora I set down, coiling its chain loosely about it. I dipped my cupped hand into the stream's icy water and, with a whispered command, spilled the water over the Amphora.

The cascade and its pool became as still as ice, the forest itself silencing in shock. Then the rush of water returned, faint, like a mighty roar heard from a distance. Water seeped from the stone bridge up the wall formed by the coiled chain until it flowed over the Amphora's lip.

When the last drop slipped into the Amphora, the rush of water returned to its normal volume, and the stream beyond the bridge meandered as happily through the woods as it ever had, seemingly birthed from a spring under the bridge. The pool and cascade were dry.

Standing, I cast a sideways glance at Marcel. He stood at the foot of the bridge, gawking. A path paved of the same stone as the bridge now spread from his feet, cutting into the bank's slope and running to an ornately carved arched doorway leading through the nearer of the twin boulders. The stone arch and the ancient wooden doors with their decorative hinges blended with the boulder until one wasn't sure if one saw a boulder or a doorway, or both at once.

The Amphora hummed as I slipped it over my head. It was the same icy cold as the stream. "Eva, would you open the way?"

She gave me a disapproving look but proceeded to the boulder-door, pulling out her keys and choosing a long iron one. She seemed intent on striking the key against a crevice in the boulder, but as the key neared it, the crevice resolved into an antique lock. The arched doorway won out over the boulder, and the inscription *Marie's Glen, For Potion Making and Spell Casting* darkened letter by letter across the arch.

Marcel caught my gaze, delight dancing in his eyes. "Not bad. How do you keep people from following you inside?"

I pressed my lips together to keep from laughing at Aunt Helene's offended gasp. "The doorway and path to it disappear once we lock it from the inside," I answered.

"Well then"—Marcel hoisted the crate back to his shoulder—"lead on, Fair Water Spirit."

Ignoring Aunt Helene's huff, I led him through the archway and into the narrow, rock-bottomed valley some fifty feet long. The valley terminated at a waterfall, though the falls were silent now. Something akin to a pulse, the thrum of water against rock, beat in my little blue jar. Only a touch of algae here and there gave away the valley's secret.

Marcel settled the crate on a ten-foot stone workbench and looked around. Another workbench sat not far off, near a fire pit. A wire cage holding small clay jars was attached to the steep bank across from the fire pit.

Marcel stepped to me and inclined his head toward the cage, an inquisitive expression on his face that gave him a kind of boyish charm. How would he look after he regained the weight lost during his illness? "In case your little jar doesn't hold everything?" he asked.

"For pools with fish that sometimes get left behind."

He nodded, and with another glance around, bowed. "I am duly impressed." He looked as if he were about to say more, but instead, he glanced at Aunt Helene, then tipped his hat to me. "Thank you for showing me this."

"Thank you for helping us. Making this potion is important to me; it's a clue of my brother's."

He nodded in acknowledgment, wished my sister and aunt a good day, then left without so much as looking over his shoulder.

As I locked the door behind him, I found myself wondering what he'd been about to say. His opinions with regard to Brammar's books had been definite indeed and unapologetically given, as had his opinions of the Floraisons since the night of our meeting. There was something to be said for his honesty. Even if his opinions happened to be wrong.

"I'm going to move them." Aunt Helene, standing next to a boulder jutting from the bank, waved her hands in the shape of a cube. "Here will do nicely."

"Move what?" Eva and I looked up from the potion apparatus, now set up on the workbench, the first stage of the potion well underway. It had taken a few days to get this far, partly due to the weather and partly to the complexity of the recipe and the time required to gather the ingredients.

"The Place Changers," Aunt said. "We can't leave them hovering about where anyone might find them. The Duke of Lofton and I agree they should be moved. I'll put both here."

"You can do that?" Eva questioned as she peered over the glass flasks and tubing of the potion-making setup.

"Oh yes. The trick is getting the cube of air to grab. Once you've done that, it's not difficult to change what's in its claws, so to speak. However, we're shifting them, not changing where they go in case Frederick intends for them to be used later. You'll help me, of course, tomorrow. It's time to return to the house for tea. Take the potion off the heat, dear. It should be good for tonight."

As Eva took care of the potion, I cleared the workspace of loose items, returning them to the crate stashed in a compartment in the rock. Fred's clue lay on the bench next to the open potion book. I slipped it into the book, and stowed them. We'd not flood the area again until we were finished, but I wanted little left out for any inquisitive animals to investigate.

The next day, we helped Aunt move the Changer from the ford, depositing it between the jutting boulder and the smaller workbench, and continued on with the potion. It was a dull, windy day, but I rather fancied such days, with the low, full clouds in their multitude of grays. Down in the glen, we were out of the wind, and overhead, the birds chirped merrily and flitted about the trees and shrubs. I must admit to convincing Aunt to use a spell to draw them to us.

Listening contentedly, I used a pestle to grind brightly colored leaves for the potion. The brighter the better, the book had said. After all, the potion was to make visible the next clue on the blank paper Fred included along with a riddle about a potion to make the blind see and read.

At the agreed upon time, Eva and Aunt Helene left the potion to me and used a reveal spell to watch the Changer, waiting for the Duke of Lofton to appear beside the one in the garden. Instead of transporting the second one through the gardens and on a lengthy, easily observed trip here, the duke was going to attempt to turn it in on itself and send it here through itself. Aunt, wand in hand, waited to retrieve it and tether it next to the other.

An angry twittering of birds drew my attention to the glen's entrance, near where Sterling, along with Eva and Aunt's horses, munched on hay in the pen Harvey had built them.

Marcel stood near the boulders, an uneasy expression on his face, something like a *please don't scream* look.

"Lord Ellsworth." I set aside the mortar and pestle and went to meet him. My victory a few days ago seemed less substantial now with him standing inside our private glen. Not that we didn't know anyone could climb the glen's banks and descend since the stream was still bound up in the Amphora. The forest around the glen had been bespelled to make that difficult and to alert us *before* someone entered.

"Good day, Lady Gabriella," he replied as he strode toward Aunt Helene and Eva. I changed direction to join them by the Changer.

"This is an unexpected surprise," Aunt Helene said coolly with a glance at the archway, which was locked and resembled a boulder.

Marcel bowed as he reached her. "Please forgive the liberty I take in returning to your private place uninvited." He drew a letter from his coat pocket and handed it to her. "I bear a message from the Duke of Lofton. He wished it brought speedily, and a traveling ring"—he twisted his wrist so his ring faced her—"allows that. I knocked on the boulder—door—by the bridge, but no one answered. Thus, I took the liberty of letting myself in."

Aunt's scowl deepened as she eyed the ring. "A ring that allows the wearer to travel anywhere he's been before. I've heard of such a pair. I didn't realize the duke would lend such a valuable thing."

Marcel's eyes widened, but whatever correction he intended to make died as Aunt Helene took the letter and continued talking even as she skimmed it. A muscle in his jaw twitched.

"Of course, this glen wasn't designed to be impregnable, Lord Ellsworth, merely less likely for people or animals to stumble into and ruin a potion or hurt themselves. You must think little of my brother's lectures to so readily accept errands. Nonetheless, thank you for delivering the Duke of Lofton's message." She paused, then reread the letter in silence.

"I assure you, Countess," Marcel said, "I have the highest regard for your brother's lectures. It was only because I could come and return during the break that Lofton asked, and I accepted, this task."

Something about the way he said "task" gave me the impression he was not happy about it. Was it the message or a wish not to involve himself with us? He hadn't so much as approached me in friendly greeting since the day I showed him the glen. Not that I wanted him to. It simply seemed odd that he would be so concerned about my safety at the statue, concerned enough to insultingly question my actions, and then ignore me. It's true we talked when we were seated next to one another at dinner, as had happened twice, but those conversations hardly counted since he was forced into them by politeness and Lord Tyndale.

Aunt, lifting her chin, folded the letter. "I'm sorry the duke was detained. As to the other matter, I do not think there is any danger from *that* quarter or ever was."

"What danger? The Magic Thief?" A feeling of unease, such as I'd had when the duke and I examined the fallen tree, crept over me.

"Yes, specifically a half-magic one," Marcel said. "The duke asked that you not leave the potion, any stage of it, or the book, unattended."

"We are not carrying the potion to and from the house every day, young man." Aunt Helene huffed.

"I understand," Marcel began, his manner stiff and formal, "that your family holds the common view that half-magics are the fictitious imaginings of idle minds, but I do wish you would heed Lofton's advice to be cautious. Potions, with the magic enchantresses infuse into them, hold particular allure to some ... troublemakers, shall we say."

"Girls," Aunt Helene said, "get back to the potion. We wouldn't want it to overheat." With a tight smile, she handed Marcel the letter. "You see, Lord Ellsworth, we Floraisons are always careful."

"I have no doubt."

The birds chirped angrily again, and as if in response, a crack sounded behind us, at the main workbench. The potion apparatus hissed, steam bursting from the joints of the glass tubing.

"I lowered the flame!" Eva groused and sprang toward it.

Aunt Helene grabbed her arm. "Get back."

The glass rattled, the hiss building to a scream. Marcel and I ducked behind the second workbench. Aunt Helene, wand out, stood straight, pulling Eva to her side.

"Get down," Marcel shouted at her.

"A Floraison does not cower."

A blast shook the glen, and bright light rolled over us as Aunt cast a shield spell. Glass, leaves, and hot liquid shot above us, but none breached her shield.

The shower ceased, and the shield dropped, a puff of debris shooting up in its wake. One tumbled flask near the workbench belched green vapor. Sterling snorted furiously as the other horses whinnied. I coughed from the dust and the spilt potion's foul fumes. My racing heart slowed, and I blinked against a sudden weariness, an unnatural tiredness. I raised my head, nearly bumping into Marcel's chin. With a jolt, I realized I was tucked against his chest under the protective shelter of his arms.

Aunt flourished her wand, and the air cleared of the fumes. The weariness left with it. She complimented Eva for standing bravely with her and gave me a disdainful look as she put away her wand, a look that said "You're not a real Floraison." It wasn't the first time I'd seen that look. I had the pale hair of my mother's mother, but I had my father's facial features. It wasn't bloodline she questioned. It was me. In her eyes, I was lacking in the Floraison attributes—courage, resourcefulness, dignity, and so on.

I fought the feeling of shame that look usually brought. Whatever she thought, I wasn't lacking in any of the true Floraison virtues. Without a wand to defend myself, I would've been a pincushion if I hadn't sought shelter. That was sound Floraison sense, not cowardice, and behind the rock was just as good as beside her.

I raised my chin and let Marcel assist me up. Sterling snorted to let me know he was exceedingly put out with the noise and excitement. I started toward him, but Aunt's voice stopped me.

"You see," she said haughtily as she pulled out her handkerchief. "Floraisons have no reason to fear, even when *distractions* result in accidents." She coughed into her handkerchief, then waved it in front of her, fanning away the dust. She took a step back toward the shimmering Place Changer. "We—"

"Look out!" Eva's warning came too late.

Aunt Helene's heel caught a shard of glass, and she jerked back. She grabbed for Eva as Eva grabbed for her. They both fell straight for the Place Changer as if being dragged toward it. I lunged for Eva's hand, but Marcel yanked me back. Eva and Aunt Helene disappeared.

"Stay away. That thing's got a pull like a riptide to it," Marcel yelled over the screeching hiss of another flask. We ducked behind the stone bench as the flask burst.

I flinched at the spray of glass and hot liquid shooting over the bench, but I couldn't take my gaze from that horrid, shimmering box. As soon as the spray ended, I tried to get up, but Marcel stopped me with a hand on my arm.

I gave him a frantic look. "What if it sent them to the cave like it did you? Someone must warn them about—" My throat constricted. I could almost see them stumbling through the dark of the cave right into the gaping opening of that accursed chamber, or into the empty air of the chasm. I gulped in shallow breaths. *It was only a nightmare. A Floraison does not give in to fear. A Floraison does not give in to fear.* I staggered up again.

Marcel squeezed my hand in a comforting way. "They're fine, Lady Gabriella. They're fine." His confidence gave me pause. "I saw a bit of the gardens over the toe of your aunt's boot as she fell." He pointed to the shimmering, faintly green edge of the Changer. "See the color? It'd be black if it were linked to the cave." He gave me a lopsided grin. "I would know. Besides, it would hardly help if you went through now and fell on them."

I stared at the Changer. It was green. I slid down the side of the workbench and cradled my head in my hands. *Eva's safe in the garden. Aunt's safe. We're all safe.* I looked up when Marcel laughed. He covered his mouth with his hand, but laughter filtered through his fingers.

"What are you laughing at?"

He pointed to my head. "Other than the new fashion in hair accessories?" His grin, broad and mischievous, broke through the darkness shrouding my spirit.

I ran my hand over the crown of my head and extracted a leaf from my hair. I tossed it away, grateful it was a leaf and not glass or boiling potion. "I don't know why you should laugh. It also seems to be the new fashion in men's hats."

"But of course I wear a leaf hat," he said as he brushed the leaves from his hair. "Like the Floraisons, the Ellsworths are always up on the latest fashions, especially in hats. In that department, I flatter myself we are among the avant-garde."

"I can see that you are. Pray tell, who is your haberdasher? I must recommend him to my brother."

"It's a local shop called Forest Mayhem. You may have heard of it?"

"Naturally."

"I suspected one of your taste would have." He plucked a missed leaf from my hair, handed it to me, then settled back against the stone bench.

We fell silent, and I was content to sit and let my trembling limbs regain their strength.

"Actually," Marcel began after a moment, his eyes twinkling with amusement, "I was picturing her landing." His apologetic smile turned to one of gleeful delight. "I hope she plops down in the middle of the shrubbery as a large group of your father's guests walk by. Can't you see

their faces at her sudden appearance and dreadfully undignified position? And her look of mortification ... delightful."

I stared at him, aghast. "Eva?"

He laughed outright. "There would be some small satisfaction there, but I was referring to your Aunt Helene."

"Really, Lord Ellsworth, that's not—"

He continued to smile at me, and in his eyes I saw
what he saw: Aunt's ungainly landing, her bewildered expression, the surprised stares of everyone who happened
to be around. I felt the triumph of every person whose
preferred name she'd deliberately ignored, of those she'd
snubbed or lectured on the dignity of the Floraisons. I bit
my lip but the chuckles building in my chest burst forth.
Marcel and I both doubled over with laughter.

"That's not kind of you," I finally finished when I
caught my breath, but there was no censure in my voice.

"Really, Lady Gabriella." He winked and pushed himself up. "I know it's not." He held out his hands and
helped me up. "However"—he paused as he held me out
in front of him, looking at me in mock reproach—"if you
are to scold, you must call me 'Marcel Gustave,' as my
aunt does."

"Does she call you that often?"

He gave a soft snort as if to say "very often," and I
laughed, my smile lingering. He stared at me a moment,
then a pained expression flitted across his face so quickly
I might have imagined it.

"'Marcel,'" he added, assuming a merry grin, "will do
nicely for all other occasions." He dropped my hands and
gestured to the wreckage that had been our potion apparatus. "I make it a point of allowing anyone with whom I
have survived an explosion the privilege of calling me by
my first name."

"That's generous of you, I must say."

"Generosity is the chief virtue of the Ellsworths." He turned to the main workbench, and we picked our way over to it.

He whistled as he inspected a dent in the workbench's top. "Since I'm here, neither Lofton nor Olan could blame me for investigating," he muttered.

"What's that?"

"Nothing. I was thinking aloud." He picked up the open potion book, which, fortunately, had an anti-spill spell on it. Holding it by one end, he let it drape open, then shook the dust and leaves from it.

Shards of glass glittered in the sunlight. A cast iron pot, the receptacle for one of the two mixtures needed for the potion, rocked on its side on the workbench's edge, liquid sloshing over its brim and flowing down the stone in a slurry of reds, oranges, and yellows. I righted the pot and considered all the work lost and what needed to be redone. It would take days to catch up, and it would interfere with my writing schedule, but we *would* complete the potion and find the tresor box and my wand.

I picked up my empty mortar and pestle with a frustrated sigh, adding the need to collect leaves to my to-do list. Why had this happened? The temperature, as Eva said, had been sufficiently low, rather like that used to let a soup simmer. It had nothing to do with the leaves I was grinding.

"Yes," Marcel said with a sly glance at me as he flipped through the book, "it was kind of you to arrange it. Very entertaining and educational experience."

"What? This was not my fault." I sat the mortar and pestle down with deliberate slowness, his cunning glance putting me on the alert. What was he playing at?

"Oh?" He raised his eyebrows, then scanned an entry in the book, running his finger along the page like a speed reader. "No. No, I don't see 'stand back and cover your ears for an explosion' in the directions." He snapped the book shut and set it on the bench. "Must have been a mistake in the preparation, but perhaps it was due to your aunt or sister."

"It was nothing of the sort. We followed the instructions exactly."

"Are you implying the instructions were incorrect?"

"Of course not."

"You couldn't have made a mistake?"

"No. Well, it's possible but not in this instance. We were most careful. It was an accident." Wasn't it? Why had the birds twittered so fiercely before the apparatus exploded? They did the same when Marcel appeared. That wasn't the alarm. The forest should have misdirected anyone who tried to go over the bank and warned us with a boom like that of a crashing tree.

I gave myself a mental shake. *A Floraison does not engage in idle speculations.* After all, no one could have caused the explosion from the bank. But what if someone could have gotten to the apparatus and moved away in the blink of an eye? Or come earlier and tampered with it, purposefully or accidently setting up the conditions for the explosion? But why bother? A prank? No, there was the sleeping gas Aunt blew away. With us asleep, our wands and the Amphora were fair game.

"You don't sound so sure. Someone could have tampered with it." Marcel picked up a rock, which looked more like a piece of gravel than a pebble, then dropped it, shaking his hand as if he'd touched something hot. His ring glinted in the light.

A passage from my ancestor's book came to mind: *Weak enchanters tried to pass themselves off as half-magics to make themselves special, to justify the thieving that earned them the second name of Magic Collectors.*

I'd wondered before if Marcel were an enchanter. It would explain his ring and the things he knew that a non-magic wouldn't. But he couldn't be the Thief. He'd returned my wand, and he had a genuine purpose for coming to Henly. Or were both lies to gain my trust? Every time he was near, something happened. How could he be innocent? At the very least, he was a troublemaking meddler. The duke warned me against misjudging Marcel. I thought I'd judged him too harshly. Did I now judge him too highly? "What do you know about potions, Lord Ellsworth?"

"Not much. My godfather—" Marcel glanced up at me and startled. "Now, don't look at me like that. I only moved the crate. Your aunt would never let me near the actual setup. Not the right bloodline, remember?"

"But you have that ring and could come here without us knowing it. You could've played around with the apparatus and accidently set it right for exploding."

"I'd never dream of even asking to observe the potion making, much less fiddle with it. What reason would I have to? It's not as if I could do anything with the potion since I don't know what it is. I'm not an enchanter or a half-magic."

"Don't give me that half-magic rot," I said, taking a step toward him. "Every time I see you, there's trouble. The very night you arrived, I lost my wand to a Place Changer and was nearly abducted."

He stood and backed away, holding his hands out as if to keep me at bay. "That was not my fault. Okay, the first bit may have been, but I got your wand back."

"The Duke of Lofton told you to return it." I took another step, all my interactions with Marcel churning through my mind, trying to reconcile everything that had happened with the "kind man of integrity" I'd almost judged him as. "Then the Duke of Lofton is nearly crushed at the spot where *you* set up his easel, and I have to track you down in a cave I shouldn't go nea—that you shouldn't have been in."

He kept backing away. "Now that was definitely not my fault."

"Half-magics, I suppose?"

He glanced at the piece of gravel he'd dropped. "I've been thinking about the falling tree. All a half-magic would have to do is add extra water under the tree and freeze it, pushing the tree up. The wind would take care of the rest with little help from him. Any Magic Collector with a decent supply of magic could handle that."

"As easy as that, huh?"

"How do you think a non-magic like me could do it?"

"I—" What if he were a non-magic? How were we to know?

He lowered his hands, an infuriating smugness about him.

"That's a weak defense and you know it," I said. "You can't prove you're a non-magic. That's a talent only your beloved half-magics are said to have, and legends can't prove your innocence." Reason argued he could've used his ring to escape the bandits, yet he stayed as if ready to help Harvey and me. Why must his presence presume his involvement? Yet even the return of my nightmares followed his arrival. I cradled my scarred hand to my chest. What had happened to Henly? My wand was gone, people were in danger, and I couldn't trust my own judgment.

Marcel looked from my cradled hand to my eyes, his expression troubled. I forced my hand down to my side and lifted my chin.

"I'm not an enchanter, Lady Gabriella," he said softly, "and you have my word that I had nothing to do with this incident or any of the others. I would never endanger you or your family either willfully or by fooling with a volatile potion apparatus. The only reason I came here today was because Lofton received an urgent message from the Council of Enchanters right as he was preparing to assist with moving the Place Changer. He left for Gersemere directly and asked me to deliver the note out of necessity. You can ask him when he returns."

I stared at him, trying to read his face. It was tired but open. I could trace no deceit, and only a fool or an honest man would risk such an inquiry. I wanted to believe him, but still I couldn't be easy. What if I judged him wrongly? 'Twas better to think too ill of someone than too highly and prove myself a fool. Lacking in the Floraison sense, Aunt would say.

"Shall I collect Sterling for you?" he asked. "I'll help you return your aunt and sister's horses to the stable."

I glanced at Sterling, then gasped as a sudden connection formed in my mind. "The toy wand. The night Sterling got loose, I had it with me when I captured the bandits. I couldn't work magic with a toy wand. You must have had a wand, and I used it to direct the magic. That explains why I was warm all through with magic instead of only in my wand hand. Or could your magical ring direct it? I felt it against my back, but no, only wands can direct magic." Alarm flashed across his face, driving me to continue voicing my burgeoning suspicion. "And then at the archer, when the spells broke—"

"And you conveniently fell into my arms. Lady Gabriella, I repeat, I had nothing to do with any of it. 'Magic Thief' is an old accusation, and I'm tired of it."

"You give your word you had nothing to do with it, that you didn't interfere with the spells in some way that could've caused my wand to be sucked away when the spells ended? Nor did you take it? Forgive me. I must ask."

"I doubt my word is worth much to you or your family, but you have it. I did not. I didn't lure the bandits here, I didn't filch a wand, and I didn't arrange any of the other incidents."

If insolence and thinly veiled indignation were indicators of innocence, then he was innocent. "Your humility makes your assurance so much more convincing. Please, help me saddle the horses."

He nodded and walked ahead of me toward the pen. "Wait," he cried, spinning around and hurrying toward me. "Your wand is gone?"

His gaze fixed on my face, he stumbled against a boulder and hit the ground with a thud. He jumped up and skirted the boulder, erasing any concern I may have felt. Was it possible the great Magic Thief could be clumsy?

"Fred's spell sent the wand to the tresor box with the rest of the items he purloined—my wand lost a second time because of you."

Instead of the accusation angering him and reassuring me of his innocence, or drawing up a guilty reaction, it distressed him, for his face drained of color. One less prize to steal?

"Lady Gabriella! Gabby Marie!"

I sucked in a breath at the familiar, but unexpected, voice bellowing through the glen.

"Harvey?" I hurried toward the archway, but Marcel dashed around me and blocked my way, a startling intensity to his eyes.

"You're sure of this?" he asked.

"Of what?" I snapped, trying unsuccessfully to get around him.

"That your wand went to the tresor box?"

"Yes. 'To the wrong you shall belong,' the clue said. I dropped the chip on the wrong statue, and the statue grabbed me. I broke free after a time, but the wand was taken."

I refused to consider how the stone spell and Fred's spell broke at the same time, before the stone spell's twenty minutes were up. Marcel was sure to start spouting legends at me if I did.

"You're absolutely positive? You were stone yourself for a while. Have you talked to Lofton about this?"

"It's none of his concern." Must I embarrass myself in front of him again?

"But the rumors of the Magic Thief—"

"Are no more than rumors of legends. Let me pass."

Marcel did as I asked, his mouth a firm line.

"Gabbie Marie," Harvey yelled again.

"Coming." I opened the boulders, and Harvey strode in leading a horse behind him.

"You okay?" he asked gruffly. He dropped the reins to the ground and cupped his hands over my shoulders. Despite my answer to the affirmative, he looked me over before releasing me with a satisfied grunt.

He startled as Marcel walked up. "Ellsworth? What the devil are you doing here?"

"Ask the Duke of Lofton."

Harvey looked at him with raised eyebrows, then shrugged. "What happened here?"

While I explained, he checked the horses and walked over to stare at the Place Changer, the biggest grin I'd ever seen wrinkling his weather-beaten face. He chuckled but sobered at a look from me. I retrieved the potion book as the men gathered the horses.

Harvey rode behind with Marcel as we left. They kept their voices low, but I could still hear them.

"You should have seen it, lad," Harvey said. "I was cutting through the gardens looking for that no-account Cox—thank heavens he's one of the temporary servants—when I hear a scream. I run around the corner, and the old girl falls out of nowhere, lands arms and legs akimbo on the hedges, then slides kerplunk into the dirt with Lady Eva landing on top of her."

Harvey laughed boisterously. Marcel's laughter sounded forced, but Harvey didn't seem to notice.

"'Harold,' she cries, 'Help us up,'" he mimicked. "'Harold,' I say, 'doesn't work here,' and keep going."

"You left them?"

"Well, I did walk to the bench to put down my dirty gloves before helping. It wasn't as if they were hurt. Such a small fall would never hurt a Floraison."

And Floraisons never lost wands. Or let them be stolen. I flexed my palms. The warmth of magic flowed through me and into my fingers, but there it stopped without a wand to amplify and direct the power. My hands tingled and began to burn from my palm to my fingertips. When my hands turned a bright red, I fisted them and ended the flow of magic.

Perhaps Aunt Helene was right. Perhaps the Floraison blood was watered down in me. Or tainted beyond recognition. The white scar on the tip of my finger stood out against my red skin as I slipped my gloves back on.

Chapter 10

They were feeding a half-magic, not with food, but with their paltry attempts to use magic to protect themselves. And this half-magic was using the power of the collected spells to aid the sorcerers.

The Fall of Bevvelian by Edgar Frock

MARCEL ELLSWORTH

GABRIELLA FLORAISON MADE the Ceurian inspector seem gracious in his judgments. However, I'd still catch the Magic Thief to clear my own name and find her wand to save it from the sorcerers.

I huffed out a silver breath. It was a chilly day to be out and about, but it was a more appealing kind of chill than what I would've experienced if I'd accepted the invitation to take the carriage with Gabriella and Harvey. The three of us were to testify to the village constable about the kidnapping incident.

What had I gotten myself into coming here? Thieves of people. Thieves of magic. I'd only wanted to learn how to run an estate better than the former overseer—a thief of money hired by Lady Ellsworth at Uncle Mauldin's suggestion—had done for the past twelve years.

Henry, who like me enjoyed a brisk walk in the crisp air, walked beside me on the narrow forest trail. To my left, the ground fell away steeply to the river some ways below, providing a magnificent vista where the bank-clinging trees and shrubs were thin. I hated to spoil the view with gossip, but if I wanted to clear my name we'd have to discuss the Thief and our investigations. "All right, Henry, down to business. You're the Thief—"

"You've caught me already, sir? How clever of you," he said drily.

"Work with me, Henry."

"Yes, sir."

"Now, pretend you're a thief of magic." I stepped over a muddy patch, then swatted away an overhanging branch. This path was unexpectedly overgrown, little more than a deer trail at times.

"A Magic Collector?" Henry used a sturdy stick to clear away a spider web.

"Undoubtedly, a half-magic, yes. That should be easy for you."

He nodded curtly. "Continue."

"You arrived at the beginning of the mentoring season with the rest of the guests and servants. You feel it wisest to leave with them at the end of the month. What do you do in the mean time?"

"What sort of a man am I?"

"You're a thief, Henry."

"But am I a debauched one or one who lives only for his trade? If the former, I would be engaging in flirtations with the local women and over-indulging in the local brew. If the latter, I would be studying the Floraisons' treasures, reading through their magic library, and touring the local sites of importance to the history of magic."

"You would?"

"Yes, sir."

"Are there any places of importance here?"

"Several great battles were fought nearby, and it's believed the sorcerers had a hideout or two about."

"Destroyed?"

"That would be a mystery." He paused to let me cross a particularly narrow part of the path, where a section of the bank had fallen away into the river below. Hating heights, he kept his gaze firmly on the path ahead. When the trail broadened, he asked, "Do you wish to know what I've learned about the servants and masters here?"

"Of course. That was the purpose of you accompanying me."

"Well then." He tucked the stick under his arm and pulled out a small notepad from his pocket. He flipped it open. "This is what I've discovered: absolutely nothing." He snapped the notepad shut and put it away. "I can't find a scandal worthy of the gossip column. Well, maybe a few of those but nothing of relevance to us."

"Me neither. However, I've been thinking that we might be going about this from the wrong angle." I caught the twist of a smile on Henry's lips. "Oh, so you've considered that already, have you?"

"Far be it from me, a humble servant, to be ahead of my master."

"Henry ..." I said with enough edge in my voice to make him fully smile.

"Well," he began enthusiastically, pulling out his notebook again, "it occurred to me we should consider what the Thief intends to steal, where those items are located, and how he purposes to carry them off undetected."

"Logical. What have you got on that so far?"

He flipped a few pages in his notebook, and his finger came to rest on a page scribbled over with notes. "I haven't been able to do a full investigation," he said modestly, "but I have noted a chest in the stable tack room that looks promising, a number of items in the library, a—"

"Help! Help!" a man cried from ahead.

Henry and I took off down the trail, stumbling over roots and pushing through dense laurels. I soon drew ahead of him. Shouts blasted my ears as I rounded a bend. I slowed, considering the best way to cross the rain-fed stream carving a rut down the bank. A few feet beyond the stream lay a stocky man, a hunting trap clamping his ankle. A metal walking stick jutted out of its jaws, hopefully having jammed the trap, preventing its sharp teeth from doing full damage to the man's ankle. A thick chain tethered the trap to the ground.

"Henry, stop!" I skidded to a halt, black spots dotting my vision as I fought my weakness. I forced myself to consider what needed to be done. "There are poacher's traps about. Watch your step."

Snap!

Henry yelped. I spun around in time to see him jump back, broken stick in hand, from a trap I'd miraculously avoided. But he leapt too far and landed badly, skidding on fallen leaves at the bank's edge. Lunging forward, I grabbed him by the jacket as he slipped backward off the bank. I couldn't stop his fall, and as I landed on my stomach on the path, his legs and chest disappeared over the ledge. I grunted as I took his weight while he grabbed hold of a sapling jutting from the bank. His weight eased off me.

"I'm secure. You can let go." He let out a long breath and laid his forehead against the dirt. "I hate heights."

"I imagine you hate falling from them even more," I said shakily as I got to my knees. As I took in his healthy bulk, I got the feeling my stitches were going to rip out again, if they hadn't already. "We didn't think this through properly."

"How is that?"

"I'd be easier to pull up."

"Get out of my way, and I'll pull myself up."

I did as directed, and he began to hoist himself up. His eyes widened, and taking that as a bad sign, I grabbed him by the arms as he began to slide down again. He eased back to his starting point.

"The blasted plants in the bank keep slipping out from under my feet," he said. "I feel like a wagon stuck in the mud."

"What about me?" the injured man demanded. "I'll say you didn't think things through. I feel like a man stuck in a poacher's trap." He snorted, then his face pinched in pain. Even so, he was recognizable as the unlucky suitor, Lord Mavern. Would it be too much to hope freeing him would encourage him to stop glaring at me every time he saw me? Of course, leaving him here would accomplish the same thing.

"We'll get to you, Lord Mavern. Hold on." Leaning over the bank, I grabbed Henry under the arms, and we tried again.

"Maybe you should get a rope and a horse to attach it to," he offered after the next failed attempt.

"How about a pry bar to get me out of this?" Mavern jabbed a trembling finger toward the trap.

"Bubbling cauldrons, man! What are you doing?" The cry came from above but was too irritated to be an angel.

Barely keeping my grip on Henry in my surprise, I craned my neck to see the top of the rise behind us. Harvey's hulking figure loomed down. Gabriella stood beside him.

"Ohhhh. Ohhhh," Mavern moaned dramatically.

The ham. I hoped Gabriella didn't fall for his show.

"I'm coming down," Harvey said. "Hold on."

"*Hold on.* That's all everybody says. As if we would do anything else," Henry muttered.

"How badly are you hurt, Lord Mavern?" Gabriella eased her way down the bank on Mavern's side of the stream while Harvey came toward us.

"Ohhhh," Mavern moaned again.

That does it. I tugged my ring off and shoved it onto Henry's finger.

His eyes bulged. "You know I don't like—"

"The bank beside me." I twisted the ring while pulling him up.

Henry sprawled beside me, groaning and pale-faced. "—traveling by magic," he finished.

"Why don't you go help Mavern, Harvey?" I removed my ring from Henry's finger and patted him on the back. "We're okay here." Henry glared at me.

Harvey stopped short, his eyebrows high, and then backtracked up the bank and over to Mavern's side. "Gabbie Marie, do *not* touch that trap."

Snap!

I jumped.

"It's sprung now and harmless," she said of a trap to the left of Mavern's. A hefty branch stuck out of it. "There are no others here."

As soon as I could get Henry to stop groaning and clutching his stomach like a seasick sailor, we made our way over to the others, going up the bank a bit to cross the stream. I slipped on leaves going down. Henry and I collided and rolled down the final few feet, landing like a tossed clump of weeds next to Mavern, who started bellowing like a wounded bull calf.

"Oh hush. They didn't touch you," Harvey groused as he hauled my servant to his feet.

When I scrambled up, I found myself pinned under Gabriella's critical gaze. Her hard look faltered when it met my wrist, my bandage exposed but not, as I'd feared, stained with fresh blood. Her eyes quickly shuttered again.

"No worse for the theatrics, I hope, Lord Ellsworth? You tumble so well you could join a circus."

"Anything to entertain a lady."

She scoffed and turned away to speak to Mavern. I dusted myself off, not that it improved the state of my clothes, and moved aside to watch Harvey free the trapped creature. Mavern. I meant Mavern.

Vehemently spewing curses against poachers and their traps under his breath, Harvey grabbed the trap's chain and yanked it out of the ground. "You could've used a rock and dug this out yourself, Lord Mavern." Harvey grunted as he went to work prying the trap open from around Mavern's ankle and ruined walking stick.

"How was I to know?" Mavern whimpered. "Could I have? It must've been the shock of the event, and the ruckus caused by those two lumbering buffoons, that drove the idea from me."

"I like that. We came to help—" I bit back the rest of my comment and blocked it in my chest behind crossed arms.

"Lord Ellsworth and *an accident*. What an unusual combination," Gabriella said only loud enough for me to hear as she passed behind me.

"Gabriella." Harvey's voice held all the command of a general.

The lady stopped and turned toward him, her face half hidden by the branches of the overgrown path.

"This is not the place to explore."

"No, it's not. You're right." With an unusual flush of embarrassment and one hand cradled against her chest, she retreated to Harvey's side. There, she turned to me. "What were all of you doing on this path? It hasn't been in use for years. From what I understand, it's completely gone in places. The new path is up there and enjoys the same view." She indicated the top of the bank she and Harvey had descended.

"What do you mean *gone*?" Mavern asked as Harvey helped him up. "To the river?"

"Or lost in growth."

"Yes to both, and full of wolves and wild hogs and vine-covered holes to fall in," Harvey added as if additional reason to avoid the path was needed.

"But this is where I was sent," Mavern said, tugging at his collar.

Henry closed his eyes. "We should never have come."

"Relax, Henry. I'm sure there's another explanation than us being purposefully sent to our doom." Despite my words, my fists clenched at my side. "As to why we're here, Henry and I are on our way to the village for the same reason as you and Harvey. I inquired of a stable hand about a scenic walk and was directed to this path."

"Same here." Mavern grimaced as he tried to take a step without putting too much weight on his ankle. I offered him my arm, and he leaned heavily on it.

"Oi, down there."

Once again, I craned my neck to see the source of the heavenward voice. It was the stable hand with the scraggly beard, the one I wanted to get my hands on.

"Cox, what the blazes are you doing here?" Harvey said. "Why aren't you doing what you were hired to do?"

"Come to right a wrong, I shouldn't wonder," I said through gritted teeth.

Cox drew back, chagrin evident on his face. "I ... um ... came to be of assistance to the baron and his manservant. "I—" He cleared his throat.

"Spit it out, man," Harvey said.

"Some of the other stable hands," Cox rushed the words, "thought to make a joke of me, telling me about this path, saying how pretty it was and all, the place to take a sweetheart. But I never came out here, and so when his lordship inquired about a scenic path along the river, I told him about it. After he left, I mentioned it to one of the others, and he called me all kinds of names. Anyway, I thought I'd better come rescue them. I didn't tell Lord Mavern, though."

"Why ... I heard you mentioning it and thought how nice a day it was for a walk to the village," Mavern said, glancing at Gabriella. I harrumphed, but was pleased by the cold look Gabriella gave the swain.

"Anyway, that's what happened. I swear it," Cox pleaded sincerely enough for me to unclench my fists. He tugged on the lead of a horse, bringing two muzzles into view. "I have two mounts, if they're needed."

Harvey shut his mouth for a moment before responding, grinding out the words as if they tasted like vinegar. "Good work, Cox. I suppose it wasn't your fault. Now, come down and help us."

With a little effort, we all made it up the bank, Gabriella refusing all assistance but making it without difficulty. I envied her surefootedness.

With a few threats against whoever deceived Cox, Harvey sent Mavern, Henry, and Cox back to the manor. I took the spare horse and joined him and Gabriella on the ride to the village. After I'd refused to join them in the carriage, they'd decided to travel on horseback. This was fortunate for us, as they were able to hear Mavern's bellowing when they drew near.

After the others left us, they allowed me a few moments to use my ring to return to the house and change. When I rejoined them, Harvey asked again about the incident with the trap, but Gabriella said not a word then or during the whole of the afternoon, except when called on to answer questions by the constable.

The local constable was a friendly man, but conscientious of the respect due to the Floraisons. The specifics of how the villains were tied up like geese in the marketplace was noticeably skimmed over. I, however, was thoroughly examined for any evidence that would indicate the men had fouled precious Henly soil because of me. Several times, Gabriella looked as if she wanted to say something, whether in my defense or not I couldn't tell. Something about her eyes made me wonder if she knew herself. It gave me a painful kind of hope.

Thanks to Harvey's comments in my defense, or an unspoken wish of the duke's not to have a guest of his involved in a scandal that might damage his own reputation, the constable decided the ruffians were thieves of opportunity who had unwittingly come across Henly. He supported this with the poacher's trap found around Mavern's ankle. I wondered how Mavern would feel if he knew how useful he'd been to me. There was also a report that one of the caves the duke employed for winemaking had been broken into and relieved of a cask of wine.

For the second time in half a year, I walked outside an establishment of the law and sucked in a breath of cold air, tasting a freedom that seemed all too shaky of late.

Donning my hat, I followed Harvey and Gabriella out to the street. Tension dropped from my shoulders like rain from a thundercloud. "I'm glad that matter is settled," I said by way of gaining my companions' attention. I gave a small bow of farewell. "If you'll excuse me, I'll take this opportunity to mail a letter to my cousin and call on Lord Tyndale's son. I promised the lad the loan of a book."

"I'm afraid you'll have to return to Henly with us, Lord Ellsworth," Harvey said firmly.

The tension clapped itself back on my shoulders. I hadn't been exonerated in their eyes, had I? I looked from Harvey to Gabriella. Of all the residents of Henly, these were the two I'd thought most likely, that I'd hoped, would look past my rank and clumsiness and give me the benefit of the doubt, as a friend might. But that was part of *A Floraison never* statement, it seemed.

"Why is that?" I demanded. They might treat barons with the contempt given to rodents, but it didn't mean I had to act like a mouse.

"The duke doesn't want anything else to happen to you during your stay at Henly," Harvey said.

"Shouldn't you save that guff for Lord Mavern? He's the one who was caught in a trap."

"That's the only thing that's happened to him," Gabriella said. "We're to return together." As if on cue, a carriage bearing the duke's livery rumbled up the narrow village lane.

"Then the carriage will have to wait. I have errands to run."

"We're returning to Henly, Lord Ellsworth. Now." Harvey's mien indicated he'd see me into the carriage whether I agreed to it or not.

"No." I widened my stance. Being manhandled into the duke's carriage would be quite the tale, and there were plenty of people around to tell it. It'd be worth every bruise.

"Ellsworth." There was enough threat in Harvey's lowered voice for a sensible man to rethink his decisions.

"*Harold.*"

Harvey's eyes flashed as he stepped forward.

"We'll wait." Harvey pulled up sharply at Gabriella's command. She put a hand on his arm, then indicated a tearoom a few buildings down before turning to me, her eyes as friendly as dragon fire. "You have one hour, Lord Ellsworth. Try not to cause a scene." She walked away with all the arrogant disdain I'd witnessed daily in my youth from Lady Ellsworth.

I'd been a fool to think Gabriella better than my grandmother. Or had I? There were times when she'd treated me as a friend. What had changed? Me challenging her ancestor's book? Had her family's prejudices so blinded her that she believed I was responsible for all this trouble? The dark anger I thought I'd buried when I forgave my grandmother blackened my mind. I strode after Gabriella. "I'm not the one you should be concerned for, Lady Gabriella."

She halted before the tearoom and turned to me looking as beautiful and cold as only a Floraison could. Without asking permission, I took her arm and directed her inside, ignoring Harvey's growl.

"In the great dukedom of the Floraisons," I continued in a low voice, "no one would notice a humble baron such as myself. The villagers of this idyllic place would find only one of your beauty and noble birth worthy of their attention. You should take care lest they see you interacting with someone of lesser ilk. *That* would be a scene worth recounting. Friendliness toward such a one would be treachery against your unblemished ancestry. By all means, treat him with as much disdain and disrespect as only a Floraison is capable of. 'Tis the only way to preserve your heritage."

"Don't worry. I know whose company to avoid." She tried to move away, but I kept her at my side.

The matron of the shop, a well-built, sandy-haired woman, greeted us with wide eyes that bounced between Gabriella, me, and Harvey.

"I'll take our usual private room, Matilda," Gabriella said, her voice perfectly composed. "Harvey will speak to our coachman and join me in a few moments."

"And the gentleman, my lady?" The older woman looked dubiously at me. I grinned back.

"The gentleman will not be joining us." Gabriella again pulled away from me, and I let her go, keeping hold of one hand. I bowed low and kissed it.

"A proper dismissal, Lady Gabriella," I said softly, releasing her hand. "Your aunt would be proud. After all, all the world is guilty and untrustworthy. Blemished. The Floraisons alone are as pure as doves."

Gabriella flushed, then walked to the stairs as quickly as propriety allowed. Matilda jogged to catch up to her.

"Sorcerers take you, Ellsworth," Harvey whispered. "Sometimes I wish the bandits had gotten away with you."

I laughed coldly. "Would it not be the greater insult to the famed, beautiful daughter of the Floraisons to be ignored by the lowly man she rescued from bandits? No, he must be hopelessly smitten and decidedly rebuffed for the story to play out as it should—the Perfect Floraison and the Unworthy Admirer."

Harvey muttered something ungentlemanly, then strode outside. I trailed after him, forcing all thoughts but those concerning my errands from my mind.

Gabriella kept her face averted as we rode home in the carriage. Harvey looked like he wanted to tear me limb from limb. With each spin of the wheels, I came under greater and greater conviction that I'd inherited more than I cared to admit from Lady Ellsworth. The circumstances might be different, but I could be just as selfish and cruel.

That evening, Alfred Floraison called me to his study. Sitting in the shadows at the back of the room were three men, none of whom, I conjectured from their figures, were guests for the mentoring season.

No smile of greeting softened the duke's face as he motioned for me to take a seat. "I learned from my daughter, and from the constable's report, that the matter of the attempted abduction has been settled to our satisfaction. It's a relief to have that taken care of."

He spoke with a contentment that irked me. The matter may have concluded satisfactorily, but it certainly hadn't been conducted satisfactorily. "I was not found guilty of my own abduction, which, as you might imagine, was a strong relief indeed."

The duke arched an eyebrow. "I understand," he said slowly, "that the constable exemplified a strong curiosity as to your background and habits. Did his inquisitiveness bother you?"

"Yes." I might have elaborated but for the interest of the strangers watching me from their dark corner.

"Ah," he said expressively. "I did not intend for that to happen, I assure you. The constable, like most of the villagers, is as jealous of the reputation of the Floraisons as our own family could be. Many of the villagers have close connections to Henly Manor. The woman who owns the

tearoom, for instance"—he shot me a knowing glance—
"is Harvey's sister."

I swallowed a spasm of guilt-ridden regret.

"That is beside the point," he continued. "Are you satisfied with the verdict and the punishment of the bandits?"

"Yes, sir, with those I am satisfied."

"Good. That brings us to another matter. Gentlemen?"
He rose and gestured to the three men in the corner.
They drew near, and my insides went cold. Two of the
three were associates of the Ceurian inspector.

The duke motioned to the man on the right, a Sonserian by his dress. "This is Inspector Duban of Florenburg."
The man bowed rigidly. "And Assistant Inspector Chead
and Mr. Polad of Ceur. You are acquainted with these
two, are you not?"

"Yes." The traveling ring warmed about my finger, as if
sensing my urge to flee. Olan had done as he'd warned. I
was bound for Ceur and no amount of justice would save
me, for it didn't exist there. Emil was missing and
couldn't save me this time.

How like my life. Orphaned, maimed, criticized, and
accused. Never good enough. Would they treat me like
this if I were a prince or a duke? Or even a handsome,
charming baron? The fairytale life at Silvestris Castle—of
being loved and treated as an equal—was over. Back to
the real thing, with the Lady Ellsworths, the Aunt Hele-
nes, and the Ceurian inspectors with their dank, lightless
prisons.

*Oh shut up. You're not imprisoned yet. Do what you've
always done: fight.* Fight the self-pity. Fight the bitterness. Fight the lies about myself other people, and my
own self-pity, would have me believe.

I flexed my fingers, aware the three men of the law were watching me with a hungry expression. I would not disgrace myself by running. I forced a smile, albeit a flippant one.

The duke eyed me narrowly, glancing at my ring before seating himself with the air of a judge. He didn't invite the rest of us to sit. "You're aware that Inspector Olan of Ceur ordered you to stay away from enchanters, are you not, Lord Ellsworth?"

"I am. I am also aware, and grateful, for the fact that I am a citizen of Sonser, that the inspector has no authority over me here. It should be noted, however, that I did not know your family possessed the power of enchantment when I applied to come here three years ago, or even until the very night of my arrival. It's not commonly known."

"No, it's not," he replied with an unreadable look at the visitors.

"But you stayed." Assistant Inspector Chead's meaning was clear: jump and run every time you see an enchanter, like a slave doing his master's bidding.

"It appears I did."

"Ignorance will not save you, I'm afraid, lad." The fake friendly manner of the good Inspector Duban of Florenburg set my teeth on edge.

"How unfortunate for me. It's the second-best argument I have, after innocence of the theft, of course. The third would be an unawareness of anything that's happened concerning Emil Farro since I left Ceur, as I have twice informed the inspector."

Duban gave a tight smile. "You can tell Inspector Olan yourself. He requested you be taken back to Ceur for questioning as well as for possible involvement in the attempted thefts against Emil Farro and the disappearance of the inventor himself. The office in Florenburg has agreed to his request."

I'd known it was coming, but still the world beneath me rocked. Betrayed by my own kingdom. If that didn't beat all. *Oh hush.*

"How long will Lord Ellsworth be gone?" the Duke of Henly asked.

"It's hard to say in these matters." Duban shrugged. "A couple of months, if found innocent?" I barely kept from snorting. "These things take time," he continued, "and we haven't found Emil Farro yet."

"Of course. These things take time," the duke repeated with a polite smile. "If you'll excuse us, gentlemen, I'd like to speak with Lord Ellsworth alone."

"Your Grace, I—" Chead stopped as the duke motioned to the door. The three men left.

As the door swished shut behind them, the duke motioned to a chair, and I sank into it, testing the bandages on my wrist, wondering idly whether I should take Henry with me or send him to his family at Silvestris.

"Well, Lord Ellsworth," the duke said, "for someone who is quiet and attentive during my lectures, you cause quite a stir outside them."

A cold splash of empathy hit me. How would a respectable duke with dozens of guests feel about having to deal with the law multiple times?

"I apologize for the inconvenience and trouble I've involved you in," I said, "however unintentional it was on my part."

He nodded and continued to examine me for a moment before turning his attention to some papers on his desk. Silence reigned for several minutes. Apparently, he didn't have anything to say to me after all.

"If you'll excuse me," I said. "I won't disturb you any longer. I must return to my room to tell Henry to pack and to write to my aunt." My heart, already heavy, plummeted at the thought of what I had to tell them. I spared a moment to consider what the others would say about my departure. What would Gabriella think? *Good riddance,* probably. If she even noticed I'd gone. *Don't be so harsh on the girl,* I scolded myself.

The duke looked up, and his face, so similar to Gabriella's, gave me additional pain. He pushed away from his desk. "Going so soon?"

"I fear the inspector will not want a delay."

"He didn't." The duke's flash of a grin took me aback. "But he must endure it."

"Endure it?" They weren't going to drag me away?

"I told them you couldn't leave before the end of the month."

"Oh." The end of the mentoring season. Must preserve the duke's reputation. Wouldn't want any rumors about the quality of his guests. Still, I was grateful for the little time given me.

"It's best for all of us if you depart at the expected time. You have more to learn to save Carrington, after all." His half-smile sank into sternness, the sort of expression I'd imagine my own father might have given me before advising. He looked pointedly at my ring. "Where you go when you leave is up to you, but I would recommend accompanying Assistant Inspector Chead to Ceur. If you find justice there is a farce, then use your ring, but not before. You'd lose respect and credibility if you did."

"Yes, sir," I said, surprised and cheered that he cared enough to advise me.

"You never know," he continued. "Jonathan Lofton might find the Thief after all and be able to clear your name so they can't use that excuse any longer."

I managed a weak smile. *Might* ...

"But don't try to help him in the hunt, Ellsworth. The Ceurians are staying in the village but implied they'd be keeping an eye on you. Everyone knows Farro is a daring inventor and that his inventions do not need to fall into the hands of the emperor of Ceur. They want him back; hence, they want you. Don't give them a reason to drag you away sooner than agreed upon. A reason such as consorting with a prominent enchanter like Jonathan Lofton."

"Yes, sir."

"You may go now."

My hand was on the door knob when he stopped me again.

"And Ellsworth," he said as I faced him. "If you can't treat my daughter with the respect she deserves—no matter how you feel she or anyone else has treated you—don't speak with her at all."

I dipped my chin, as much in shame as in acknowledgment. "Yes, Your Grace."

"I'm glad we understand one another. I'll see you in the morning."

Chapter 11

Don't ever let a half-magic touch you. By touch he casts or takes spells.

The Fall of Bevvelian by Edgar Frock

GABRIELLA FLORAISON

SLENDER ICICLES HUNG from the branches and jutting rocks of the glen, and early morning birdsong took the place of the usual rush of water. If only the glen smelled as pristine as it looked. The scent of rotting leaves and a strange mixture of other odors assaulted me as I picked up our toppled cauldron and flung the muck filling it onto the glen's rock floor.

"It's not damaged, is it?" Alexandria swept pieces of a broken flask into a larger pile of debris.

Holding the pot out from me, I flipped it over and examined it. "No."

"One cauldron then," she said, "and one potion book. We'll have to find replacements for everything else."

As I helped Alexandria straighten the glen, I wondered how long it would take to complete Fred's game and what might happen in the meantime. What if the Thief did steal my wand and give me that strange chill while I was stone? He could've tried to steal Eva and Aunt Helene's wands here by turning our potion into a sleeping gas. How long would it take us to find the tresor box now to determine if my wand was in it or not? Should I ... No, there was no need to resort to using the mirror. That plain, spiteful baron was not right about the half-magics and my wand. It was all an accident or Fred's mischief.

Your aunt would be proud. I paused in my sweeping as Marcel's accusation stung anew. His implication that it was the role of the Floraison ladies to scornfully reject gentlemen was uncalled for. And unjust. He'd never been more than friendly. I'd never rejected him or had a cause to. I'd been friendlier to him than my relatives had. Why purposefully embarrass me in front of half the village? His anger and jabs were unpardonable.

But had he no right to be angry? How must it feel to be the one wronged and yet be treated as a suspect? I could have spoken in his defense, but I remained silent. Of course, I hadn't decided whether he was innocent or not. In either case, the Duke of Lofton and Papa could handle the Thief. I would finish Fred's game, find my wand, finish my books, and stay away from troublesome barons.

Sterling neighed and pranced around his pen. I flexed my hand, then rubbed my gloved fingers against my palm. "Calm down, Sterling. We'll leave this unwholesome-smelling place soon."

"How much of what we need do we have in storage?" Alexandria asked as we were finishing up.

"Not much." I helped her sweep debris into a burlap sack, for we couldn't let the remnants wash downstream when we flooded the glen again. "This particular setup requires a large number of pieces and some specialty."

"We can get a few from the apothecary. I'll write a letter to the shop in Gersemere for the others."

I rubbed my fingertip over the rough stone bench. The air in the glen was foul. I needed a walk. The woods would be lovely with a crisp, white layer of snow and the fresh scent of pines.

"Are you ready?" Alexandria asked.

"Why don't you go ahead and write the letter? I'd enjoy a walk."

"Better make that a ride. Sterling's making a racket over there."

"He's certainly antsy." Not the best mood for riding.

After Alexandria left, I walked out of the glen alone. Sterling's protests carried through the forest behind me as I strode toward the old river path. When I remembered the traps and the stream cutting through the trail where we'd found Marcel and the others, I considered changing direction for the upper trail, but something kept my feet moving toward the old.

Bare branches tried to snag my cloak, but the sturdy fabric wouldn't be caught. The view of the river to my left was forgotten as I passed along, my gaze searching the shrubs and vines on the bank to my right.

Birds.

I was looking for birds. It was a pity I hadn't brought my sketchbook.

A metal trap, poorly concealed, caught my eye. I needed to change paths. I had no business on this particular one anyway. But still I stared at the overgrown way ahead. Only after promising myself to return to it at the spot where we'd found Mavern was I able to turn and scramble up the bank. I'd have to go up to skirt the stream anyway, I told myself. Another part of me insisted I return to Sterling, but I ignored it.

On the upper trail, I walked close to the rim, surveying the bank below. How long before I could descend again? Was I missing any birds?

"Lady Gabriella." Lord Tyndale stepped from behind a holly not ten feet from me.

My hand was nearly to my chest before I caught it and forced it to hang loosely by my side. "Lord Tyndale. I didn't expect to see anyone here. I was out for a walk. I was looking for birds for a book I am writing and illustrating. Isn't it a lovely day for a walk?" *Hush, you're babbling. You've done nothing wrong.*

"It is a fine day for a walk," he said slowly, his expression clouding. He joined me where I stood. Where I'd been rooted to the path since seeing him. "Do you often walk this way alone, so far from the house?"

"Yes. That is, no. I walk wherever I want to. It's my father's estate."

He startled but quickly collected himself and eyed me narrowly. "Forgive me, I wasn't questioning your right. After the incident with the bandits and the traps, I was merely concerned and expressed myself poorly. Do forgive me."

"I-I apologize as well," I stammered, blushing at my outburst and his scrutiny. "You gave me quite a fright, that's all. I was lost in thought."

"I came out for a solitary ramble myself." He stared down at me, his expression that of a man bent on solving an enigma.

I broke his gaze, my eyes lighting on a golden-brown leaf clinging to his sleeve. It was a leaf like those adhering the whole winter long to the beech trees lining the path below. What business had he on the lower way? Was he planning to prevent my walk? I rebuked the ridiculous thought. "What brings you out, Lord Tyndale? You are far from the house as well."

He caught my gaze and flicked off the leaf. "Lord Mavern asked me to recover his toothpick case." He held up a small, silver box but returned it to his pocket before I could examine it. "And I wanted a walk to ponder some unfortunate news I received this morning." He continued to stare at me as if trying by the pressure of his gaze to wrench some secret from me.

I scrubbed my fingers against my palm, ignoring the neighing coming from the direction of the glen, though not that far away. "I'm sorry for your bad news. Don't let me disturb your ponderings." I made to walk around him. He stepped into my path.

"Might I accompany you to the house instead? I wouldn't be at all surprised if those ruffians locked up in town have accomplices on the loose." He moved to take my arm, but I drew away.

"I thank you for your concern, but I'm quite safe. There's nothing of value in this area to draw them."

"Unless they are also poachers." He looked over my shoulder at another, closer neigh.

I pressed my lips together. Bossy men and a clingy horse. Would I have no peace this month?

"If you'll excuse me." I hurried around Tyndale, aiming for a good spot to descend to the lower path.

"Where are you going?" he demanded as he caught up with me.

"For a walk."

"The lower path is dangerous."

"I am fully capable of avoiding poacher's traps and animal dens." I sped my steps. Sterling was almost upon us, but I could nearly touch the branches beside the gentle descent Harvey and I had taken. I could get down before he reached us.

"Wait." Tyndale snagged my arm, and I jerked away, but to no avail.

"Let me go. You have no right to—Oh!"

Sterling's head loomed into view, and I stepped back into Tyndale. He tried to get in front of me as if to protect me, but Sterling butted him with his head, knocking him to the side.

"Sterling, behave!" I cried. He lunged forward, snapping at my hand with precision. I jumped back, nearly tripping over Tyndale, and reached for a limb with my right hand to steady myself. Sterling snapped at that hand, breaking the limb when I dodged his bite.

"What kind of a horse is that?" Tyndale demanded as he pushed to his feet.

"A temperamental one." I escaped Sterling's large mouth again.

"Gabriella," he said brusquely, closing in behind me like a shadow. "What kind of a horse is that?" I slid on the trampled grass. He caught me and pulled me to his chest. "What kind? Answer me! Is that a Pyren?"

"What does it matter? Let me go." I pushed against him, trying to get him to move us away from my crazed horse.

He whirled me around, putting himself between Sterling and me. Sterling's neigh pained my ears. I just needed to get to the woods, where the air was better. Damp and cool. Cave-like. Why did Sterling always object so? I had to get to where I *belonged*.

You belong to us now. The hag's scream turned to a cackle in my mind, and fear nearly stopped my heart.

It was true.

The cave, the hag, the pricking of my finger. It hadn't been a nightmare I'd dreamed but one I'd lived. I'd spilt my blood on a sorcerer's altar. I was doomed to become their slave. If it wasn't true, I wouldn't be where I was. Sterling wouldn't be trying to stop me.

One more drop of blood on their altar would seal my fate, and I was heading toward that accursed cave.

"Answer me!" Tyndale shook me by the shoulders as he pivoted us out of Sterling's way. "Is that a Pyren?"

"Yes!" I turned my face away from him. "He's a Pyren."

He shook me again. "Then, blast it, woman, let the horse do what he was bred to do! Do you want to answer the Call?"

"No!"

"Then stand still."

Mustering all my strength and courage, I stilled and slowly reached out my hand. Tyndale yanked off my glove just before Sterling's teeth found their mark, and I screamed.

How many scars was this? *You're not a true Floraison.* Aunt's voice in my thoughts overshadowed my own. *No true Floraison would need a Pyren.* No true Floraison would try to escape her Pyren either. How close had I come to pricking my finger the final time?

Tyndale called my name. I felt the support of his arms as he leaned me against Sterling's side. Sterling nuzzled me until my head cleared.

Summoning what little pride I had left, I patted his neck and stood by my own strength. "Forgive me, Lord Tyndale, for—" I couldn't say the flippant phrase I wanted to: *for acting a fool.* I wasn't a fool, I was a monster in the making. "I mean, thank you for—"

"Of course," he said hastily with a glance over his shoulder. That was all the man who'd only just stopped yelling at me had to say?

He snagged Sterling's reins with one hand and positioned me beside the stirrups with his other. He didn't have to say *up* for me to realize his intent. Before I had staunched the flow of blood from my finger, I was seated atop Sterling, and we were walking at a fast clip toward the house. Tyndale said nothing, guiding us with a firm hand on Sterling's bridle and often looking over his shoulder.

"How did you know?" I asked.

"That you're a Sorcerer's Called?"

"That's not tr—but it is true. I can't deny it any more, can I?" The last of my pride slipped away. For the first time, I saw clearly my fate and the flaws that seemed determined to speed me to it.

"To deny it would be your undoing, Lady Gabriella. You can't fight a thing until you acknowledge it," he said bitterly.

A wet laugh escaped me. "I, Lady Gabriella Floraison, daughter of the Duke of Henly, am a Sorcerer's Called. There, it's said. How long have I desired to admit it? But I feel no relief. Do you know what that means, Lord Tyndale?"

"Yes. You might become nothing more than the personal slave and entertainment of a wealthy, disinterested sorcerer. Or you might become the priestess to a devout one, a collector of blood for their hellish rites, an assassin, anything."

I could commit any number of evil deeds, harm so many people, my family even. I choked back a sob. "By rights you could turn me over to the king. Sorcery's punishable by death in Sonser."

"You're not a sorceress nor can they make you one. You alone decide whom or what you will worship. They could make you *do* anything but never change that. Now, pull yourself together." He handed me his handkerchief. I blew my nose and was quiet for some time.

"How many times?" he asked suddenly. "When were they? Is there any pattern to the Call?"

"Four times," I answered, managing to sniffle only once. "Twice since my father's guests arrived. No pattern." I told him of the earlier times, finishing my tale with a scoff. "Only four times, and they nearly won. I've never made Sterling's job easy." Aunt Helene was right. I wasn't a true Floraison.

"Pity and loathing for yourself won't help, Gabriella," Tyndale said harshly. "I suggest you get over those emotions as quickly as you can if you want to survive."

"I'm sorry. I'm so ashamed. I—"

"You should be."

I gasped at his coldness. Tyndale startled and looked up at me, horror in his eyes.

"That was cruel. Forgive me," he said quickly. "You didn't bring this curse on yourself, though you must fight it as if you did. I was thinking of myself. You don't deserve the trouble you're in, but I know your strength of character will see you through it." He released Sterling's bridle as we left the woods for the road connecting the house and the village. This was not the short route I'd taken to the river. "I should leave you now before I injure you more," he said. "I must check on my son in the village before it gets late. This is the best route for both of us."

I looked around frantically. The way home was so long. Anything could happen between where we were and the shelter of the stable. "But, Lord Tyndale—"

"Courage, Gabriella." He took my hand and regarded me with surprising tenderness. He quickly dropped his gaze to my hand. "You had quite a shock today. Give yourself time to recover." He met my gaze again. "You're a fighter. I see it in you. You can make it home without me. Give Sterling his head, and you'll be fine."

Giving him a weak nod, I stiffened my back and turned Sterling toward home. Tyndale slapped Sterling on the rump, as if we needed encouragement to hurry home, and watched us ride away.

Sterling thundered into the stable some minutes later. Hiding my gloved hand from Harvey, I asked him to give Sterling a special treat, then took refuge in my room.

To know my life and freedom rested uneasily with a horse and myself, my weak self, did not allow a peaceful afternoon. I wanted to go out, yet I feared leaving the house lest the Call take me unprepared. I couldn't have Sterling trotting around after me everywhere. Of course, there was no guarantee the Call wouldn't strike while I was inside. Sterling couldn't help me then unless I went to the stable.

Unless I ... The phrase took me aback. I looked at the scars and the fresh bite marks on my finger and for once found comfort there. I'd stood my ground and let my Pyren protect me. Granted, I'd had encouragement, but I'd stood, and I would keep doing so.

If only that single declaration could prevent the temptation, but I feared mine might well be a long-lasting fight. Could I endure?

I tossed and turned all night. How could I have left Sterling in the glen knowing it was his purpose to protect me? At some level, I'd known where I was trying to go, what my danger was. Why hadn't I fought it? Was I such a coward? Or was I so blindly proud, believing that if I didn't consciously acknowledge the Call, it couldn't hurt me and I couldn't be considered flawed?

That my beloved parents hadn't left me to half believe Aunt Helene's claim it was merely my imagination? Why hadn't they told me?

What if courage failed me? It was hard to be courageous. It was so much easier to give in. But the Floraisons didn't take the easy way.

"That's it. You're coming with me." The next morning, Alexandria plucked the book from my hands and tugged me up by the arm.

"What—" I began, but she cut me off.

"You haven't turned a page in five minutes. I'll not have you moping about your wand all morning. Grab your sketchpad."

I was *not* moping. Beside me sat a stack of books on Sorcerer's Calleds, Pyrens, and magic thieves. Questions plagued me, and I had to fight the desire to ignore them in fear of the answers. Why had I tried to get to the cave twice in the last few weeks while in my whole history since my first visit there, I'd only tried twice before? I should talk with my parents about it, but I wanted to know everything I could about the Call and magic thieves to convince them I could handle the truth. Yet as far as Alexandria was concerned, I was moping, and I didn't want to explain yet.

We were soon on horseback roaming the forest, listening and watching for new subjects for my book on birds. A light snowfall lingered over the ground and draped itself over the trees. The crunch of snow under our horses' hooves dominated the wood. It was an eerie, lonely sound. The forest felt less alive than usual. Or, perhaps, I was less at ease than usual. None of the hounds had accompanied us, and it was possible that somewhere in the forest was the wolf, or the poachers, I might have seen when the tree fell. Unless one believed Marcel's claim that it was a half-magic who'd turned to stone and then escaped. I almost did now. There was a sorcerer's lair at my beloved Henly, and my parents hadn't told me. Why shouldn't there be half-magics and half-magic thieves as well? The Thief may have stolen my wand.

"Is it one you need?" Alexandria asked, pointing to a rust-bellied bird atop a high branch.

"Yes," I answered after confirming the white bars on its black wings.

The chaffinch dove off the branch as if planning to swoop between us, then stopped. If possible, I would've said there was as much surprise in its tiny eyes as in mine. It simply hung in the air, perfectly positioned for a gorgeous illustration.

"You're welcome." Wand out, Alexandria grinned at me.

"Thank you," I chimed, shaking off my astonishment. I hastily retrieved my sketchpad and pencils from my saddlebag and began work. "Is that the first time you've used the spell? It's not one we learned from Mama or Papa."

"I looked it up this morning because I thought it might be useful." She grimaced, her wand still extended toward the bird. "I wish I knew how to make it stay on its own. I have to keep holding it."

"I won't dawdle."

Tension eased from me as I pulled the pencil across the paper, though the questions lingered in my mind. One thought became clear: What would it mean if the Magic Thief were a half-magic? What of my wand? Could he, a servant of the sorcerers, activate the Call on me?

"Alexandria," I began slowly, "do you ever wonder if the legends of the Magic Collectors aren't legends?"

"Fred and I discussed that the last time he was here. It seems that in Gersemere, though it's not readily admitted, the enchanters believe they exist. He hasn't found proof, however. The enchanters there are very hush-hush." She shrugged. "I don't know, but I rather hope so. I've always found the idea fascinating."

What would that mean for me?

The sketch quickly took shape, but then a shadow's movement gave me pause. I reached for my empty wand pocket. "Alexandria!"

A wolf charged from between the trees and then stopped, the same look in its eyes as in the bird's. Alexandria, her wand pointed toward the bird and her other arm stretched toward the wolf, stared at her latest capture.

"Stand," I ordered the prancing horses. They stood, their muscles twitching in readiness to bolt. I suppressed a tremble. "You were right about that spell coming in handy."

"Yes." She smiled, but her voice shook.

Returning my attention to my drawing, I quickened my pace, since Alexandria refused to let the bird go until I was completely finished and satisfied with the results. I was almost done when the crunch of snow announced company. The voice that accompanied it identified *human* company.

"Lady Gabriella. Lady Alexandria. May we be of assistance?" The Duke of Lofton and Marcel, both on foot and well-bundled against the cold, strolled the forest path. How would a more knowledgeable enchanter, such as the duke, have handled the wolf?

He joined Alexandria, but Marcel stopped near me, though not too near. He cast a dubious glance my way, his usual friendly, open look shuttered, but it wasn't clouded by anger today. My accusations seemed silly now. Nothing about him suggested a scheming mindset or a lack of integrity. If only I could settle the half-magic issue, I'd know whether to trust him and panic about my wand or to continue the tresor box hunt at my leisure.

Even so, Marcel and I were not on friendly terms. I returned his tip of his hat with a cool nod and went back to drawing. My pencil paused mid-stroke, an unexpected connection forming in my mind. The Duke of Lofton was an enchanter from Gersemere. He might be able to provide the proof of half-magics Fred had been unable to find.

"Good heavens!" Marcel jabbed a finger at the wolf, then rounded on me. "Why haven't you fled?" he demanded. "That's a wolf, not some overgrown box, I mean fox. It ... it could easily take down your horse and you with it."

I managed to shut my gaping mouth, but no reply, no reproof would form. He was terrified—for my sake. Hardly the sort of person to arrange an explosion or steal a wand.

Alexandria scolded Marcel for his outburst, but I couldn't help but smile as he sheepishly agreed with Alexandria that the wolf hadn't moved, much less attacked anyone. He certainly wasn't handsome, but there was something sweet and endearing about him. Who was I to judge anyway? A Sorcerer's Called?

The duke laughed, then spoke to Alexandria, freeing Marcel from her look of reproach. "Haven't you been trained to leave a lasting spell? Release the wolf. I'll take care of him."

I held my breath as Alexandria dropped the spell. The wolf barely had time to snarl before it shrank and puffed into a fluffy sheep at the duke's command.

Marveling, I looked at Marcel. His slack-jawed stare quickly changed to a grin of pure amusement. He glanced at me, sharing his enjoyment as if I were the friend he knew would understand and reciprocate.

"Marcel Gustave," I said quietly. He walked hesitantly to Sterling's side. I drew his attention to the wolf-sheep, reminding him of his earlier outburst. "We can take care of ourselves, you know."

He sighed heavily and rubbed his forehead. "I'm sorry. My cousin Giles says I'm as bad a worrier as my aunt. I can't seem to help getting upset when anyone I—when people put themselves at risk. Or when I *think* they've put themselves at risk."

In that trait, he reminded me of my mother's sister, and I much preferred her to Aunt Helene.

"My great-grandfather," he continued in a tone that said he was half lost in thought, "died in a wolf attack. My grandfather nearly did as well." I caught a glimpse of horror in his eyes before he looked away. "I was, well"—he cleared his throat and met my gaze—"I should trust you know what you're doing."

"Since worriers aren't likely to cause potion-making equipment to explode, I suppose I'll have to find another scapegoat for the incident in the glen."

His eyes widened. "Thank you for believing me. I—I only wish there were a scapegoat for my behavior in the village."

"I understand your anger and frustration. There's no need to speak of it. Neither of us behaved as we ought. I should have spoken up for you at the trial."

"I'm forgiven?"

When I nodded, his green eyes shone as if I'd given him unexpected grace. I wondered at the seeming power I had over this man. I felt oddly accountable. "Am I forgiven for false accusations?"

He bowed gallantly. "It never happened."

"Then you're forgiven."

"I'm relieved to hear it." He turned away to pat Sterling's neck but soon gave me a sideways glance. "Have you anyone else in mind for the incident at the glen?"

"I'm investigating possibilities."

"Even *unlikely* ones?" he asked with meaning.

"Even unlikely ones," I answered, blushing at how I'd previously scorned him for suggesting half-magics. Marcel was an intelligent man; even Papa had commented he was among his brightest and most promising students. Why had I dismissed his ideas so readily?

He smiled, and I smiled back without meaning to, grateful he could forgive my petulance. The heroine of a favorite novel had proclaimed she'd rather be happy than proud, rather have mended relationships than the pride found in unforgiveness, or in saving face by refusing to admit a wrong. I understood what she meant.

"I'd be happy to help in any way I'm able," he said. Regret flashed across his face. "That is, I would, but I should focus on your father's lectures. I have so much to learn in order to run Carrington the way it should be run. I've no business intruding in your family's affairs."

"Of course." I barely covered my astonishment at his sudden change and the hurtful sense of dismissal. Perhaps he forgave but didn't forget offenses. "You did come as my father's guest." I forced a bright smile and handed him my sketchpad and pencils. "Since you offered to help, would you return these to my saddlebag?"

"It would hardly be wise to refuse an enchantress." He jerked his chin toward the *wolf in sheep's clothing* as if to back up his statement.

"Decidedly not."

He asked about the bird, and I explained our mission in the woods and the wolf's interference. "Is it wise to view an enchantress's artwork?" He returned the pencils to the saddlebag but held on to the sketchpad.

"Only if compliments alone are given."

"You'd better take it then. I never give false praise."

With a laugh, I pushed the proffered sketchpad back to him. "None is required, sir. I give you leave to voice your honest opinions, good and ill."

"I am honored." He opened the sketchpad. I caught myself waiting for his scrutiny to end and for him to say what he thought of it. His wasn't a skimming glance and hurried, insincere praise. He gave a quick nod and turned a page, then it struck me: he understood art. How much did this man, a stranger mere weeks ago, and I have in common?

"Do you draw?" I asked.

"Story illustrations mainly, but yes," he said and continued his perusal of my work.

"Shall we return to the house?" Alexandria suggested with a significant look at me. "The wolf's condition is temporary after all." Without waiting for a reply, she nudged her horse back onto the forest path, encouraging us to do likewise. To my disappointment, Marcel stowed the sketchpad in my saddlebag without comment.

The four of us set out, the duke and Marcel walking beside the horses. The duke explained to Alexandria the details of making a spell a lasting spell, that is, timed or long-lasting, not everlasting.

Marcel walked beside me, though he looked around often enough. One would think both he and Tyndale were afraid to be seen with me. Or was he concerned there might be another wolf?

Out of curiosity, I asked Marcel his opinion of my work. He gave an artistically sound and overall complimentary critique, and we fell easily into conversation on other matters.

As we spoke, the tension between us drained away, leaving only two people engaged in conversation. It was surprisingly enjoyable conversation. He was well-read and well-traveled and his opinions were sound.

Alexandria gave me a few questioning looks, but I ignored her. It would be dreadfully rude to ignore Marcel. I would not have him think so poorly of us.

Sooner than I expected, Harvey greeted us at the stable.

"Lady Alexandria," he said as he took my sister's horse. "The duchess has been asking for you. She's going to Lady Tannon's soon and wants to know if you're coming."

"Yes. I'll go change." Alexandria paused in adjusting her hat. "Gabriella, won't you join us?"

Keenly aware of Marcel's presence beside me, for he'd helped me from my horse, I shook my head. "Not today. I really must continue the hunt for the tresor box." I also intended to question the duke and Marcel about half-magics.

"Very well then." Her brow furrowed, but she put on a smile before she curtsied to the duke. Yet when she took leave of Marcel, there was more frost in her manner than on the ground on a winter's morn. Marcel bowed to her, and I fancied both hurt and contempt flashed in his eyes.

"I must l-leave you as well," he said before Alexandria had even left the stable. His color rose as he spoke, and he grimaced like he'd bitten his tongue.

He was just going to leave? Was he so easily affronted? I suddenly found I preferred the angry man at the village teashop. He stood his ground and didn't stutter while he was about it. To leave because Alexandria hinted her displeasure at him! Was my company worth so little? "Go then if you must."

He would've been out of the stable in a thrice had not Harvey's voice arrested him.

"You aren't going to visit your hound?" Harvey asked, more in censure than in question.

Marcel slowly twisted back around. "I must speak with Henry before the lecture begins."

A stony silence followed this. I almost shooed the fickle friend on his way.

"A few more minutes will do you no harm, Ellsworth," the duke said.

"If you say so."

Wondering at the strained look Marcel gave the duke, I joined them in visiting the puppies.

"What do you intend to call your dog? 'Bitsy' will sound strange when she's a full-grown wolfhound," I asked as I greeted Nympha at the stall gate.

Marcel scooped up Bitsy and rubbed her tiny head. "I haven't given it much thought."

Feeling a weight on my foot, I picked up one of the other puppies. The air grew stale. I needed a walk along the breezy river path. *Not now. Please not now.*

Sterling neighed. The Duke of Lofton and Marcel startled at the fierceness of his cry. Must they witness my shame? I could walk to the meadow. Sterling would follow. All would be well. They needn't see.

Shifting the puppy into my other hand, I rubbed my fingertip against my thumb. Sterling's neigh filled the air. I started toward the stall door.

"Lady Gabriella, are you ill?" Marcel asked as I passed.

"Perfectly well, thank you." I slipped my wiggling puppy into his empty hand. When I caught his look of concern, a bit of the haze cleared.

Get a hold of yourself, Gabriella. Fight it. The cool of the river walk would feel lovely compared to the stuffy stable. I could meet Sterling in the meadow or the edge of the forest. There was no need to let the duke and Marcel know. *Oh, hang it all.* I yanked off my glove. "If you'll excuse me, gentlemen, I must see to my horse."

"Gabbie Marie, are you still here?" Harvey bellowed as his heavy boots thudded down the straw-dusted floor.

"I'm coming, Harvey."

Avoiding the duke's and Marcel's looks, I hurried to Harvey. For good measure, I gave him my hand, and he pulled me along to Sterling.

I steeled myself for a fifth ring of horse's teeth marks. A third new one within a couple of weeks. It was time to stop playing games. Change had come to Henly, and it wasn't good.

Several minutes later, finger bandaged and hidden under my glove, I returned to Nympha's stall. The duke alone waited for me, and I couldn't ignore the disappointment that Marcel wasn't with him. He might have had useful information.

"Is there something you'd like to talk with me about?" the duke asked even before I greeted him. He glanced at my hand.

"Indeed, I—" The words caught in my throat. Did I really want to know if my family had believed a lie for generations? That the book we were revered for was a monstrous untruth? To admit to him I was a Sorcerer's Called? Intuition told me he knew the latter, but I wasn't ready to discuss it. *Truth is more important than pride.* But one truth at a time. I raised my chin, like a boxer ready to take a blow. "Tell me about half-magics."

"Tell you if they have your wand?"

"You know it's missing?" What must he think of me, an enchantress who'd twice lost her wand?

"Ellsworth told me of your adventures at the statue and the glen."

"Then he left. How considerate of him. It will save me from having to tell him what I think of him."

"I would reserve judgment for a while longer if I were you. Ellsworth did what he could for you by informing me of something you should've confessed yourself. He has troubles of his own to deal with and doesn't need to be involved in yours." The duke offered me his arm. "Is there somewhere private where we can talk?"

My cheeks stung at the duke's reprimand, but I took his arm and let him lead me from the stable. "We can go to my father's study while he's out lecturing."

As soon as we entered the privacy of the study, he asked me to tell him the details of the incident in the glen and at the statue.

"It's Ellsworth's opinion," he said when I was done, "that someone shot a heated piece of gravel at the potion apparatus, which caused the apparatus to explode. Previous tampering with the potion led to the sleeping gas your aunt cleared away. The Thief might have hoped to steal the remaining wands and Ellsworth's ring in one fell swoop."

"That was my thought as well. About his purpose, that is." I brushed aside an ungenerous aggravation that I had Aunt Helene to thank for us avoiding such a fate, and turned the conversation back to my original inquiry. "As a half-magic, the Thief would know there were protective spells on our enchanted objects, correct?"

A quirk of a smile crossed his face. "I was hoping you'd forgotten that question. As strange as it may seem, half-magics—I personally know several and am very fond of them—don't mind being called legends. Your ancestor's book was a blessing in disguise to them. Sometimes I wonder if he knew it himself."

I nodded slowly, not surprised to find how easily I accepted the reversal of long-held beliefs after yesterday's breach. "Why would they want to be hidden?"

"That's a story for another day. I only mentioned them to your father and aunt out of desperation, and after my failure with them decided not to try with the rest of you. I'm glad one of you understands, but you'll keep it in confidence, I trust?"

"I will," I answered reluctantly.

"Good girl. The point is the Thief knows where your treasures are and that they are safeguarded by your family's old protections and, ahem, some of my own."

"Then we're safe. Our treasures are safe."

"I'm afraid not. You recall how the stone spell left you suddenly, when someone touched you?"

"Yes."

His eyes, always piercing, took on a new intensity, but instead of trying to search my soul, they were trying to put something there. My mind ran once more over what he'd asked, and my heart nearly stopped. Magic leaving suddenly ... at a touch. Half-magics were often called Magic Collectors because they could collect magic by touch.

"Oh no. What's to stop the Thief from collecting the protective spells?" I asked. He'd reached the glen unnoticed because he'd stolen the alarm spells. Was it too much to hope some spells were un-stealable?

"That, my dear, is the question," he said approvingly. "Not all spells are easily removed. Fortunately, your ancestors knew enough to use multiple layers of sturdy spells. Given enough time, he likely could remove them, however."

"The month of Papa's mentoring season?"

"Would be sufficient. He could take some and leave others weakened so we'd believe they were still functioning."

I stifled a groan. "Have you any idea who the Thief might be?"

"I couldn't say."

Wouldn't, more likely. But discretion and honor urged the concealment of unproved accusations; he was wise in his reticence. Then his question came back to me: *You recall how the stone spell left you suddenly, when someone touched you?* It left when Tyndale touched me. Hadn't the cold also left when he scooted my feet onto the bench? Was he collecting spells he'd put on me? Surely not. He might be a half-magic, but he was not the Magic Thief. He had gentleman written all over him, in his manners, his appearance, and his concern for me. He'd saved me from the Call.

I felt the duke's attention on me, and I wondered if he knew my train of thought, for his expression was grave.

"Now about this wand of yours," he said, "that you claim is in the tresor box."

Chapter 12

If the magic thief was a servant of the sorcerers, they would not long tolerate failure on his part. If he did not accomplish what they sent him for, they would join him and see that he did.

The Fall of Bevvelian by Edgar Frock

Marcel Ellsworth

NOTEBOOK AND PENCIL in my hand, I hurried to my chambers at the close of the day. A large package had arrived for me. I hoped it was the reports from Carrington. With the thieving estate manager gone, I was anxious to see how the new manager's reports looked. Had any of the changes we'd implemented had an effect yet?

"Henry, has it finally come?" I asked as I opened the door. From the desk by the window, the two Ceurians watched me like hawks their prey. Cold dread rushed over me, only to be replaced with indignation at the sight of my mail, open and scattered on the desk before them.

"Well, well. This is a larger package than I expected." I closed the door behind me and strode to the desk. The men never bothered to rise. "Would it be inquisitive to ask what you're doing here and where my servant is? I should like to ask him what he means by letting foreigners read my private mail." Eying the open letters, I laid my notebook and pencil on the desk.

"He agreed that he had work to do elsewhere." Assistant Inspector Chead observed me coolly as I slid the opened envelopes and papers around to see what the men had seen. "Your estate could be in better shape, Lord Ellsworth."

I hated the way the Ceurian accent made my name sound like a sea creature's.

"How clever of you to figure that out. Tell me"—I tucked the financial reports back in their folder—"was it the reports themselves or my presence at an estate manager mentoring program that tipped you off? I wouldn't have thought reading complicated financial reports would be among the skills of an assistant inspector. You seem more fitted for bullying servants to leave their posts."

My fingers stilled though my heart tripled its pace. Beneath the papers from Carrington were three sheets of fine quality stationery written through with my aunt's strong, lightly flourished script. What had she said? If they knew of the inquiries about the Magic Thief and Farro she and Giles were conducting on my behalf, I'd never make it to the end of the month. Lofton wouldn't have the chance to clear my name.

"Has the sarcasm left our little Sonserian?" goaded Mr. Polad. "He's even paler than his kind usually are."

"Perhaps he's learned a bit of respect." Assistant Inspector Chead linked his fingers and rested them on the desk, his stare as coldly professional as Polad's was wickedly pleased.

Possibilities and consequences raced through my mind faster than the blood through my wildly beating heart. Would they let me write home and explain what happened before they took me? Would my family be al-

E.J. Kitchens

lowed to visit before they put me away for good, in a cell or a wooden box?

I could use the ring and go into hiding. I'd lose Carrington, but they'd not take my life. *Pull yourself together.* I struggled to steady my thoughts when a particularly strange one intruded: *An Ellsworth handles every situation with confidence and poise.* It shocked me into mental silence.

"What is it they say here?" Polad asked. "Caterpillar's got your tongue?"

"Cat," I answered absently. There had to be a start for family sayings of that variety, even for the Floraisons. It was time I started some for the Ellsworths.

Feeling the strange looks of my companions, I picked up the letter, folded the sheets together, then slipped them into my jacket pocket. "You're wrong, gentlemen. I was merely thinking how horrified my poor aunt would be to know her private correspondence had been revealed to strangers." Perching on the edge of the desk, I rested my ankle against one knee and cupped my hand around my other knee. "Now, will you tell me the reason for this unexpected visit or do I have to guess? Let's see. Have you a message from the dear inspector you conveniently forgot to deliver in the duke's presence? Another accusation too ridiculous to reveal in public?" I grimaced. Sarcasm wasn't really poise.

The assistant inspector stood, his bulk crowding the space around me. "You were seen with the enchanters again—three of them. You know our bargain." His hungry grin showed wide, yellowed teeth.

"I never bargained anything. I only know your inspector's impudent orders. What's a walk through the woods with an old man and my host's charming daughters to you? I could hardly rob all three at once, could I?" I smiled wryly. "Since they're enchanters, it'd be foolish to even consider it. Besides, I couldn't stop speaking to them without some explanation."

Polad huffed. I wondered how many times that crooked nose of his had been broken.

"Do you expect us to believe that? You and the blonde looked friendly enough when she was riding beside you. Nor did she seem inclined to leave you when you helped her from her horse." He added a lewd guffaw I suspected was designed to make me angry. The suspicion didn't stop the trick from working.

My hands fisted, and I barely kept myself seated. "Lady Gabriella was merely being polite to her father's guest." She didn't care for me and would never behave in the manner his tone implied. *An Ellsworth handles every situation with confidence and poise.* Heat rose up my neck and face. Did they really?

Only if they started now.

With a quick prayer for the strength to act as I knew I should, I unclenched my fingers and drew in a slow breath. Polite, not sarcastic. "It's true I arranged to meet with the Duke of Lofton to explain why I could no longer spend my breaks with him or meet him for billiards in the evenings, as I have often done. He deserved an explanation."

The Ceurians glanced at one another but belief didn't show in their faces. "The women?" Chead asked.

"Running into Lady Gabriella and her sister was accidental. I'd arranged to meet with the duke in the forest hoping to avoid being seen, but we came across the ladies dealing with a wolf." My thoughts went back to Gabriella's dismissal at the stable. *Go then if you must.* If I dared hope, I would say her words bore the mark of a woman cross for being abandoned. But hope was a fool's game at Henly. That was something I needed to remind myself of.

"You can be assured," I said softly, more to confirm my own purposes than to enlighten them, "that I have no intention of starting a relationship which must end when I leave with you for Ceur at the end of the month."

The assistant inspector's brow furrowed, but he nodded, his hawkish grin reappearing. For a moment, I wondered if it was his show of bravado, his way of dealing with things he didn't like, as sarcasm was mine. The darkness of soul behind Polad's eyes gave me no such illusion about him. Whatever might be their feelings, I was still their prey.

The assistant inspector moved toward the door. "So glad we've made ourselves clear. Do let us know if you hear from Emil Farro."

The door shut behind them with a pleased thunk. In a few days, it would close behind me. Despite all my troubles here at Henly, I wasn't ready to leave, especially not for the bleak future a visit to the Ceurian inspector promised.

Henry found me some time later slouched at the desk, staring at the strewn papers in a state of melancholy. He promptly started sorting the papers, a silent scolding for my wayward mind. Pulling myself together, I replied to his comments about boorish inspectors, but with less enthusiasm than usual.

Henry stopped his work and looked me in the eye. "What did they say?"

I pulled Aunt's letter from my pocket. "The usual. It's just that the time is growing shorter."

"You don't have to go with them. You can hide and petition the king, hope the Thief is caught."

"I can't risk it. Neither can the king risk an incident with Ceur right now. I must go and hope for justice."

Henry scoffed, but I shrugged and unfolded Aunt's letter, more than willing to have something else to think about. However, a thick missive plopped down in front of me, one also postmarked Silvestris. Picking it up, I turned an inquisitive eye to Henry.

"From Prince Giles." He smiled smugly. "I swiped it from the desk before they noticed."

"Henry, you're a wonder. Go buy yourself a book at the village bookstore."

"I already have one in mind." He handed me the letter opener, then left.

I skimmed Giles's letter, then reread it slowly. After contacting several of the Thief's victims, Giles discovered something peculiar. Some of the stolen items had found their way back to their owners, unharmed, sometimes in better shape than before. With each item was a note scolding the enchanter for his carelessness and encouraging him toward diligence in protecting his treasures. There was also a request that the return not be reported.

In addition, Giles discovered that certain people in Ceur were upset about the sudden disappearance of items they'd purchased. What the items were and where they'd purchased them, they wouldn't say.

Had the Magic Thief been double-crossing the sorcerers? I reread Giles's closing comments: "Some of the sorcerers are displeased with their Magic Thief. He's in trouble. They'll want to keep an eye on him. Yet I suspect at least one powerful sorcerer supports him still for some special purpose, but that's merely my instinct. I have no evidence."

That would bring the sorcerers to Henly. Heaven help Lofton help the Floraisons. I could not.

Chapter 13

*ACKMAN ESCAPES TORMIR PRISON. For once, the head-
line reads not as a cry for attention but as a whisper of
horror. ACKMAN ESCAPES the towering letters say, and
they tremble. O that we had listened to Sonser's king! The
Council of Enchanters and that of the Half-Magics, we
should have listened. The young king of Tormir was too
naïve to understand sorcerers, but the enchanters and half-
magics? We should have hanged all prisoners of that bru-
tal battle to destroy the reactivated sorcerer's lair plaguing
Tormir those fifteen years ago. But we were weary of
bloodshed and longing for mercy, for twenty enchanters
and half-magics, good men all, died that day. We locked
away the surviving sorcerers and placed magical protections on the prison. What fools we were. Where was our
mercy to the other prisoners? Where was our mercy to the
poor Sorcerer's Called who became a prison guard and
servant of the sorcerers there? Where is the mercy to those
Ackman left his prison to find?*

The Duke of Lofton, a letter to a colleague

GABRIELLA FLORAISON

THE DAY WAS cold with a barren sky. The light
crawling through the library window fell short of
the drawer I was tremulously unlocking.

"Your trepidation does you credit." The Duke of
Lofton smiled down at me as I knelt by the section of
drawers and slowly inserted my key into the lock of the

bottom drawer. "I wish more respected the enchanted objects."

"My wand is lost. I must know where it is and if a half-magic has it."

"You are courageous to search for the truth, but I fear your courage will get you little reward."

"My wand would be reward enough." The key clicked into place, and the drawer glided forward. I removed the key, letting it slip into my lap along with the other keys attached to my chatelaine. The keys reminded me of the matching ones my parents and siblings carried. "Why do you insist my family not be told?" I asked softly. With my curse and now this hunt for a half-magic thief, I was weary of secrets and missing my family's support and usual unreserve.

"They'd not be easy to convince, and their efforts to help would interfere with my schemes."

I almost smiled at his confidence in his plans, even though pained by the truth of his statements. My family had many virtues, but openness to ideas that diminished the family glory was not one. "The Thief would have to be a half-magic, not an ordinary thief we could set a watch for at the library door and under the outside window."

"Where would be the challenge in that?" the duke replied mildly. "It won't be long, child. When your family *checks* the locks every six months, you're actually pulsing them with magic, resetting them. They're weakest right before you do that."

"And the time to check them always falls on Papa's birthday—the end of the mentoring season," I mused.

"The Magic Thief would sense the locks losing power and know that. But it also means we know when he must strike. All will be well come the dawn of your father's birthday. You'll see."

Would it? With a sigh, I regarded the open drawer. A silver mirror with roses that twined up its handle and cascaded down its back rested quietly in its velvet-lined home of deep purple.

"Shall I?" the duke asked when I didn't pick up the mirror.

"No." I scooped it up. This mirror was Papa's pride and joy. "If Papa decides to show you our collection of mirrors—"

"I'll feign awe." The duke's tone suggested amusement.

"I forget you're Head of Enchanters in Gersemere. What marvelous things you've seen I can't begin to fathom." Gently, I trailed my fingers over the roses backing the mirror. "Living here in the country, far from any who might compete with us, has inflated our opinion of ourselves, I fear."

"To think so is a sign of growth. Nevertheless, it would be quite a journey to find any to compare with you, and a Demandez à Voir mirror would command respect even in Gersemere. I say so with partiality: my wife is Keeper of a set."

"Is she?" The connection kindled a new respect and affection for the Loftons.

"Yes." His smile faded, leaving a somber expression. It was time.

I raised the mirror. It sparkled at the edges of its blank, silver face; it was awake. "Mirror, mirror, in my hand, I ask to see the enchantress's glory, the wand of Gabriella Floraison." I often wondered if the mirrors required such flowery speeches or if we made them to remind ourselves not to take their power lightly.

The sparkle raced like a sunlit river across the mirror's face, and the silver burned with iridescent color in the center, but it immediately faded back to flat silver. The sparkle shot around the edges again and bolted across the surface, bouncing back and forth as if trying to escape the mirror's lip.

I squinted against the blinding flashes. "Mirror, show me my wand—the wand of Gabriella Floraison." White spots flared in my vision, and I covered the mirror with my hand. Why wasn't it responding as asked?

"Enough, mirror." It went blank at the duke's command.

"I'm sorry. It's been troublesome since its mate disappeared seventy years ago, but it's always answered my father."

"It's not the mirror." There was something odd and unsettling in his tone.

"It's answered me before. Papa trained it to respond to each of us." I frowned. "He was with us, however." Papa said it was a cantankerous mirror.

"It's not you either, though I almost wish it were. Ask it to show you the tresor box."

I held up the mirror again, doubtful it would do more than flash and fade as before. "Show me the tresor box of Frederick Floraison, future Duke of Henly."

The sparkle split the mirror's face in two, clearing away the silver to reveal a long, low wooden chest crouched against a curving rock wall. Dim light reflected off the wall's crevices. "Enough, mirror." I shoved it back in its place, my heart sick within me.

"What is it? You're paler than the statue your brother stuck you to."

I blushed at his concern and at the excuse that escaped before I recognized the lie in the familiar self-deception. "It's in one of the caves where we store wine. I'm not fond of it, that's all. Fred and I were caught in an earthquake there when I was young."

"In the cave where the unstable Place Changer deposited Ellsworth?" the duke prodded, sparing me from correcting the falsehood.

"Yes, the Dreydon Caves."

He added quietly, "Where he met Tyndale."

"The Changer"—I swallowed a choking lump of fear—"deposited Lord Ellsworth in one of the tunnels. I imagine the tresor box is in the main chamber, but it's of little consequence. I can send one of the servants after it."

He nodded, considering. "It makes sense the Changer would link there. Your brother must've had a third Changer in the cave and used it and one of the others to transport the box. The unstable Changer by the river remembered it vaguely."

I slid the drawer into the darkness of its home, feeling as if I were burying my hopes with it. I still didn't know where my wand was, and without a wand, I couldn't practice magic beyond potion making and taboo power bursts. Without a wand, I was as defenseless as I was bereft of dignity in the eyes of enchanters.

The duke offered me his hand and helped me up. "Would you show me the cave?"

"No." The answer came out quick and sharp. I clutched my hand to my chest, conscious of how strange and vulnerable the action made me appear, but I was unable to coax my hand down to my side. "My wand's not there." I forced myself to speak calmly. "The Thief took it. It would be a needless trip for you."

He eyed me narrowly. "'Needless' is for me to say, unless you have some reason for not going to the caves?"

He knew what he was asking, but he was going to force me to admit it. My pride revolted against one more admission of my flaws, but what did it matter? If he suspected but hadn't changed in his treatment of me, why would he change now? And he might be able to give wisdom or protection.

I took a deep breath and let it out slowly, suddenly wondering if this shame-laced embarrassment also burdened Marcel when he stuttered in front of my aunt or sisters. How had he not soured under it?

"Sleeping Beauty," I said, forcing myself to look the duke in the eye, "pricked her finger on a spinning wheel and fell into a one-hundred-year sleep while all about her grew old and died natural deaths." I held up my hand, fingers spread so he could see the scars. "I pricked my finger on a sorcerer's altar, and if I do it again, I'll fall into a living nightmare and could be forced to kill all those I know and love."

With compassion in his eyes, the duke took my hand in his. "You won't, my dear. You won't."

Despite his comfort, or perhaps because of it, I laughed bitterly and sank into the nearest chair. I buried my face in my hands but then straightened. I could at least sit with dignity. "It's ironic, isn't it?" Another bitter laugh escaped. "Aunt Helene and my sisters so enjoy criticizing the plain, bumbling Baron of Carrington, yet I am so much worse—a Sorcerer's Called. Such a blow to the Floraison pride! Not something to be acknowledged: No. Let her believe her experience was a wicked dream so the family could forget the shame themselves."

"No parents want to admit, least of all to themselves, that their beloved daughter might become the slave of sorcerers."

"Why did they leave me to think it'd been a nightmare? Did they not consider what danger it might lead to? Or the reprehensible self-deception I've lived in?" My voice cracked with buried hurt.

"Who can say? A nightmare might be easier for a child to recover from than the fear of sorcerers. They did everything they could to prevent the possibility of you returning to the cave."

I looked up, doubtful. I couldn't question my parents' love, but their wisdom in this area was hurtfully lacking.

"Your father made a report of the incident. I found it in my research before coming here. He did everything he could to protect you, Gabriella, as you must know. He gave you a Pyren stallion, which is not an easy acquisition. The earthquake destroyed the main path to the lair and, he'd hoped, the lair itself, maybe even the altar. He suspected a second entrance to the cave from the river cliffs, but no one could find it. He arranged for that area to suffer landslides to make the path inaccessible and to, perhaps, even destroy the outlet."

He held out his hand. "Now that I know, officially, that you're a Sorcerer's Called—and think no less of you for it—will you show me the cave? Between the pit, Sterling, and myself, you will be safe. When this business with the Thief is over, we'll find and destroy the lair. The Thief may even lead us to it."

Frowning, I considered his offer. He wouldn't suggest the trip if he believed we'd see danger there now, or if it weren't worth the danger. "I will take you. Forgive me for my self-pity."

He took my hand and gave it a comforting squeeze. "Don't judge yourself solely by your faults, my dear. Fight them when they call, but remember they are not what define you. Nor what defines anyone else, for that matter. You are flawed, and yet you are loved, and that is the great contradiction."

"Why," I began, dragging the duke's attention away from the snowcapped mountains beyond the fields bordering the road to the cave, "wouldn't the mirror show my wand when it would show the box?" Horror dragged my breath out of me in a sharp gasp. "Was the wand destroyed? The mirror showed nothing because there was nothing to show?"

He shook his head but then stared at the mountains for a moment longer as if choosing what to say. "The mirror was prevented from showing your wand."

"Prevented? One of the most powerful enchanted objects from the Caffin Wars *prevented*? How so?"

"There's no seeing spell more powerful than that captured in the very makeup of the Demandez à Voir mirror, Lady Gabriella, but it is still an enchanted object and thus capable of being manipulated, of being deceived in what it sees or blocked from revealing what it sees."

"You knew this when I called on the mirror, didn't you?" He hadn't been surprised when the mirror was burning itself up trying to show the wand.

A look of chagrin passed over his face. "I have one of my wife's mirrors with me. I asked about your wand immediately after I learned of its disappearance, but I wanted to make sure. There have been many magic thieves, Lady Gabriella, but over the last few years, one has set himself apart by his choice of items and by the fact the items, and he himself, could not be traced with the mirror."

"Is there any way to undo this spell? Put the mirror under one more powerful than that on the stolen objects?"

"I'm afraid not. At least, one of the most gifted Spell Writers since the Caffin Wars hasn't been able to create one." There was an odd mix of pride and sadness in his expression. "The spell that can block an enchanted mirror is a powerful one, so much so it's only stable in potion form, and as such it doesn't wear off for some time."

My puzzlement must have shown, for he quickly explained, "My wife invented it along with one of my nephews. Over twenty years it's been since they mastered it and put it away as a challenge overcome, an amusement, nothing they thought would ever see the light of day in another's hands."

"Your wife and nephew weren't alone in experimenting then."

That sad smile appeared again as his eyes took on a faraway look. "Perhaps."

We rode the rest of the way to the Dreydon Caves in thoughtful silence. When we arrived, the lock on the cave's portcullis-style gate was hanging open, but only so slightly that I didn't realize it until it fell open as I inserted the key.

The duke cursed and dragged me back to the tree where the horses were tethered. "Does your family normally leave this unlocked? Anyone could be in there."

"No," I said, shaken. "But the bandits who tried to abduct Lord Ellsworth supposedly broke into one of the caves and stole a cask of wine. This could be their work. That would explain why it was open the day I found Lord Ellsworth here and how Lord Tyndale and his son entered."

"Tyndale and the boy," he mused, rolling his wrist. "Bring Sterling. We'll leave the gate open, and if someone other than they are in there, or if you feel the least bit *in need of air*, ride Sterling out in all haste."

"What about you?"

His blue eyes flashed. "I can take care of myself."

With surprisingly steady movements, I untied Sterling and followed the duke into the main chamber. With a flick of his wrist, his wand was in his hand, and he led our way with a pale blue light.

As soon as the dark ceiling of the cave covered our heads, the years of fooling myself into believing it was the earthquake that scarred me took their effect. I felt my way forward with my feet. *Was it steady? Was it solid? Would the floor give way beneath us?* The frantic questions deafened me even as the true, worse ones followed. *Had the hag escaped over the pit? Was my scar burning?* Sterling nudged me comfortingly, and I adjusted my skirt, covertly wiping my sweaty palms.

The main cavern was large, roughly circular, and had three passages branching off from it. Two passages held more wine and one the bones of Nympha's grandmother. The duke led us cautiously around rows of stacked wine casks to the chamber's rear wall. My eyes at once caught the old wooden chest we called the tresor box resting at the foot of the wall not far from the hated passage.

"There it is," I said, pointing a shaky finger at it.

"*What* did the young marquis take from your sisters?" the duke asked, his gaze arrested by the two unmarked barrels flanking the box. Standing on end, they were each about six feet high.

"Nothing so large as that." Ignoring the gaping mouth of the tunnel not ten feet from the tresor chest, I knelt before the chest in the comforting aura of the wand's light. I chose the only key from my collection that folded over into itself, unfolded it, and quickly unlocked the chest, sad in a childlike way that I was finding it like this instead of in the triumph of a game well played.

I shifted Alexandria's lute and Eva's collection of rare shells before uncovering my book on birds. Nothing else save cloth and cotton batting for padding filled the box. No wand. Fred hadn't even had the decency to put my other purloined manuscript there.

I gently lifted my book. At a foot in height and two inches thick, it was a hefty piece by itself. Nonetheless, a weight fluttered away from me as I flipped through its undamaged pages. I'd never have time to finish all the sketches and have it properly bound before the celebration, but a few weeks' delay wasn't a disaster. Having something so mundane and easily accomplished to work toward somehow shifted the loss of my wand and everything else plaguing me from the realm of *completely hopeless* to only *mostly hopeless*.

"You're certain these barrels aren't part of your brother's game?" the duke asked.

"Everything I know he took is in the tresor box. Unless his last clue pertains to the barrels, I don't know what interest he'd have in them."

Hugging the book to my chest, I locked the box. "Alexandria and Eva can finish the riddle on their own. My wand isn't here. Let's go."

The duke circled the massive barrels, testing the metal bands, tapping the staves. They had no bunghole and bore no family crest.

"Your Grace?"

Sterling snorted behind me, but not the snort of a Pyren to his Called. I was safe.

"Indulge me a moment more, my dear." Kneeling, he touched the rope encircling one of the casks. The rope, darkened in such a manner that one almost didn't notice it against the cave floor, snaked to the wall and along the tunnel leading to the pit. "Do you have any idea where this rope might be leading and for what purpose?" He gave it a tug.

"Not unless it belongs to the boy Lord Ellsworth mentioned." I traced the rope with my eyes to the wall, around the corner, and up the tunnel. The duke did the same, and I knew what he was about to say. *Remember you're a Floraison. Don't make the duke drag you where a little boy bravely walks. You have Sterling.* "Shall we go meet this young adventurer?" If my voice shook, the duke didn't comment on it.

"You read my thoughts, Lady Gabriella." He rose and offered me his arm. I took it with more gratitude than I cared to admit. Sterling's hooves clapped against the rock, echoing up the tunnel, as he followed obediently behind us.

"How far to this pit?" the duke questioned.

"Why do you ask?" Why couldn't the boy be along the tunnel somewhere?

There was laughter in his voice when he replied, "Where else would a boy go but to a pit?"

My stomach knotted. "Where else?"

My finger was raw from me rubbing it to convince myself it wasn't burning by the time we came to another cavern. It was slightly wider than the tunnel and about forty feet long. Most of the forty feet had dropped into the deadly chasm ahead of us. A ray of light rose from the hole to lose itself in the darkness before reaching the cavern's roof. Time had eaten away at the pit until its jagged teeth had fallen in, leaving a relatively even brink, like a toothless gum. I supposed that meant the unsupported shelf had caved in, that it was safe for the boy to climb down, for our rope guide dipped out of sight at the brink.

The duke released my arm and knelt at the edge. "Hello there."

"Hello," a boy answered.

"What are you doing down there?"

"Exploring, of course, and burying this poor wolf."

"Hound." I surprised myself by correcting him.

"What?" the boy called from below. The rope shifted and went taut.

The duke looked over his shoulder at me.

"Wolfhound. Not wolf." An odd sense of relief filled me, like an old guilt had been forgiven. Roma was getting her burial at last. I scooted to the edge, and with one hand on the duke's shoulder and the other clutching my book to my chest, I peered over. The wand lit the chasm, clashing with the boy's lantern light. On its floor, resting against the base of the solid bank below me, was a pile of stones, a burial mound for a prize dog who'd unwittingly given her life for two children.

The crag Fred had clung to, with me weighing him down until the workers found us and we all fled, was still there. A convenient foothold for the boy, no doubt. I backed away.

The boy's tawny head soon appeared. "Give me a hand, won't you?"

The duke gripped his forearm and heaved him over the side. The boy pulled his knees underneath him and pushed himself up. He did a double take on us, a triple on Sterling.

"Hello." He drew out the word to indicate surprise. "I thought it was the other gent." He ran a hand through his neatly trimmed hair before replacing his cap. "I wasn't expecting a lady. Or a horse. I'd wondered what that racket was echoing up the tunnel. How do you do, miss?" He straightened his jacket and bowed with the air of a little gentleman.

Sterling snorted and shook his mane. Biting back a smile, I curtsied. "I'm doing well, good sir. And you?"

"Topping." He grinned as he unlatched his lantern from his belt and held it up to look at us. The duke's wand had dimmed, and he'd stepped back into the shadows, seeming to say the little gentleman was mine.

"You and your father helped Lord Ellsworth over the pit, didn't you?" I asked.

"Yes." He waved his arm toward the sickeningly thin shelf opposite us. "He'd stumbled into the cave without so much as a lantern or a rope. I'd never do that." He gave the duke a confident, man-to-man look that would rival one of the duke's own. The older man nodded to him, and the boy turned his attention back to me.

"I'm glad you were prepared and thus able to help him," I continued. "He said your name, but I've forgotten. It was something like a bird's, I believe."

"It's Ryn, my lady, but it's spelled R-Y-N, not W-R-E-N. I'm honored you'd remember he even spoke of me." A charming twinkle lit his eye.

From the shadows, the duke cleared his throat. "It wouldn't be short for *Devryn*, would it?"

"That's right." Ryn's face brightened. "No one else has ever known that. They all think I'm named after the bird. If you'll excuse me a moment, I must collect my things, then we can be on our way." He retrieved a bag of supplies from against the wall, then leaned over the ledge, no doubt to have a look at his handiwork as a grave builder.

"Is your mother fond of birds, Ryn? Was the similarity in sound purposeful?" I took a step away from the ledge, which encouraged Ryn to do the same.

"I expect she was. She died before I was born."

"I'm sor—you mean she died *when* you were born?"

"No, before."

"But that's—"

"Oh, I don't count my birth mother. I don't remember her, but Papa's told me all about my mo—that is, his late wife." He scuffed a toe against the smooth rock. "I sort of know her, so I count her."

"You're adopted then?" Stepping forward, the duke raised his wand, returning it to its blue glow, and illuminated the boy's face. Ryn watched the wand but a moment before accepting it as perfectly normal.

"Yep. He picked me up off the streets of Gilden years ago." Ryn's chest puffed up as if he were proud of having been chosen. "Shall we go?"

I snapped my mouth shut, then nodded. Off the streets? This little gentleman was a former street urchin? And probably a pickpocket at that, as many urchins were.

The duke huffed as if having expected that. "I'm surprised there aren't more of you." He offered me his arm, and we walked after Ryn, who was busy coiling the rope guiding us back to the main cavern.

"There are." Ryn slowed until we were even with him, Sterling behind us. "The other four are too young to take care of themselves while Papa's busy, except Bessie—she's ten. Papa says old Mrs. Morcos, our housekeeper, never'd survive our absence without Bessie, so she stays at the cottage and helps with the young ones when Papa and I travel."

The duke faltered, his expression unaccountably sad. "What of your grandparents? Those you *know* through your father. Or does he not speak of them?"

"Oh, they were wonderful." The natural ease of Ryn's voice dissolved.

"Were?"

His gaze lingered somewhere over the duke's shoulder. "Near as I can figure." He turned to me. "You're Lady Gabriella, aren't you?"

"Yes. You're very clever."

"My father, Lord Tyndale, told me who you were when we saw you here looking for Lord Ellsworth." He regarded the duke a moment. "You're the Duke of Lofton, aren't you?"

"Right again, but I didn't come to the cave that day. How do you know me?"

"My father described all the guests. I run around the gardens sometimes and watch them and try to figure out who's who."

"Why have I never seen you?" I asked in surprise.

"I try not to disturb anyone." There was a self-consciousness to his expression that confirmed my earlier suspicion. He was quiet, fast, and clever, and had used those talents in his life on the street.

"Do you happen to know," the duke said as the tunnel opened into the main cavern, "anything about those casks you've secured your rope to?"

"They're heavy enough to support my weight." Ryn untied the rope from the base of the unmarked barrel and stuffed the coil into his pack. "I have to go now. Thanks for keeping me company in the tunnel. I'm happy to have met you at last." He tugged his pack higher on his shoulder, waved goodbye, and ran off between the casks as quickly and silently as a woodland sprite.

"Ryn," I cried after him, "don't ever cross that pit!"

"I won't. Don't worry!"

A screech tore through the house as I entered it. A maid waving her hands above her head sprinted down the main stairs.

"Belinda, whatever is the matter?" I shoved my book into the hands of the disheveled footman who'd opened the front door, and ran after my maid.

"They've been set free, my lady. They're *everywhere.*" Despite her haste, Belinda was pale as bleached linen when I caught up to her.

I grabbed her by the shoulders. "What's free?"

Chirp!

Belinda screamed again and ducked through a doorway, barely giving me time to follow. She slammed the door shut just as I caught sight of a rosy-colored finch diving for the nearest window, proclaiming his freedom in a warbling song.

"The birds," Belinda rasped and fell back against the door as if it held off ten legions of sorcerers. "They were put in cages in the conservatory while the aviary was being cleaned. Now, they're all loose."

"But they're—" *harmless songbirds.* Surely she wasn't ... I bit my lip to keep from laughing as she glanced wide-eyed around the room. She was. "How many are loose?"

"*All* of them. Has your family bewitched them and given them terrible powers, my lady?"

I choked back a laugh. "No, Belinda. They're quite harmless, ordinary birds."

She narrowed her eyes.

I smiled reassuringly and patted her arm. "We'd never endanger our servants. You go rest in the kitchen. I'll see what I can do about them." Motioning her aside, I peeked out the doorway. Pixter the Tiny Terror hopped along the windowsill opposite us.

Belinda squealed. "Be careful, my lady."

"I will. Don't worry."

I slipped out. Belinda pushed the door shut behind me, sending me stumbling into the hallway. Pixter cheeped and zoomed over my head. With no idea of how to catch him without my wand, I chased him through the house and nearly collided with Eva and Alexandria.

"Oh, Gabriella," Eva said between giggles. Beside her, Alexandria smirked, her eyes twinkling. Two footmen followed them, one with a long-handled net and the other with two birdcages, one of which held several oddly stiff and silent residents.

"I haven't had this much fun in ages," Eva continued. "The ridiculous maids are terrified of a bunch of song masters. We've had to chase the birds down ourselves."

"The cages were all unlocked sometime this afternoon, and the house has been in chaos ever since," Alexandria said.

"By whom?"

"Some fool guest probably. Papa changed the schedule to keep them out of the house until we catch the birds and the servants clean up any droppings." She darted around me, her wand in her hand. "*Defixus.*"

Twelve feet up, Pixter came to an abrupt halt. Grinning, Alexandria twirled her wand. "It's a lasting spell now thanks to the Duke of Lofton's training."

A silent footman swung his net and gathered Pixter to him.

"Put him in the empty cage," Alexandria ordered. "That's twelve of twenty. Do you want to join us, Gabriella?" Her smile fell, as did mine. "You can use my wand. I'm two up on Eva."

"Only one," Eva retorted.

"Two, counting Pixter." Alexandria held her wand out to me.

I waved it aside. "You two go ahead. I must check on something. I'll join you later." A strange foreboding twisted my insides as I ran to the library, hesitating at the door. No sound filtered through the dense wood. Taking a deep breath, I unlocked the door and stepped inside.

The fire burned low, and the slight wear on the seat cushions was plainly visible. No form or shadow obscured the drawers, armor, or bookshelves. Nevertheless, I couldn't shake a feeling of unease. For the second time that day, I unlocked and opened the drawer holding the Demandez à Voir mirror. It lay undisturbed. I quickly shut the drawer and locked it.

A rustling jerked my attention to the window as the curtain shifted. Heart thumping, I slowly pushed to my feet. A bird hopped from behind the curtain and chirped. Laughing in relief, I watched the little fellow as he hopped and sang his way over the windowsill. This was one bird I didn't need a wand for. Whistling, I held out my hand. Harrison trilled in response and alighted on my finger, his tiny claws tickling.

"I wish you could tell us what happened," I crooned as I stroked his chest. He twittered and fluffed his feathers. Laughing, I rubbed his head. When he tired of the attention and hopped away down my finger, I took another look around. I couldn't find anything amiss, except ... was that a shimmer about five feet in the air above the sofa? Blinking, I looked again. The book titles on the shelves behind the sofa were plainly visible. I was only imagining things.

Harrison sang a jaunty tune, and I lifted my hand to better watch his chest rise with each note. When he finished, I said, "Come on. Let's get you home, little friend."

Harrison chirped as the library door shut softly behind me. I rocked back on my heels and stared at Harrison's tiny yellow head. The door had been shut when I arrived. How did he get inside?

Chapter 14

"It's not a place you can get to by a step, or a hop, or even a jump. You must take my hand," my cousin ordered.
"H-h-how do you get there th-th-then?" I asked as I took his hand.
"By magic." Familial pride shown in Emil's eyes. "My father and grandfather built it. When I'm grown, I'm going to keep all my most wonderful inventions there." He looked at me sternly, impressing me with the enormity of the secret he was about to share. "Now promise me not to tell anyone."

Marcel Ellsworth, a childhood memory

MARCEL ELLSWORTH

W HAT ARE YOU going to do about her?" Tyndale broke the silence that had pocketed us as we leaned against the mantle in the drawing room, a bastion of quiet amid the after-dinner chatter.

"Her?" I looked up reluctantly from the dance of flames.

"Lady Gabriella." Tyndale smiled as if I'd known exactly whom he meant. He was right.

"There's nothing to be done except hope her family doesn't get burgled, or worse."

"I'm sure they've taken precautions," Tyndale said.

"They don't believe in your type."

He chuckled. "So I've read."

I'd run into him after leaving Gabriella and Lofton in the stable a few days before, and with my mind full of the Magic Thief and half-magics, I'd bluntly asked him about the statue episode and whether or not he was a half-magic. He'd admitted it without a blink of the eye.

"I should have said, 'I know her family has taken precautions,'" he continued, "or the Duke of Lofton has taken precautions on their behalf. The library alone has several items a half-magic would notice, and many the Magic Thief would want, but they're all protected by powerful locking spells. Anyone who tried to get into the drawers or cabinets housing the items would get the equivalent of a nasty burn—at the least." He flexed his hand and frowned as if he were thinking aloud. "The locking spells could be whittled away over time, but the Duke of Lofton would've taken that into consideration."

"Is he so familiar with the ways of half-magics?"

Tyndale shifted his attention to a carving on the mantle, rubbing his thumb slowly over it. "I would say there is no enchanter as familiar, except his sister. She married one. And reared several. However," he added hastily, "the Duke of Lofton loves a game of cat and mouse. He will have considered every angle.

"What you need to do," he continued, "is find a way to spend more time with Lady Gabriella."

The man was a hopeless romantic and quite delusional. We had a lot in common.

"I don't think the lady would agree," I said. "Besides, her family would never approve of me. I'm not a show horse." Not to mention I could get locked away permanently—sooner—for interacting with her. The Ceurians would consider it disobedience and proof of my villainous intentions. Would I risk it if Gabriella wanted my help?

What was I thinking? I was the last person a Floraison would ask for help.

Tyndale chuckled as if something were funny, though I couldn't figure out what. "Their disapproval would be a nuisance to a happy marriage. A man doesn't just marry a woman, he marries her family as well. They're his for the next fifty years or so." Tyndale scrubbed a hand over his forehead. "Sometimes they're all you have and you wish you could be free of them, free of promises made," he mumbled.

Some of the crowd drifted toward the library, and I stepped away from the fireplace to join them. Tyndale followed, and from his melancholy expression, I judged that his mind was still on the subject of ladies, chiefly his own.

"Did your wife's family not approve of you?" I asked as we passed into the library. A cheery fire blazed in the hearth and numerous candles lit the room.

He startled as if having forgotten our conversation. Quickly recovering, he said, "Oh no. Nothing like that. She had but one brother, a likable scoundrel with a silver tongue. Society might have expected my family to disapprove of her. She was a commoner, but my family loved her. How could they not? She was as kind, clever, and honorable as she was beautiful. And she was a brilliant half-magic."

"How did you meet?" As we wandered the library, I tried to guess where the precious objects Tyndale had mentioned were. Alas, I had no sense or skill to discern them. I felt it impertinent of me to ask.

"She owned the hat shop my mother and sisters frequented. I went with my older sister to the shop one day and developed a sudden interest in hats. For the next seven weeks, I was busy convincing some female member of my family—sisters, mother, aunts, cousins—of their need for a hat and my readiness to escort them. By the eighth week, I couldn't convince anyone to go with me, so I went alone on the pretense of buying my mother a hat for her birthday."

Tyndale and I came to a stop in front of a suit of armor supported and hung as if it were worn by an invisible knight. Not for the first time in this grand and ancient house, I wished for plaques to explain the history of what I was seeing. And not seeing. Where was the knight's sword?

"By that time, she'd caught on," Tyndale continued with a wistful look. "She refused to serve me and lectured me on how a gentleman doesn't pursue the attention of a woman he could never intend to marry. I asked her why I could never intend to marry her. 'Because you're a lord and I'm a shopkeeper,' she said. I told her my family knew and respected her, that they wouldn't object, and that if she would agree to walk with me in the park on Sunday afternoon, I'd no longer call on her at her shop. She agreed, and we were married a year later."

"You're fortunate to have such a family." I gestured to the suspended suit of armor, barely resisting the urge to run my hand through the gap between the helmet and the breastplate to make sure no one was there. "How in the world do they keep it upright? I can't see any strings or hanging equipment."

"Magic." Tyndale's eyes twinkled when I shot him a look of skepticism.

"How would they keep the spell going for so long? Why waste magic to do that? I can understand it for a locking spell but not for a decorative spell."

He laughed and carefully worked his hand under the breastplate and tapped at a particular spot. "I meant the illusionary kind." He removed his hand, and I felt where he indicated and noted the supports.

"You know," he continued, "if you find a way to spend time with her, you'll have more opportunity to make certain the Magic Thief doesn't get near her."

"Is *Persistence* your middle name?"

"*Tenacious* actually. Tenacious Tyndale. You must concede I have a point."

Much as I wanted to frown at him, I couldn't, not when the thought of a genuine reason to seek Gabriella's company was threatening me with a hopeless happiness. "All right, I concede," I said, momentarily lost in a memory of Gabriella's smile as she'd looked down at me from Sterling. When I realized what I'd said, I wanted to kick myself.

"Wonderful. Let me know if I can be of assistance," Tyndale said.

"Get her a hat shop I can visit."

"Now, Ellsworth, don't be cynical."

I opened and then shut my mouth. It was time to change subjects. Any controversial titles on the shelves to debate? A quick glance around revealed more than one ancient or rare volume worth a small fortune. Alfred Floraison wasn't worried about one of them disappearing during his mentoring sessions?

"Tyndale"—I shook my friend's arm, distracting him from his scrutiny of the armor—"if most of the valuables are here in the library, all we need is someone to guard the room and keep an eye out for whoever comes to chip away at the locking spells." It was so simple. We could arrest the man before he had time to harm Gabriella or Lofton. Forget all this magic stuff. He was still a thief and could be caught with the usual methods. Releasing Tyndale, I scanned the room. Did the Duke of Henly have a guard here I hadn't noticed? Or was there a magical alarm of some sort?

Tyndale shook his head, his smile incredulous. Apparently, it wasn't so simple.

I rested one hand flat against the wide wooden beam next to the armor and leaned against it. "What's wrong with the idea?" I drummed my fingers against the beam. My ring slipped a hair, and I used my thumb to straighten it. If it turned without me directing it somewhere, there'd be no telling where I'd end up.

Tyndale perused the titles on the nearest shelf. "Do you really think the Duke of Henly would suffer a guard in or at the door of his favorite room? It would not only insult his guests' integrity, and therefore his wisdom in accepting them, but also any precautions he or his ancestors took to protect the items."

A groan escaped me. "You're right. How foolish of me not to have taken their pride into account."

The library door swished open. I turned to see who it was, and my ring twisted against the beam. The library, the firelight and candlelight, the beam supporting me, all vanished. My breath left in a whoosh as I stumbled into a bare room no bigger than a small chapel. I stopped my sideways tumble with a hand to the wall and waited for my vision to clear of its gray haze. It didn't. The walls, floor, and ceiling were all the same mild gray.

No candle or sunlit window provided light. The only luminescence seemed to filter through the walls, and the single deviation from the gray was the sword resting horizontally on a mount at head-height along the wall to my right. It was silver, like the armor I'd admired, with rubies in the hilt. It was beautiful and tempting, for all swords tempted me to try a few maneuvers, but not enough to stay in this gray purgatory. My hand twitched for a door handle to turn, but there were none. No windows either.

"Thunderation. But the ring got you here, the ring'll get you out." It'd better, or I'd melt it for scrap. I took hold of my ring. Now, I just needed to know where I was so I could tell it where to take me. Simple, I was ... in the beam in the library?

"From the beam in the duke's library to my former position beside the armor—no." If my disappearance hadn't started a commotion, my reappearance would. "From the beam in the duke's library to my chambers." I twisted the ring and prepared for the slight tug that always accompanied jumps. No tug came. "From the duke's library to my chambers." Nothing. "From Henly Manor to the garden, by the cedar."

On and on I went, naming any location I could think of from beam to sword room to dungeon, but I never moved. I began to feel my way around the room, testing for a hidden door. Was this some sort of challenge? Only those who escaped alive were worthy of consideration for the Floraison family? Perhaps the beam was one of the treasures and sucking people into a room with no way out was the protection. No, there was too much potential for accidents. There were no skeletons lying about, however, which was comforting.

Perhaps Gabriella would come looking for me again. Tyndale would doubtless have noticed my disappearance, and the schemer would like nothing better than to tell her. But I didn't want to be the enchantress's *bachelor in a bind* any more than she wanted to be the supposedly criminally inclined non-magic's *damsel in distress*. Well, this was one man who was not going to require rescuing. The only object in the room was the sword. Obviously, I'd have to fight my way out. Would I be required to hack through the walls? Or would a warrior, or the suit of armor, step through a magical door to challenge me? Time to find out.

I pocketed my ring and stepped up to the weapon. It was a knight's sword, keen of edge and bearing a few dents. I put one hand on the hilt. It was cool to the touch. Adding my other hand to the hilt, I lifted the blade and stepped away from the wall, quickly shifting into a fighting stance, reveling in the whoosh of displaced air. The stale place needed a bit of stirring up. No other sound disturbed the room. I waited. Still nothing. Maybe it wasn't a testing room, simply a storage room.

The tension in my shoulders eased, and I held the sword out and tested its balance. It was heavier and broader than the ones I fenced with. This was a weapon for battle, not for sport. And, oh, it felt good to swing it, even though I had to compensate for the difference in size and weight. I worked through several of the forms, surprised that I never ran out of space. It was as if the room expanded to accommodate my lunges and swings.

Breathing deeper and moving faster than I had since before my illness, I danced back and forth across the room until I was breathless. My chest heaved as I lowered the blade and leaned it against the wall. I removed my jacket and turned to hang it on the sword's mount, and found two golden eyes the size of my fists staring at me. Hunger was plainly visible in their depths. Of course, the lion was probably an illusion, but I wasn't taking that chance.

"If I promise to put the sword back, will you let me live?"

It bared its teeth in a snarl. With my free hand, I reached for the sword. As I grabbed it, the lion roared. I flung my jacket in its face, lunged to the left, and swung the sword to block the massive paw coming my way.

Sword and paw collided, but the paw faded. A cub growled playfully from the floor three feet away, my jacket beside it. Gaping at the cub, I failed to adjust my weight for the swing and stumbled after the sword. Lowering the blade, I threw myself into the wall, hitting it squarely with my shoulder. I jumped up and spun around to be blasted by the roar of an adult lion. I swung at its incoming paw. The beast shrank to a cub. I hopped over it and dashed to the center of the room.

There had to be a door, or a lever to release a hidden access, somewhere. I yanked on the sword's wall mount, jerking it this way and that, until a hot breath warned me to turn.

Ducking, I thrust at cub-height. A young lion leapt over me. I tucked, rolled, and bounded up. Again, it charged, and again I swung. It toyed with me, chasing me around the room and swatting at me as a cat plays with a chipmunk.

If I swung high, it was a cub. If I swung low, it was a leaping young lion. Why couldn't I age it forward to a pile of gnawed bones? Once more, I tucked and rolled as the young lion leapt. A tuft of golden fur wafted in the air beside me and settled onto the smooth, gray floor. Did that mean the lion was tiring? Did it lose fur the way I lost water, as through the sweat now flowing down my back and face?

The adult lion in all its maned glory reappeared and roared its strength, the force of it nearly knocking me over. Apparently, the lion never tired of its toy. I considered putting away my sword and declaring the lion an illusion, but then I smelled meat on its hot breath. The guardian of the sword was flesh and blood.

Where was Tyndale with that enchantress to save me? My pride, like my strength, was wearing thin. My limp was becoming more pronounced with each step.

"Is this how you protect your treasures," I cried to the blank, gray walls after yet another fruitless stroke. "With a crazy lion?" I thrust and then lunged toward the wall mount. "No one wants your worthless sword—it won't cut anything!"

A clang rang through the room as I rammed the sword on its mount, thinking to try my ring again, from the lion's den to my chambers. But as the clang echoed through the room, I truly noticed the mount for the first time. It was made of the same metal as the sword and inscribed with runes, ancient ones of magic. Did the blade not hit anything because the lion was untouchable, or because the blade was untouchable to all but the mount? If the lion changed with each stroke, vanishing before me, would the walls dissolve as well?

I grabbed the hilt and jumped for the wall, throwing my whole weight behind the blade. The wall didn't give way before me; it simply wasn't there. My momentum slowed. The wall faded, and I stumbled to a halt, blade down, back at my spot next to the armor in the library. Men chatted in groups or sat alone reading in the brightly lit room wonderfully colored by the rainbow of book-bindings.

Half laughing, half gasping for breath, I sank back against the beam. I'd made it out without a scratch. I was free. I was alive. I was in one piece.

I was jacketless and sweat-drenched in the duke's library holding a magical sword that was doubtless supposed to stay hidden. My joy dropped from full flame to simmer.

Tyndale stared at me from his earlier position by the bookcase, a book in his hand. "Where the devil did you g—you're missing your jacket."

"That's not nearly as scandalous as missing my head. Keep your voice down."

Shutting his book, he glanced around, but no one else seemed to have noticed my reappearance, thank heavens. "What did you do?" he whispered, stepping closer. "Get chased around the estate by the wolfhounds? And where did you get that sword? Out of a stone?"

"Something like that. Listen, I need you to fetch the Duke of Henly. I need a Floraison."

"Why? And in your state?"

"Never mind why, just bring one. Please. And a jacket."

He gave me a roguish grin. "The Lady Gabriella it is."

"I didn't ask for—"

But he'd left. Five minutes passed, during which the excitement of my lion taming experience left, leaving me with the full force of exhaustion and sore, trembling muscles and an aching leg. Then Tyndale reappeared, alone, a bulge under his arm, and casually walked to me.

He slipped me a folded jacket. "You're in luck."

"How so?" I shrugged on the jacket and ran my fingers through my hair.

"She'll walk inside in a minute with a book, and I'll ask her to explain the armor's history. How's that? I didn't want to make it obvious she was coming to see you and expose either of you to gossip."

"Perfect. I can't thank you enough, Tyndale," I said sarcastically as I buttoned the borrowed jacket.

"Don't mention it. It was a great deal easier than dragging you out of that pit. Here she is."

Gabriella, tome in hand, entered the library and was greeted by several of the gentlemen stationed near the door. I slipped my ring back on, feeling more at ease wearing it.

Tyndale glanced from her to me. "The jacket's not a perfect match, but you look less bedraggled than before." He patted me on the shoulder and approached Gabriella.

Without any appearance of pre-arranged design, the two of them soon made their way to the armor. Unfortunately, a woman of Gabriella's beauty attracted a great deal of attention.

Still concealing the sword, and using it as a cane, I stepped partially out from behind the armor in order to form a natural part of the group when Tyndale and Gabriella arrived.

Bowing carefully, I greeted Gabriella. "Thank you for coming," I added in a lowered voice.

"I was under the impression, Lord Ellsworth"—she eyed me with a mix of annoyance and curiosity as she indicated pieces of armor and pretended to direct her comments to Tyndale—"that you didn't wish to be involved in the affairs of the Floraisons."

"It's not a matter of *not* wanting to be involved," I said as I stepped forward, but Tyndale motioned for me to be still. He moved closer to the armor, angling himself so as to block a view of me and the sword.

Gabriella met my eye for the first time since arriving, and I instantly regretted my words. To be admired by someone as marred in the Floraison eyes as I was would only be repugnant to her. A plain, lowly baron soon to be on trial for complicity in a theft and murder, and with a troubled estate to boot. I looked away before I could read her response and lifted the sword to draw her attention to it. "But occurrences do seem to keep throwing your family's affairs my way. I believe this belongs with the armor."

Gabriella gasped. "Where did you get that?" Her gaze jumped to the wooden beam and back to the sword, then up to my face. "*How* did you get that?"

"I was hoping you could tell me. I was leaning against the beam when my ring twisted accidently. I found myself, quite to my dismay, in a gray room with this hanging on the wall."

"But that shouldn't have happened. The realm is locked." Alarm flashed in her eyes, then vanished as she fought for composure.

"The what?"

"The realm where the Sword of Ora is supposed to be safe."

I almost laughed. "A magical realm for sword storage? No wonder I couldn't get the ring to take me out. I thought I was in a secret room within the beam. I was about ready to melt the cantankerous ring down for scrap." Not that I ever would. It connected me to my mother's family, to their love and acceptance. I hated being without it and its reminder of them.

Gabriella's mouth snapped shut, and both she and Tyndale stared at me. The clock's chime reverberated through the room, reminding us of the lateness of the hour. The room's inhabitants filtered out, but we stayed, unmoving. Unease worked its way up my spine at Gabriella and Tyndale's shocked expression.

"How do you know so much about magic?" Gabriella asked warily. There was something new in her eyes. Unfortunately, it looked more like distrust than admiration for my knowledge.

"Sometimes it's who you know, not what you are," I answered flippantly, hoping to lighten the mood. Neither she nor Tyndale laughed. Tyndale studied my ring. Instinctively, I slipped my hand into my pocket.

"Your ring has the king's seal on it." There was as much wonder as accusation in his words. "It could have unlocked the realm."

Gabriella paled. "Where did you get that?" She asked it as if the ring were something new and terrible to her.

"I've had it all along. You know this."

"But where? How did you come by a king's ring? You're only the son of a baron."

My cheeks flushed. How did her family come by a sword that cuts between realms?, I wanted to demand.

"And a princess," I said through clenched teeth. "A baron and a princess. Lady Gabriella, if I'd wanted to steal the sword, I wouldn't have gone to the trouble of arranging this conference. I would simply have used"—I held up my ring hand—"one of my family's treasures and taken this monstrosity of a letter opener to a hiding place of my choosing."

Surprise flashed through Gabriella's eyes. "She was a princess?"

That's all she had to say? She'd switched from wanting evidence to convict me of being the Magic Thief to wanting to know my family history? My jaw tightened. The proud, petty Floraisons. It pained me more than I cared to admit that Gabriella was no different than the rest of her family. Theirs was the same sort of pride that had nearly destroyed my maternal grandfather before he relinquished it, and which had made Lady Ellsworth critical and unloving to the end.

"My mother," I said, "was the daughter of Prince Gérard Bête. It's a hereditary title now, but the founder of our family line was a favored nephew of a king, and the king who gave him his title and estate also gave him a pair of enchanted rings. My cousin Giles carries the title of prince, as well as the other ring, but I am still the grandson of Prince Gérard Bête of Silvestris Castle."

"Why didn't you say so? Why did you let Aunt Helene belittle you and assume your mother was a commoner, or a mistress, because you wouldn't speak of her?" Gabriella looked up into my face as she spoke, those mesmerizing blue eyes fastened on me, and I almost thought I saw hurt there, but that couldn't be.

"I refuse to use my heritage to buy respect. But now that you find me worthy of speaking to, might I remind you of the question necessitating your appearance here: how is the sword to be returned? I entered the gray realm by accident using my ring. I exited, after much peril involving a rather unusual lion, by running the sword through a wall. Surely, given that your family arranged the room and presumably the guard, you have a better way of returning the sword and getting out."

Gabriella had blushed as I began to speak, but as she reached for the sword—it came up to her waist—her gaze was as cool and hard as the double-edged blade. "I will return it."

I handed the weapon off to her with relish. "I apologize once again for inconveniencing you through my blunders. If you'll excuse me?" I bowed and left her.

Tyndale followed me out. Though I could feel Gabriella watching us, she kept her pretty little lips pressed together and never said a word.

Tyndale stopped my march up the stairs with a hand on my arm. "I spoke out of turn, Ellsworth. Forgive me. One doesn't often see items with the king's seal outside the palace, and certainly not powerful ones worn like common jewelry."

Instinctively, I touched my ring. I knew wearing it was risky, but I didn't want to part with it. "I have nothing to hide. You only spoke an observation." I turned and continued up, clutching the banister as a limp threw me off balance.

"You would've told her soon, I hope." Tyndale followed a step or two behind.

"She knows I have a traveling ring."

"About your mother."

"If it came up in conversation, but I refuse to puff up like a peacock for everyone, especially women like her Aunt Helene." I hadn't meant for the last statement to slip out, revealing a bitterness in my heart I'd never uprooted.

"Why do you dislike her so?"

"She reminds me of my paternal grandmother, Lady Ellsworth." I bit my cheek. Anger and tiredness made a fool's tongue wag.

Tyndale snagged my sleeve. "That's hardly a reason."

I fought down the bitter memories of my father's family's scorn, birthed of my weaknesses and their jealousy of my mother's rank. Keeping my voice even, barely, I continued, "I was a broken wreck, body and soul, when I left Lady Ellsworth's for my maternal grandfather's home at Silvestris. I-I-I have fought for every s-scrap of s-s-self-respect, every s-sense of worth I have, just as I-I-I fought to walk and run. I-I-I will not let the Floraisons' conceited arrogance tear down what I've s-struggled for."

Tyndale released me, and I jabbed my finger at the marble stairs beneath our feet, hating my weak tongue. I would control it. "Since I came here," I said slowly, focusing on each syllable before I uttered it, "I've been snapped at, sneered at, scorned, treated like a mistrusted servant, and accused of being a thief and a fugitive. Gabriella can keep her Floraison pride. I desire neither her company nor her good opinion." Grabbing the banister, I stomped up the stairs as fast as my limp would allow.

"Ellsworth." The command in Tyndale's voice stopped my upward march. It was a different man I saw as I turned, one older, sterner, and not given to idle chatter. His gaze bored into me as if he could force me by sheer will to think and do as he wished.

I narrowed my eyes at him. I was not one to be controlled.

"I don't play cupid by nature," he said. "When I suggested you find a way to spend time with Lady Gabriella, it was for her protection. You, non-magic though you are, will act as her guardian."

"I will do nothing of the kind. Have one of the fools you've arranged to guard her sisters take the job."

His face darkened in an anger that quickly melted away, leaving a troubled expression. "Lady Gabriella's connected herself with the Duke of Lofton, and she has no wand, and she's ... she's vulnerable where her sisters are not."

I bounded down the stairs until I was only two above him. "How do you know about her wand?" Gritting my teeth against the pain in my weak leg, I gripped the banister for support, wanting to grab Tyndale by the shirt-front instead.

"I'm a half-magic." He held my glare until I was certain I detected no threat in him. There was something in his eyes I couldn't make out. Guilt maybe, or concern, but not malice.

"I'm sorry, but I cannot help you. I will not play the smitten fool, or the obsessive stalker, for her or anyone else. You're a half-magic. You look after her." I spun around and hobbled up the stairs.

"There's a magic thief here," Tyndale called out behind me in a voice that tried, and failed, to command me to stop and listen, "as well as others of a more violent and unforgiving nature."

"You know so much, Tyndale. What are you going to do about it?"

When he didn't answer, I stopped and twisted to look at him. He stared at me, his jaw working.

"Well?" I asked.

"What I can, which is what I'm asking of you."

His sudden avoidance of my gaze worried me, but I shook off the feeling. Jonathan Lofton and Alfred Florai-son were enchanters; they would see to the safety of the house and family. They had the power to do so. I did not.

"Bah." I waved my hand, as if freeing myself from Tyndale's spell. "You're a lonely man trying to create an unequal romance to remind yourself of your late wife." I was almost to the top of the stairs before Tyndale spoke again, his voice pitched low so as not to carry into the rooms nearby.

"There's a chip on your shoulder, Ellsworth, as big as the Floraison pride. Don't let it be Lady Gabriella's undoing as well as your own. None of the people here have the sense or the knowledge to fight the danger that's come, except you."

I flexed my fingers, felt the pulse thrumming through my injured wrist, and remembered every time I'd tripped over my feet or my words or ended up some place I didn't belong. "I've bungled everything I've touched since I've been here. I'd be of no help, not that they'd accept it."

It would also send me to prison and leave Carrington and its villages to rot.

Chapter 15

The power of enchantment always held an allure stronger than any other. As a half-magic, I could manipulate magic as I liked, but always the magic was limited to what I was given or dared collect. A magic thief would have no such restrictions of quantity. He would only be limited by his own talents and cunning in thievery. His abilities would be used in full, collecting magic from enchanters too careless to properly secure their treasures and spells.
Would not such challenges and daring ventures bring back the colors of life to one who has fallen into the shadows of despair?

Diary of a magic thief

GABRIELLA FLORAISON

THE NEXT DAY dawned fair. As Alexandria was very fond of walking, she and I, accompanied by a couple of the wolfhounds, took a pleasant stroll to the village to buy supplies for Fred's potion. The duke and I had decided it was best to pretend to keep playing Fred's game. Pretend everything was normal. I was to leave everything to him. I wasn't happy about that, but without a wand there was little I could do except keep my eyes open. He suspected the Thief wouldn't strike until the night before Papa's birthday, and he had a plan ready. That he was unhappy about this mysterious plan but determined to carry it through was evident.

Until then, however, I was to watch for any slipups on the Thief's part and keep away from the sorcerer's lair. In connection to the latter, I'd warned Harvey to let Sterling loose should he become agitated, and I made a promise to myself to run for the stable should I feel the least *in need of air*. In truth, there was always a slight desire *for air* now, and had been since the first of the recent Calls, like a minor annoyance growing worse with each attempt. I feared it would soon cease to be minor and become a constant arthritis of the soul, but I was determined not to dwell on it or let fear of the curse control me.

As Alexandria and I neared the village I was reminded that I was the only one in my family who enjoyed visiting there. Though plain of face and often drably dressed, the villagers always smiled kindly when they greeted us. In contrast, Alexandria's face was slightly pinched the entire time. Her expression only eased when we visited the bookshop and the stationer.

We soon left the apothecary with a bag of herbs and various pieces of glassware and headed home along the public footpath. At the edge of the village was a meadow where children, and even adults, gathered to play on fine days. The cheerful sound of such merrymakers greeted us as we approached it. Games of battledore and shuttlecock, bowling, and tag dominated the area. I watched with a smile as a little girl with bright blue ribbons tying back brown braids chased after first one child, then another, zigzagging between the older children and adults playing their less exuberant games.

A head of light red hair among the players caught my eye. Marcel, Tyndale, and Ryn batted a shuttlecock between them, deliberately making it difficult for the next to reach, laughing and taunting one another all the while.

Without meaning to, I slowed to a stop to watch the game. Around and around the shuttlecock went, almost flying out of reach or dipping to the ground before one of them reached it. I'd seen Marcel stumble, though not always fall, several times, including once when he fell up the stairs (I may have been the unintentional cause of that by distracting him). But now he darted to and fro, leapt, and lunged with quick, sure movements.

The path of the shuttlecock took him out of the ring of play. Marcel jumped up and back, batted the shuttlecock, and landed on Ryn's discarded jacket. It slid beneath him, and he fell onto the grass, but the shuttlecock flew to his friends, and it was Ryn who missed it.

"I was waiting for that to happen," Alexandria said smugly, looking at Marcel on the ground.

I startled at her voice, and then again at the way her tone rankled. I pushed the feeling aside, remembering instead Marcel's expression when he said it wasn't a matter of *not* wanting involvement with us. Why avoid or ignore us then? Run when Alexandria scowls? Get angry when I question him? Finicky man. His mother must have been the princess kept awake by the pea under her mattress.

"Gabriella, whatever are you doing?" Alexandria asked in irritated dismay.

"I'll be back in a minute." Leaving the dirt path and Alexandria behind, I marched through the meadow's thick grass.

"Lady Gabriella, have you come to play?" Ryn ran to me. After greeting him with a hug, I walked with him back to his father and Marcel.

Tyndale, after laughing at Marcel as he pulled him up, received me with pleasure in his voice, though without the slightest surprise. He was a half-magic—how strange an admission for me!—and must suspect I knew it. I could never sneak up on him. His feigned shock at the statue had been convincing.

One of the wolfhounds, Freya, greeted Tyndale and Ryn with a wagging tail.

Frowning, Marcel dusted himself off. "Lady Gabriella." There was a strained look about his eyes to go with their shuttered coldness. Had I offended him by my honest questions about his mother and the ring, or was something else amiss?

"Good afternoon, gentlemen. I hope you're enjoying the unusually warm weather."

"Very much." Tyndale wrapped an arm around Ryn's shoulders as the boy moved to stand beside him. "Though I enjoy your father's lectures, I never regret the breaks he gives on such lovely days."

Tyndale gave Marcel a significant look, which, from Marcel's expression, he seemed determined to ignore. Marcel glanced at the packages cradled between my arm and hip.

"Are you in need of anything? A servant to carry your parcels?" he asked.

My fingers twitched. If ever there was a man who tempted me to turn him into a frog, it was Marcel Ellsworth. Not even Fred compared. "We are well able to carry them ourselves, Lord Ellsworth. I merely wanted to wish you all a good day, particularly Ryn." I offered Ryn my hand, and he took it. "I never thanked you for burying Roma. It's pained me many years that such an excellent hound did not have a proper place of rest. I'm grateful to you."

"I was happy to do it, Lady Gabriella."

"You didn't tell me this." Tyndale gave his son a proud smile. "When was it?"

Ryn glanced at me before looking down. "A few days ago. I met Lady Gabriella and the Duke of Lofton in the caves."

Tyndale stilled, then swallowed hard before speaking in a strained voice. "What did you think of the Duke of Lofton?"

"I liked him."

Tyndale smiled faintly, then focused on me, his eyes sharpening. "Lady Gabriella, what brings you out this way, if I might ask? I've heard your family seldom visits the village ... or the caves."

A shiver ran up my spine. "My sister and I came to purchase a few supplies for a project. As for the caves, the duke wished to visit them, and Sterling needed exercise, so we joined him."

"She brought her horse right up to the pit! His hooves made a horrible racket against the rock," Ryn said. "I didn't know what was coming up the tunnel."

Tyndale continued to stare at me, as if impressing me with the danger of what I'd done. A knot tightened in my stomach as I considered it, and it occurred to me to wonder how Tyndale knew so much about the caves and my danger there.

"A horse would allow for a fast exit in case of an earthquake," he said, turning away at last to Ryn. "You've played in the caves enough, son. Why don't we find another place for you to explore? Perhaps Lady Gabriella would be so kind as to suggest some?"

"Happily. I believe I know exactly the spots you'd love, Ryn. I'll prepare a list, complete with directions, and give it to your father tonight."

Ryn bobbed his head in thanks. "I'm sure I'll like them."

"Perhaps"—Tyndale gave Marcel that peculiar look again, and Marcel set his jaw—"we could convince Lady Gabriella and her sisters to join us on an outing during one of the breaks, eh, Ellsworth?"

"I doubt the ladies could spare the time from their brother's game," Marcel said.

"We might be able to arrange it, nonetheless," I said, curious as to the silent exchange between Tyndale and the sullen Marcel. "Lord Ellsworth." The frustrating man finally met my gaze and held it. The sunlight hitting his eyes made them almost the color of lush grass, but there was no smile in his eyes as there used to be. "Have you a particular interest in birds? Songbirds, for instance?"

"Not especially. Why?"

I arched an eyebrow. "Someone opened the birdcages in the conservatory a few days ago. My sisters and I had to chase the birds all over the house to capture them. I even found one shut up in the library."

Marcel's face and neck reddened to match his hair at the perceived accusation while his friends, oblivious, laughed at the incident.

"I wondered why the Duke of Henly delayed the afternoon break," Tyndale said.

"That would be why." Ignoring the anger flaring in Marcel's eyes, I continued. "Alexandria claims it was one of the guests, but I don't believe so." I shifted the parcels on my hip and curtsied. "Forgive me for interrupting your game. Please return to it. Alexandria and I must get back to our work."

Without looking at Marcel, I accepted Tyndale's farewell, hugged Ryn again, and turned to leave. Marcel didn't say anything beyond the barest of polite farewells, but when I glanced back as I reached the footpath, he was watching me, and his expression wasn't the stony one he'd worn earlier. I waved, and he gave me a half a wave before stopping himself and turning away with a scowl.

I couldn't help the mischievous grin curling my lips as I walked away. He wasn't as indifferent as he'd have me believe. So *that* wasn't the issue. I likely did give offense in the library when I questioned how he got the ring and thus the sword. But if he was the kind of man I thought he was, and if he did think me a friend, he'd seek a reconciliation. After all, *he* abandoned *me* in the library, yet I made the effort to speak with him today and to apologize in a way. It was his turn. And I had so much to say to him. I wanted to consult with him about my writing project, find out what he thought of Papa's latest lectures, ask about the report from Carrington he was expecting, and so many other things. But I couldn't if he insisted on avoiding me or playing the distant, sardonic gentleman whenever we met.

"What are you smiling at?" The disapproval in Alexandria's voice brought me quickly back to the present, to the real Henly, where young ladies of Floraison blood didn't pursue friendship with plain, stuttering barons. But was that the true Henly or merely a warped version of what it meant to be a noble, pure Floraison?

"I was inquiring if they knew anything about the loosed birds."

Alexandria's brows dipped into a *V*. "We'd better hurry if we want to get started on the potion today."

The next day, Mama asked us to stay near the house since we were expecting a visit from a cousin. Working in the glen then being out of the question, Alexandria and Eva wiled away the morning at the archery field while I worked on my manuscripts. I collected Sterling mid-morning and joined them to practice hitting the targets while riding astride. I had just sent an arrow into the center of each of the three targets when a burst of applause drew my attention from the practice field.

Several of Papa's guests walking the path bordering the field slowed to watch and applaud. Among them was Marcel. He tipped his hat to me, for a moment forgetting the hard look he'd schooled himself into giving me whenever we'd passed of late. I hadn't given up hope he'd come round and reconcile. Was that why the stress around his eyes at those times, proving the uncaring look forced, pleased me so? Feminine vanity was not a Floraison virtue, but I couldn't seem to conquer it where Marcel was concerned. He was the only friend of similar age and interests I had among the guests, and I didn't want to lose him. I returned his acknowledgement with a smile and a wave.

Tyndale, walking behind Marcel, bumped into him. With good-natured laughter, the pair apologized to each other and walked on. For once, it hadn't been Marcel who tripped. There was something admirable in his resilience, in how he always bounced back from whatever happened. I rubbed my scarred fingertip. That was a virtue I was developing.

"That Lord Ellsworth makes me glad I'm too young for suitors," Eva said as I joined her and Alexandria around the table holding the archery equipment.

"What a thing to say, Eva. It's not as if he's pursuing you," I said. She was far too young for his attention. Besides, he seemed determined not to pursue any of us.

"The man looks rather like a stork," Alexandria added, "and is about as intelligible. He stutters and stammers so that one cannot get a full sentence out of him."

"That's simply not true. He can talk coherently, especially when you're not glaring at him. Marcel, Lord Ellsworth, I mean, may not match the Floraison standard of beauty and poise, yet I find him an agreeable companion. You might like him too if you would speak to him kindly and get to know him. Give him a chance, Alexandria. You too, Eva."

Alexandria gave me an appraising look. "An artistic critique is the only notice Lord Ellsworth deserves to receive from the daughters of the Duke of Henly, Gabriella." She paused, her gaze making me uncomfortable. "You always did have an odd attraction to the runts of the wolfhound's litters. You don't extend those feelings to gentlemen, do you?"

"Certainly not!" Sterling pranced under me in recognition of the displeasure churning in me. I'd never settle for a runt of a man. What an insinuation! I tightened my grip on the bow and cantered off to shoot, letting the arrows fly into the targets, relishing the thunk as they hit.

"Imagine Marcel's portrait," Alexandria said when I returned, "hanging in the family gallery next to the one of Grandfather, who was considered the epitome of manly beauty. Or next to Papa's, for he's almost the exact image of Grandfather and is known far and wide for his skill as an orator and statesman."

I resisted the urge to roll my eyes. Marcel's portrait had no business there, so it was a moot point. Alexandria and I gasped as a magical image of a portrait, a cruelly caricatured one of Marcel, suspended itself in the air. Eva snickered, and something in me snapped. I sent an arrow through her callous misuse of magic. The illusion drifted like mist to the ground.

"Yes, I get it," I said. "He's no Adonis. And though he's not nearly as unattractive in appearance as you make him out to be, he would look plain next to Papa or Grandfather. But have you nothing better to accuse him of?" He wasn't cruelly arrogant. Or a Sorcerer's Called. I glared at them, but when they didn't answer, I touched my heels to Sterling's sides. "Sterling and I are going for a ride."

MARCEL ELLSWORTH, THE NEXT MORNING

A wet, red stain marked a path before me along the gravel drive. My nose burned with a coppery odor, dredging up memories that nearly drowned out the yelling coming from the house. Whose blood was that? Tyndale had warned that Gabriella was in danger, and I'd ignored him. Was this the consequence? I stared at the discolored gravel, unable to move as visions of Gabriella, unconscious and bleeding, being carted back to the house on her horse, mingled with scenes of my parents' fateful carriage crash.

A need to help her shot through me, dissolving the shock and freeing my limbs. I raced into the house and promptly rammed into Alexandria as I rounded a corner. With trembling hands, I pulled her from the wall I'd accidently knocked her into. "Forgive me, Lady Alexandria."

She stumbled a step before getting her balance and glared up at me. "Release me, sir, before you do more harm. What is the meaning of this?"

More bloody visions flashed before me. "That's what I want to know. I mean, your father sent me to fetch something, and I heard yelling and saw blood on the ground outside. I was so worried. Is Lady Gab—everyone in the family well?"

"A peasant's been hurt. We're about to do surgery, and you've broken the pain relief."

It wasn't Gabriella's blood. I nearly laughed as relief flooded me. She was fine. She was unhurt. The Thief hadn't gotten her. Life was wonderful. Why was Alexandria still scowling at me? The pain relief. I'd broken it.

The spirit of criticism so familiar from my grandmother, as well as a justifiable anger, burned in Alexandria's eyes. I felt myself falling back into old habits.

"I'm s-so very, very sorry." I took a step back and slipped on the floor made slick by the spilled brandy.

Alexandria caught my arm and helped me regain my balance. Embarrassment fought for dominion with my usual light-headedness around blood and injuries. *Get ahold of yourself. Remember, Gabriella is safe.* The thought steadied me. "I'm s-sorry again. Th-thank you." I made an effort to slow and control my speech. "Is there anything I can do to help? Comfort the family? Get your father? I'm so happy your family is well."

"No—yes! Fetch another bottle of brandy and meet me in the surgery."

My chest went silent, my heart too horrified to beat. Alexandria wore a determined frown, and I got the strange notion she was somehow giving me a chance by ordering me to the surgery. A chance to prove myself worthy of her sister's friendship or to prove myself as far beneath the family dignity as she thought I was?

Either way, I nodded but couldn't seem to move until she snapped her fingers and pointed down the hallway. As I struggled to walk steadily in the indicated direction, she hurried off toward the surgery, wherever that was.

Getting ahold of myself, I inquired of the first servant I passed, and he directed me to the brandy and from there to the surgery. I bade him take the Duke of Henly the items he'd sent me to get.

The smell of blood and cleaners turned my stomach as I entered the surgery. The bottle of brandy cracked softly against a metal tray as I set it with unsteady hands on the small table near where Alexandria stood at the foot of the patient. The physician, a distinguished looking, white-haired man of fifty or so paused in his examination of the patient's leg to give me an assessing glance.

"Thank you." He hunched back over the boulder-sized man on the table in a kind of dismissal.

"Lord Ellsworth asked if he could help. Have you any use for him?" Alexandria said, to my horror. Wasn't getting to the surgery enough for me?

The physician quirked a brow and gave me another up-and-down examination. "Can you handle a sick room, young man? It's not pleasant."

"I know it's not." I remembered my own surgery after the crash, and the delusions caused by the trauma and pain. *If the physician takes my leg, will it go to heaven with my parents?*, my six-year-old self had wondered. The room hadn't been as well-lit and clean as this, but it had the same aura of fear and pain. The current patient was unconscious, so perhaps the fear was all mine. What use would I be? Alexandria's smile was smug. She was waiting for me to fail. "I-I don't know if I can handle it or not, but I'd like to try, if I can do so without endangering the patient."

He nodded to a basin of steaming water. "Scrub up."

The surgery was a blur. I fetched this and that, handed Alexandria different items, and fought to keep my thoughts in place and away from ones of pain and death. A small part of me admired the physician's skill and Alexandria's calm capability and her willingness to help a peasant. But even those thoughts couldn't stop the light-headedness plaguing me or steady my hands, which were all too likely to release whatever they held before Alexandria could receive it.

After the third time I dropped a pair of forceps, Alexandria's words, sharp as a scalpel in their derision and irritation, pierced the haze in my mind. "You're worse than useless, Ellsworth. Leave."

An Ellsworth handles every situation with confidence and poise.

No, they didn't.

I made it out the door before I had to seek the wall for support. Memories and my natural weakness around blood assailed me. I despised my weakness and clumsiness as much as I hated the Floraisons' insistence that everyone not sharing their talents and gifts in equal measure be inferior in worth, fit only for derision. I thought I'd conquered my verbal glitches and forgiven Lady Ellsworth's cruelty, and ceased to care what others thought of me. Yet coming to Henly had revealed I'd merely buried them in a shallow grave. I hated that most of all. Would I ever be free?

I don't know how long I leaned against the wall before Alexandria came out, for I was lost to the sickness and the haze of light-headedness. She paused to stretch as if relieving herself of hours of tension, and I felt her almost human. Then she noticed the blood on her dress and whined about the peasant ruining her garment. She was a Floraison through and through. Dutiful but heartless.

"You must have a lung of stone." My thoughts escaped through the haze. She startled before turning to sneer at me. I only half cared I had, in my typical fashion, butchered the wording.

"You mean a *heart* of stone?" she said, and then she was gone.

The weakness clung to me still, made worse by fleeting visions of my parents before and after the crash. My stomach turned, but I managed to make my way out of the house into the gardens, where I collapsed onto the stone steps leading to a sunken walk. Resting my head against the wall of the walk, I let the memories flow over me, hoping they would then drain away. The odor of the surgery clung to my clothes, keeping the horror of the place with me, but I was too miserable to care.

Sometime later soft footsteps approached from the sunken walk, startling me despite their lightness. Gabriella stopped before me, hands clasped in front of her, silently watching the man who couldn't handle blood. Another proof of my unsuitability for even admission to her father's mentoring season.

"The surgery was successful," she said.

"I'm glad to hear it." I didn't rise, but she didn't seem to expect me to. I rubbed my hand over my face, trying to clear my vision. The black spots began to fade and the twists of my stomach to straighten. She waited, though I didn't know what for. Staying to watch me in yet another display of weakness? Closing my eyes, I leaned my head against the wall again, ignoring her as she shifted from one foot to the other and ignoring the inner voice that chided me for being so critical of her.

"The physician said you held out better than some who wanted to be physicians themselves," she said after a moment. "He once had to stop a surgery to stitch up the head of an assistant who'd fainted."

I snorted. He didn't know how close he'd come to repeating that. That would have perfected their picture of me. "But I didn't handle it like a Floraison. That's all that counts, isn't it?"

"Is it?" There was challenge in her voice, and it irked me. She knew it was.

Tyndale's words came back: *You've got a chip on your shoulder, Ellsworth, as big as the Floraison pride.* So maybe I had, but considering my situation with the Ceurian inspector, it didn't matter. I was forbidden from interaction.

"You've sought me out, Lady Gabriella. You can congratulate yourself that you've done your Floraison duty. Your guest is safe. He hasn't fainted and split his head. Feel free to return to suitable society."

Her offended gasp tempted me to look at her, but if I did I'd only apologize and prolong a conversation I'd likely regret.

"If you're so determined to judge us," she snapped, "then you can hardly blame us for doing the same. If you had any sense, you'd see that—oh never mind." Her skirts swished as she swept away over the paving stones, her steps not as soft as before. I finally dared open my eyes.

A pebble skittered over the stones. Gabriella had kicked it, and that was not a thing an untouchable Floraison would do. My eyes followed the pebble's path. That's when realization hit me, and I couldn't have been more surprised if she'd kicked me: She was hurt. Her seeking me out wasn't solely Floraison duty, or even feminine vanity wanting to string along an admirer. Somehow, Gabriella Floraison had developed an affection for me. How and what kind I couldn't fathom unless it was that which drew her to the pitiable runt Bitsy. But somehow she had, and my rudeness hurt.

I laughed bitterly to myself. What a triumph. The plain, lowly baron had a chance to reject the universally adored, flawless Floraison, even if only for friendship. To let her believe it was my choice to scorn her instead of the order of the Ceurian inspector and my own sense of hopelessness with regard to anything serious between us ever being allowed.

Yes, let her believe I was the one who thought her not good enough. I smiled grimly in a twisted kind of satisfaction as Gabriella marched away.

Chapter 16

"Beware a thief," Lettie's mother warned. "Not all seek treasures of gold and silver. Some, though perhaps unknowing and unwilling, will steal your heart and leave theirs in return. In them the greatest danger lies, for who can replace a heart?"

The Magic Thief by Charlotte James

GABRIELLA FLORAISON

M Y SNIFFLE CAUGHT me off guard, and I hurried my steps. Why had I bothered to find him at all? He'd never believe any of us had a heart. Half-magics, that's why. I needed information from him. Not that I wanted to see him.

But, truth be told, when Alexandria told me she'd coerced him into helping with the surgery—if only she'd known what she was asking of him!—I felt a need to see that he was all right. Why had he done it anyway, when he'd known the memories it would bring back? But it didn't matter. He was miserable, and I was the last person to encourage him, it seemed. He could respond to Aunt Helene with more politeness than to me. I detested the man!

No, I detested the bitterness he clung to. I didn't detest him at all.

"Gabriella!"

I'd heard my name a thousand times before, but never spoken like that. Now it was a single word that could have brought a comet to a halt had the comet a heart to feel.

How does one respond to a sound like that? It says a thousand things. It speaks of remorse and apology, of yearning and affection. It said there was something between us he desperately wanted to make right. Yet most of all it begged me to stop and hear him.

I blinked away a tear. The wretched man didn't deserve the consideration. Still, the echo of my name brought me around anyway. When I turned, he was in front of me, a look on his face to match the tone of his voice. He caught my hand in his.

"I'm a wanted man, Gabriella, in the criminal sort of way. Your father didn't tell you after all then?" He rushed his words so I could barely make them out.

"I don't understand. You were cleared at the village trial."

"That wasn't my first trial. Officers from Ceur and an official from Florenburg have come to take me back to Ceur. Gabriella, I can't be—"

His gaze darted to the shrubbery, and he stepped back, dropping my hand as if it burned him. Then his demeanor changed. Like a chameleon that had found itself in a house of the arrogant and heartless, he bowed stiffly, his face a cold mask.

"I regret to inform my lady I must be as a leper to her, one to be avoided for the good of all." With a furious, determined look he spun on his heel and left me staring after him, unsure whether to hate him or follow him and demand an explanation.

Something moved on the other side of the walk. Suspicion boiled a noxious brew, and I dashed up the stairs and around to the other path. It was empty, but there were depressions in the earth to match man-sized boots.

My fists clenched at my sides. If I had a wand, I'd be tempted to use it on whoever had been spying on us. Marcel had intimated that Papa knew something. When opportunity presented, I would ask him about it.

For now, I wanted to ride. I could still hear the screams of the injured man's wife. She'd been difficult to comfort, poor thing. Then there was Marcel's mercurial behavior and the Duke of Lofton's sudden decision to spend the day in Florenburg. Sterling, at least, I understood.

"Harvey's gone with Sterling?" I stared dumbfounded at Cox, the temporary stable hand formerly bearing the disgraceful beard. In vain I glanced around for Harvey. Cox rattled off some excuse about shoeing and going out for exercise, but I was still reeling. Harvey never took Sterling out without telling me, especially not now. I pressed my hand against my chest. What if the Call came before they returned? I scolded myself. They were still on the estate. If the Call came, Sterling would find me. "Do you know where they went?" I asked.

He pointed toward the river. "That way, my lady."

Of course they went that way. Most of the paths went *that way*, toward the river and the village. The meadow before the river path would be a good place to check Sterling's gait, however.

"Shall I saddle another horse for you?" he asked.

"No, thank you. I'll walk."

He bowed and returned to his work.

Soon, I was shading my eyes to look across the meadow. There was no sign of them. I changed course for the village lane. Not far along the path, I spotted two men, one tall and trim, the other not so tall or trim. My feet sped up of their own accord. Was the tall one Marcel? He had some explaining to do. My steps slowed. No, it wasn't him. The stride wasn't the same. As they approached, I recognized Tyndale. His companion was a stranger.

"Good afternoon, Lady Gabriella." Tyndale bowed, his eyes bright with a charming twinkle that reminded me why my sisters had declared him the handsomest of Papa's guests. "I hope you're having a pleasant walk."

"Pleasant enough, yes. Have my father's lectures ended so early?" Or was it later than I realized? I *would* find Sterling soon.

"Unfortunately, duty demanded my absence; otherwise, I would never miss your father's excellent lectures." He indicated the stranger. "May I have the honor of introducing my solicitor, Mr. Keldan?"

"How do you do, sir?" I curtsied to Mr. Keldan, my gaze catching on the wild brown hair poking out from underneath his hat. He was a far cry from the polished gentleman my father employed.

"Good, thank you, my lady." As if sensing my scrutiny, he brushed a hand over his collar and rolled his shoulders, adjusting the fit of his jacket. Though his clothes were of good quality, suitable for a solicitor, he wore them uncomfortably, like a man lifted from a lower station. From the fields of an uneducated farmer, perhaps. He must be a clever man to have managed that.

I turned my attention once again to Tyndale and was startled by the look in his eyes, one similar to the tender one I'd seen when he took my hand and assured me I could fight the curse. His expression shuttered, but not quickly enough to prevent the heat from rising to my cheeks.

"I hope it's nothing serious that brings your solicitor here," I said.

"Just urgent."

My lips pursed at his lack of explanation. No one, it seemed, was capable, or willing, to explain anything. Tyndale's business was not my own to warrant an explanation, but the frequency of dissembling among my acquaintances was vexing in the extreme.

"I won't detain you then. Good day to you, gentlemen." I curtsied and stepped forward, but my boot heel proved unsteady. I stumbled, and Mr. Keldan caught my arm.

"Are you all right, my lady?" he asked, a Tormirian accent breaking through his words. A wave of nausea passed over me. Blinking against sunlight—I hadn't realized it was so bright this afternoon—I swallowed hard and covered my mouth. Tyndale took my other arm as Keldan moved around to face me.

"Take a deep breath, through your nose now," Keldan said comfortingly. "That's right. Feel better?"

My gaze flew to his. Surprisingly, I did. "Much better, thank you."

"Did the accident earlier make you ill?" he continued in his soothing way. "Poor man. We all heard about it."

"You're sure you're better?" Tyndale asked with a light touch on my hand before releasing me.

My cheeks flushed as I tugged my arm from Keldan's grip and away from Tyndale. What on earth had come over me? But it was the incident earlier of course. "Quite well." As if to prove myself, I straightened my hat.

"Want us to accompany you back to the house?" the solicitor asked.

"Bosh," Tyndale said with a wave of his hand, as if shooing the idea away. "You don't know the stamina of the Floraisons, Keldan. They can handle anything, can't they, Lady Gabriella? No passing sickness deters them."

"Thank you, Lord Tyndale, but I have no intention of returning to the house at present."

"I thought not. We'll leave you to your walk, but call out if you need us."

After bidding one another good day, we parted. No sooner had I turned my back to them than their conversation recommenced, something about an old shack on Tyndale's estate. A boy playing there had been hurt when a plank broke off in his hand. One of Ryn's adopted siblings?

"Are you sure you want to tear it down, sir?" the solicitor asked. "It's got quite a bit of history to it."

"It's a danger," Tyndale replied firmly. "I'll not let a danger linger on my property no matter the consequences to myself. The children's safety comes first."

They walked out of hearing, but I couldn't forget their conversation. Visions of the cave formed a background to their words. How could I suffer the altar to remain? What if some other child wandered there? One of my own nieces or nephews one day? I couldn't let that happen. Papa had tried to block it off, but that hadn't worked. My dreams revealed another entrance; I only had to find it and then smash the altar. I should have thought of that before. How could I, a Floraison, have been content to merely survive the Call? I should have fought it!

Purpose filled me and put a spring in my step. I only just remembered to check my finger—the scar was white. The cave was empty then. I would cleanse the property of this danger and free myself of its curse.

After a short detour back to the stable to secure a hammer, I made for the old path, joining it beyond the traps. My feet didn't falter until I stood before the gate from my dreams. How I knew it was there I couldn't fathom, for I couldn't make out its rusted hinges from where I stood. I stepped off the path and a distant part of my mind cried out, *Why are you doing this? Get help. Don't go in there alone!* I tripped on a vine, and the hammer struck my leg. I fell to one knee and dropped the hammer in the underbrush. Released by the pain, the cries of my mind burst forth, and I saw the shadowed patch of stunted shrubs and twisted vines as if through new eyes. I gasped. "What am I doing here? Alone?"

You must destroy the altar and save Henly. Alone? Only a fool would go in there unaccompanied in my condition. Shaking my head, I picked up the hammer and turned around, but a wave of nausea struck me. I fell to my knees again, the hammer landing beside me. *The children's safety is first.* How could I suffer the altar to remain? I could do it. A Floraison is courageous after all. A Floraison can handle anything. I wasn't under the Call; therefore, I had nothing to fear. If I hurried.

Picking myself up, I stumbled over the bulging roots and twisted vines. Shoving aside the limbs shielding the gaping hole, I caught hold of a rusted hinge long enough to let my eyes adjust to the dim light of the cave's mouth. Flakes of rust stuck to my hand or dusted down to the ground as I shuffled forward. The air staled immediately. Hadn't I always thought it would be cool and fresh? A lie. Another reason to destroy the altar.

One hand over another, I moved along the wall deeper and deeper into the hillside. The air grew damp, and the staleness vanished. Had I ever thought it stale? It was cool and pleasant to breathe. At last the dark space about me widened, the walls moving apart and the ceiling rising. I paused to get my bearings. The primitive altar had been cut into a wall. Which one?

Fumbling in the dark, I hugged the wall to my left. My fingers shied over the rock, jumping back to my chest at the least hint of the altar's depression. Again, I questioned what I was doing. What could I accomplish here in the dark? *Keep searching. You must destroy it!*

I couldn't find and destroy it without light, not without the risk of pricking my finger again. I couldn't chance it. I shouldn't be here. I had to get out. Clutching my hands to my chest, I pivoted and pressed my shoulder lightly against the wall to guide me out.

"Out," I repeated to myself. The air felt heavy again, full of something foul. *You'll find it.* "With help," I snapped at that inner voice.

"Did you ask for help?" a man said. Biting back a squeal, I fell against the wall. "Forgive me for alarming you, Lady Gabriella. There's no need to be afraid."

I gasped. How could anyone know I was here? It was as black as a night without stars. Footsteps trod softly over rock in my direction. One would think it trod on my heart for the rate at which that organ beat. Could I move away quietly enough that he wouldn't know where I was?

Where was my courage? He might not be a foe. "Who are you?"

"The Duke of Lofton ... my dear."

"You left Henly for Florenburg. You couldn't possibly have returned."

The soft tread circled nearer. "Left? With the Magic Thief around? Don't be daft. I only wanted everyone to think so."

"Oh." I could see the logic of that, but failed to see why he couldn't have told me. I felt safer when he was around. Usually.

"I'm glad I saw you come in here," he continued before I could ask more. "You're right in that you can free yourself and help me against the Magic Thief by breaking the altar."

"How did you know why I came?"

"Why else would you when not under the Call?" His voice calmed me, like the soft pacing, yet I felt a need to struggle against it.

"How would it help you against the Thief?" I shook my head to clear it.

"Why ... so his sorcerer accomplices couldn't use it to aid him, of course."

"Oh." Sliding along the wall, I moved back a few feet, deeper into the cavernous room, away from those footsteps. "Would you light the cavern with your wand?"

"I would but it's not *safe* to use a wand in a sorcerer's lair. Don't you know?"

"Not safe?" Hadn't I used mine that horrible day?

"No. Safety is important, isn't it?"

The children's safety is first. You must destroy it. The thoughts flew like swarming locust through my mind.

"All you have to do is smash it, Lady Gabriella. Then you'll be free. Henly will be safe. You needn't worry for yourself or anyone else then."

Needn't worry. Wouldn't that be lovely? No more bites. No more scars.

"Turn around, Gabriella. A few more steps. You're almost there."

Just a few steps. I could make that in the dark.

"Don't you want to know what it feels like to be free?"

"Free—but I forgot the hammer." Jerking to a halt, I reached out around me to the air and the wall as if I could somehow find the hammer there.

"You can use a power burst on it."

"I don't know how."

"You're an enchantress. There's power in your touch. Strike it with your hand."

With my hand. I remembered my attempts in the glen, and my hand warmed in response. I took a step forward.

"Go ahead, Lady Gabriella. Strike it with your hand. End it. End the fight."

Yes, that's what I'd do. My finger burned as I raised my hand.

"No!" a man cried. I stilled, my hand hovering near the wall. No?

"Leave her—" The Duke of Lofton's command screamed passed me as the air in front of me hissed with motion.

Pain shot through my head, and all went blacker than even a cave should be.

The air smelled of lavender and freshly laundered linens and my mother's perfume.

The feel of my bed had never been so welcome, though I couldn't recall why I should be so relieved to be here. I opened my eyes and looked for Mama. Her face was a blend of shadows and soft light from the firelight. How had I passed the afternoon and into the night? She saw me stirring, and some of the shadows of worry left her face.

"Mama."

"Yes, darling." She moved gracefully to my bedside, the familiar swish of her skirts a beautiful sound.

Groaning against the pain in my head, I sat up and leaned back against the pillows. "Have I made you miss dinner?"

Smiling, she tucked the covers around my waist. "What if you had? Do you think I would melt away?"

"'Too good to be true, the fey lady vanished in the night, and his heart was never again whole,'" I quoted from one of our favorite childhood story books.

She kissed my forehead, and with a featherlike touch, smoothed wild strands of hair away from my face. "I would never do that." A hint of color bloomed in her cheeks. "I might spend too much time with Lady Tannon," she added sheepishly.

My head aching, I closed my eyes and let out a long breath. "She needed you. But, Mama, what did I do to myself?"

Her fingers stilled. "Harvey found you with Sterling in the meadow." She hesitated. "Your finger was bleeding."

With a gasp, I jerked my hand up for inspection, but Mama caught it between both of hers.

"It's white, but it does have another impression of Sterling's teeth."

The sudden panic and its relief drained my energy, and I sank back against the pillows. Memories tried to surface, but all I could recall was the darkness surrounding me. Later, when my head cleared, I *would* remember. Then something came back on its own. I tried to sit up, but Mama gently encouraged me to rest.

"Harvey was gone with Sterling when I went to the stable," I protested. "Something about a shoe or exercise. Sterling wouldn't have been with me."

Mama's dark brows drew together. "No, Sterling escaped his stall during the chaos of the surgery. Harvey went to look for him alone since you were needed here. He'd looked everywhere, going to the village even, and had given up when he chanced to spot him in the meadow." She smiled faintly. "He said you gave him the fright of his life when he saw you lying there beside Sterling."

A twinge of guilt assailed me for enjoying Harvey's concern. "You'll send Harvey up later, won't you?"

"How could I not? He and Sterling are both treasures. I can almost be glad Sterling managed to free himself so he could find you when you needed him."

"But my head?"

"Harvey said there were some rocks in that part of the meadow. You may have tripped and hit your head. But now I should relieve your father's mind." She rose, a fond smile on her lips. "I'm not sure if having him entertain the guests was a useful distraction for him or simply cruel to the guests. Your father can be quite testy when he's worried."

When she was at the door, she called over her shoulder, "The Duke of Lofton left you a note. It's on your nightstand."

"Has he—" I hesitated, a concern I couldn't recall a reason for building in me. "Has he returned from Florenburg yet?"

"He's gone, Gabriella," she said softly, and I wondered for the first time how she felt about the rumors of the Magic Thief. "He received word that his wife is ill."

"He did go to Florenburg today, didn't he?" Why did the answer seem so vitally important?

"Yes. We received the message about his wife and sent a servant to meet him in town and tell him, to save him the additional time traveling back and forth. He sent the letter for you back with the servant. He also sent us a note. Gabriella, your father and I are sorry we weren't forthright with you about what happened in the cave that day. It's a little late, but we will talk with you about the Sorcerer's Call when you've rested."

Chapter 17

There were two brothers in the Caffin Wars, twins and in-
separable as ever any twins were. This pleased their wives,
for they were twins themselves. Dandies they were, with
lace cuffs and coats of scarlet and gold, with jewels on their
belts and swords, but brave and bold all. In a sorcerer's
hold the four fought to free their lord. Two lost their wands
in a daring venture there. When all hope seemed gone they
recalled what had been said in days long past: stolen wands
could be recalled, though the wands would be weakened.
The two called, and the wands obeyed their masters and
returned, and on they fought. Together, the four slew the
creatures of evil, but great was the cost. For they died on
their wands those two, one brother, one sister, their hands
clasped, their wands shattered on the stones. Those pre-
cious fragments the others took and bound in scarlet and
gold, a pair of rings. It is said that deep within the rings,
the wands, broken though they are, have never forgotten
their mates in the hands of the living brother and sister,
and are ever anxious to find them. That if you asked, the
rings might take you wherever you wished to go in hopes of
finding their lost mates. Neither did they forget they were
once wands.

A legend of the Caffin Wars

MARCEL ELLSWORTH

T HE SCRIBBLED WORDS in front of me made as much sense as the trill of a cardinal's song, though I wrote them. I massaged my temples. The Duke of Henly's lectures were brilliant, and I needed to transpose my notes into a more legible form before I forgot everything he taught. Did it really matter anymore? I shushed the pessimistic thought. One way or the other, I *would* soon be free to pursue Carrington's bright future.

Covered over by those notes was one to Gabriella apologizing for my own pride and bitter, critical behavior and explaining why I could no longer talk with her. Tyndale was right about that chip on my shoulder. I'd have to shrug it off if I ever hoped to be happy, and Henly Manor was the perfect place to do that. But how was I to get the message to her without aggravating the situation with the inspector?

I looked up as Henry cleared his throat. He didn't usually use such meek arts to gain my attention. "Yes?"

He shoved a small note toward me. "Um."

It must be the firelight, but I could almost swear he blushed. I looked closer. No, it wasn't the firelight. He was red-cheeked. Panic seized me. "Are you resigning, Henry?"

"Oh no, sir."

His wide-eyed start reassured me, and I settled back in my chair, my shoulders falling in relief. "Thank goodness for that. What is it then?"

"It's just that I've never delivered a note like this before."

I almost laughed at his distress and took another look at the folded square of paper. "Does it bear the pirate's black spot?"

With a disgruntled smirk, he thrust the letter into my hand. "It might as well. Lady Gabriella's maid passed it to me to give to you. Such dealings. Even if they weren't likely to get us into trouble, would get us into trouble, if you know what I mean, sir."

Gabriella? The unaddressed paper, folded over as an envelope, stared up at me. I knew better than to blush with a lover's shyness. I had almost told her the truth. What must she think of me now? The whole truth would have been bad enough, but only managing to tell her half was far worse. *I'm wanted. In a criminal sort of way.* Brilliant. I could at least have told her I was innocent! The pride and acrimony of my earlier behavior was reason enough for her to hate me without a criminal background to add to it. Well, to that and my plain face, tendency to stutter around the females of her family, and low rank.

Cringing, I worked up my nerve and unfolded the letter.

Dear Marcel,

I went to my father for an explanation of your behavior. If you believe I believe the Ceurians' accusations, you're a nincompoop. The truth is, I require your assistance. I must learn more about the half-magics. To my great sorrow and consternation, the Duke of Lofton left yesterday. He commissioned me to question you and your servant Henry about them.

If you wish to remain in a state of nincompoopery, then by all means burn this letter without reply. But if you wish to return to the status of a sensible gentleman, and friend, then during the breaks or before dinner, when none of us will be missed, betake yourself—and Henry, if he is agreeable to it—to the glen. Discreetly, of course.

Yours truly,

G

"Is *nincompoopery* a word, sir?"

Covering my start with a scowl, I glanced over my shoulder, the one Henry was leaning over. He backed away, and I skimmed the letter again, not quite certain what to make of it. That she hadn't blasted me as a worm of a man was a wonder. That she wished to see me—and Henry—was nothing short of a miracle. "She doesn't think I'm a criminal," I muttered in awe, "and she called me a friend." Gabriella Floraison was goodness itself, and I'd never deserve even her friendship. But I would no longer be too stupid to accept it.

"*Nincompoopery* is a word, sir. The plural form is *nincompooperies*." The dictionary shut with a soft thump.

"Thank you, Henry," I said drily. But what if the letter was a fake, a trap set by the Ceurians? What had made Lofton change his mind about me getting involved with the enchanters? And since when did a Floraison use words like *nincompoop* and its derivatives?

A grin barreled through my defenses. Since she became a horse lover and started spending time in the stable with the likes of Harvey. The letter was hers, all right.

"What of the inspector, sir?" Henry's question threatened to rip my joy from me, but I held it fast.

"Our clever correspondent has solved the problem for us. The glen's a wonderful place. You'll like it. The inspector won't discover us there." Even if he did, Gabriella was worth the risk.

"You're determined to participate in these clandestine lessons then, despite the inspector's warnings and all the family has accused you of?"

"Yes. I didn't take Tyndale's hint of Gabriella's danger and his order to look after her seriously, but I'll not make that mistake again, especially not with Lofton implicitly saying the same thing. Are you willing?"

"To be sure. As you say, the duke's request should not be ignored."

"Good man. Meet me at the stable during the first break tomorrow, and I'll show you where the glen is."

"Very good, sir." There was a surprising amount of satisfaction in his voice.

"And if you can handle one more scandalous exchange of letters, I'll get you my reply in a moment." I pulled out my earlier missive to Gabriella and added a postscript to it.

"Very good, sir." There was no satisfaction in his voice this time.

Henry and I stopped at the stone bridge. The archway in the boulder was barely visible if I squinted and looked at it just right. Water swirled in the pool, then flowed away through the forest.

"Shall I knock, sir?" Henry moved to the boulder as if he knew exactly where the doorway was.

"It didn't do any good the last time I tried, but they weren't expecting me then. Go ahead."

He lifted his hand to knock, then hesitated, his attention drawn to the path beyond the bridge. It went steeply uphill and around a bend to disappear behind the trees of the ridge bordering the glen.

"Henry?"

He slipped his hands into his pockets with a wry smile. "A moment, sir."

The clip-clop of a horse treading a rocky trail reached my ears, but then it halted and was followed by Sterling's distinctive neigh. My servant and I exchanged glances.

I set off across the bridge, Henry following. We moved quickly up the bank and were nearing the bend before we heard Sterling again, coming from a magnolia with two thick trunks diverging from a single base. The horse was nowhere to be seen.

This didn't deter Henry. Chuckling like he'd discovered some secret, he marched off the path for the divided tree. "Now this is the sort of tree I would have enjoyed climbing growing up," he murmured. He walked right into it and disappeared.

I paused, gaping, but then marched on. I was not to be outdone by my servant. I strode up to the tree, right up to it, but instead of bumping into it, I bumped into Henry and fell back against a towering boulder—the boulder-gate formerly attained near the bridge.

"I do apologize," Henry began, but quieted at the sound of a horsey laugh. Before us stretched the once water-bound glen, now dry. A few feet away, Sterling shook his mane at us and then trotted off to a pen accompanied by one of the wolfhounds.

"The Duke of Lofton and Papa fitted the glen with a new entrance." Gabriella stood at the boulder's edge, one hand resting on it, the other cradling the blue Amphora on its long necklace. "It opens and closes at the tree now with a mild power burst or the Amphora. It's nothing fancy, but it should allow us to come and go less visibly than at the arch." She pulled her hand away from the rock. "That's one reason the Duke of Lofton suggested I meet with you."

"To learn power bursts?" I queried, following her further into the glen.

She came to a stop beside the massive stone work-bench, on which rested two books, her ancestor's definitive *Half-Magics: Only a Legend* and the fictional *The Fall of Bevvelian,* often ridiculed for the amazing feats accomplished by its characters, the half-magics in particular.

"And general knowledge of half-magics." A hint of self-consciousness broke through her normal confidence but was soundly squashed as she tapped a finger on the novel. "It occurred to me while reading that one cannot fight half-magics with magic. It would feed them with magic unless one knew spells to prevent that."

"*Feed* them," Henry muttered under his breath.

Snickering, I stuck my hands in my pockets. "We can teach you those, Lady Gabriella. But before we begin, have you ever seen a half-magic at work?"

Her eyebrow rose as if to say, *why would you ask such a ridiculous thing?* It quickly lowered. "No, I have not. I have felt the effects of spell removal, I believe."

I gave my servant a significant look.

Henry bowed. "My pleasure, sir."

Gabriella's brows furrowed as she took in the both of us with one glance. "Oh."

"Yes, my lady." Henry moved in front of her and extended his hand, palm up. "Would you care to *feed* the half-magic?" There was no malice in his words.

With a laugh, she laid her hand in his. "I have much to learn, I fear."

"No more than most beginners." He guided her to a spot a few feet from the bench and took both her hands in his. Then my impudent servant winked at me.

"Henry, don't forget about that charming little schoolmistress in Silvestris waiting for you to come back." Scooting the books to one side, I hopped up on the bench and sat.

When I looked up, he'd dropped one of Gabriella's hands, a look of distress fleeting across his face.

"How did you know about her?" he asked in mock concern.

"I have my ways, Henry. I have my ways." Had I imagined his unease? Something told me it wasn't about the schoolmistress.

Henry tentatively took again the hand he'd released. "If you'll let the power flow gently into your hands, my lady."

Gabriella's amused expression morphed into one of concentration.

After a moment, he said, "That reminds me. I have something for you, my lady." He reached into his jacket, and when he pulled out his fist, Gabriella turned to me with a look of suspicion. I shrugged and nodded in Henry's direction.

He opened his fist, and a bluebird, ethereal and brilliantly colored, leapt into the air, circled the awed Gabriella and then me before disappearing in a blue poof.

Gabriella took her hand from Henry and felt her palm. "My hand is cool to the touch. You used the magic I directed there to create the illusion." It was three-quarters statement, one-quarter question. "Like I would use a wand to cast a spell."

"Just so." Henry's eyes gleamed. "It wasn't a typical spell or anything useful, but illusions are entertaining. A good introduction to what a half-magic can do."

"It was beautifully done," she said.

He shrugged, then jerked his chin in my direction. She followed his gaze and smiled at me.

"His grandfather," Henry said, "is fond of saying, 'There are two kinds of beauty; beware which one you treasure, for lasting beauty lies within.'" He took her hands again. "But I maintain there are three types: external being the most easily observed, internal the most desirable to sensible people, and illusions"—he winked—"being the most fun. Wouldn't you agree?"

"It is a wise saying," she said, blushing faintly. "Tell me, have you often trained enchanters?"

"No, my lady."

"Despite his talent, he prefers other activities," I added.

"I prefer teaching people how to read," Henry said.

"And to read himself."

"A noble purpose," she said. "Shall we begin in earnest?"

It wasn't long before I needed to return to the duke's lectures. Using my ring, I was able to get to my room and from there to the lecture hall *in a twist,* as we often said.

Since learning power bursts is an arduous task and difficult on the flesh, Gabriella and Henry ended the lesson when I left them. We agreed to meet again during the next break.

GABRIELLA FLORAISON

It scared me how easy it was to ignore the seriousness of my missing wand. A horde of armed sorcerers were not before me to fill me with anxiety. Nor did I see more evidence of the lurking Magic Thief to keep me on my guard. So rarely did we use our powers that retaining the ability to do potions would have seemed enough to me but for a small voice inside, a persistent whisper justified by the duke's warnings and the occasional snippets of the sorcerers' evil doings in the newspaper. It was a voice that reminded me that gifts were for a purpose and should not be neglected, even if the purpose wasn't readily visible. That caution and preparation shouldn't be neglected.

Thus, every night for the week remaining until Papa's birthday, I covered my stinging palms with lotion, and every morning, I met Marcel and Henry in the glen. We met three times that first day and the days that followed.

I gathered that while Henry possessed the skills of a half-magic and a great deal of knowledge, it was Marcel who loved to lecture, who loved the history and the ins and outs of how magic worked. He paced around the stone bench, his shoulders relaxed, his hands behind his back, reminding me very much of a dear old professor in his lecture hall, and of Papa, though Papa's manner was more commanding. Marcel caught my look once, seemed to read it, and smiled with a slight shrug as if to say he didn't care if he did look like an old professor.

The friendly banter between Marcel and his servant initially surprised me, but I soon came to enjoy it. The three of us had lively conversations that often threatened to make Marcel late to Papa's lessons. Henry kept him on schedule, however, and no one seemed to notice our private tutoring sessions, for we were careful to arrive and depart separately. Henry walked, I rode, and Marcel, after seemingly going to his room, traveled by his ring's power.

After dinner on the third day of our training, several of the guests requested that my sisters and I sing for them. As I was singing, a burst of laughter nearly threw me off-key. As it had that first night, the despicable sound came from the direction of a certain lanky man with red hair.

Marcel turned, and I prepared to glower at him, but the look of utter horror on his face took me aback. It was then I noted his lips were closed but the laughing continued. He moved aside to reveal a diminutive man with his head thrown back in laughter.

After gaping at the man's blatant rudeness, a break in the music allowing me to do so, I wanted to give him an appropriate look, to instruct him that his ways were not the ways of polite society. Yet I found I couldn't help but smile instead at Marcel's horrified expression, one pleading for recognition of his innocence. He did nothing, yet was blamed for everything.

MARCEL ELLSWORTH

Two nights before the duke's celebration, Henry sat quietly at a small side table absently shuffling a deck of playing cards. A book lay on the table, unopened.

"Are you troubled about something, Henry?" I glanced up from the stationery in front of me, dated and addressed to my aunt but otherwise blank. I hated the thought of upsetting her almost as much as I hated what lay ahead.

Without stopping the rhythmic movement of his hands, Henry replied, "I've been studying up on horses."

I put my pen away. Perhaps I should let Henry tell Aunt Coraline after I left for Ceur. "I didn't know you were interested in horses."

"I'm not usually."

"Why the sudden interest? Planning a horse farm for your retirement?" I scrubbed a hand over my face. It'd been a long day.

"The duke's stable houses some magnificent horses," Henry said, his voice lacking the excitement of an enthusiast. "Some rare breeds too. You might want to think about adding a horse farm to Carrington."

There was something cunning in his solemn tone and seemingly careless movements. He was leading the conversation somewhere he didn't want to approach directly.

"Which breeds would you recommend?" I asked, assuming my role as follower in the conversation.

He cupped the deck in one hand and moved cards from the back of the deck to the front, feathering them in, the circular motion of the cards almost hypnotic in my tired state. He named off a few breeds, all but one I recognized.

"What's a Pyren? I've not heard of them." Leaning back in my chair, I fought to keep my eyes open.

"I'm not surprised." He broke his forward stare for a sidelong glance at the book near him. "It took a bit of research to find mention of them in the duke's library. It's an ancient breed now only raised on the White Mountain of Tormir. During the Caffin Wars they were fairly common in areas that had sorcerer's lairs, for the sorcerers often stole enchanters' children and made them prick their finger on their altar. Sometimes they kept the children, but sometimes they sent them home to be trained in magic by their parents and given a wand before calling them back. A Pyren could sense and stop the Call, if the sorcerers didn't find and poison the horse first."

"That's quite the horse. You said there was a sorcerers' hideout around Henly that had never been destroyed, didn't you?" I pressed my thumb over the engravings in the thick gold band of my traveling ring, remembering the story of how a wand was shattered in a lair.

He gave a quick nod.

"It's wise of the duke to keep a Pyren on hand in case some poor child finds the lair," I said.

In case? My skin crawled at the remembrance of the foul chamber I'd stumbled upon in the cave Gabriella disliked so. Was it the lair? It felt evil enough to be. Thank heavens the pit would keep everyone away.

"They are also excellent horses in general—strong, loyal, intelligent," Henry continued.

"Which horse in the stable is a Pyren?"

He stopped shuffling. "Sterling."

The word shot through me and was echoed by another. *Gabriella.* She hated the cave. She adored Sterling. The blood drained from my face. "What chance would a Sorcerer's Called have if something happened to her Pyren?"

"Ordinarily," he said, "none."

"None at all?"

"If a half-magic chanced to see her scar change colors, he might be able to do something. Or if she knew what was happening and had a wand, she might stand a small chance. I read of a Called who broke from the haze in his mind long enough to use his wand to blast the altar, but even he barely escaped from the sorcerers who initiated the Call."

My hand trembled as I gripped the chair arm. "That sounds like a worthwhile breed to invest in. Thank you for telling me about it."

"I thought you'd like to know," he said quietly.

When I nodded and picked up my aunt's letter, he laid aside the cards and went about his normal duties. The night drew on, yet I hunched over the writing desk, holding the pen but unable to think of anything except that Gabriella had no wand and I was going to prison in Ceur.

"Henry," I said at last, lifting my stub of a candle to light another. He stopped polishing my boots and looked up. Though my throat constricted, I forced a light tone as I pulled out a fresh sheet of paper. "I need you to do two things for me."

He joined me at the desk, a questioning look on his face.

"I need you to write a letter."

"Is the cut on your wrist bothering you?" he asked. "You always see to your own correspondence."

"Nothing's wrong. It's a letter to Lady Gabriella."

He looked askance at me, and I remembered his flush when he delivered her earlier message.

"It's not that kind of a letter."

He quirked an eyebrow. Not caring to argue, I settled the inkstand and pen beside the paper. "The other matter?" he asked.

I slipped off my traveling ring and laid it on the paper.

"Ah," he said slowly. "It is that kind of a letter."

Chapter 18

It is worse even than I feared. Ackman was no prisoner in the Tormir Penitentiary. He was a king. Politics among the sorcerers themselves made it expedient for him to stay away for a time, and what better place to hide than in a prison? Through the assistance of a Sorcerer's Called and a few others, Ackman took control of his entire cellblock, somehow creating an illusion of normalcy to any checking in.

Some turn to the dark ways purely to grow their magic and avoid the blood sacrifices as much as possible, but some worship the dark. Ackman is one of the latter. The Sorcerer's Called, in his assumed role as head guard of that floor, provided Ackman with prisoners and other articles, and Ackman built his own lair with the blood and tortured cries of those poor men. And now he has left his home. Vanished like a thief in the night. Or a thief's prize.

The Duke of Lofton to a colleague

GABRIELLA FLORAISON

THE DAY DAWNED a thunderous gray, lit only by streaks of lightning. Stifling a moan, I pushed up and leaned against my headboard. We couldn't possibly meet at the glen in this weather. Fumbling on my nightstand for my hand lotion, I grimaced as I bumped different objects, unable to see much in the dark room. My skin hadn't calloused to the power bursts yet. I had so much training left, and Marcel and Henry were leaving tomorrow with the rest of the guests.

Would Papa let them stay awhile to train me? No, Marcel had to travel to Ceur to answer questions for that horrible inspector. Perhaps Papa could bring in a tutor? That wouldn't be the same.

I found the jar and rubbed the lotion over my hands, slowly working it in, focusing on the unusual roughness of my skin, hoping to drown out the thoughts reverberating through my mind. *The Thief will strike today. The Duke of Lofton promised to take care of the Thief and the sorcerers, but will he succeed? Will the Call take me today? Marcel's leaving. Will I see him again? How will his meeting with the Ceurians go? The Thief will strike today.*

After returning the jar to its place, I scooted out from under the covers and slipped into my dressing gown. Curling up in the cushioned window seat, I watched the storm play out and wondered how this day would end. The duke, through his letter, had entreated me to keep myself safe and within Sterling's reach, and oddly enough, to keep an eye on Marcel. Did he fear the Thief would attempt to steal Marcel's ring? The duke asked Papa to ensure Marcel did not leave with the Ceurians before the end of the celebration tomorrow. I was to keep Papa accountable to that.

While I was considering how to accomplish the duke's requests, my maid came in with a candle, stooping just inside the doorway to pick up something. "What's that, Belinda?"

"A note and a parcel, miss. Someone must have slipped them under your door." She lit a lamp on the mantel, then passed me a folded square of stationery and a long, narrow parcel clumsily wrapped in the same paper before going to make the bed.

My eyes traced the *G* written in a man's script on both, and my heart picked up its pace, seeming to think I was twirling around a dance floor instead of sitting still. Aware of Belinda's presence, I laid the note and parcel on the seat beside me and hurried to dress.

A few minutes later, Belinda paused in arranging my hair. "Does the storm disturb you, my lady?"

"No, why do you ask?"

"You keep looking toward the window."

My gaze darted away from the parcel on the window seat, and I cleared my throat. "And making it difficult for you to do my hair. I apologize. I will be still."

She left a few minutes later, and I returned to the window seat. My hand hovered over the parcel but finally picked up the note. The seal cracked as I slid my thumb under it and unfolded the letter. It bore no signature and only a few sentences: *Yours until your own is returned. It is weak. Use it only in great need. Tell no one.*

The waltz playing in my chest slowed; it wasn't Marcel's handwriting. Curiosity soon overcame the break in my heart's rhythm, however, and I picked up the parcel and tore it open. Dark gold glinted from a break in the tissue wrapping the contents. Slowing my fingers, I carefully stripped off the tissue and then gasped. A gold wand with scarlet markings warmed in my palm.

I stared at it in awe. Who would give me a wand? The Duke of Lofton, of course. A powerful enchanter such as he might have access to a spare wand, for you couldn't buy one. Was that why he went to Florenburg, to pick it up? Thanking him in my heart, I hugged the wand to my chest, relishing in the flow of magic. There was a slight sense of distress in it, though, like a fractured vase. Thunder cracked the air, rattling the windowpanes, but the day seemed less dark.

The first break came and went, but I went nowhere. The rain still poured and lightning threatened to split in two anyone who ventured out. I paced my room, stopping frequently to touch my borrowed wand. Once, I ventured to the library, using my key to get in, to read for a time. I remembered Henry and the duke telling me of the spells on the library's enchanted objects, spells that should stop the Thief. For a while. Nothing seemed able to stop the Magic Thief for good. How would the duke succeed against him? I wanted to help, to do something, but I understood the danger of an interloper in a carefully laid plan.

The storm ceased by noon, though the rain continued, slacking off to a drizzle by mid-afternoon. I left the library and watched the remnant of the storm from one of the windows near a door leading to the gardens. The doorway beckoned, luring me with promises of a world hung with rainbow-laced droplets and scented with the pleasing fragrances released from water-beaten plants in well-tended gardens. And reminded me of a friend who needed attention. I wouldn't risk riding Sterling on the soft, slick ground, but the rain was light enough for me to visit him in the stable, the path to which, conveniently, wound through the gardens.

When I returned from fetching my cloak and gloves, I found Marcel staring out the window at the spot I'd vacated. *Do you take as much pleasure in rain-drenched gardens and storm-cleansed air as I? I have a feeling you do.* But I locked my question away, remembering his danger if the insufferable inspector's men saw us together. But as I prepared to slip away to another exit, my heel clicked against the floor.

"The weather's improved dramatically since this morning, hasn't it, Lady Gabriella?" Marcel's gaze moved from my reflection in the window to me. He smiled, and my heart warmed in response, the anxiety and questions that had plagued me since the morning melting away.

"Yes," I answered, surprised at my reaction to his simple gesture.

"Henry was disappointed he didn't get his usual walk this morning."

"And I my ride." *Did you miss anything?*

An unreadable expression passed over his face, and I had the oddest feeling he was trying not to look at my hands. "Sterling's a magnificent creature."

"I was about to visit him, by way of the gardens." I raised my hood, despising the necessity of running away from Marcel as if he were some criminal. *Sorcerers take Ceurian inspectors with their threats and false accusations.* "If you'll excuse—"

"Gabriella." He stepped to my side and offered me his arm. "May I walk you to the stable?"

"But the inspector ..." I trailed off lest anyone be around to hear.

"Tomorrow is the end of my stay anyway." He tucked my hand into the crook of his arm. "The only thing I have to lose is the pleasure of your company today."

Not allowing for further argument, he ushered me outside. We were soon strolling down my favorite path, though, in truth, it was some time before I truly noticed it. *The only thing I have to lose is the pleasure of your company today.* He delighted in my company. Why did that please me so? A voice whispered the reason was deeper than an inclination for flattery, but I shushed it. Why shouldn't I be glad he didn't consider me a nuisance? Me, the proud enchantress whose very presence could cause him trouble?

"Tell me more about this theft that brought you to the inspector's notice," I said. He told of his cousin and his fateful visit to the inventor-enchanter's house.

"They kept demanding to know how I got into Emil's house," he said. "I used the ring, of course, but I couldn't tell them that. Magical items are forbidden to non-magics there. They would've confiscated it."

"Your ring means more to you than your freedom?"

"I can be very stubborn."

I frowned at him.

"It's too valuable to fall into the hands of the Ceurians. There are too many sorcerers there with too great an influence—they would get it. I couldn't risk that."

"You would use it, as my father suggested, if it came down to it, wouldn't you?"

"I won't give up without a fight, if that's what worries you." The spirit that had shone in his eyes when he'd faced Harvey in the village lit them now. His expression, unclouded by anger this time, cheered me.

"That's good. I wouldn't want Bitsy to be abandoned."

"She'll be well-cared for, I assure you. I have too much fear of, and respect for, a certain enchantress to neglect the pup. I've been pondering her name. What do you think of *Leah*?"

"It's a lovely name. Wasn't she one of the heroines of the Caffin Wars? One of the twins in the story of the broken wands?"

"Yes. That was her."

"Leah," I repeated slowly. "A heroine's name. I approve," I said archly. "Leah it is then."

He laughed, and we walked on. Too soon our walkway gave out and the meadow ahead peeked in through the last archway of the garden path.

"Tell me about this garden," Marcel said, swiftly turning me about so that we faced the gardens again. "Which are your favorite plants? Your favorite paths to walk or benches on which to sit and read? Your favorite statues ..."

I shot him a glare. "You know my *least* favorite statue, but I'll gladly show you the others."

We wandered through the gardens again, talking and laughing. Once, I thought I saw a figure in one of the upstairs windows watching us, but as Marcel said, it was too late to matter anymore. The rain soon began to pitter-patter around us, and we hurried to the shelter of the stable. After talking to Harvey for a few minutes and making arrangements for Leah to be sent to Marcel's family at Silvestris Castle, Marcel left for Papa's last session.

"I'm going to miss that lad," Harvey said as Marcel disappeared out into the misting rain. "Henly's going to be dreadfully dull without him around to stir up trouble."

"Harvey! None of those things were his fault."

The stable master shrugged. "Whatever the cause, he was involved. Go see to your horse. I don't want Sterling causing mischief because he doesn't like to be cooped up when it rains."

"I'll walk him around the stable."

"Good girl," Harvey said before he went off to his work.

After walking Sterling, I went to say goodbye to the puppies before returning to the house. Promising myself I'd only stay a minute, I sat beside Freya and let the puppies clamber into my lap. They yipped as Harvey bellowed at Cox. I hadn't noticed the stable hand since the day Sterling supposedly found me in the meadow. Despite a sudden, strange urge to return to the house, I closed my eyes and tried to remember what happened after I left the stable that day. Voices and the shadows of two men swam at the edge of my mind, but I couldn't draw them to the surface. The mere thought made me nauseous.

Shaking my head, I pulled the brush I'd borrowed from Harvey from my pocket and brushed Freya's coarse fur. The nagging sensation I was forgetting something important wouldn't leave, nor the feeling I should depart the stable. I put aside the brush and stood. I needed to dress for dinner anyway. As soon as I was able, I'd visit the library for the Mirror of Memory. It could reach memories I could not.

When my family and the guests adjourned to the drawing room after dinner, I found myself drawn into Marcel and Tyndale's company. Tyndale discreetly asked about the Sword of Ora, and I assured him it was safe. Marcel gave a lively account of his adventure with the lion, and we laughed over the incident that had once caused so much tension between us.

We shook hands before we separated for the evening, and I wondered if, in the busyness of Papa's celebration, I'd be able to speak with them again. For the first time I could remember, I was sad for the month's end.

Upon leaving the drawing room, I slipped into the library for the Mirror of Memory and smuggled it to my room where I wouldn't be disturbed. Curling up among the pillows at the head of my bed, I placed the ebony mirror in my lap. It warmed in my hand, and an image of Cox working in the stable filled the silver surface. His voice, smooth and oddly cultured for a stable hand's, sounded once more in my ears. I followed my journey along the river path and was surprised to see Tyndale and another gentleman, whom he introduced as his solicitor, Mr. Keldan. I listened to their conversation and felt again the strange nausea, the whispering of a suggestion to go to the cave that was so much stronger than a mere hint. Then I saw the cave, its hidden entrance from the old river path, and heard the man who sounded like the Duke of Lofton. The mirror's surface went blank. My head remembered the sharp discomfort of a blow as a blow of a different kind struck my heart.

I'll not let a danger linger on my property no matter the consequences to myself. The children's safety is first. The words that set me on my path. They were no mere statement: there was magic in them.

They were Tyndale's words.

Didn't he find me at the statue when my wand disappeared? Didn't I know him to be a half-magic? I shook my head against the monstrous accusation. No, Tyndale was not the Thief. He'd never involve himself with the sorcerers. He'd rescued me.

But the mirror didn't lie. Had I not twice seen him go out of his way to avoid the Duke of Lofton? Did I not meet him near the lair's secret entrance that day in the woods? I squeezed the mirror's handle, vainly hoping it would spring to life with some image of Tyndale to confirm his friendship, but none emerged from the jumble of my thoughts. I tossed the mirror aside, and it bounced on the thick bedding before I buried my face in my hands. Was I so very blind and easily misled? Willingly deceived because of his handsome looks and charming manner?

I pushed off the bed and paced the room. No. No, I was not such a fool. It must have been Keldan who planted the suggestion. I would never had sought the cave alone when not under the Call's compulsion unless bespelled and given the subconscious prompt.

But Tyndale brought Keldan here. Leaning against the bedpost, I pressed my cheek against the smooth wood. Perhaps ... perhaps it was by some accident I went to the cave after meeting Tyndale. I bit my lip as an inner voice dared me to face the truth: I was a fool, and Tyndale was the heartless Thief, a friend of sorcerers. I slapped the bedpost, using the sting of my hand to fight a sob. I'd thought Tyndale a friend. A stranger's selfish callousness I could fathom, but not a friend's. How could he count my life of such little value as to damn me to my fate as a Sorcerer's Called? Was I so lacking in worth and likeability?

Blinking away moisture, I picked up the mirror and suffered through the memory twice more, a hollowness growing in my chest each time. I laid the mirror on the bed, gently this time. They'd said the Magic Thief was charming and the master of deception. I could attest to that.

Tyndale, the handsome, charming Magic Thief. A bitter laugh nearly choked me. Swallowing hard, I reached for my handkerchief, but when my fingers touched the soft material, I balled it up and tossed it aside. Floraisons did not wallow in self-pity.

Tyndale was the villain who stole my wand—I *would* get it back. He'd nearly sold my life to the sorcerers—I'd see him hanged before I let him stay free to do that to anyone else.

Pulling my borrowed wand from its pocket, I tapped it against my palm as I paced. Tyndale knew where most of our treasures were, and I'd told him of the Sword of Ora's hiding place myself. By now he'd know how to break the protective spells on them. According to the Duke of Lofton, we couldn't, and shouldn't, stop him from stealing them, for we needed to catch him red-handed. But how would he get them out of the house?

I thought back to the few rumors of the Magic Thief I'd listened to. He'd stolen several items too large to carry out by himself. Therefore, he must have transported them by magic to a nearby location where he could collect them later. Where would that be for this theft? I paused at the window and stared out into the lightless night. What could I do about it even if I knew? I was weak and largely untrained in such matters. Even my borrowed wand was weak.

Growling my frustration in a most unladylike manner, I rang for my maid, then strode to my desk and began shuffling things around with more force than necessary. Where was the letter the duke sent me? I yanked open drawer after drawer until I found the name and address of his contact at the village inn.

Henry had been right that day we talked in the glen: there were thieves and there were murderers, but if pressed by the sorcerers, the thieves would become murderers. Tyndale may have tried to save me once—unless it'd been a ruse to gain my trust—but he'd been in the sorcerer's lair mimicking the duke's voice, I was sure of it. That's where he would send our treasures. What better place than a lair whose surviving entrance was hidden from all eyes but those willed to see it?

Eyes like mine.

And what I had seen was captured in the mirror for the duke to see. For Papa to see. With the mirror's evidence, Papa would have to believe in the Magic Thief.

"Yes, my lady?" Belinda asked as she entered a moment later.

I tossed a heavy cloak onto my bed, beside a riding outfit and the mirror. "Ask my father to meet me in his private study as soon as possible. Also, find out whether Lord Tyndale is still in the house or if he's returned to the village for the night. I don't wish to see him. I simply want to know if he's here."

"I saw Lord Tyndale leave not half an hour ago, my lady, and your father's not here either."

"What?" I cradled my scarred hand against my chest. Papa had to be here. I needed him.

"The physician called him away to help with a delicate surgery," Belinda hastened to explain. "They say he protested but Sir Guy would have none of it. He's the only man alive who can command your father. Mrs. Baxter says it's on account of Sir Guy having once saved the duchess's life."

Reaching out with my free hand, I eased onto my bed, my initial fear being torn apart by concern for the patient and an unreasonable anger that someone got hurt tonight of all nights.

A glimmer of the evening sky peeked through a gap in the window curtains, its dark presence an unwelcome intrusion in my well-lit chambers. Tonight was not the night, if there ever was one, for fear to command me. "Never mind, Belinda," I said, rising. "Find out where Papa has gone and tell Harvey. Ask him to saddle Sterling and a horse for himself."

"Saddle Sterling, my lady?" she asked, aghast.

"Yes, and one more thing." I moved to my desk and dashed off a note to Marcel asking him and Henry to meet me at the stable. I sealed it as she waited patiently beside me. "Deliver this to Henry or Lord Ellsworth."

She recoiled from the letter, but with a stern look, I pushed it toward her. "It's nothing scandalous."

She looked at me dubiously as she took it. "Are you sure you've recovered from your accident the other day?"

"Perfectly," I said through clenched teeth. "Please hurry, Belinda."

Still regarding me strangely, she curtsied, then hurried away. I quickly changed into a riding dress and placed the mirror and the duke's letter into a pocket of my cloak. Fastening the cloak about my shoulders, I passed swiftly down the hallway.

"Gabriella." Mama's voice stopped me as I approached the stairs. "Would you join us in the drawing room?

"Forgive me, Mama, but I must—"

"This won't take long, dearest. Your aunt insists."

An unpleasant sensation settled over me at Mama's pinched expression. Impatience fought with respect, but I followed her into the drawing room. Harvey would need time to prepare anyway.

"Please sit, dear." Mama motioned to a chair and then settled onto the settee next to Alexandria. She folded her hands in her lap. Papa was absent, of course, but Mama, Alexandria, Eva, Uncle Bertram, and Aunt Helene were there. I looked from Mama to Aunt Helene, wishing to get whatever scolding I was in for over with so I could deliver my information.

"Gabriella." Mama looked as uncomfortable as I felt. "I must confess I'm disappointed in your choice of companions of late. The Baron of Carrington is not a suitable friend for a young woman of your status, and we know so little of Lord Tyndale."

"Mama ..." Biting my tongue at her stern look, I pulled my cloak into my lap, placing the concealed mirror on my knees. This was about Marcel? The man who returned a wand to a woman who'd only scorned and blamed him? Unfortunately, I understood their concern over Tyndale.

"I recognize," she continued, raising her hand to Aunt Helene, who looked ready to take over, "that your shared experience with the bandits and the falling tree"—she paused and sighed—"and the explosion in the glen would give you a sense of connection to Lord Ellsworth, but his feelings for you are obvious. It's not kind to encourage him by befriending him."

I stiffened. His feelings were obvious? I'd seen his friendliness and anger and even suspected the tenderness of affection she implied, and vainly had I wanted to prove it to him when he was avoiding me. Yet I'd never taken it seriously, insisting it was nothing more than the friendliness I selfishly wanted it to be.

Breaking from her gaze, I stared at the bunched fabric of my cloak. Her confirmation of Marcel's affection made it real in a way that could not be comfortable. What had I done?

Or had I done wrong in simply getting to know a man who was neither lacking in character nor pledged to another? Would him caring for me, or me for him, be so very terrible?

"In the man's defense," Uncle Bertram said, "I must say it's understandable he would admire her. She does have the beauty, intelligence, and wealth of the Floraisons, but he has no business making it known, being only a poor baron."

Only a poor baron. I huffed. I was only an arrogant Sorcerer's Called.

"All the more reason why she should be careful." Aunt Helene turned on me. "What are you thinking encouraging the man the way you do? Talking to him, walking with him through the gardens as though he were your equal? Who knows who may have seen you? You'll be the tittle-tattle of the household and all the guests. 'Lady Gabriella and the Bumbling Baron of Carrington, favorite of the constable.'"

I bit my lip to keep from striking out in anger. Feeling the passing of every precious second, I scrunched the cloak between my fingers. I *had* to keep quiet. The sooner they had their say, the sooner I could go to the duke's associate. How I wished I could turn Aunt Helene into something without a mouth to condemn with, without a face to show disdain with!

Aunt continued speaking, criticizing Marcel, even blaming him for the incident in the glen and her subsequent humiliation, and then scolding me. But I fought down every reaction until I was numb with the effort. Even for a woman of her age, Aunt Helene was beautiful and graceful, a talented pianist, and often an engaging conversationalist. Yet in that moment I found Marcel's plainness, even his stumbling and stuttering, easier to bear than her beauty and pride.

Tears stung my eyes, and I almost laughed at the irony. *There are two kinds of beauty; beware which one you treasure, for lasting beauty lies within.* Marcel's grandfather had spoken rightly. Catching Alexandria's concerned look, I realized I had murmured the words.

"You can't possibly have formed an attachment to that man," Aunt said.

Oh couldn't I? The question born of rebellion shocked me, and I shoved it aside to be buried along with my anger. Marcel was leaving, and even if he wasn't, he knew my family's opinion of him. He'd never seek to know my own. What did the question matter in the end? I turned away from my aunt.

"That's enough, Helene. I'm sure she understands." Mama shot her sister-in-law a warning look. "Gabriella." Her voice was soft, yet firm. Somehow I knew what she had to say would be worse than Aunt Helene's blustering. "Lord Ellsworth is under suspicion of a serious crime. He may be guilty."

A defense of Marcel nearly broke my resolve to remain quiet, but Mama wasn't watching me. Head bent, she watched the play of light in the diamonds on her wedding band as she nudged the ring back and forth with her fingers. "Even if he's innocent, he might never return. Don't make his leaving any more painful than it has to be." Her fingers stilled, and when she met my gaze, I saw sorrow there.

My throat constricted. "May I go now?"

"Yes." Mama rose, giving me permission to do so as well.

"You're wearing riding clothes," Aunt Helene exclaimed. "Surely you're not going out at this hour?"

I whirled about to face her. "I'm running away with Lord Ellsworth."

"Gabriella." Mama's voice was as sharp as mine had been sarcastic.

Dipping my chin, I turned back to the door. "Forgive me. I must take Sterling for a ride."

Aunt Helene started to object, but Mama stopped her. "Sterling is her horse. If he needs exercise, she is right to go." Her voice softened. "Do be careful, and take Harvey with you."

When I arrived at the stable, Sterling was saddled, but Harvey, as immovable as any mountain, blocked the open stall door.

"Are you going to tell me what this is all about, or do I have to guess?" he said.

Something about his familiar surliness, which so often masked concern, put a crack in my already fragile heart. I wanted to throw my arms around the stable master and weep against his shoulder, but I set my jaw. Tonight was not the night for weeping. Tonight was the night for justice, though the anger burning in my chest felt dangerously like vengeance.

"We're going to The Rose and Thorn." Hanging my lantern on a hook beside the stall door, I eased past Harvey into the stall. "We're going to deliver a message to a friend of the Duke of Lofton's and then find my father." Then the Thief would be captured and punished, the altar destroyed, and Marcel exonerated. And Aunt Helene forced to take back everything she'd ever said about either of us.

Harvey eyed me narrowly. "Is that all?"

"Yes, unless the Duke of Lofton's contact tells us otherwise." I stroked Sterling's neck, focusing on his silky mane and the playful nudge he gave me.

Harvey harrumphed but didn't uncross his arms or move to help me mount Sterling. "Then why was Belinda crying?"

"Crying? I don't—" I sucked in a breath. The note to Marcel. That's what brought about the family meeting. Aunt Helene must have seen Belinda with it, suspected the recipient after seeing Marcel and I walking together in the garden, and confiscated it. Thank goodness she had too much honor to read it.

"As near to weeping as any niece of mine gets in public," Harvey said. "She was carrying on to Mabel and me about the Count and Countess and Lord Ellsworth and how both you and she were in trouble."

With a groan, I leaned my head against Sterling's neck, letting his mane cover my face, and murmured the things I wanted to say but knew shouldn't be spoken aloud.

"I take it the baron was supposed to join us but won't be now?" Harvey said.

With a sigh, I straightened and brushed loose strands of my own hair from my face. "No, Harvey. He won't be. I doubt he ever got the message, and we don't have time to wait for him. I'm sorry Belinda was upset. I'll see that everything is set right."

He nodded, satisfied, and thumbed in the direction of a neighboring stall. "Thunderbolt is saddled and ready, but considering Lord Ellsworth is still in the vicinity, I'd better fetch a gun. Make that two. There's no telling what will happen." He strode away toward the stairs leading to his apartment above the stable.

"Really, Harvey. That was not his fault."

He harrumphed again and kept walking, disappearing into the darkness of the building he knew too well to require light to navigate.

One of Nympha's puppies whined as a door shut behind Harvey. The pup quickly quieted, and the stable fell into the peaceful silence of undisturbed dreams, the quiet flight of mice, and the stalking of the stable cats. And the startling, demanding meow of a plump tomcat I knew well, one that loved nothing better than a rub behind the ear. An icy chill ran down my spine. The tack room, from which the sound had come, should be empty of stable hands for the cat to bully for petting.

A hiss escaped me. The Midnight Ride—not all our treasures were in the house. I stared down the darkened stable, unsure whether to call for Harvey or to hide in Sterling's stall. But if the Thief were here now, there was no need to wait for the duke to act. I'd captured the bandits. I could capture this Thief while he was distracted with breaking the locking spells.

Softly shutting Sterling's stall, I drew my borrowed wand and crept over the straw-covered stones. The stable was a long building divided into two wings by the main doors, which were set opposite one another to create a breezeway on hot summer nights when both were open. Beside the rear doorway was the tack room. With a glance at its door, fast shut and near where Harvey, armed and ready, would soon be coming downstairs, I felt my way to the rear exit and groped for the latch. I found it as the tomcat meowed again. Quickly lifting the latch, I pushed open the door and scooted outside.

The land fell away behind the stable, and at the base of the bank ran a broad strip of forest, the shade of its lofty trees plunging the stable's rear into a deeper darkness than its front. Into that darkness passed a slit of light from the tack room window. I fumbled my way toward it in the scarce moonlight, nearly tripping over flagstones piled near the window. Hardly daring to breathe, I pressed against the side of the building and peered through the tear in the curtains.

In the dimly lit tack room lined with saddles and bridles, Tyndale, with the cat rubbing against his legs, knelt beside a chest emblazoned with the Floraison crest, the only chest family members alone had keys to. I pressed my own set of keys against my side, grateful they hung from my waist in such a way as to not jangle when I moved. Without the counterspell in the keys, the protective spells on that particular chest ought to toss anyone tampering with it across the room and nearly burn the flesh off his hands in the process. Fred, always curious, still had scars from an attempt. But Fred wasn't a half-magic and certainly not the Magic Thief.

Tyndale pressed a strip of cloth against the lock with one hand and pushed against the trunk's side with the flat of his other hand. He pressed, rested for a few seconds, then pressed again, harder. The chest shuddered, and Tyndale sat back, stuffing the cloth into his jacket pocket and wiping a hand across his forehead. The lock fell open. I rued the day half-magics discovered their abilities.

Tyndale removed the lock and opened the lid. Ignoring the non-magical items, he pulled out the Midnight Ride set, the velvet-like horseshoe covers and the bit and bridle with magic worked into them that would give a horse unnatural speed and silence. There would be no catching him if he rode away with those on his horse.

"Gabriella?" Harvey's anxious call escaped the stable. "Gabbie Marie, get back here."

With a glance my way, Tyndale hastily shut the trunk and put out his light. My stomach tightened. He was coming out the window. Putting away my wand, I spun around and reached for one of the old flagstones. My fingers recoiled as an image of Tyndale unconscious on the ground by my hand flashed through my mind.

Growling, I snatched a hand-sized flagstone. *For the safety of Henly.* But I wouldn't hit him harder than necessary, though it was tempting. *Papa will see that justice is—*

Tyndale stood empty-handed across from me, the window at my back.

My grip on the flagstone slackened. What a fool I was! A half-magic senses the presence of an enchanter: he'd known I was there. *Call for help.* But my throat wouldn't cooperate.

Tyndale lunged at me, and my muscles startled to life. I slung the rock at him, crying out for Harvey. The Thief dodged, caught my wrist, and jerked me around into his chest. Pain shot through me as he twisted my arms behind me and clamped a hand over my mouth. I kicked him, and he dug his elbow into my back. He picked me up, raising my feet off the ground, and loped toward the forest.

"Be still," he hissed as I dug my heel into his shin. Then he softened his tone, raspy though it was in his exertion. "I won't take you to the sorcerers, Gabriella. Give me the keys, and I'll leave you."

Liar. I shook my head, trying to dispel his soft voice.

"Don't believe me? Then come with me." His voice soothed despite the danger I knew it carried. "Follow me and catch your Thief." My stomach roiled.

The ground began its downward tilt to the forest. I hooked my foot around his leg and pulled. He swayed, and in my desperate, frantic state, the ground itself seemed to aid me with a sudden, shuddering rumble. Tyndale lost his balance, and we tumbled down the bank. Fallen branches broke underneath me, stabbing me in their vengeance.

From the stable gate, Harvey cried out and Sterling screamed. Other horses whinnied in reply, from the stable and the forest. Tyndale leapt up almost as soon as we landed, but instead of running, he grabbed for my keys. A shot cracked the air, and a bullet whistled as it flew over my head. Tyndale yelped and dove beside me.

"Touch her and you die," Harvey shouted.

Tyndale clutched my hand and whispered, "Catch me if you can. Prove yourself to your family."

With the grace of a cat, he sprang up. I rolled flat on my stomach and snagged his trouser leg, but he kicked me off and dashed into the shadows. I almost thought he called after me.

Harvey fired his second pistol. Tyndale pivoted and fell backward to the ground. The rolling light of a shield spell flared in front of him, and a nearby sapling shook as the redirected bullet struck it. Again, he jumped up and lost himself among the trees, but the shadows played tricks on me, making him seem shorter, stouter, and less agile than before.

"Go back to the house, Gabriella," Harvey yelled, gun in hand, as he jogged down the bank, picking up speed as the bank leveled off to meet the forest floor.

"Not till he's caught. He would've sent me to the sorcerers." Sterling skidded to a halt beside me as I gained my feet. A wave of nausea hit me. Pressing a hand to my stomach, I steadied myself against Sterling's side. My heart pounded with a mix of fear and fury and Floraison determination that left me shaking when the nausea passed. I snatched Sterling's loose reins and swung up into the saddle. "I must catch the Thief."

"Gabbie Marie." The warning in Harvey's voice stopped me from digging my heels into Sterling's sides. "Use your sense, girl, and wait for me." Reloading his pistol as he went, he hurried back toward the stable and Thunderbolt.

But I had Sterling and the air felt clear. And I had a wand. "He has a horse hidden in the forest. We can't wait." I prodded Sterling with my heels. "Hurry after me, Harvey."

Sterling plunged into the forest, where moonlight was little more than a memory. Trees with low, swooping limbs attempted to hem us in, and I leaned into Sterling, ducking under their branches, zigzagging to find the best way through until the stable was lost and only woods surrounded us. Though I strained to see, I pushed Sterling to go faster. The Thief couldn't have gotten that far. I would catch him. I would prove myself to my family. *Catch me if you can.*

My stomach roiled as it had the day I'd walked into the cave. With a gasp, I reined in Sterling. What had I done? Oh heavens. What had I done?

Chapter 19

Before the dagger struck home, he looked into his brother's eyes and knew the truth: The sorcerers had learned the Spell of Imitation. His brother's murderer would become his own.

The Fall of Bevvelian by Edgar Frock

MARCEL ELLSWORTH

I WANTED TO punch someone. But I couldn't decide whether it should be Inspector Olan or the Magic Thief. Or Jonathan Lofton.

I paced around my chambers, which had never felt so small and constricted. "I can't believe he convinced the Duke of Henly to have me locked in my room. Tonight of all nights!"

"What would've been the point on the other nights?" Henry said nonchalantly. I glared at him over my shoulder. Undisturbed, he continued packing.

"Tonight of all nights, I *can't* leave," I murmured, and then prayed Gabriella would never need to use my ring in its weakened form of a gold wand.

I finally picked up a book and slumped onto a chair, yet concentration eluded me. What was happening in the library? Was Gabriella safe? I jumped up at a knock on the door. Reaching the door before Henry, I tried the handle before remembering it was locked from the outside. The head butler's keys jangled in a mortifying tune before the door opened halfway and his balding pate appeared.

"Forgive me, Lord Ellsworth." Despite the polite tenor of his words, his expression pinched as if he were observing a mangy stray. "These gentlemen have come to … see you." He sniffed and then swung open the door. Assistant Inspector Chead and Mr. Polad flanked him.

The time had come. My feet stuck to the floor, and I stared at Chead's stoic face, trying to find the courage I'd put aside for this moment. Alas, if courage could be counted in coins, there'd barely be a rattle in the bank of my heart.

Swallowing hard, I held out my hand to greet them. "Good evening, gentlemen." *When at a loss, be polite,* Aunt Coraline always said.

Chead glanced at my hand before taking it hesitantly. "Good evening." He took in Henry and the room. "Are you packed?"

"I have a small bag packed that will do. My servant will take care of the rest." I gestured from Mr. Polad to the bag at the foot of my bed. Doubtless, they would want to search it for weapons or items of enchantment. "I am ready when you are."

Not wanting to see the expression on my old friend's face, I strode to the hallway without looking back. "I'll write you instructions, Henry. Greet my family for me." *Watch over Gabriella tonight.*

Chead hurried to catch up with me as I led the way, jogging down the stairs and nearly running into the duchess as I entered the main hallway.

"Forgive me," I stammered, stumbling to a halt with Chead bumping into me. Polad caught up to us, my bag at his side.

E.J. Kitchens

"Lord Ellsworth." Something like sorrow flashed through the duchess's eyes. Then her expression shuttered and a calm politeness took its place. "You aren't staying for the celebration tomorrow?"

"Circumstances will not allow me to, I'm afraid." Ignoring the men beside me, I rushed on with a request before I could convince myself otherwise. "May I have a moment of your daughter's time?"

Her delicate, dark brows drew together. "I'm sorry, Lord Ellsworth, but Gabriella is out."

"Out!" If anyone needed to be locked in a room tonight, it was Gabriella. Didn't they care that she was a Sorcerer's Called?

The duchess drew herself up, and her eyes, one sapphire and one emerald, flashed up at me. "Yes, she is *out*. She's exercising Sterling."

"With Sterling—thank heavens," I muttered, scrubbing a hand over my face. *An Ellsworth handles every situation with confidence and poise.* I gave the duchess an apologetic smile. "Forgive me. I'm a bit on edge tonight."

A strange mix of expressions clouded her face as she nodded her acceptance. "I will tell her you wish her a goodbye."

"I appreciate your kindness, and I hope you'll forgive me one more request. I know the duke is from home, and Henry has a note for him that explains things better, but I would like to ask you in his stead.

"I may be away for some time, and the duke has expressed an interest in the plans for Carrington and for using it as a case study for his lectures. Lady Gabriella also asked to use its history and improvements in her book. Might I be so bold as to ask if the duke would consider overseeing it while I'm away? I don't expect much direct oversight, for I have an excellent steward now and know the duke has numerous responsibilities, but if he would occasionally check on it, I would be most grateful. I'm certain Lady Gabriella would be happy to assist him, if he wished. I believe she would enjoy the opportunity and responsibility."

That odd mix of expressions came over the duchess's face again, a bit of shock quickly hidden beneath inscrutable thoughts. "I will speak with him about it." She held out her hand, and I took it in mine.

"That's all I can ask of you. You are most kind."

"If you'll excuse us, my lady," Chead interrupted, "the carriage is waiting out front."

Releasing her hand, I bowed. "Goodbye, Duchess."

"Goodbye, Lord Ellsworth."

Following Chead and flanked by Polad, I marched to the door, halting at a word from the duchess.

"Lord Ellsworth." Her face was drawn in concern. "May your trip be short and safe."

The carriage sloshed along the village lane. Seated across from Chead and Polad, I kept my hands folded in my lap, an odd sense of gratitude that they hadn't handcuffed me settling in my chest.

Not much was visible out the square window in the little light from the carriage's swinging lanterns, but I had a feeling we were nearing the spot where Gabriella and Harvey had accosted my kidnappers. If it would help in the long run, I'd wish they'd do it again.

I rotated my forearm, the makeshift wand harness and that ridiculous toy wand chafing my skin. Henry didn't say exactly what Lofton had done to the toy he'd made me promise to hang on to, but he'd hinted Lofton had infused it with enough magic to do damage. As long as it didn't do damage to me, it might come in handy if I needed to break out of a Ceurian prison. Henry also said it had been set to respond to me alone, so I couldn't give it to Gabriella.

The carriage suddenly braked, flinging me forward into Polad. He cursed as Chead yelled at the coachman. Somehow his anger slowed my racing heart—it wasn't the terror of a man who sees a wreck coming. Pressing back unwelcome memories, I fought to decipher the coachman's reply over the chorus of shouts and horses' neighs.

Grabbing the seat edge, I held on as the carriage slammed to a halt. Apparently one abduction wasn't enough for a visit to Henly Manor. Was it too much to hope this one was for my freedom?

Chead pulled out a pistol and kicked open the carriage door. As fast as a striking snake, a garden hoe whipped inside and knocked Chead's gun aside and then thwacked both him and Polad in the side of the head. The formidable weapon retreated as the two collapsed onto the seat. I tensed for another strike from this strange serpent, but none came.

A broad shouldered, dark-haired man in simple clothes stuck his head in the doorway. Even if he'd still had his patchy beard, his would be one of my favorite faces from now on.

"Cox! What the blazes are you doing? Did Harvey send you?" At some point, I must go to Ceur, but tonight, I wanted to make sure Gabriella was safe and Lofton successful.

The stable hand grabbed my sleeve and pulled me out of the carriage. "No, the Duke of Lofton did." He pushed me toward a horse.

"Lofton?" Taking the reins in one hand, I swung into the saddle, then gave my hat a thump, pressing it down in preparation for the ride.

"You don't think he planned to catch the Thief alone, did you?" One of the coach's lanterns in his hand, Cox clumsily mounted his horse.

Laughing, I replied, "He didn't seem to want my help." In vain, I looked around for Gabriella and Sterling. "Say, Cox, have you seen a woman on a large horse anywhere abouts?"

"No, and we don't have time to look for one. This way. Duke's orders." Cox kicked his horse and shot off through the darkness, the lantern sloshing an eerie glow about him.

Chapter 20

There is no hiding from a half-magic, for magic is as a scent to them. Such is the claim of proponents of this legend. Yet a clever woman may guess which among her brothers and sisters is an enchanter, and a well-trained man may discern the presence of a hidden foe. No special power is required for what keenness of mind and the physical senses can tell.

Half-Magics: Only a Legend by Charles Floraison, 10th Duke of Henly

GABRIELLA FLORAISON

HARVEY!" SEIZING MY wand, I lit up the woods. Darkness did me no favors, for Tyndale was a half-magic. My power of enchantment betrayed me to him. What a rash, rash fool I was to run after him! A bespelled fool. And since it was a spell and not the Call, Sterling couldn't help me. "Harvey!" I cried again.

Catch the Thief. The command pulled at me. I clenched my hands around Sterling's reins, resisting the urge to dash further in after my quarry. I needed a way out, but the thick trees, many full evergreens, gave nothing away. No Thief, no stable, no Harvey. *A Floraison can handle any situation with confidence and poise.* Even calamities they caused themselves. I visualized a map of Henly, noting the shape of the forest. Unless I lost my sense of direction along with my common sense when I raced into the woods, the stable should be on my right.

"Right. Ride to the right," I murmured and directed Sterling that way. We rode a few paces, and then I found us heading deeper into the forest again. I pulled Sterling's head toward the right and dug my heels into his side. "Out, Sterling. Go!"

"This way, Gabriella." Sterling slowed at a man's call. Or did I slow him?

"Gabbie Marie, get back here."

"This way, Gabriella."

"Harvey?" I spun Sterling around, trying to find the sources of the two voices.

"Gabbie Marie?"

"Harvey!" Fighting the tug of the Thief's command, Sterling and I dove back through the trees toward the stable master's voice. Then the ground shuddered. My head swam and the trees whirled and rearranged. Sterling neighed and reared, and I slipped off, the air leaving me in a rush as I thudded to the leaf-littered forest floor. The wand rolled from my grasp. Above me, the treetops still twirled, their bare limbs or evergreen needles highlighted by a sliver of moon.

When the air returned to my lungs and the forest ceased its motion, I flung myself over and felt for my wand. Sterling whinnied from somewhere behind, and I knew he was cut off from me. Soft footsteps approached. I didn't need to look up to know whose they were.

"Let me touch your hand, Lady Gabriella," Tyndale said.

Don't ever let a half-magic touch you. By touch he casts or takes spells, warned *The Fall of Bevvelian*.

"Never." I reached out desperately, crushing leaves and brushing stubby woodland plants away. Where was it?

"Please let me touch you. You've been bespelled."

"I wonder by whom." After one final, fruitless search for my borrowed wand, I sprang up and faced him. "Give me my wand, Thief."

Tyndale, the bridle of the Midnight Ride thrown over his shoulder, took one step closer. "No."

I edged away, but the circular clearing kept me always near its center. I curled my scarred finger protectively against my palm. "Give it to me," I demanded, forcing more courage into my voice than I possessed.

"No." He circled after me as I moved away. "Not now."

With a sardonic laugh, I dared a glance at the forest floor for the wand. "You'll give it to me if I follow you to the sorcerer's altar? Is that the promise now?"

"I didn't send you to the cave. Please believe me. Please let me touch your hand. I can help."

"Help me to my doom, you mean. Thanks, but I'd rather you didn't."

"Gabriella, please listen—"

Gold shimmered beneath a withered fern a few feet away. He caught the motion of my eyes, and we darted forward at the same time. But instead of going for the wand, I threw myself at him, both surprising him and knocking him off balance. We toppled. I sprang up and snatched the wand.

"Get back," I warned, pointing the wand at him as he sprang up. An acute awareness that I had no idea what I could do against a half-magic, who could capture the power of a spell and use it however he liked, didn't stop my desperate attempt at bravado. *Where are you, Harvey?*

But Tyndale drew back, alarm on his face. "Where did you get that?"

"From a true friend. Now, give me my own wand."

"It's not one of your sisters'?"

"It's none of your concern." *Catch the Thief.* I dug my fingernails into my palm. I would. No, no. I wouldn't. Or would I? I shook my head, trying to focus on the Thief in front of me.

"I ask you again: where did you get that? Floraison wands are silver not ... gold and scarlet." His voice shook.

I pressed my lips together.

"The fool," he cursed. Gunshot split the air, and we both ducked. Tyndale hissed with pain and grasped his upper arm. He knelt with one hand flat on the ground, the other touching the blue Amphora hanging from a chain about his neck. *My* Amphora.

The earth groaned, and Harvey cried out. Fear seized me. I spoke the stone spell at Tyndale, not caring it would be but a momentary diversion for a half-magic. Praying that moment might be enough for Harvey. Tyndale snagged the air like a boy snagging a ball in flight. His fisted hand paled to gray. He opened his fist. The gray melted back to the color of flesh.

He turned his angry gaze to me, and the ground shook beneath me. My legs gave way, and I collapsed. I scrambled to get up, to take steady aim at him, but the shaking sent me reeling onto my back. The Amphora was only supposed to open the glen. What was he doing to it?

Follow me. Catch the Thief and prove yourself to your family. "Stop!" I screamed as much to him as to the voice in my head.

Tyndale stood slowly, clutching his bleeding shoulder. "When you put up that wand that is not yours."

"No." I tried to capture him in a vine, but he tossed it away, sending it back to its tree, and took another step toward me.

"Please, Gabriella. I haven't much time."

"It's *Lady* Gabriella to you, Thief."

A jolt sent me into the air. I fell back with a thud that knocked the breath from me and the wand from my hand. The ground dipped around me, leaving me in a crater and my wand above the crater's lip. I reached for it, and the earth rippled from the border of trees toward me. I crawled back and scrambled to get out of the depression, but roots shot out of the ground, spraying dirt and bits of rock, and clamped around my arms and skirt, dragging me flat against the dark soil of the crater.

Tyndale fell to his knees beside the crater. It flattened out, and I was beside him, free but unable to move from shock. He took my hand between both of his. Nausea rose up, and I heaved, but nothing came. The nausea left.

"Tyndale, I'll get in there," Harvey bellowed, the sound beautiful to my ears.

Tyndale squeezed my hand and tugged it toward him in a manner that instinctively made me face him. "Listen to me, Gabriella. Take Sterling and Harvey and go to the glen tonight. Lock yourselves in, and don't let anyone in. Not Ellsworth or Lofton or anyone you think you know. Especially not me."

"Do you honestly think I'd listen to you?" I trembled too much from exhaustion and shock to fight back as Tyndale took the Mirror of Memory from my cloak's pocket. "After you sent me to the lair yourself? You know what could've happened to me. Why did you do it?"

"I—"

Sterling neighed, and the tightly woven trees shook as he and Harvey pressed against them. Tyndale looked back at me, his gaze boring into mine with an intensity I'd not seen there before. "Go to the glen."

I glared at him, hoping he saw all the enmity and disdain I felt for him. Something that might have been pain deepened the lines of his face. He ran a finger down my cheek, his touch and look as tender as a lover's, yet I wasn't certain I was the one he saw.

"I have some honor left," he said. Then his gaze snapped back into focus, and he drew back. "Please trust me."

He pressed my hand again, then snatched up the fallen bridle and dashed to the edge of the clearing. Clutching where the bullet had grazed his upper arm, he brushed aside a limb, and the trees spun once more, knocking me flat again.

When the world stilled, I was beside a pine's scaly trunk, a fallen cone poking my side. Harvey and Sterling stared at me from a few feet away. Tyndale was gone.

Harvey pulled me to my feet, and I clung to him and cried against his chest, sobbing disgracefully about how I should have listened to him. He patted my back and gruffly agreed I'd acted a fool. Then he pushed me away and walked off. Taking that as a cue to get a hold of myself, I pulled out a handkerchief and dried my eyes.

"I'll be a monkey's uncle." Kneeling beside a sapling, he held the gold wand in one hand and the Mirror of Memory in his other.

As if the horses had wings on their heels, we flew down the village lane, thundering past a carriage bound for Henly. The pounding reminded my head of my previous injury, the night's adventures, and our reason for the ride to the village. Harvey agreed we must get word to the Duke of Lofton and that once we returned I would remain with him and Sterling at the stable for the night.

Slathered in foam, Sterling huffed as we reined in at The Rose and Thorn. A surprised groom met us and took the horses to get cooled down and curried off as Harvey and I hurried into the inn. I started to raise my hood to avoid being recognized, but with Harvey's presence, I couldn't avoid it. A Floraison lady visiting the inn at night, and in such dirt-streaked attire? Not even Marcel's ploy could cause as much gossip.

"My lady." The innkeeper bowed as he greeted us, his eyes bulging. "How may I help you?"

"I have an urgent message from Henly for one of your guests." I held out the letter and let him read the name on the envelope.

His face reddened. "Forgive me, my lady, but he specifically asked not to be disturbed."

"I understand. You are a considerate innkeeper, but I must insist. He would want to see me. My message cannot wait until the morning."

The innkeeper sputtered something, and Harvey ground his teeth and stepped forward, lowering his voice. "This gentleman's helping us in a plot to catch more of the bandits. There was a ... er ... mishap earlier"—he looked pointedly at me—"and we must let him know. The duke's away assisting with a surgery, or he would've come."

Relief stole over the innkeeper's face, and then mine flushed as I realized what he must have been thinking. "This way, my lady." He led us upstairs, and I noted the private stairwell leading out of the inn to the alley beside it. He indicated the third door and then excused himself.

When the innkeeper had disappeared down the stairs, Harvey rapped on the door. A man about my own age answered, cracking the door only enough to show his face, which was a handsome one. The young man, though with midnight eyes and darker-toned skin than the Duke of Lofton, favored my old friend, even in his keen gaze as he examined us and the rest of the empty hallway.

I stepped forward. "I have a message for Jonathan Lofton."

"You must be Lady Gabriella." His mouth quirked into a half-smile at my evident surprise. "I was told you might appear. Do come in." He opened the door the rest of the way and moved aside for us to enter.

"And you are?" Harvey touched a hand to my arm, stilling me.

He flashed a cocky smile. "Jonathan." Ignoring Harvey's growl, he motioned for us to enter the room. "Christened after someone we both know."

Harvey moved me behind him. "Wait here." Glaring a warning at the stranger, he walked in ahead. To our host's amusement, Harvey inspected the room and then waved for me to enter.

When the door shut behind us, the young Jonathan's expression sobered, as did mine when I noticed the room was empty save for a small suitcase resting on the floor and a stained travel cloak thrown over a chair.

"The Duke of Lofton isn't here," he said. "What can I do for you?"

Pulling the ebony mirror from my cloak's pocket, I wondered at my situation. The young man was either an associate of the duke's or, if the duke's letter had been a fraud, was in league with our enemies. If the latter, he already knew what I had to reveal. "You know how to reach him, don't you?"

"Perhaps." That cocky grin returned.

"I have reason to believe the Magic Thief will make use of a sorcerer's lair in a local cave tonight. I can show you the lair's secret entrance in the mirror. I believe the duke has searched for the entrance before but to no avail."

His eyes narrowed as he examined the mirror. "A Demandez à Voir mirror will not reveal a sorcerer's entrance, Lady Gabriella."

"This is not an ask-to-see mirror, but the Mirror of Memory, and I've seen the entrance myself. The mirror will reveal it to me."

The young Jonathan's eyes flashed. He swiftly pulled up a chair for me, slinging his traveling coat off it and onto the bed. "I'll hold you to that boast. Please sit."

As I complied, he and Harvey positioned themselves on either side of me. "Mirror of"—I blinked against glaring sunlight—"Memory, a memory I ask ..."

Were those men's voices coming from the mirror? In it, several of Papa's guests walked down a lane near the meadow. They laughed, and a chuckle rumbled deep but sad in response, and the mirror shook with it. It was a man's chuckle.

"That's not—" I began, but stopped as my throat constricted. Would all my efforts tonight be in vain? The mirror bewitched, some memory of Tyndale's given to prevent me from showing mine? Exhaustion, and the sense of despair so often coupled with it, dropped onto me like another cloak as Sterling's neigh echoed from the mirror. It was the cry of a Pyren to his Called.

The men around the memory-giver exclaimed and pointed, and he followed their gaze. Through the trees, Sterling could be seen trotting into the meadow, saddled but loose, tossing his mane like he does when he's frustrated.

The memory-giver's breath caught, and he ran toward Sterling.

"Where are you going?" someone called after him. "Leave the horse to the stable master," another said. "You'll never catch him, Tyndale."

Closing my eyes, I turned the mirror over, my movements heavy and slow. "Harvey, is it possible to use a memory to block another's access to the mirror?"

"Magic mirrors are beyond my reckoning, Gabbie Marie." Harvey rested a hand comfortingly on my shoulder.

"Whose memory is that?" Young Jonathan asked, his tone laced with suspicion.

"A guest of my father's: Lord Tyndale. At least that's the name he gives."

"Please," Young Jonathan begged as I started to rise. "Let me see the rest."

I wanted to protest but was too weary to do so. Seating myself, I held the mirror once again where the three of us could watch it.

Tyndale rode Sterling hard toward the cave's main entrance. Leaving Sterling outside the gate, he lit a torch and hurried through the cave's main chamber, stopping only to pull a rope from behind one of the two large barrels. He ran to the pit and slung the rope onto a torch holder attached to the wall midway across the pit. With the rope secured, he swung across and then attached the end of the rope to another holder, one of many along the path. "Let me be in time," he breathed as if in prayer. "Please let me be in time."

"Can mirrors be made to lie?" I asked.

"Yes," Young Jonathan said. He added softly, "But I pray this one wasn't."

Some distance down the tunnel, Tyndale left the torch and ran on, feeling his way until he crossed a brick wall.

I heard my own voice and the one that sounded like the duke's. Beside me, Young Jonathan stiffened.

Tyndale moved forward without a sound, guided toward me in the dark by his half-magic's ability to sense enchanters and enchantresses. Somehow, I sensed it too through the mirror and knew I stood before the altar.

"No!" Tyndale screamed. He sprang, his head knocking into mine. Then I fell back against the wall, hitting my head against it and crumpling to the floor beneath him. Tyndale lifted me into his arms and carried me back the way he came.

The glow of a lantern cast new shadows around the lair. "Leave her," the other man cried as he rushed at Tyndale.

"Keep away, Damien," Tyndale warned, the fierceness of his voice a shock to me.

Heedless, Damien pressed forward. "I need her. What's one less pretty face flaunting her power of enchantment? Give her back."

Cradling me to his chest, Tyndale kicked the shorter man in the thigh and thrust him backward. Hurriedly but gently, he settled me into a corner made from the cave wall and the partially fallen brick partition. Just as he straightened, Damien barreled into him. He shoved him off, but the shorter man grabbed him. They fell to the floor, grappling.

Tyndale got in a punch and broke free. He backed toward me, crouched and tense, as the other man rose. "I'll kill you before I let you give her or anyone else to the sorcerers. I swear it, Damien."

"Would you really, *brother*?" Damien taunted as he stalked toward Tyndale. "You'll have to then because I've made my choice. I don't need you anymore. They've promised me the power of enchantment—Emil Farro's invention will give it to me."

"They always promise that. Lies are all they give."

"You've lived on lies for the past fifteen years and never complained."

Tyndale growled low in his throat, and Damien lunged. Tyndale lithely stepped aside, grabbed Damien by the collar, and threw him down.

Damien landed roughly, panting, and clumsily righted himself. "'Teach me the ways of the elite half-magics, David.'" Damien mimicked a high, pleading voice. "'My talent's not equal to yours, but it would distract you from your grief.'" He huffed out a laugh as he rose. "And you fell for it. David, the handsome, the rich, the talented—a gullible fool."

"Save your breath," Tyndale warned.

Damien inched forward, herding Tyndale toward my corner. "Doesn't it bother you? Or is it merely Lady Gabriella who brought you to your senses at last? Her blonde hair and nightingale's voice remind you of someone? Does she stir up feelings you swore never to have again?"

"Shut up, Damien, or I'll—"

"Or you'll what?" Damien said contemptuously, moving dangerously close to Tyndale. "I heard your promise to my sister as she lay dying—your promise to look after me—and I've made the most of it."

Damien sprang, but Tyndale caught him, and together they fell. Damien's head smashed against the cave floor, and he went limp. A small cry escaped Tyndale. He knelt beside Damien and felt for a pulse, his shoulders sagging in relief as he found it. Quickly, he patted Damien's pockets, felt his sleeves, and pulled a wand from his cuff. He slipped the wand into his own jacket pocket, picked up the lantern, and hurried back to me.

He knelt beside me and gently brushed my hair from my face. "Forgive me, Gabriella. For once, this isn't for him, for that stupid promise. It's to catch the Magic Thief and destroy this place and its sorcerers—at the proper time." He covered my eyes with his hand, and I had a sense he was putting some spell on me. "You won't remember this afternoon, Lady Gabriella, and you will avoid Damien's company." Tyndale lifted me into his arms and carried me out of the cave to Sterling. The memory ended.

"I shot him," Harvey said, his tone a mix of shock and remorse.

"You grazed his arm," I corrected, not sure whether I was disappointed it was only Tyndale's arm or relieved.

"*David*," Harvey mused. It galled me he accepted the man's innocence so readily. Hadn't Tyndale and Keldan bespelled me to go to the cave? Hadn't he tried to kidnap me behind the stable? What if this "memory" was another act of deceit, the product of a bewitched mirror?

"His name is David Ashby." Young Jonathan's eyes shimmered. "Nephew of the Duke of Lofton, and he's not dead." He huffed out a breath that was almost a laugh. "And he's not the Magic Thief."

"But he had the Amphora," I protested, "the Midnight Ride, and he admitted having my wand. You saw him take it from Damien. He never returned it to me."

"Then he had his reasons," Young Jonathan said sharply.

"He left you the gold wand and the mirror," Harvey said softly.

I glared at them both before lifting the mirror again. "Let's not forget why we came." I called upon the mirror to show my memory of the cave's entrance.

Young Jonathan stood dutifully beside me, his gaze fastened on the mirror, but I doubted he was watching it with the attention it merited. He had a smile of quiet joy on his face I didn't quite like.

Swallowing hard, I rubbed my arm, the grit of dirt reminding me of the strange circle in the forest, of the Tyndale with the stolen tack and the empty-handed Tyndale who'd bespelled me to follow him—the one who'd appeared to shorten after using a spell to shield himself from Harvey's bullet.

How could David Ashby not be the Magic Thief? How could he be the one who saved me and the one who put me in danger?

The memory of my trip to the tunnel played out without me realizing it.

"At the very least you can use the dropped hammer as a marker for the lair's entrance." Harvey picked up the blank mirror from my lap. "All those vines and trees look the same to me."

"Who is Damien then?" I asked. Could he be Mr. Damien *Keldan?* The memory was too dark to tell.

"Brother-in-law to David Ashby," Young Jonathan replied.

"What's he like?"

"I don't know. I never met him. They said he was a talented actor but didn't have the looks to play the only role he wanted, that of the leading man. He wanted too much to be famous and admired."

I thought back to my meeting with Tyndale and Keldan. Tyndale was quite handsome, and Keldan, with the right haircut, would have something of a rugged handsomeness that would suit the stage if he had the acting skills to match. Keldan also put me in mind of the people of Tormir. Damien wasn't Keldan. Then who was Keldan?

"Who is Damien pretending to be here?" I asked.

"That no one has told me." Young Jonathan offered his hand and helped me rise. "But as you said"—he stepped away, his tone turning merry as he surged into motion—

"your mission was to provide knowledge, and you've done so admirably."

He snatched his travel cloak from the bed, slung it over his shoulders, and then took my hand with a bow. "You are as full of information as you are beautiful, Lady Gabriella. I only wish we'd met under pleasanter circumstances. If you'll excuse me, I have vital news to convey." He kissed my hand and then rushed out, his footsteps light as he jogged down the private stairwell.

My lips twitched as I watched him go. Doubtless, the elder Jonathan would not be pleased I'd given his young relative an excuse to leave the safety of the inn. But at least someone was enjoying the evening's adventures.

I scrubbed my arms as if I could dust off the night's events. The duke told me all I needed to do was look after myself and Marcel. I'd failed with regard to myself. I could only hope the Ceurians hadn't tried to take Marcel while Papa and I were gone.

I smiled despite myself and wished Marcel and Henry were here to talk over the night's occurrences with. They could tell me if the mirror had been bewitched with a false memory.

I took Harvey's arm and guided him toward the front stairway. "Come. Let's hurry home."

"I thought you wanted to find your father?"

"He may have returned by now. Besides, I know someone else who can help."

Harvey eyed me a moment, then surprised me with a wink. "And the nosy Countess will have gone home. Just bring Ellsworth out to the stable where I can keep an eye on him and hear what he has to say."

Chapter 21

Never underestimate your enemies. Or your friends.

The Art of War with Magic, a tactical handbook from the
Caffin Wars, by General Aiden Floraison

GABRIELLA FLORAISON

MY RIDING DRESS hung heavy and damp, weighted by the muddy water slung from the horses' hooves, as Harvey and I walked the horses back into the stable.

"If you'll go upstairs"—Harvey nodded toward his apartment above the stable—"Mabel will help you clean up. She's got a dress of yours up there that she's mending."

With a laugh, I brushed wild hair from my face. "Do I look such a fright?"

"Well, some would say you've got a becoming color to your cheeks."

Noting his pointed look as he took Sterling's reins, I wiped a hand across my cheek and came away with mud smearing my fingers. "You mean Aunt Helene would have a conniption if she saw me. 'A Floraison never looks like that: wet and muddied and red-cheeked,'" I mimicked.

He huffed a laugh. "Yep, and the duchess would scold me for letting you get cold."

"In that case, I hope your wife won't mind the intrusion."

"Mabel never minds you, you know that. Now, go on up. I'll see to the horses and fetch Ellsworth myself."

Shivering in my damp dress, I approached the stairs, stopping short at the sight of the tack room. There were two sets of the Midnight Ride. I detoured to the tack room and found the trunk marked with the family crest back where it should be and locked. After choosing the proper key from my set, I unlocked the trunk and rummaged through its contents. Inhaling the scent of leather, I picked up the bridle belonging to the second Midnight Ride set. Tyndale hadn't taken everything, only one set. *Then he had his reasons*, Young Jonathan had said. Or perhaps he left it because he knew Harvey and I were about to find him. I replaced the bridle, locked the trunk, and went upstairs.

Mabel greeted me affectionately, exclaimed over my cold hands, and sent me to her bedchamber with a basin of warm water, a towel, and my own mended gown to change into.

When I was presentable, I joined her in the kitchen for a wonderfully warm cup of tea.

"I don't know what's taking that husband of mine so long to see to the horses," she said later as she offered me a second cup. "But as I was saying, I don't hold with telling falsehoods, but when the footman came to ask about the gun shots, I told him my husband was aiming at 'some thief preying too close to the house.' 'A wolf?' he asked. 'I can't say either way,' I said. That seemed to satisfy him."

I squeezed her work-roughened hand. "Thank you, Mabel. It would be complicated and unpleasant to explain what happened. Do you know if Papa's returned?"

"Oh yes. Let's see." She paused as she added sugar to her tea, her forehead wrinkling in thought for a brief moment before smoothing out. "I'd say not half an hour before you did. I took care of his horse myself. He got back, and before that, Lord Ellsworth left, or so the footman told me."

My teacup clinked as it collided with the saucer. "Left? With the Ceurians?"

"I don't know, my dear. The footman said it was quite a scandal, for he left with not one but two men of the law, one an assistant inspector. But I don't half credit what that man says."

"When was this?"

"Let's see. I heard a carriage roll in half an hour or so after you and Harvey left, but when they didn't come here, I forgot about them."

"This was while my father was absent, wasn't it?" Papa promised to keep Marcel here until after the Duke of Lofton had a chance to catch the Thief. Papa would have to do something.

"To be sure. It's a pity the young lord had to leave before the celebration, and without his pup."

Rising, I set aside my cup and saucer. "If you'll excuse me, Mabel, I must speak with Papa."

"Of course, dear," she said, a bewildered smile on her pleasant, round face. She rose and followed me to the door. "Shall I walk with you to the house?"

"I'll be fine. I'll take a lantern." I kissed her on the cheek. "Thank you for everything."

"You're more than welcome, love." She hugged me and watched me down the stairs before closing her door.

A cold wind swept through the gardens, and I brought the lantern closer to me for its little warmth. I picked up my pace, my boot heels clicking against the paving stones, my thoughts alternating between raging at myself for not keeping Marcel here and praying for his safety.

"Lady Gabriella," whispered a masculine voice.

Sucking in a breath, I spun around. The walk was empty except for shadowed corners and tree-sheltered crannies my lantern could not illuminate.

"Gabriella?" The low whisper was unrecognizable.

I ground my teeth, furious at my thudding heart and this fool's game of hide-and-seek. "I do not speak with disembodied spirits. If you desire my attention, reveal yourself."

The chuckle following my declaration was dearly familiar.

"Marcel?" I spun again, searching for him. My lantern's golden glow tangled in the limbs and needles of the cedar hiding the alcove with the bench to which Marcel had once sent me.

"Yes, but you'll have to forgive me for remaining *disembodied*," he said with humor in his voice as I hurried around the cedar and then stopped short. He stood beside the bench in the tree's shadows.

"Mabel told me you'd gone," I said, straining to keep my relief from being blatantly obvious.

"I couldn't leave without saying goodbye." He stepped in front of the bench and held out his hand.

Goodbye. A smile faded from my lips as I took his hand and let him guide me to a seat on the bench. "Mabel said the inspectors ..."

"Yes, I'm afraid so. I've already left, officially, that is. The Ceurians took me away this evening, but I managed to sneak back. That's why I can't reveal myself in the house, why I must stay disembodied." He smiled but didn't look me in the eye. "I must leave for my estate tomorrow."

"Oh." I fidgeted with the hem of my cloak, not sure what to say. Would he get into more trouble, at least partly on my account? I wasn't vain enough to believe he returned solely to see me.

When he squinted against the lantern light, I lowered the flame and set the light at my feet. He seated himself in the corner of the bench, watching me from the shadows.

"I thought you'd decided to go to Ceur, if need be, after tomorrow," I said slowly, countering my wish for his safety with reason and integrity, and the duke's warning. "That you believed facing the inspector was the only way to eventually be free and able to save Carrington." The only way to not end up a fugitive who could never show himself at Henly again.

He slapped the air in an angry gesture. "That was a fool speaking. The inspector would never let me go, not when I know where Emil Farro is."

"Farro? I thought this was about the Magic Thief? The inspector suspects you of being the Magic Thief."

"You're right, certainly," he answered quickly, "but it was the theft at Farro's that drew me to his notice. Gabriella." He leaned forward and took my hand in a pleading gesture. "If we catch the Thief tonight, I could prove my innocence and not have to go to Ceur. That's why I couldn't leave tonight." He smiled slyly. "One reason."

My heart did a strange flip-flop, and I remembered my mother's warning, but I smiled back at him anyway. Yet I was done trying to catch the Thief. "That would be wonderful, of course, but—"

"That's my girl. I've discovered some information that will help us capture him, but I need your help. I need you to let me into the library."

"You can't use your ring?" I stood and paced in a small circle in front of the bench.

He blinked and might have thrown a glance at his hands. "The magic protecting the library blocks my attempts."

"Of course." My keys dragged against my skirt liked lead weights. What would helping Marcel hurt? He wouldn't do anything foolhardy, especially not with Henry there to give his half-magic expertise. My skin prickled, but not from cold. *Into the library.* Where the Thief wanted to be. What about the Duke of Lofton's carefully laid plans? "Into the library, Marcel? Our goal is to keep people out."

He cocked his head. The lantern light caught his face, but shadows still darkened his eyes. I missed the openness of his green-eyed gaze.

"They've put a Place Changer in the library, Gabriella. You can't keep them out."

"A Place Changer!" I hadn't imagined the telltale shimmer there the day the birds were let loose. "But that would mean ..." I cradled my hand to my chest.

"There's a link between the library and the caves, which is why we must steal the treasures before they do. Help me, Gabriella. Help me save your family's treasures and gain my freedom."

He held out his hand to me, but I kept pacing, rubbing my fingertip out of habit. I wanted to help. I wanted our treasures safe and out of the hands of the sorcerers. I wanted Marcel to be free. I wanted to accomplish something great to make up for losing my wand. I wanted the altar destroyed. But I'd learned enough tonight to make me hesitate.

"I don't know, Marcel. How would we keep the items safe if we got them out before the Thief did?" What if they called me to the altar through the Changer? Letting my hands fall to my sides, I faced him. "I think we should trust the Duke of Lofton. It could endanger him and his associates as well as ruin his arrangements if we interfere. We can't go rushing in for the sake of our pride. You're exonerated if the Thief is caught by him just as if he were caught by you."

"Lofton? After all we've been through together, you'd follow him over me?"

"That's not fair."

He threw up his hands. "The duke left us, Gabriella. He knew he couldn't catch the Thief. He's an old man. His days for heroics are over. It's our turn."

"And how can you catch the Thief? You're a non-magic. I'm not diminishing your worth by saying that but reminding you of the inequality in fighting capacity between you and *the old man*. You didn't see him disintegrate half a tree. He's not defenseless. And he's our friend. How can you disrespect him so?"

"I didn't say he was defenseless, but he is gone."

"He's not."

"Where is he then?"

"I don't know." I didn't, did I? Only that a young man knew where he was.

Marcel rose slowly and moved to stand in front of me. He cupped his hands over my shoulders and gazed down at me with a look so serious it tempted me to change my mind. "Will you not help me?"

"No. Not in this."

His grip on my shoulders tightened. "What can I say to make you change your mind?"

"Nothing. I ask that you respect my decision."

He frowned, his grip becoming vise-like as I tried to pull away. My breath hissed through my teeth as much in pain as shock. "Are you sure?" he asked.

"Let me go. You're hurting me and disgracing your-self."

Instead of releasing me and apologizing, he dug his fingers into my arms until I was certain he was trying to scratch my bones. "Will you let me into the library?"

Speechless, I stared up at the man I thought I knew. My imagination had taken a few good deeds and made this worm into a man of noble character. What a blind fool I was.

Once again.

Clenching my fists, I glared up at him. "It's true you never know a person until trouble hits him. I should've listened to Aunt Helene. You're no better than Tyndale, only honorable so long as it's not unpleasant for you. But that's not honor at all. You're a bully and a coward, Marcel Ellsworth, and I hope they keep you in the Ceurian prison." I choked back a sob. How could the death of a friend's character hurt so much? I'd rather he'd died a noble death! "Let. Me. Go." I pushed against his chest and kicked his leg, but Marcel only laughed a strange and un-familiar laugh.

I stilled, my true mistake bursting on me. I did know Marcel, and he'd never hurt anyone. It was this man I didn't know, like I hadn't known the Jonathon Lofton calling to me in the lair. That had been Tyndale's brother-in-law Damien, the actor. But it was only the duke's voice Damien imitated. I *saw* this villainous version of Marcel. I gasped as a line from *The Fall of Bevvelian* breached the barrier of my memory: *The sorcerers had learned the Spell of Imitation.*

If a sorcerer or an enchanter could wield the Spell of Imitation to look like another, so could a half-magic with a source of power. Tyndale—David Ashby—was my protector, and Damien—the actor—my enemy, a usurper of Tyndale's image, the Magic Thief.

And Marcel?

"I'm sorry you made this decision." The peculiar edge to Marcel's soft tone drew my gaze to his face. It wasn't the shadow of filtered light darkening his eyes: it was the black mark of sorcery. "Things could have been so much more pleasant—for you."

"No!" I punched him in the chest and jerked away, but he grabbed my wrists and yanked me back. I kicked his leg and strained to free my arms. He knocked his head against mine, and spots danced in my vision as he wrenched my arms behind me. Pain stole my breath and shot into my shoulders. The fake Marcel clamped my wrists together with one large hand and groped for my keys with his other.

The power of enchantment flared in my chest, waiting to react. I shunted it into my wrists. He cried out as the power burst hit his hand. I grabbed for my wand, but he shoved me forward. I toppled to the ground, jarring my teeth and gouging my hands on the wet gravel as I landed.

Polished black shoes stepped within a foot of me, and I looked up into the black eyes of Tyndale's supposed solicitor. Keldan drew back his hand into a cedar behind him and whispered strange words that needed no translation to be known as sorcery. From the green needles he pulled a thin black spine the length of a man's hand—a dart of pure sorcerer's poison.

I pushed to my feet, fighting for footing against the slick stones, desperate to get out of the range of the spine, but I slipped. Falling prone, I stretched out, pushing power into my hand, and reached for Keldan's leg. He scooted back and jammed the spine into my forearm as the man I'd thought Marcel clamped a hand over my mouth.

My arm went slack, and I slumped to the stone pavement. A bird of carrion screeched into my thoughts, carrying a searing pain in its claws and nausea on its wings, the darkness of nightmares in its wake. The warmth of my power faded to an ember that couldn't be flamed to defend me against the beasts warring in my head.

Images of Mama being chased by a wolf flashed through my mind. I felt her panic, the tear of her flesh, and smelled the coppery odor of her blood. A cry caught and gurgled in my throat as agony radiated through my body. *It's not real. It's not real.*

I fought to take in everything around me. The cold wind, the jerk on the chatelaine, the release of its weight, the kick to my legs, the frustrated curse.

"Haven't you learned to walk in that form yet?" Keldan asked. The pressure of their footsteps around me passed through the ground and pounded against my head like the collapse of a mountain. But even that was better than the image of Sterling trampling Eva or Marcel drowning in the glen, the red of his hair always turning to blood on my hands.

"It's harder than you'd think. I don't know how that devil of a Magic Thief manages it as well as he does. One of the reasons Lord Ackman values him, I suppose."

"One of his many talents," Keldan said, his tone venomous. "Put her on the bench, Jace."

Jace picked me up, dumped me onto the bench, and pulled my legs down so that I lay on my side. My head cracked against the seat, and my arms lolled, one across my waist and the other draping over the bench's edge.

Keldan grasped my dangling wrist and lifted my arm into the lantern light, tilting it as if to get a better look at the spine.

Jace peered over his shoulder, a sadistic look on his face. "Not even a quarter gone. I wonder how she'll feel at the full dose?"

Keldan's lips thinned. He rotated my arm, examining it and then my hand. The light passed over a scar running down the side of his little finger. It was black. He was a Sorcerer's Called who didn't escape.

Horrified, my gaze found my own scar, and Keldan noticed. He grabbed my finger and examined the nick.

"So it's true. You are a Chosen One." He clumsily folded my fingers over his, like a gentleman would take a lady's hand before kissing it. "To be Chosen isn't a curse, Lady Gabriella." His voice was kind, sympathetic. "They've told you it is, that you're a monster, but you're not what they've named you. You know that, don't you?"

I did, didn't I? Aunt Helene's critical looks and jibes were baseless. Even as a Called—a Chosen—I was not less than my sisters.

"It's a blessing," he continued in that calming tone of his. "The sorcerers don't take the will and kill the dreams of their special ones. Oh no, they give both. To you, Lady Gabriella. They'd give you everything you desire or give you the strength to take it for yourself, which is far better."

He cocked his head, bringing his face close to mine. There was kindness in his voice, and it dulled the nightmares. "How does that sound, sister? Even with all your wealth and beauty there's something you want. Isn't there? What is it? Let us give it to you."

He let my arm fall back against the bench, then cupped his hand under my chin. His rough fingers slid softly over the side of my face and came to rest near my eye. He stared at it, not at me, but at my eye.

Then he blinked, his black eyes hidden for a brief second. He drew back his hand.

Many from Tormir have blue eyes, similar in color to mine. *The touch of sorcery darkens the soul and the eyes show it*, a history on sorcerers said.

"You've no need of money or food," he mused, his gaze momentarily averted. "The admiration of men? The love of family? No, you'd have those." He paused again and began to scrub the palm of his hand. "The Countess Helene to never berate you again?" Something like a smile curved his lips. It sent a shiver down my spine. "You could take care of her yourself. You'd enjoy that, wouldn't you? She'd never hurt anyone again, like my father never hurt anyone again."

What would it be like to be free of her? To be free of any I disliked, of any who made me feel inadequate? To get rid of Damien for tricking me and attempting to send me to the sorcerers.

Terrified of the thought, I stopped resisting the nightmares and let them overrun the dangerously enticing scene Keldan presented.

"No," the Called said at last. "That wouldn't do it. You're not strong enough for vengeance. Not yet." He rested the palm of his hand on my forearm, his thumb touching the base of the spine with no seeming ill effect. Though he stared ahead, his eyes flickered.

He was watching my nightmares. He saw and yet no trace of dismay or pity showed in his face. And I hated him for it. Had he no compassion?

He smiled. He knew what I felt for him.

Horror filled me. Then anger and pity and, finally, terror. Horror at my own hatred. Anger and pity at what had been done to him. Terror for myself, at what he could make me. The spine did him no harm. He could take me to the cave and force me to finish what I'd unintentionally begun so long ago. The spine wouldn't harm me then. I would live, and I would be theirs.

He drew his hand away at last, a knowing look on his face. "Aside from the foolish wish to be free of the Choosing, it's that troublesome Lord Ellsworth you want. I thought I saw it in your eyes when you spoke to *him* earlier, and now he's in your nightmares. But your family would never approve, would they?" He lowered his voice. "We could give him to you, after he's told us what we want to know. We could give him to you and make sure your family never spoke a word against him. How would you like that?"

His voice dulled, as if he were lost in memory and talking to himself. "The sorcerers can give you whatever you want, be it food or revenge or love. The sorcerers give so much and ask so little. They value their Chosen. Even the children of the drunks, the abusers, the desperately poor. They would take you and provide for you so you could provide for those you love. All you need do is serve them, and you would live and live well."

Live. I stared back at the Called, though in my mind's eye Marcel's limp body once more slipped from my grasp into the foaming waters of the flooded glen. I thought my heart had died too many times that night to care about another death, but it lurched in a pain that jolted even my paralyzed limbs.

Serve them. I could be free of the nightmares. I could stop the Ceurians from taking Marcel, and the sorcerers themselves wouldn't harm him if they gave him to me.

But no, the sorcerers fed on the lies and deceit and death they dealt. They worshiped the dark. No gift of theirs was worth that cost.

Keldan cupped my chin again. "Answer the Call, Lady Gabriella. The poison won't hurt a Called. Choose them freely and be free. Those who choose freely are favored."

I'd rather die, my eyes told him.

He released me and rocked back on his heels. "So be it." He tapped the spine deeper into my forearm. Again I tried to scream but couldn't.

"Doesn't Ackman want her?" Jace asked.

"Do you think I don't know what my lord commands?" Keldan snapped, one hand closing over his scar. He forced his hands apart and continued in a milder tone. "He wants an enchantress for the experiments, but there's no time to deal with an unwilling Chosen." He darted another glance at my eyes, then rose, scouring his palm. "They're unresponsive while the transformation takes hold. We'll find another, or see if she's willing after the poison's eaten all her enchanter pride."

"She may be dead by the time we finish tonight," Jace said warily.

Keldan shrugged. "Or she may be wishing she were. If the inventor succeeds in doing what Ackman claims, we won't need any unwilling ones. We can give what's needed to any, magic or non-magic, with sense enough to understand what they're offered."

They left, taking the lantern and my last bit of distraction with them. Save for the light of a few stars, there was nothing to raise my senses above the horror playing out in my mind. Everyone I loved, even some I hadn't realized I did, had died a hundred gruesome deaths, some by my own hand. Yet I couldn't move beyond a shudder.

Instinct told me the spine was growing shorter, my life and sanity shrinking with it. Despite that, the thrum of my own power was still there, however dampened it was by the sorcerer's poison, and that thrumming gave me hope. After all, *a Floraison does not die easily.*

Pushing and calling and begging, I pulled a faint line of power into my fingers. Blindly, taking minutes for each tiny jerk of movement, my fingers groped for the spine. My skin was cold and hard, barely recognizable, as I found my wrist and began working my way up my arm.

Somewhere over the nightmares, I thought I heard my name, but it could only be the cry of one of the players in my dreams. The outside world had faded but for the half-feel of touch in my fingers. They pinched around the spine, but it burned and my hand recoiled, losing its place.

I wanted to cry but couldn't. I had to get the spine out. I had to warn my family and see that Marcel was safe. Once again, I tried to find my fingers in the darkness and move them.

Henry rose up in the forefront of my mind as the prey of a dozen hungry cannibals who all looked like me. His screams struck my mind relentlessly but never numbed it. Other words mixed with his pleas. More words joined those, and my stomach told me the world was shifting, but it was just the tremor of an earthquake bringing down Henly's stones atop everyone here, crushing them limb by limb, letting them watch one another die. Then, slowly, the world stilled. Light crept over the horizon of my dreams. Then voices. The smell of the well-oiled furniture of our drawing room.

"If you're going to be sick, do it in the fireplace." A man. Not someone I loved or hated. Not someone from my nightmares.

"I don't care about their rug. Will she live? Tell me she'll live, Mavern."

Henry?

Mavern harrumphed. "Not if she has to depend on half-magics of your abilities."

The sound of retching was followed by moans and the brush of material as a heavy hand patted a shoulder.

"I didn't mean it, lad," Mavern said. "If she does, and I think she might, it will be because you saved her. Pulling sorcerer's poison out of an enchantress isn't easy. That you can do it at all is a testament to your grandfather's training. That you can't stomach the sorcerer's magic is a testament to your integrity."

Henry muttered something inarticulate, then retched again.

Mavern sighed, and I recognized the clink of the brandy tray against the table. Liquid splashed into a glass, but I couldn't gather enough light to make out more than the outline of Mavern's stout figure against the fireplace. "Drink this and rest. I'll work on her after I get the emergency kit from my room," he said and then left.

The clock ticked and Henry moaned. I couldn't even join him in that.

The door clicked shut behind Mavern as he returned. He poked and prodded my arm, lifted my lids, and then poured a thin liquid tasting of watermelons down my throat. When I spit it up into his waiting cup, it was black. After the next forced draught, it had specks of green. After the tenth, it was as green as I felt.

He lay my head back on the settee and wiped my face with a damp cloth as he knelt beside me. I could see him clearly now. He didn't look at all like the man who'd been caught in the poacher's trap or sound like the man who'd wanted to declare his three-day love for me.

As if feeling my stare, he smiled. "Don't worry, my dear. I'm not about to propose to you. I hope you'll forgive the silliness of my disguise."

"Disguise?" The word slurred over my numb tongue.

"Yes." His eyes twinkled as he dipped the cloth into a glass of water. "My wife's always said I have a flair for the theatric. I thought I'd put it to use while I could. I had to have some reason to wander about and see what I could find out."

Henry, pale-faced with blood-shot eyes, sat at my feet. He held a half-finished glass of something I suspected Mavern had given him. "Lord Mavern came with the Duke of Lofton as a representative from the Council of Half-Magics. I thought I recognized him."

"Fortunately, you got around to introducing yourself before the spine completely disappeared into the lady's arm." Mavern rocked back on his heels and stood, his damp handkerchief dangling from his hand. "Now, don't use any magic for a few days or get any more sorcery put into you. It will interfere with the counter-magic potion I gave you."

Wonderful.

"Do you know where the duke is?" I rasped. Mavern gave me a drink of water, holding the glass for me. "The sorcerers have a way into the library."

"I know—the Place Changer."

"You know?" The words screeched out.

"Certainly. Why else send a half-magic along but to discover things like that?" Mavern dipped the handkerchief in his glass of water and laid it on my neck. His expression turned solemn. "They have to be stolen, Lady Gabriella, but they'll be returned. My job here tonight is to make certain no one comes out of the library."

"But they took my keys."

He hissed through his teeth. "That wasn't how I expected them to get the stuff. It's too fast."

"Someone bearing Lord Ellsworth's image stole them from me"—I lifted my arm, rejoicing in the small ability to do that—"and helped do this."

Mavern's jaw clenched. "They've got him then. Blast it. Your father agreed to keep him locked in his room tonight." He turned on Henry. "How did this happen?"

"Assistant Inspector Chead came for him. The Duke of Henly was gone. I suppose the duchess didn't know about the agreement."

Even if I didn't owe Henry my life, I would have loved him for the stricken look on his face. He was a true friend and a worthy man.

"He could escape using his ring, couldn't he?" I said, wanting reassurance against the gnawing fear inside me. "You haven't hidden him away somewhere, have you, Henry?"

He shook his head sadly, and my hopes sputtered out. "He hasn't got the ring."

"What?" Mavern bellowed. "Did the sorcerers get that too? The lot of you should just give them everything, why don't you! As if Lofton doesn't have enough to worry about."

"They didn't get it, though heaven only knows how they missed it," Henry said calmly. He drew the gold wand from my skirt pocket. "Lord Ellsworth, noble fool that he is, gave it to a woman."

Mavern rolled his eyes and pivoted toward the door. "Stay put, you two. I've got to signal Lofton the latest catastrophe."

"How?" Henry asked.

"Colored smoke up the fireplace, of course." Mavern stomped out. The door slammed behind him, and pain flared through my head.

Marcel gave up his beloved ring for me.

And now the sorcerers had him. Keldan was right. I couldn't let anything happen to Marcel. But helping him would put me back in the way of the sorcerers, possibly in the lair itself. I trembled at the thought. I had every reason not to do anything. I was recovering from sorcerer's poison, for goodness sake. I'd nearly died. Mavern had told me to stay put and not use magic.

But I sounded like what I'd accused Tyndale of—noble so long as it wasn't inconvenient. I professed such fine sentiments, but what did they mean to me?

I turned my head into the cushions of the settee's back. Who was Gabriella Floraison truly? The spoiled daughter of a duke who accepted admiration and selfless protection as her due but never returned them, if inopportune? Or a woman who expected honor and nobleness of herself no matter the cost? I knew which one I wanted to be.

With effort, I twisted back around to face the room. Henry watched me. No matter how much I wanted to help Marcel directly, though the thought terrified me, I had to be sensible. I could very well lose myself to the Sorcerer's Call and become a weapon. Then everyone would be better off if I'd stayed on the settee all night. Yet, with the help of a half-magic, I might be able to do something useful and not merely foolishly brave.

"The fastest way to the cave," Henry said, "would be through the Place Changer in the library."

I nodded, deliberating.

"After they're through using it themselves, naturally."

"Naturally." I pushed myself into a sitting position and held out my scarred finger. "Henry, I must tell you something. I—"

"I know—you're a Sorcerer's Called." He shrugged at my surprised expression. "I am a half-magic. I sensed something when I touched your hand the first day in the glen, but it was Sterling that gave away your secret."

"Does—"

"Yes."

"That's why he gave me the wand," I said softly. Why he couldn't escape the sorcerers by himself. "Could you stop the Call if it took me?"

He examined the tip of his finger as if it bore the telltale scar. "I might. At the very least I could use some of your own power of enchantment to cause you to sleep or be unable to move to get to the altar."

"Just don't turn me to stone."

He smiled as if he'd already considered the idea and rejected it.

"Would you help me up?" For some minutes, I'd felt the edges of darkness in my mind beaten back until they were almost gone and the heat of magic once more welling up, albeit weak like my body. Henry wobbled on his feet but managed to help me to mine.

"We make a fine pair of rescuers." I grasped a table for support, my legs prickling but slowly regaining their strength.

"It evens the odds."

I hobbled a few steps with Henry's help, then shook off his hand and managed to make it to the chair in front of a broad beam similar to the one in the library and a few other rooms of the house.

Taking Henry's hand again, I scooted around the chair and relaxed against the beam. "We can get to the library from here. There's always a chance they missed the storage realm."

Whispering the entry spell, I let myself sink through the cushion between the realms, pulling Henry with me. Gray light wrapped around us as we entered the storage realm.

Giving a murmur of approval, Henry followed as I worked my way around toward the invisible library door, grateful Papa had us memorize the location of each exit. We froze halfway there as a hot breath rolled over us.

"Oh no," Henry muttered as we turned.

Sarcodinas bounded into the gray realm in a flurry of golden hair, but he stopped short and roared irritably at the sight of me. Then he eyed Henry, who was as stiff as a frozen fish. I took Henry's hand and held it palm out to the lion. Sarcodinas sniffed it, repeated his mild roar of annoyance, flopped onto his haunches, and began grooming his paws, eyeing us every now and then with his large, honey-colored eyes.

My heart leapt. If Sarcodinas were here and eager for a fight, then no one else had been here. My gaze shot around the room, landing on the sword hanging on the wall a little ways away.

"Beautiful beast! I'd hug you, but you're not that tame. Maybe I'll find someone for you to devour instead." I turned from Sarcodinas to lift the sword from the wall, staggering under its weight. Henry placed a steadying hand on my back, and I let him take the weapon from me. Bargaining chip or walking stick, it might be useful.

Henry and I stationed ourselves before the library door. Henry flattened his face against the wall as a boy might press his to a windowpane. He drew back and rubbed his nose. "No one is in the library."

"How would you steal a person from a den of sorcerers, Henry?" I asked, staring at the wall and making no move to pass through.

"'Snatch and grab' has always seemed the most expedient method of theft to my mind." Sighing heavily, he looked at his feet. "However, and I may only be speaking for myself, I do not feel particularly spry at the moment."

I wished I didn't agree with him. "We'll have to find someone who is then."

In the room's center, Sarcodinas stretched out like a statue of the sphinx and yawned. Henry threw his gaze heavenward. "We never should have come. We should have stayed at Silvestris."

As quickly as we could, we passed into Sarcodinas's realm, found the harness used to walk him when his quarters were being cleaned, and then returned.

Sarcodinas padded along behind us, ears perked up, alert with curiosity. He allowed me to harness him and even knelt for us to climb onto his back with little more than a couple of growls and a few twitches of his tail for show. He knew which way excitement lay.

Henry took one look at the great beast stretched out before us, let out a great, mournful sigh, and took his seat. Then he stiffened his back as if Sarcodinas were a show horse on parade, and he the festooned rider. "You're not trained properly," he said to me, a slight tremor to his deep voice, "nor are you well enough for a direct assault on the sorcerers." He placed the sword on his lap and extended a hand to assist me in getting situated in front of him.

I adjusted my skirts as best I could and then lurched forward as the golden beast rose beneath us. "Careful." I tugged on Sarcodinas's harness, directing his padding steps toward the library exit. "What do you recommend?"

"An indirect attack, not magic versus magic."

"Sensible plan." What would a half-magic count as an indirect attack?

Feeling the power of Sarcodinas's muscles beneath me, I relaxed, took hold of his mane, and swayed with his movement. "I've always wanted to ride a lion."

"*I* never have," Henry said as Sarcodinas's fur rippled beneath us. The animal growled as if to say he'd never desired riders.

"Sword, please," I said. The solid gray wall wouldn't give way even for the lion without the sword or my touch. I held the heavy Sword of Ora unsteadily before us as Sarcodinas stuck his soft nose up to the wall and pressed through. "You're a brave man, Henry, to do what you do not fancy for the sake of your friend."

"My lady is kind to say so, but it's really a matter of self-preservation. My mother works for his aunt. If anything happened to him, I'd never hear the end of it." Henry held out his hand, his fingers spread as if feeling the realms pass like wind through his fingers. "And if anything happened to you, Lord Ellsworth would kill me even if he had to come back from the dead to do it."

I laughed, my spirits lifting as we passed from the gray realm into the library with its brilliantly colored wall hanging and book bindings.

Sarcodinas halted just inside and sniffed the air. With a low growl, he began to stalk about the boundaries of the room. Behind me, Henry sucked in his breath. Tucked into the handle of the Demandez à Voir mirror's resting place was a silk blossom, the token of the charming Magic Thief. The room was empty of every magical item, save for the Place Changer, and it was shrinking.

Before I realized it, Henry was dashing across the room for the Changer high above the sofa.

"Move, Beast," he cried over his shoulder. Sarcodinas leapt forward as Henry leapt for the Changer. Henry grabbed its shrinking, dark edge. It flickered, expanded to half its normal size, and stilled. "Hurry," he cried. "It won't hold forever."

"Move, Sarcodinas." I prodded the cat for greater speed and clutched his fur as he gathered himself and sprang for the Changer.

We flew from candlelight to darkness, and Sarcodinas skidded to a halt over the slick cave rock. Pressing into his sides with my legs, I lurched forward but managed to hang on.

"Gabriella!" Henry called from the library.

"Henry!" I toppled from the lion's back and ran as fast as my weak legs would carry me to the shrinking square of eerie candlelight and color hanging before the cave wall. Henry's forehead and fingers rose to block the light. I grabbed for his hand to help pull him through.

The Changer's shimmering edges flared a solid white-hot. Henry screamed.

Chapter 22

There is no promise more foolish than one to look after a man bent on his own selfish ways.

Sonserian Proverb

MARCEL ELLSWORTH

I should have known better than to trust a man with a patchy beard. As soon as I realized where the vine-covered tunnel was heading, Cox employed his multi-purpose garden instrument on me. My head was still ringing.

Forcing one eye open, I peered around the foul cave chamber. It had been less threatening in the pitch dark. When it was empty. Its current yellowed lantern light and smell of sawdust and lumber didn't alleviate my unease. It reminded me of a coffin maker's workshop. The freshly made coffin resting at the foot of the stone table didn't help either. Several crates filled it, as if keeping it warm until its occupant was ready for it. Compared to that long box and whatever prelude it would have, the Ceurian prison didn't look so bad. I flexed my wrist, letting the wand holster chafe my skin. The toy wand and whatever magic Lofton infused it with might come in handy earlier than planned.

Unfortunately, the villainous crowd scattered about the domed, circular chamber numbered over a dozen. Not promising odds. Some worked at the stone table carefully packaging the items their comrades brought from the partially bricked-up tunnel leading deeper into the caves. The packed crates were then relayed to others who hurried them out the tunnel to the river path, and, from what I gathered, up the bank to carts on the main path.

My captors were young to middle-aged, except for one bent old woman who could have stepped from any children's story, so perfectly did she fit the wart-covered, evil sorceress persona. The rest could have stepped from the shops of Gersemere or Ceur or Tormir and never have been noticed.

The old woman crooned with a mother's pride over various elements of the chamber to a couple of the men, who seemed less awed by its ancient evil history than she did. The taller of the two men had the dark complexion typical of those from eastern Ceur, the other the exceptionally pale skin of the people of Tormir, though his eyes weren't the typical blue.

Yet even their interest waxed when she hobbled over to a cleft in the wall. The rock dipped in and then jutted out in a primitive altar, the kind that suggested a mouth by which the rock drank blood. The trough's lower lip bore teeth, deadly sharp and bound with sorcery.

The cave wall also had convenient iron rings and chains the sorcerers had thoughtfully oiled in expectation of me. The bonds that rattled behind me every time I moved were all that kept me from smashing the accursed altar with everything I could find. In my imagination, it was in a million splinters, charred, and buried, and Sterling was out of a job, retired to a riding horse.

Sighing, I leaned my aching head against the rock. What was the use of futile dreams? I was the sorcerers' prisoner. Even if I were free, I didn't have the power to destroy the altar.

An Ellsworth never gives up.

I wanted to laugh at the irony. My life was about to *give out*, and I was spouting new family mottos. But I shifted into a position that didn't scream *hopeless prisoner* and prayed for courage and deliverance. Self-pity and complaining had never brought me anything but depression, bitterness, and missed opportunities. If I had to become a fountain of family mottos and hopeful dreams to keep my mental enemies at bay, so be it.

"That's the last of it." The traitor Cox stepped around the remains of the brick wall. He carried one end of the knight's armor. Two other men followed, attending to the rest of the empty knight.

"The Place Changer?" the old woman asked.

"Disintegrating," Cox answered.

One of the men tossed the smaller crates out of the coffin, and then they lowered the knight into the coffin. Somehow, I wasn't as comforted that the long crate wasn't for me as I thought I'd be. Protracted torture instead? My mind broken in an attempt to get information on Emil Farro's whereabouts? My broken body dumped in the river? I added endurance to my prayer list.

"You didn't make certain it was gone?" The woman scowled, her furrowed brow giving her an even more hooded look.

Puffing out breaths, Cox released the knight into the crate. "It was going that way. No one could have stopped it," he said defensively as he wiped his sweaty brow on his sleeve.

"You don't look so good, Damien." The Tormirian escorting the old woman didn't hide the cruel pleasure in his voice as he addressed the Magic Thief. "Are you sure this job isn't too much for you?"

Thick-shouldered Cox reddened as he tweaked the knight's padding. "The keys didn't work on everything, Keldan. Those protective spells could've killed your men, but *I* broke through them. I also told you how to get the keys. Don't forget that. You can be sure Ackman won't."

Keldan's jaw clenched. I momentarily forgot my discomfort, intrigued as I was by the jealousy playing out between the head sorcerer's two favorites, the old and the new.

"You also lost us the girl earlier," Keldan said. "We could've had her as our slave."

"I did not."

"Your associate then. He's always had a weakness for women, hasn't he?"

Cox jerked upright. "He's not—"

He yelped. The old woman screamed. The chamber shook. A lion roared. The guardian of the storage realm leapt over the broken wall, magic even I could see gleaming in his fur. Gabriella was bent low over his back. My heart stuttered.

Keldan, his black wand out, screamed words of sorcery as the lion reared and Gabriella jumped off. She ducked behind a crate, and whatever spell Keldan used against the lion did little more than turn the beast into a cub for a split second. Then it was upon them again, distracting them from the woman in pale blue.

As one of the sorcerers fell beneath the lion's paw, I shook my right arm, bound behind me, but the toy wand held fast in its holster. I jerked against the chains. *Work free, blast it!*

Gabriella, her face as pale as death, slid along the wall using the Sword of Ora like a cane. She clutched a gold and scarlet wand, but the wand was more scarlet than gold. What had happened to them both?

"Would it do any good if I told you to go away?" I asked. She was close enough to touch had my hands been free. Her eyes, always a beautiful blue, were bright like patches of sunlit sky, full of the courage and strength I admired in her.

With a half-smile, she shook her head and raised the Sword of Ora. "Close your eyes."

My attention shot to the sword's keen edge. "Close my—"

"Well, well." Keldan's accented words echoed through the chamber. "It seems the Chosen has chosen us after all." Wand out, Keldan strutted toward us.

The lion's roars were getting fainter, coming from the tunnel to the river instead of the chamber, a fact no doubt adding to Keldan's swagger. Cursing lion guards and wand holsters, I shook my arm again.

"In that case," Keldan continued, "I can say I'm happy to see you alive, sister."

Gabriella stiffened. "I'm not your sister, nor will I ever be." She raised the sword and nodded to me. "Now!" Her command was followed by words I didn't understand. I closed my eyes and still squinted against a flash. A round of screams and profanities assaulted us, but close behind me was Gabriella's sweet, firm voice. "Sword that knows no bounds, cut not through time but human bindings, make this prisoner a man unbound and free."

She plunged the sword into the chains, and the manacles fell from my wrists. Gabriella grabbed my arm, and I staggered up, my head reeling from the earlier blow, my legs numb. Light pulsed through the chamber, and I glimpsed a floating ball of brilliant white before common sense forced me to look away.

"Don't look at it." Gabriella wrapped my arm over her shoulder and her arm around my waist and urged me forward. "Sarcodinas, come back!"

Getting my feet firmly underneath me, I shrugged off her hold and took her hand instead. We clambered over the brick pile, but then Gabriella pulled me to a stop behind the shelter of the remaining wall. She grabbed her waist and doubled over.

"Gabriella! Are you hurt?" I wrapped an arm around her and prepared to lift her up and carry her to the Changer, but she waved me off. A yell and a lion's roar echoed in the chamber.

"I'm weak, that's all."

"Then let me help you. The Changer should be close." I offered her my hand, but she moved away, that wonderful, terrible determination flaring in her eyes. "Gabriella, we must leave."

"Look out!" she cried.

I turned as a sorcerer vaulted over the brick pile and tumbled to his knees. Hardly thinking, I snatched a loose brick, smashed it into his head, and shoved him back over the pile. Spinning around, I grabbed Gabriella by the arm. "Come on."

But she yelled over the cacophony, "The Changer's gone. Our goal isn't so much to get away as to keep our distance."

Chapter 23

*A weakness should never be ignored. You can be assured
your enemies will not neglect it.*

The Art of War with Magic by General Aiden Floraison

GABRIELLA FLORAISON

THE LITTLE LIGHT brave enough to venture into our tunnel was enough for me to see Marcel blink.

"At least that's clear," he said as I pushed the Sword of Ora into his hands.

"Make sure no one gets over the brick pile. I'm going to repair the wall. We'll be safe in the tunnel until the Duke of Lofton gets here. Sarcodinas will see to it." It was a nice thought anyway.

"Yes, General," he quipped. Sword in one hand, he picked up a brick in his other. "This sword doesn't sever heads, does it?"

"Not readily." Fighting back the nightmarish visions using magic had released, I forced the power of enchantment to the wand. So much for the simple snatch and grab.

"Pity."

I turned my attention to the power thrumming in my chest. There was so little available because of the poison's dulling effect. Mavern had warned me not to use magic at all, but what else could I do? I swallowed hard against the horror once more playing out in my mind and focused on what needed to be done.

I raised the wand, glowing strangely, to the edge of the intact wall, and whispered the command. As ordered, a brick flew from the pile and cemented itself against the wall, so I dismissed the wand's glow from my thoughts. Two more bricks flew up. Then five. Then twenty.

The lion roared and gave chase to the nearly blinded sorcerers. Keldan screamed for the half-magic to stop the light. They wanted the lion alive. *Be wary, Sarcodinas.*

My hand burned, my body ached, but I had to keep going. The wall, with some added magic in it, might stop them long enough for the duke to do whatever he was going to do, if he'd found the secret entrance. Maybe the sorcerers would think we weren't worth the effort.

Beside me, Marcel chucked another brick at a sorcerer running too close to our exit. "Cox snagged the light," he said. "He'll be able to absorb the power in it, the—" He broke off and muttered something about a gun Emil Farro had promised him.

Another brick slid into place, and a hiss escaped me as the warmth of magic seared my palm. Scarlet light streamed from fissures in the wand. That definitely shouldn't be happening.

"Stop!" Marcel snagged my wrist. "The wand is cracking. How much have you used it?"

I shunted the power already going toward it to warm my muscles, then stopped the flow. "It took a lot to protect Sarcodinas and make the light globe. Then the bricks." Shaking, I slipped my wrist from his grip. What had I nearly done?

"It's had its emergency use then. It'll explode if you use it anymore."

"But we can't leave this op—"

"Move!" He shoved me forward, then pivoted back toward the wall. I winced as another brick thudded against a head. He grabbed my hand, and we dashed through the dark.

"But the tunnel ends—" I began.

"I know. Now go. Move to the left," he warned before maneuvering me in that direction. "We'll feel our way along the wall." A crash sounded behind us, followed by a roar. We picked up our pace, my finger trailing along the rock as our guide.

"You're supposed to be safe at home," Marcel growled. "I'll fire Henry for this."

"Henry saved my life," I said quietly. Would I ever get to thank him for it?

"He *what*?"

A spark of warmth that had nothing to do with the flow of magic flared in my chest. It didn't matter that I'd just saved him, his protectiveness still pleased me. How could I have ever thought he'd hurt me? Believed the man in the garden was truly Marcel? "Sorcerer's poison, but I'll explain later."

"I'll give him a bonus and then fire him."

"You will not. I like Henry," I said archly, grateful for the distraction from my nightmares.

"I did too until today. Why didn't you bring him with you?"

"I tried. He held the Place Changer open long enough for Sarcodinas to carry me through, but it must have reached a critical point in its disintegration after we passed through. It vanished before he could follow us."

"Remind me to have a word with your brother about littering Henly with those things. Stop." He gave me no choice but to comply, his arm holding me back. "Did you hear that?"

"What?"

"Our voices are warbling with echoes. We must be nearing the pit."

We'd gone as far as we could. No rope lay on this side of the chasm. In my memory, the ground trembled, and I heard again my own screams and Roma's final yelp. They rolled into the poison's nightmares, and my knees went weak. I buried my shoulder against Marcel's side. He wrapped an arm about me, offering strength as well as comfort.

"The floor near the pit is a thin shelf. I think we've reached it." He tapped his heel against the rock, noted the hollow reply, and backed us up a few feet. "We must be careful, but we'll be safe. I have a plan."

I laughed weakly, struggling to get the nightmares under control. "Why do I have a feeling those words usually ended with a 'Marcel Gustave' talk from your aunt?"

"I have no idea." The sword, glowing with a blue light, lit our path as he swung it in front of us. "Um, Gabriella, why is the sword glowing?"

I rubbed my forehead as if that simple act could cleanse my mind. "I don't know. Magical swords tend to do that."

"When there's trouble about?"

"Swords generally go where trouble is, so that's possible, or maybe it likes your scheme."

He rested the flat of the blade against his shoulder, illuminating his face, highlighting his drawn brows. "I'll go with the last one." His arm tightened about me in a hug. Then he stepped cautiously forward, leaving me behind.

I grabbed his sleeve. "What are you planning?"

"Nothing you'd want to hear about. Stay on the solid rock." He pried my fingers from his jacket and sprang forward. "Forgive me if this doesn't work."

The thin shelf vibrated as he dashed over it. I scooted back against the tunnel wall as the vibrations swelled, the clapping of footfalls joining with the cracking of rock. Marcel leapt, sliding his legs forward and ramming the sword into the air beneath him. Several feet of shelf crashed into the pit behind him, deafening in its wake.

Sword beneath him, Marcel skimmed across the chasm like a fallen skater over ice. The solid rock of the other side loomed in front of him, and he jerked the sword up at the last moment and rolled onto the tunnel.

He'd used the sword to find the solid rock from the past, before the floor had collapsed in the earthquake.

The air in the cave suddenly found its way into my lungs. It was stale. I pressed a hand to my chest, rubbing my fingers against my collar.

How could you want to kiss someone and strangle him at the same time? He could have died!

"It worked!" Marcel exclaimed, laughing. "It actually worked!"

"Don't you ever do that again, Marcel Gustave Ellsworth," I said through clenched teeth as I tiptoed forward, testing the rock, somehow hoping the air quality would improve in that short distance.

A warning of some kind tried to pierce the wall in my mind I'd built to keep the nightmares at bay. I shook my head. I had to focus. I had to get Marcel away from the sorcerers. And myself, of course.

"You know," he said. "I think both of your explanations fit the sword's glowing habit." He pushed to his feet and raised the sword. "Stand clear. Just in case this thing is like my ring and only tolerates one person at a time, I'm going to toss it to you. You can probably walk over with it. I ... well ... running helped me get my courage up."

And prevented me from stopping you.

He raised and lowered the sword a few times, testing its weight. "You might not believe it, but I'm pretty good at shot put." His expression pinched in the sword's light as he looked over the chasm.

I rubbed my itching finger against my palm. "I believe you, but it would help if you asked it to land at my feet."

If he made an exclamation of relief at my statement, it was lost to my breathing. When had the air fouled so? I gulped another breath as the sword flew toward me. It landed with a clang a foot away, but I only stared at it. I tugged at my collar, scratching my finger against it. I couldn't go over the pit. The air ... it was too ... hollow ... over the pit.

"Gabriella?" Marcel's call was shrouded in a haze. I heard it, but it didn't register a response. "Gabriella! Stop!"

MARCEL ELLSWORTH

"Fight it, Gabriella! Fight it!"

But she made no response. How could I have been so stupid! Of course they would put the Call on her to bring her back. What chance of fighting it did she have this close? I should have tested the sword for a foot or so and then sent her across instead of leaving her, but I'd feared she wouldn't go unless I crossed first, proving it possible despite her childhood experience.

As she disappeared beyond the sword's radiance I knelt at the pit's edge. Fingers curled around its jagged rim, I swung my feet over. I had enough bruises from the last time I crossed to know the rock face was littered with sufficient protruding rocks for handholds and footholds.

My feet found some, and I lowered myself down until the stones under my feet seesawed like those on a pile, or a dog's burial mound.

I leapt down the mound and stumbled over the rubble until hitting the opposite wall. Some instinct warned me of the thin shelf extending over my head. I needed to break it off so I'd have a steady face to climb over. Backing up a ways, I blindly searched the rubble for a suitable bombardment. Finding a sizable rock, I launched it at the shelf. It cracked against it, and the whole shelf rumbled. That was unexpected.

I scrambled out of the way and crouched, covering my head with my arms as the shelf crashed into the pit. A glow disturbed the darkness. I clambered over the debris and kicked rocks aside until I could pick up the sword. I jammed it into the air half a foot above the cave floor and stepped onto the air beside it. The sword held fast, and my foot found rock I couldn't see to stand on. Trailing the sword beside me to create an invisible ramp, I ascended the pit and climbed out onto the tunnel floor.

For all its magic, the sword was cumbersome and didn't readily cleave heads. I left it beside the wall and sprinted after Gabriella.

I ran through the dark, touching the walls occasionally for guidance and loosening the clasp holding the toy wand in its place. Lantern light floated toward me over the remains of the brick barrier. Why hadn't whoever first discovered the lair destroyed it as the law demanded!

A couple of men stood near the entrance, and I tensed in preparation for a fight, but they made no move to stop me. Their smug look almost gave me pause. They still wanted me. And I had come back of my own free will.

So be it.

I bounded over the rubble and pulled the toy wand from my sleeve. Not a dozen feet from the altar, Gabriella inched forward, her struggle evident in the taut lines of her body and the slowness of her steps. The old woman walked backward before her, crooning to her, leading her toward the altar.

My grip tightened around the silver-painted wand—a toy, but it was all I had. That and trust in the foresight of the one who had given it to me. I darted to the right for a clear line of sight and hurled the wand at the altar.

"Destroy!"

Pivoting, I tackled Gabriella, tucking her beneath me as the altar exploded.

Chapter 24

An enchanter can gift a half-magic a finite store of magic to manipulate at will. Few things are as dangerous as an angry half-magic with access to an enchanter's power.

The Fall of Bevvelian by Edgar Frock

GABRIELLA FLORAISON

THE CHAMBER WAS quiet when consciousness found its way back to me. Despite that, I woke to the feeling one of my nightmares was about to play out. Two sorcerers stood at the ready, armed with spine-loaded crossbows since wands were, thank heavens, scarcer to them than to us. The old woman and two men lay on the floor, unmoving. Keldan and the rest, I assumed, had followed the tunnel out to the river path.

A moan acknowledging the aching of my entire body found its way to my lips. Marcel quietly shushed me. I realized with a start that I was sitting in his lap, and that he was once more chained to the cave wall, only with his hands bound in front of him this time. Ropes bound my own wrists and ankles.

"They don't need to know you're awake," he whispered against my forehead. He adjusted his arm about me, and I relaxed against him once more.

The guards moved farther from us, closer to the tunnel, and began to talk amongst themselves.

"It should be safe to speak now," Marcel whispered. He lifted my hands just enough to show me the blood-stained tip of my scarred finger.

I sucked in a breath.

"You're free, Gabriella," he assured me. "You didn't touch the altar. The scar tore open when the altar shattered. You passed out."

"Shattered?"

"Yes." He turned his head, mine moving with it until a gaping hole in the wall showed itself. "You're free."

My heart stilled like a diver at the brink, afraid to leap. "Of that altar anyway."

"I did a little reading after learning of your affliction, my dear pessimist. That was the only altar that could call you. Unless you go searching for another, you're safe. Nevertheless, try not to pick up any splinters off the floor."

My heart thumped. Was it true? My greatest shame and fear was no more? But if the scar opened and bled, it must be. I waited for some great joy to well up in me, or tears of relief and gratitude, but none came, only a heavy sort of peace shielding me from any strong emotion. One day I might be able to rejoice in my freedom, but for now it was little more than a fact I knew, rather than felt, I should be grateful for.

Nonetheless, I moved my hands over Marcel's. "Thank you."

He linked his fingers through mine. "Don't mention it. An Ellsworth always settles his scores."

"Only those repaying good, I hope?"

He chuckled. "You should know better than to ask that, after all the displays of temper I've shown you." A chorus of harsh cries flooded into the chamber from the tunnel leading to the river path. "Lofton's men are attacking the carts outside," Marcel whispered. "With the pit behind and Lofton's men ahead, and likely at the cave entrance too, the sorcerers are trapped. We're bargaining tools. They don't dare harm us." I heard a smile form in his voice. "The duke will get us out, return the treasure, and no one will be the wiser. Tomorrow, they'll say you look tired but as beautiful as ever and never guess what a heroine you are." He prattled on. "I do hope they find Sarcodinas before your father's birthday celebration. How they'll catch the lion though, I don't know; he'd slip out of any rope. I do believe the sword has worn off on him."

His words held all the beauty of a jewel, one that, I feared, would turn out to be a counterfeit. Yet they gave some comfort as well as a sense of purpose. It was mortifying to admit, but the sorcerers hadn't signaled the Call merely to get me back but to get Marcel, and through him, Emil Farro's inventions.

Slowly, I inched my fingers to my wand pocket. I came here to get Marcel out, and I would.

"It's not there," he whispered against my forehead. "I managed to hide it before they searched you. You can't use it anymore, you know."

Not as a wand. "Where is it?"

"I'm sitting on it." Checking to make sure no one was watching, he rolled slightly, and I slipped the wand from beneath him and stuffed it up my sleeve before settling back against him.

He pressed my hand. I closed my eyes and lowered my chin. Footsteps approached, then moved away in a nervous staccato. More footfalls followed, pounding into the chamber from the tunnel to the river path.

"Hurry up. The support's about to give," a sorcerer said, his breathing heavy.

Marcel tensed, and I dared open my eyes, then immediately wished I'd remained in ignorance. Two men pushed Tyndale, his hands bound, into the chamber. His jaw was set, but when he saw us, he blanched. Blood stained his jacket at his shoulder.

David Ashby.

Keldan and several others bearing crates hurried past him. Cox was with them. *So that's where Damien's been hiding.* I wished Harvey had done more than yell at the groom. I wished I had gotten in a better kick when he was masquerading as Tyndale behind the stable.

Keldan glanced between the bound Tyndale and the free Damien, a strange light in his eyes.

The chamber shook and dust gushed from the tunnel. Coughing, the men stumbled further into the chamber.

"What now, Keldan?" the young blond sorcerer demanded. "They've trapped us in here. The hostages won't be any good if we've no way to escape. Lofton will never just let us go."

Another explosion shook the lair, coming once again from the river path. It was soon followed by the crash of falling rocks. The Duke of Lofton must've put his own block in place to ensure the sorcerers didn't undo theirs.

"Don't worry so, Jace." Keldan toed the old woman's body, a bloody mess from having taken the brunt of the altar's bursting, unintentionally sparing Marcel and me. "She said this place is littered with secret rooms and passages shrouded by doors that blend with the cave wall. Find one that goes to the main chamber. Lofton won't sicken his half-magics by having them take our blocking spell from the river tunnel. He'll come round by the main entrance and the pit."

"The duke always did prefer a frontal attack," Jace said with a wicked grin. "What are these doors like?"

"How the devil should I know? Take Damien and find out." Keldan twisted around to study Tyndale. He prominently balanced his black wand between his palms as he strode toward him. Did sorcerers normally give their Calleds wands? Or had his master given him his for tonight so he could stay safely away? "Well, well, if it isn't the *real* Magic Thief." He gestured to Tyndale's guards, and they chained Tyndale to the wall a ways down from us. "Thought you'd get away with leading Lofton and his men here, did you?"

When Tyndale didn't reply, Keldan continued, with a sideways glance at Damien, "You're awfully modest for such a famous thief."

Leaving off examining the wall, Damien bounded toward them, poking a finger to his own chest and shooting a look of bitter jealousy at Tyndale. "He's not the Magic Thief. I am."

"You're just a bungler, Damien." Keldan sneered, and a few of the others laughed. "You couldn't make it as a shopkeeper or as an actor. Even as a thief, you'd be nothing without *Lord Tyndale*."

"That's not true, and you know—"

"Know what? That you tricked him into training you? That you copied confidential entries from his journals on half-magic research?"

To my surprise, Damien's lips drew back in an expression of pride and contempt that would rival Aunt Helene's. "I am a thief, aren't I?" His confidence quickly reverted to bluster at Keldan's contemptuous snort. "I made more use of his knowledge than he ever would have. And I'm not a bungling half-magic—or even a bungling Sorcerer's Called. I'm a legend across the continents. I'm the Magic Thief."

Praying they would stay distracted, I pressed the wand hidden in my sleeve against my skin. It warmed with the contact but still warned of fragility. How could I make it revert to a ring?

Keldan threw his head back and laughed. "Not you, Damien. You made Tyndale a legend."

Damien bristled, and Tyndale dropped his gaze. A look of pain wreathed Tyndale's features before he hid his face, reminding me of his earlier declaration in this very place that he would see the Thief caught and the altar destroyed. How could he accomplish that when he was in chains? Marcel and I both trapped with him? How could I get this bothersome wand to change back to a ring?

Keldan motioned for the others to return to the search for the doors. "Come now, Damien," he said, pacing toward him. "Whose doppelganger is it that you use when you steal? I admit it's a clever disguise, but is that all it is? Is it that you're the proverbial bull in the china shop while Tyndale has the grace of a panther?"

Short, stout, squint-eyed Damien reddened with every barb Keldan sent his way, while Keldan's hungry eyes feasted on Damien's rage and pain. I almost pitied the Thief. Had life always been this way, him falling short in every comparison?

Marcel's cheek was warm against my forehead. *The plain, bumbling Baron of Carrington* some called him. How often had he felt the short end of a comparison? Yet it didn't define or drive him even if it did bother him.

Damien could have been so much more than what nature and circumstances, and his own choices, had made him. He could have been like Marcel, always fighting his weaknesses and bettering himself, becoming a man anyone would be proud to know.

"And when you mess things up," Keldan continued, "your faithful brother-in-law fixes them for you. He's the legend who charmed even those you robbed." Scoffing, Keldan flipped his wand and grasped it in one hand like a dagger he was eager to use. "Failure and doppelganger spells are your only true talents. Lord Ackman could find a much better half-magic to give the power of enchantment to than you."

Alarm registered in Damien's eyes. "Ackman promised, and don't forget who got *your* lord out of prison."

"I won't, don't worry," Keldan snapped. "Get back to hunting for the tunnel."

Fists clenched at his side, Damien obeyed.

Grinding my teeth in frustration, I tried bending the wand, but it didn't budge. *Please, Marcel must get away.*

Keldan smirked, and his gaze slithered around the room to us. I quickly closed my eyes. "What are you doing?" he demanded.

My heart jumped, and I slowly released the wand without obviously moving my hand.

"Well?"

Marcel squeezed my hand comfortingly and asked in a superior manner, "Whom are you addressing?" He lifted his chained hands. "Neither of us is in a position to do much."

Keldan's cold silence held a threat I didn't want to consider. "Keep quiet and still," he said at last. He stalked off, barking orders at those hunting for the passageways, soon seeming to forget about us as the hunt intensified.

My chest burned, finally realizing it had neglected its job, and I took a breath. Slowly, I pinched the wand and started easing it from my sleeve. Tyndale lightly tapped the floor, gaining my attention, and nodded toward my hand. How he knew what I was trying to accomplish I didn't know, but I sensed he did.

Tyndale glanced around, then signaled an all-clear with a slight raise of his hand. I pushed the wand over the floor into his grasp. He closed both hands over it, and it disappeared. The ring's gold band became evident. He slid it silently back to me, the ring hovering over the floor. I snatched it up and leaned back against Marcel, playing the unconscious woman once again at Marcel's signal.

Dried blood pinched the skin around my temple and matted my hair though I felt no substantial wound there. Had Marcel doctored my appearance so our captors wouldn't be concerned about me, the enchantress, waking and causing trouble? Did I truly look so bad I could pass for a dying woman?

I shook off the frivolous concern. The ring was safe, and that was what mattered. I rubbed my finger over the king's seal, marveling at the craftsmanship of the metalsmith who had forged it. If I could but use it to get Marcel away ... The duke could take care of the treasures and the sorcerers. Tyndale and I would take care of each other. Somehow.

But Marcel came back for me when they enacted the Call. Where could I send him so he couldn't get back? If I sent him to the storage realm at Aunt Helene's, he wouldn't know where he was and so wouldn't be able to get back. Uncle Bertram checks their storage realms daily and would find him tomorrow. I hated to send him to Aunt Helene, but what option did I have?

Resting my hand on his, I slid the ring onto Marcel's finger and began to twist it. He grabbed my hand, nearly crushing my fingers against the ring.

"Oh no you don't," he whispered in my ear. "We're even, and I'd like to keep it that way."

"Don't be pigheaded. You've got to leave," I said, still battling him for control of the ring. "If they find out where Emil Farro is from you, we're all in trouble."

"What makes you think I know how to find him?"

"Why else would they want you?"

He stiffened, putting a sense of distance between us that hadn't been there before.

I could have bit my tongue off. "I didn't mean it like that. I meant—"

"That I'm neither an enchanter nor a half-magic. I know, and I agree with you. I didn't mean to respond like that." He relaxed somewhat. "A memory of a similar saying in a different context hit me unexpectedly, that's all."

"You know," he continued before I could reply, his voice switching to a teasing tone, "I may have been an orphaned, stuttering, crippled non-magic, but at least I was never a Sorcerer's Called. There's something to be said for that."

I elbowed him. "You were hardly a candidate for that, were you, being a non-magic?"

"'And in my weakness lay my strength.'"

"Your weakness, indeed. We should institute a new *A Floraison never* statement, and an equivalent *An Ellsworth never* one: *An Ellsworth never compares for the sake of pride or shame.*"

"Agreed." He smiled against my forehead, and our stacked hands relaxed in a kind of truce.

Floraisons didn't accept truces.

"I told you I'd explain about the sorcerer's poison, didn't I?" I said.

His arms tightened about me, and I marveled at how comfortable it was to be held by him. "Yes. Go ahead."

"It gave me nightmares—of you."

He startled, his fingers relaxing. "Of me?"

I tried twisting the ring, but he held it fast. Pursing my lips, I attempted again to pry his hand loose but failed. Instinct told me he wore a smug smile, but I refused to give him the pleasure of observing it.

He shifted, and I felt him looking down at me. "Have I ever told you how much I admire the Floraison virtues?"

"You do?" Wanting to see the truth of it in his eyes, I met his gaze, and my breath caught at the intensity there.

"Immensely." He kissed me, tugged my hand from his, and disappeared.

I plopped onto the floor, barely catching his empty chains before they clattered to the floor. He'd tricked me! He'd distracted me and sent himself away. I would *definitely* turn that man into a frog. But no princess was going to kiss him.

He admired the Floraison virtues ... He didn't thoroughly dislike my family after all. Maybe after this they wouldn't disapprove of him so, and then maybe ...

I shook my head and bent my attention to the cruel metal chains in my lap. I quietly laid them aside and glanced around. Tyndale nodded curtly, as if approving Marcel's escape. Only he seemed to have noticed.

At least Marcel was away and safe, and that warmed my heart. One side of my mouth curved up, and I drew up my knees and wrapped my arms around them. Then the smile faded, and I touched my hand to my lips. Why did I have a feeling he was not going to stay away?

"They've been blocked off, the magic taken." Damien pressed one palm against the cave wall and with his other hand indicated a door's outline. "Another half-magic's been here," he said with a snarl.

"Need we ask which one?" Keldan turned to the curve of the chamber where Tyndale and I sat. "He'll just have to put the magic ba—" His face reddened, and a vein popped out on his temple. "Where is he?" Keldan yelled, moving toward me with the ferocity of a charging bull. I pressed back against the wall, trembling despite my vow to remain defiantly courageous. He snatched a handful of my hair and jerked my head back, giving me no choice but to look up at him. "Where?"

"Through the hidden door."

He pulled me to my knees, yanking my hair until I thought it would rip out. "One dose wasn't enough for you, was it?"

Tyndale begged him to leave me alone, but Keldan ignored him and brought my face close enough to his own for me to see that not one speck of color pierced the ebony of his eyes.

"Do you think a sorcerer's lair can be so easily destroyed?" he said. "The altar may be too broken to call you to itself, but the lair lives. Don't make me find a shard of the altar for you to prick your finger on. No one's here to save you this time."

My heart quaked, but I held his gaze and wouldn't let go. "What was your name before?"

He startled, his grip loosening. "What do you mean?"

"What was your name when your eyes were as blue as mine, before the sorcerers took you? Was your name Keldan, or did they take even that?"

He stared at me, his jaw working. Then his expression hardened. He jerked my sleeve up to reveal the bruise left by the first spine.

"Surely there is hope even for a Called," I pressed. "Don't you want to be free?"

He regarded his own scar for one heartbeat before shaking his head. "There is only freedom in answering the Call." Whispering something that chilled my blood, he smashed his free hand onto the rock. Seven shining black spines were in his hand when he raised it. "Perhaps this will be enough to get rid of you."

Tensing, I put a block around my mind.

"I found one!" Damien cried.

When no spines pierced my skin or nightmares my mind, I looked up. Keldan gripped the spines, his thrust paused mid-air.

"Let her be," Tyndale pleaded. "You'll need her if you expect to get information from Ellsworth. You have to find a way to reach Farro, don't you? Your master commanded it, and you, his Called, must obey. You must spare her."

A ring of blue outlined Keldan's pupils. He looked from me to the spines, a dreadful hopelessness and yet resolve in his gaze. My heart stilled. Killing me was the real Keldan's way of sparing me. Death was the only hope he saw for a Called.

"We can use the Floraison's Demandez à Voir mirror instead," Keldan responded.

"You can't use the mirror like a treasure map," Tyndale insisted. "It may show you where Farro is—in a room—but not how to get there. He won't be easily reached."

Keldan clenched his jaw, then sent the spines sailing Tyndale's way. Tyndale dodged, kicking several out of the air. "My lord Ackman can make the mirror show him whatever he wishes. Don't forget that, half-magic."

The Called shoved me back against the wall before going to inspect the hidden passageway. He sent a man down it, and soon the sorcerer came running back. "It goes to the main chamber, which is empty, but it won't be long until the enchanters will have had time to get there."

"We'll be sure to give them a welcome then." Keldan strode around the chamber, hands on his hips, surveying the lair like a burglar his tools. He indicated the old sorceress's body. "She claimed she didn't have a wand, but search her and see if she had anything useful."

Keldan paused at the debris-strewn table and picked up an ancient stone knife. "Damien, you and the others go to the main chamber. Spread out between the two blind tunnels and the hidden one. Lofton will never risk his men by bringing them inside. They'll stay at the gate while he goes to the pit and tries to cross it."

A man who appeared to be of Ceurian descent opened his mouth, but Keldan cut him off.

"Lofton will show. He's as cocksure as they come. It's a wonder and a curse on us that he's lived this long. He also knows we have his nephew and the enchantress." He paused, his confident demeanor faltering as he ran his fingers lightly down his black scar. Clenching his fist, he looked up at his men again, his customary strength returning.

"I'll handle the duke myself, but you, Damien, will hide in the tunnel nearest the one leading to the pit and make use of those famous acting skills of yours to scream like Jonathan Lofton. His men will come running, and we'll cut them off. We *will* leave with those treasures and our baron."

He put a spell on the stone knife, tossed it to one of the younger sorcerers, and then strode around the chamber once more, indicating those he wished to command with a wave of his hand, the conductor for some horrifying symphony. "Jace, you and the girl will come with me. The half-magic we'll leave here, bound; we can't risk him getting close enough to the enchantress to use her power. Kerkly, you stay here. Guard Tyndale and pick up Ellsworth when he returns for the girl. And, Jace, see that Lady Gabriella is gagged. Chain her to the wall by her wrists and cut the bindings on her ankles. She'll need to be able to walk when we leave."

I shrank back against the wall, the threat of a gag somehow worse than the chafing of ropes or rusty chains, and started reciting what Marcel had taken to calling my family's motto during our lessons with Henry—*A Floraison can handle any situation with confidence and poise.* I would *not* cower in terror.

The sorcerers disappeared down the hidden tunnel, their scuffing footfalls echoing back, but Damien loitered at the entrance. He flexed his fingers and cast a glance at Tyndale. His brother-in-law stared back, his gaze intense.

"What's the matter, Damien?" Keldan asked. "Should I have asked permission instead of giving orders?" Damien glared at him. "Oh, that's right," Keldan continued, his tone patronizing. "You're a thief, not a warrior. Do try to make yourself as useful as you can. After all, you do want the power of enchantment, don't you? To be the most admired, most talented man alive—both a half-magic and an enchanter?"

Damien cast another glance at Tyndale, and I remembered his declaration of having made his choice. He took a few steps after the others, but Keldan stopped him.

"Wait a moment, Thief. How many street urchins did you say our rogue half-magic here adopted besides the one at the inn? Four?"

Damien's eyes bugged. "Y-yes."

"And where do they live?"

When Damien didn't immediately reply, Keldan raised his eyebrows. I wanted to scream at Damien. If the Thief had any strength of character, now was the time to show it.

Damien licked his lips. "In a cottage near a little hamlet called Lisson."

Keldan glanced between Tyndale, whose face was studiously blank, and Damien. "He's moved them or he wouldn't be so quiet." Keldan smiled. "It's no matter. We'll find them. We have the mirror, don't we? Do go on, Thief."

Damien spun on his heel and was soon swallowed by the tunnel. Tyndale remained expressionless.

"Remember I want to hear Lofton's scream," Keldan called after Damien. He knelt beside Tyndale. "Come to save your dear brother-in-law from the consequences of his actions again?"

"Not this time." The familiar sadness in Tyndale's eyes was lost to a steady determination.

"Then what did you come for?"

"To right my wrongs as far as I can."

"What wrongs would those be?"

"You've already discussed them."

Keldan snorted. "So you're taking on the guilt of his crimes now too, are you? And here I thought you were growing hard-hearted and sensible at last."

"He'll bear the guilt of his own sins as I will answer for mine, but I won't be a part of his any longer."

"Nobly spoken." Keldan bared his teeth. "There's another way to make up for training and enabling him. It's something I've been thinking about for some time."

Tyndale didn't reply.

Keldan absently scrubbed the palm of his hand. "I don't much like the Thief, so I'm willing to bargain with you. If you unlock the secrets of the items we've picked up here, I'll see to it that Ackman gives you the power of enchantment instead of him." He paused. "And we'll make sure no one takes you from your little family or them from you."

"No, thank you."

Keldan burst out laughing. "You're so amusingly righteous. I suppose you've always sworn never to work with the sorcerers?"

Tyndale shrugged.

"Damien's too arrogant by half and greedy," Keldan continued. "He was assigned to steal items from enchanters in different countries and give them to us to be sold at auction to sorcerers. He was handsomely paid, but the two-faced devil has been stealing the items back from the buyers. My lord Ackman finds this duplicity of his amusing, but not many sorcerers do. Ackman's approval could jeopardize his own safety and standing. I want you to find out what Damien did with the items, and then I'll rid Ackman of his influence."

Tyndale looked Keldan in the eye and smiled. "He didn't steal them back. I did."

"You—" Keldan's expression twisted from shock to fury to amusement. He quickly sobered. "What did you do with them, magic thief?"

"Nothing you'd approve of."

Keldan slapped him, the controlled tenor of his voice possessing a deadly undertone. "I admire your talent, but I want those items back." He jammed his wand under Tyndale's chin, forcing his head up. "We *will* find your children."

When Tyndale didn't respond, Keldan pressed the wand deeper, then stood and spun away toward Jace. "Bring her."

Jace yanked my arm, the fine tip of a black spine testing the strength of the skin at my neck, forcing me to keep pace with him as we neared the pit. He sniffed, and I stopped the power burst burning slowly through my bonds behind me, praying he blamed the torches for the odor of burning.

"When we get to the pit, keep her in front of you and close enough to me for use as a shield," Keldan said softly. Jace nodded and adjusted the pistol-sized crossbow, fitted to fire multiple spines at once, hanging from his shoulder.

Light curved around the last bend, throwing shadows our way, and my stomach knotted tighter than a street urchin's tangled hair. Would I endanger the duke, or would he save me?

Jace increased his long-legged pace. Though struggling to keep up, I began the power burst again and discreetly glanced around for the Sword of Ora.

We rounded the bend, the light of our torch pitiable against those lining the tunnel across the pit. Jace quickly settled the torch in a holder in the wall on our side and then put me in place beside Keldan.

The Duke of Lofton stood at the far ledge, feet apart, arms crossed, wand in his hand. A middle-aged man I wasn't familiar with stood to his right. He bore no wand, and some instinct told me he was a half-magic. The duke didn't spare a glance for me but fixed his attention on Keldan. "Who are you? Where's Ackman?" he asked.

My captor gave a slight bow. "Reese Keldan, at your service, Your Grace. My lord Ackman has entrusted this venture to me." *And the Thief,* the clipped manner of his declaration added. "My master regrets he could not be here to greet such an old friend. Perhaps we could arrange a meeting for tea for the two of you at another time and location?"

The duke looked Keldan up and down, his gaze finding the scar on Keldan's hand before Keldan hid it. A flash of pity softened his gaze. "So you're his Called, the prison guard."

"I have that honor."

The duke scoffed, all traces of compassion gone. "I'll deal with your master later. Right now, I want Lady Gabriella, the baron, and my nephew."

"That's most inconvenient, for so do I. However"—Keldan drew out the word—"given that you've blocked us in this damp, crumbling place, I'm willing to make a bargain."

The duke's eyes narrowed, but he motioned for Keldan to continue.

Trying to get the attention of the half-magic at the duke's side, I gently tapped my toe against the floor. I slid it in a crescent shape and then straight back to where I'd tapped. *They circled behind you.* The half-magic only furrowed his brows. I tried again, my body tense, dreading to hear Damien's scream.

"You'll gain her in exchange for not resisting our departure." Keldan held up his hand before the duke could reply. "The others we'll leave a ways out, unharmed, of course."

"Let me see her finger."

I jerked in surprise, registering a flash of anger before common sense smothered it. Once again I thanked Marcel for coming back for me. Would he do it again? He'd been gone for some time. *You wanted him safe. You wanted him gone.* But I also wanted him to be the brave, noble, self-sacrificing man he was created to be. But in perfect safety. He could make it back after the danger was over.

"Aren't you the suspicious one?" Keldan held up my scarred finger, the nearness of his scar sending a tremble through me as if the blackness were contagious. "White as any normal scar, my good duke. She made a poor choice."

A tension I hadn't noticed in the duke's shoulders eased. "I want Ellsworth up front as well."

"Nothing doing, Your Grace. If you don't like my terms, we can settle this with a good old-fashioned duel." He waved his hand toward Jace and the man accompanying the duke and then toward me. "We even have seconds and an impartial witness." I protested through my gag. "Or perhaps *prize* would be the better term for the lady," Keldan amended.

He moved closer to the pit, pushing me forward. The thin shelf trembled underneath us with each step, and I willed my knees to stay firm as they pushed me almost up to the edge. *The floor will hold. It will hold.*

Again, I lightly tapped the little section of rock jutting in front of me and circled my foot back around. Still, the half-magic stared at me blankly, but then he looked to the side. The Sword of Ora, stowed in a crevice at the base of the wall, glowed blue.

"Wands would be the weapon, of course. No inequality there tonight." Keldan pulled out his wand, and the half-magic's mouth twisted in an oath.

"I shall miss your engaging conversation when you're dead," the duke replied as he uncrossed his arms, his stance loosening for a fight.

"I'm flattered."

From beyond the tunnel's twists rolled a scream of agony that stole my breath and the duke's attention. A volley of black spines shot over my shoulder, almost reaching the duke before he threw up a shield. The spines clattered into the pit as Keldan began his own attack.

"Stand still, Gabriella," the duke yelled.

Summoning all my courage to keep myself in place, I squeezed my eyes shut, hardly daring to breathe as spines and spells hissed past, focusing instead on my feet as every movement caused the shelf to roll beneath me. It was so thin there, and they had positioned me so close to the pit. My eyes darted open. Shields worked both ways. The duke couldn't retain his protective shield and use magic to catch me if Keldan ...

I lunged backward, but Keldan caught me and thrust me over the edge.

"Catch her if you can, Lofton!" he cried.

I couldn't even scream as I fell.

Chapter 25

The enchanters say that using a killing spell against an-
other leaves a mark on a man, so they endeavor to find
other means of disabling their enemies. Sorcerers have no
such scruples, and no one can guess what a half-magic will
choose when the choice is required—in that half-magics
and non-magics are alike.

The Peculiarities of Magic by Lionel Bachman

MARCEL ELLSWORTH

I F ONLY THE ring could travel long distances. *Just one*
more jump, ring. You can handle it. I gave it a final
twist and opened my eyes.

A man with the shoulders of a blacksmith and short,
cropped hair the color of coal hunched over a workbench
manipulating the tiny mechanics of a pocket watch. A
pistol, loaded and cocked if I knew my cousin, rested at
his elbow. Mirrors hung on every wall, leaving no part of
the room unseen from Emil's workbench. Three vases of
fresh cut flowers lent color and fragrance to the room, a
lily taking a prominent place in each. A rocking horse
with faded, chipped paint ran forever in one spot at the
corner nearest the trap door that once led from the attic
workshop to the nursery of his childhood home. But so
long as the rocking horse rocked, Emil lived in a realm
reachable only by magic.

The intricate movement of delicate tools in the watch's open back paused, then resumed at a faster pace. He'd seen me in the mirrors.

Deeming it safe, I limped across the room to him. "Emil, I need it."

He laid the tools aside and snapped the watch shut. "I'm sure you do, cousin. From the looks of you, you left a brawl in a hurry. Inspector Olan still hounding you?" He rose and embraced me, and then, stepping away, said as seriously as if I'd asked for the world, "It's not for you."

"Not *that*—keep that concealed, by all means," I said. "And unfinished preferably. I need the pistol you promised." Surveying the room, I picked up the ordinary pistol on the table, un-cocked it, and slipped it into my belt. "And it's sorcerers at the moment. Olan's next."

His eyebrows rose. "Yours isn't ready yet, but I'll see what I can get you." He moved away to a locked wardrobe.

"Thanks. They all think I'll lead them to you—Olan, the sorcerers. I know there's no need to tell you, but watch out for yourself."

"Fools." He cleared his throat. "Sorry about the trouble."

I grunted in response, refraining from another lecture on the danger and arrogance of resuscitating an ancient experiment—unfinished for good reason—to give or take the power of enchantment. Instead, I walked around the room, surveying the guns positioned around it. I helped myself to powder and shot and picked up another pistol.

Emil poked his head out from behind the open wardrobe door. "You said *one*. Remember, I'm in hiding. You can't leave me defenseless."

"Defenseless?" I arched an eyebrow and glanced about the room again. "You never travel with less than a dozen weapons." Of the typical sort. That wasn't counting the magical and less typical non-magical.

He harrumphed and went back to searching the wardrobe. "I thought that ring didn't take baggage, not that my guns are baggage."

"It was a warrior's wand. Weapons are as clothes to it."

He grunted his approval. "By the way, there's a basin of water in the corner. Do something about your wrists and head, why don't you?"

"I'm in a hurry, Emil."

"Hurrying gets people killed."

I ground my teeth, but Emil was not a man to be moved, either physically or by argument. I rolled up my sleeves and went to the basin, steeling myself against the sight of my wounds. But keeping my focus on why I'd come, I kept the faintness at bay.

As I was drying off, Emil pulled a sleek blue pistol case from the wardrobe, set it on the desk, and unlocked it. He tossed me the pistol and a bag of shot. "Tell me how well this one works. I'm still sorting out the kinks."

After pocketing the bag of shot, I examined the pistol, flipping it over in my hands and testing the grip.

"No magic required to be shot but should be useful in a magics' fight," he said. "Perfect for you."

"It's a beauty, Emil. Thanks." High quality and elegant in design, it was proof Emil could be a gunsmith to a king if he wanted to be, not that he needed the job or the money. Etched into the pistol's handle were his initials, *EVF*, along with the image of a bee hovering outside a honeycomb. When I tilted the handle, the comb moved, but the bee was always after it.

"Venom in the bullets?" I asked.

His lips quirked. "Hardly."

The ring was warm, and I felt its protest against another travel so soon. "I'll be there in a twist. Just one twist," I promised it. One more travel to find the sword, and then I'd plan how to get Gabriella and Tyndale out of the lair.

The village where I'd stopped disappeared, and I collided with the blond sorcerer near the pit. I tumbled back, kicking him as I fell. Jace stumbled but caught himself and rounded on me with a crossbow loaded with spines. I rolled, cursing myself for not loading *the* gun before I traveled. Drawing the old-fashioned pistol, I twisted my ring. *Beside the sword.*

Even as I landed at the wall, I caught the twang of the crossbow and the skidding of spines on the stone floor where I'd been. Closer to me, Keldan spun around, wide-eyed, and sighted me with his wand. I fired at him and yanked up the sword. The flash of a magical shield flared in front of Keldan, and the crack of a bullet deflected into rock blasted my ears.

Across the pit, Lofton knelt at the ledge, one arm stretched over the empty air of the pit as if he were a puppeteer holding a puppet's string, the other arm he kept raised to somehow deflect Keldan and Jace's assault without a full-fledged shield. A man stood beside him, deathly pale, a black spine in his arm. He gripped Lofton's shoulder. A half-magic drawing power to fight and to counteract the poison as only half-magics could?

Cries and the strange noises of a battle between magics carried up the tunnel from the main chamber. A sorcerer crept around the bend with a loaded crossbow. Cursing the man as much for keeping me from my search for Gabriella as for sneaking up on my friends, I raised the sword, calling on it to stay in this time as Gabriella had when she cut my bonds, and twisted my ring. *Beside the sorcerer.*

Now a foot to my right, the sorcerer advanced, but my hands were empty. The Sword of Ora didn't travel. Growling, I slapped the crossbow from the sorcerer's grasp and punched him squarely on his slack-jawed chin. He hit the floor, and I rapped the butt of the spent pistol on his head for good measure.

I crouched behind him for cover, but my weak leg trembled, and I crashed to my knees. Biting my tongue against the pain, I loaded both guns.

The cry of a spell came from the path to the lair, and two men shrieked in quick succession. The half-magic collapsed with another spine in his arm. Jace doubled over and then hit the floor.

"Keldan!" Tyndale yelled. My gut tightened at the weak edge to his voice. He walked into the torchlight with the short, shuffling steps of an injured man. A spine protruded from his shoulder. He held a silver wand out before him.

Keldan twisted but for a split second before sending another spell at Lofton and then tucking and rolling toward the wall. He grabbed the Sword of Ora, rammed it into the wall, and disappeared into the stone.

"Ellsworth, get to the main chamber," Lofton yelled back to me as he felt his friend's neck for a pulse. "Find the medic and get the injured to safety."

"Not until I find Gabriella. Where is she, Tyndale?"

Hissing, Tyndale leaned against the wall and pulled a spine from his shoulder and another from his thigh. "Keldan brought her here." The concern and pain lacing his voice sent a bolt to my heart. He tried to push off from the wall but groaned and sank to the floor, unconscious.

"Tyndale!" I reached for my ring but stopped at Lofton's voice.

"Ellsworth, go for the medic. Gabriella's safe. She's in the pit." Lofton knelt beside his companion and grasped the man's hand, using it like a glove to extract the spines. "Go. I'll be right behind you."

Gabriella's safe. My heart echoed the beautiful phrase as I stood and toed the sorcerer at my feet. "Careful of this one."

In a twist I was in the main chamber. With a wand in my face. And it wasn't a black one.

"Stop! He's the real one." A green-eyed man in a worn brown coat grabbed the shoulder of a young man bearing a strong resemblance to Jonathan Lofton, despite a difference in coloration. The young man's jacket was off, stuffing a gap between the stacked barrels acting as a barrier to the spines and spells flying around the chamber.

The young-looking Jonathan lowered his wand, and the gentleman in the brown coat slumped to the ground beside a man with enough spines sticking out of him for a round of darts.

"What do you mean 'the real one'?" I asked, and then got the feeling I didn't want to know. The man in brown began picking out the spines. A half-magic. The medic?

With a sinking feeling, I realized Tyndale and the other half-magic weren't the ones most in need of attention. "Jonathan—"

"I'm Jonathan—duck!" The young man pulled me down seconds before a barrel blew out, sending splinters of wood and a spray of pungent wine over our heads. We scrambled away, helping the medic drag the downed man. When settled behind another set of barrels, Young Jonathan brushed off his sleeves. "Someone let that one get by. Did you bring a wand?"

"I'm not an enchanter."

"Oh."

I pulled Emil's custom pistol from my belt. "Will this serve instead? Lofton sent me to help get the wounded to safety."

Young Jonathan regarded the gun with an imperious lift of his brows but then shrugged. "It's not traditional, but I suppose it will do—if they don't block the lead shots or redirect them at you."

"I don't think that will happen with this one."

"Perhaps not." Young Jonathan grinned and flipped his wand. "But don't worry. We'll cover one another. Come on then. Stephan fell over there near the other tunnels."

"Wait." I tugged off my ring and held it out to the medic. He wiped his brow and looked up at me with a question in his eyes. "It's a traveling ring. You're a half-magic; I think you can make it take you and the injured to safety. Lofton's on his way from the pit. There are two men there who need you."

Young Jonathan murmured in awe as the medic took the ring with a look of interest and hope. "We'll go help the others," the former said cheerily. "Come on, non-magic. You're Lady Gabriella's friend, aren't you?" he added before he crouched and then dashed to the cover of the next row of barrels.

I took a step to follow, and my weak leg buckled. I grabbed the rack for support, took a deep breath, set my jaw, and lunged across the space between the barrels, stumbling and catching myself before I reached the relative safety behind Young Jonathan.

"Aren't you?" he prodded as I limped along beside him.

"Yes," I said, surprised by the possessiveness of my tone. I glanced over at the young man. He was handsome, almost Gabriella's age, related to a duke, and didn't trip simply getting from cover to cover. Leaving Gabriella in the pit was definitely a good idea.

Shame burned my cheeks. Was I so wrapped up in my feelings of inferiority and anger at some people's opinions of me that I was blind to the affection of others? Gabriella had relaxed in my arms as I held her and hadn't slapped me when I kissed her. Maybe she didn't judge me by the harsh standards I too often judged myself by and assumed others judged me by.

That familiar, painful kind of hope shot through my chest. Grinding my teeth, I focused on following Young Jonathan. I didn't have time for hopes or fears. Tomorrow, if we survived, she would still be a Floraison and I would still be wanted by the relentless Ceurian inspector. She was probably waiting until we were out of danger to slap me anyway.

With a few clever distractions, Young Jonathan led us safely to a stack of barrels situated barely a foot and a half from the wall. Only one stack remained between us and the blind tunnels storing more wine. Behind that stack lay Stephan, eerily still.

"Ready to go after him?" I asked.

Young Jonathan didn't reply. Crouched like a runner waiting for the signal, he watched the farther of the two tunnels.

From between the barrels, I could just see Damien in the tunnel, hunkered beside a wand-less sorcerer. While the sorcerer employed his crossbow, Damien used his half-magic abilities to direct the sorcerer's magic with dreadful accuracy and strength.

"Don't be a fool," I hissed, seizing the back of Young Jonathan's jacket. "That's a deadly pair." I pulled out Emil's gun. "At least tell me your plan so I can cover you."

He drew back and whispered, "I'm going to lean out far enough to get a shot at the crossbow. I can set it on fire and distract them long enough to give the others a break and let you use that weapon of yours."

"What makes you think fire in a chamber full of wooden casks and wine is a good idea?"

An explosion cracked the air. We ducked as shards of barrels and wine sprayed across the chamber followed by the hiss of flames.

So Keldan and Lofton had arrived.

The odor of burning oak wafted warm and acrid to me. We ducked as another explosion sent waves of debris and burning wine into the air. Yelling, an enchanter dashed from behind a stack as another cask exploded. He went down with a bevy of spines from Damien's friend. Smoke rose from the casks shielding the enchanter Stephan.

Young Jonathan started forward, but I yanked him back. "Get Stephan away from those barrels before they blow. I can't with my bad leg, but I can do something about the Thief and his sorcerer."

His eyes flashed but he shook me off and crept with enviable adeptness to Stephan, shielding him as one of the top barrels blew.

Taking a deep breath, I cocked the pistol and dove out from behind the barrels to get a good shot, then fired at the sorcerer.

A shield flashed as I shoved myself backward over the wet floor, but no bullet struck rock. I didn't hear it strike anything.

I scooted behind the cover of the rack and peered between the barrels as I hurried to reload. The shield was still in place. Damien and the sorcerer appeared frozen, their gazes locked on a spot in the shimmering shield. The sorcerer trembled like a man straining to lift a heavy weight.

A whiff of the gun's powder drifted to me despite the overpowering odor of fermented grapes. I glanced at the butt of Emil's gun. The image of the honeycomb glowed. It shifted, the bee followed, the honeycomb dimmed, and the bee caught it.

That was it. The bullet would stay on target until the sorcerer was too exhausted to maintain the shield. Then both shield and sorcerer would fall.

Drawing myself to my knees, I hurried to finish reloading the gun, but when I glanced up, Damien was reaching through the shield toward the bullet. The sorcerer, wide-eyed, watched.

No no no! I sped my hands, spilling powder in my haste. Damien grabbed the bullet and tossed it away. The shield dropped, and the sorcerer raised his crossbow. Another barrel exploded from the pile where I'd sent Young Jonathan. I crashed to the floor as debris and a collection of spines whizzed over my head. Scooting out of sight, I stood and finished reloading. Not every sorcerer here had a bloody half-magic to snatch enchanted bullets out of the air.

"Your cousin didn't think about half-magics, did he?" Young Jonathan leaned over my shoulder. I scowled at him. "What? Stephan's hidden away from the fire," he said.

I froze. Keldan's black eyes found mine above Young Jonathan's shoulder, and he smiled. "Welcome back." He thrust the boy to the floor, then tapped my chest with his wand.

I shot over the barrels, flying backward through choking fumes, but instead of smashing into the rock, I slowed, my arms jerking behind me though no one touched me. My knees hit stone, and Damien clamped a thick hand over my wrists as the sorcerer put a spine to my neck.

"Lofton," Keldan roared above the hissing and crackling of several fires. "I have the boy, and the Thief has the baron."

Chapter 26

There is some magic in the tree from which wands are made, and thus some magic exists in the wands themselves and allows them to hold and conduct the power of enchantment. But if an enchanter, having lost his wand, summons it back, the wand will use its own power to obey, losing its ability to conduct magic. This is why it will break when used powerfully afterwards. Still, the wand is not fully destroyed even then. They say only the enemies of the mother tree can do that, a tree which neither burns nor topples with the wind.

The Peculiarities of Magic by Lionel Bachman

GABRIELLA FLORAISON

STONES CRACKED AGAINST one another below me. Sweat slicked my palms, and my limbs trembled as I hung in the air. How long of a drop was it? If the Duke of Lofton released me, would I feel the impact or mercifully faint on the way?

Two men screamed, and I plummeted. Pain replaced my breath as I slammed into a pile of stones feet first and crashed backward. Someone caught my head and shoulders, and hands too small for a man's pulled me into a sitting position and untied my gag. It registered that the pain in my legs was more the throb of a bad landing than of a break.

Tyndale's voice echoed into the pit, and the hands quickened their work on my gag.

"Almost done," whispered a familiar young voice.

I spat out the rough fabric, hating the cottony feel of my mouth. "Ryn?" I croaked out.

"Yep." A lantern, suddenly free of its covering, lit our hole. From his ever-present satchel, Ryn pulled a water canteen and pressed it to my lips.

"I'm sorry I couldn't help you down," he continued as he lowered the canteen and began to cut my bindings with a pocket knife. "I don't know levitation spells yet, and I don't have a wand either, but I did help crash the shelf and bring the sword down for Lord Ellsworth to get up earlier. That shelf needed to come down anyway. It was dangerous."

I cocked my head to look at him, aware of his knife at my wrists. He was an enchanter?

Ryn grinned proudly. "Yes, we're two of a kind, you and I. But don't say anything. Not even Uncle Damien knows I'm an enchanter. Papa made sure no half-magic could know it. He didn't teach Uncle Damien *everything* he knows."

A sudden awareness of having heard both "Ellsworth" and "Tyndale" yelled from above drew my attention there. Were they safe?

"Go for the medic. Gabriella's safe. She's in the pit," the duke said.

Ryn swallowed hard, his bravado suddenly wavering, and my heart flipped between fear and pride. Marcel had come back to fight with us. And he was looking for me.

Ryn severed the ropes binding my wrists and helped me to my feet. The stones cracked sharply underneath us.

"How were you planning to get out of here?" I asked as he led me to the corner formed by the side of the tunnel and the wall rising up to the path itself. It quieted above us, and I wasn't sure what to make of that.

"The way I came. Only wait until I've crossed to the other side to follow me up." He pulled a blackened rope from the corner, hooked the lantern to his belt, and scaled the wall.

Using the same torch holder Tyndale had when he chased me to the lair, Ryn swung across to the far side. He dropped the rope end to me, and I began climbing, using the strain of my muscles to distract from nightmares and memories.

"Why did you leave Lord Ellsworth earlier? He sounded quite worried about you," he asked.

"It's a long story, Ryn." I grabbed his hand, and he pulled me over the rim. "I'll tell you tomorrow." After I caught my breath.

Dropping the rope, my arms burning, I looked around to get my bearings. Across the chasm were a sorcerer and a half-magic, the latter's face twitching in nightmares. On our side, a few yards away, lay Tyndale and Jace. Next to Tyndale's slumped form were two spines.

The blood drained from my face. Who was there to help a half-magic deal with sorcerer's poison?

"He's not dying," Ryn spat, whether sensing my concern or combating his own, or both, I wasn't sure. He sprinted forward and kicked the spines from his father's presence. Dropping to his knees, he grabbed Tyndale's hand between both of his. "Wake up, Papa. You haven't finished yet. They need you."

His father remained mute, lost in nightmares, and my heart broke for both father and son. I knelt beside Tyndale, shifted his head into my lap, and brushed his hair and bits of debris from his forehead. My hand warmed oddly at the touch.

"Papa," Ryn persisted, covering his small palm with his father's, touching hands like Henry and I had at our lessons.

I sucked in a breath and touched Tyndale's forehead again, letting my fingers linger. It wasn't the warmth of fever there but the warmth of magic, my magic. He was a half-magic even in unconsciousness: his body was drawing power from Ryn and from me to fight the poison. I grasped his jacket and began pulling it back from his shoulder. The Amphora bulged under his shirt. "Ryn, cut open his trouser leg where the spine went in and press your hand to the wound. We've got to give him magic where the poison is most concentrated."

Ryn quickly did as I asked, working with his knife at a speed that would have terrified me on any other occasion. After ripping Tyndale's shirt where the spine had torn it, I pressed my hand to his darkened wound, flinching as the contact released one of my own barely restrained nightmares. I locked the nightmare away and focused on the warm flow of magic.

"Papa, wake up. We haven't caught the Thief yet." One hand pressed to Tyndale's thigh, Ryn shook his father's uninjured shoulder.

Tyndale moaned. I breathed a prayer of gratitude and a petition for further healing. Ryn shook his shoulder again, and Tyndale opened his eyes, his brows drawing together reproachfully as he focused on his son.

"I told you you'd need me," Ryn said with a confident grin, one that faded fast. "An urchin always knows."

One corner of Tyndale's mouth curved before his gaze shifted to me. "The b-barrels ..." He swallowed hard, and his mouth worked to form words, but his lips remained silent. I cupped his jaw, and his breathing eased. "Break the barrels ... next to the chest ... main chamber. Right first ... then left." He paused and took a breath, his gaze intense. *"The forest encroaches. Night is dead. Uirgae capio."*

I nodded. "My wand—"

"The forest encroaches. Night is dead. Uirgae capio," he repeated with a shake of his head, his eyes dulling. "Hurry."

Ryn held out his knife, hilt toward me but held back, his gaze expectant until I repeated what his father had said.

We both startled as a man in a dusty brown coat materialized across the pit. He supported another whose deathly pallor outmatched even Tyndale's. Marcel had sent the medic. *Don't let him need one himself.* Barely keeping my hands steady, I took Ryn's knife.

"Gabriella." Tyndale's chin dipped sharply to his chest. Ryn pulled the Amphora from beneath Tyndale's shirt and gave it to me. "It doesn't ... work through a ... spell that ... can ... be stolen." His voice dipped to a hoarse whisper, and he shook his head, unable to finish. His gaze tried to tell me something but failed.

I nodded anyway, hoping I would figure it out in time, and settled the chain into place around my neck. I took a few steps away but then ran back, fell to my knees beside him, and kissed his cheek. "Thank you, David Ashby."

I crossed the pit with Ryn's help and then sprinted toward the main chamber.

The overpowering stench of burning casks and wine sickened me before the chamber's light, dimmed by smoke, carried down the tunnel to me. Staying close to the wall, I crept around the last bend, halting where the roof rose up and the walls flared out into the wide chamber.

Keldan stood near the blind tunnels to my left, Young Jonathan in front of him. The other sorcerers rose from their hiding places, crossbows and one other wand at the ready.

"Tell your men to lower their weapons, Lofton," Keldan shouted, raising a fist with a bit of rock showing between his fingers. "I have a shard of the altar, and the boy's not twenty-one yet. I will use this on him—twice—if you attack."

Damien and a sorcerer shoved Marcel to his knees beside Keldan.

The Duke of Lofton, hands raised, stepped from behind a triangle of barrels near the chamber's center.

I gripped Ryn's knife until my knuckles hurt. *A Floraison can handle any situation with confidence and poise.*

Any situation.

Willing my weak knees to straighten and my mind to focus on the task, I ducked around the corner and darted for the oversized barrels with no bung holes standing like sentinels around the tresor chest. I scooted behind the first of the barrels and drove the knife into a stave, repeating the saying Tyndale had given me.

Gripping the hilt with both hands, I yanked the knife out and drove it in again, twisting it as I pulled it out. The wood barely splintered around the knife's slits. I rammed the hilt into the damaged wood once, then again, cracks shooting out like veins.

"The forest encroaches. Night is dead. *Uirgae capio.* Break for heaven's sake." Throwing all my weight behind the knife, I struck the stave, and it collapsed.

A wash of air heavy with the scent of earth and forest and something else escaped into the chamber. Something about the silent darkness of the barrel's innards sent me reeling back. I scrambled to the second one and attacked it with the knife.

"Gabriella!" Marcel cried. Over the tresor chest, I watched, stunned, as Marcel flattened then rolled, kicking his guard in the chest. "Look out!"

The fabric of my dress tugged against my waist, and I dragged my gaze from the men grappling with Marcel to the dusty boots pressed against my hem and up to a man's face. This sorcerer had traded his crossbow for the bewitched stone knife.

"Gabriella!" Marcel shouted as he struggled up and lunged forward.

Snapping back to attention, I threw myself over the tresor chest, my hem ripping. I shoved the chest back as the sorcerer came over it. He stumbled, and I caught his arm and slung him onto the floor. The stone knife slid away from him. I snatched it up and drove it into the second barrel, throwing all my weight into it.

"The forest encroaches. Night is dead. *Uirgae capio.*"

My voice merged with Tyndale's. Deathly pale, he leaned against the rock of the secret tunnel with my wand raised above his head.

The stave cracked. The chamber fell silent, except for the snap and pop of the lid of the first barrel as it flipped off.

The sorcerer crawled frantically away over the tresor chest, and I tumbled back as the warmth of magic burst from the second cask. The air around me blazed the pale green of light filtering through the leaves and vines of a forest canopy.

The forest encroaches.

The Amphora shuddered against my chest and tried to rise, but I wrapped my hand around it, and it stilled. The cask groaned as the stone knife twitched in the shattered stave, dislodged itself, and flew into the first barrel.

"Secure your wands," the duke yelled above a sorcerer's startled cry.

Two black wands sailed for the barrel smelling of earth and forest. Keldan watched, a look of hopeless despair on his face: the Called had failed his master.

The first wand disappeared into the cask, and the green glow flickered at the eerie whisper of shifting leaves.

Night is dead. It claimed only things of sorcery.

Uirgae capio. Wand come.

Keldan's eyes met mine, and for a second they flashed blue, sadness beyond bearing in their depths. Then he jumped forward, his arm outstretched. *"Uirgae reditum."*

The remaining wand hung in the air and then flew back to Keldan.

My heart wrenched.

"Keldan, don't." Tyndale echoed my cry as he staggered through the chamber.

One hand still fisted around the altar's shard, Keldan caught the wand with his other and spun around to the Duke of Lofton as Tyndale stumbled to his uncle's side.

"You know what will happen if you use that wand," the duke said slowly, raising his hands as Tyndale stepped protectively in front of him. The duke slipped out to his side.

"There is no escape for a Called." Keldan uncurled his palm to reveal the small, jagged piece of altar. "Save one." The shard floated up and glided to the cask. "My lord Ackman ruined his body through the dark arts he used to increase his power. Yet he's desperate for more and believes that with the abilities of a half-magic his capacity for and control of magic could be unlimited. He thinks

Farro's invention will give him that." He raised the fractured black wand. "The Thief has the Demandez à Voir
mirror. *He* may choose not to give it to my lord Ackman."

His gaze locked on Tyndale. "But I am bound to obey
the sorcerer. I was ordered to steal the mirror, and I must
do everything in my power to see that it gets to Ackman."
He lunged forward, calling a spell of power. A flash shot
across the chamber, and the black wand cracked with a
flare that veiled Keldan.

Tyndale shoved the duke aside and took the burst
with my wand, absorbing and channeling the power that
would have destroyed an enchanter, or even a half-magic
without a wand's help. The burst disappeared with a
spray of color into my wand. Tyndale swayed and collapsed like a runner who'd run too far.

"David!" The duke caught his nephew and lowered
him to the floor, oblivious to all else. To the enchanters
quickly overtaking the remaining sorcerers. To the Thief
sprinting to the open gate, a bulge in his jacket testifying
that he carried the Demandez à Voir mirror that could
potentially lead Ackman to Emil Farro.

Marcel dashed after Damien as Young Jonathan slung
a spell at the Thief, but the half-magic used some remnant of power taken from his earlier sorcerer-accomplice
to catch the spell and shoot back a far worse one on each
of his followers. Young Jonathan ducked behind a shield,
and Marcel flattened to the ground. How could even an
enchanter fight a trained half-magic?

It doesn't work through a spell that can be stolen, Tyndale had said.

Sinking to the floor, I pulled the Amphora over my
head and set it down. My fingers spread over the worn
stone beside it but then recoiled at the sense of sorcery
tainting Henly. Rock would be hard enough to control,

much harder than water or earth, even without the sorcerers' lingering influence.

Raising my chin, I pressed my hand to the floor. "I am Gabriella Floraison, daughter of the Duke of Henly, master of Henly Manor and all its grounds. The sorcerer's altar is destroyed; they have no authority here." I took a deep breath. "Move."

The arch over the gateway shuddered and slid down to meet the wall rising from the floor.

Damien scudded to a halt and slammed his palm into the rising wall. "Open." He hit it again, but it ignored him. "Open," he screeched.

"Up," I whispered.

Stalagmites shot up around Damien, and he screamed as they encircled him.

"Leave the top open for air and uncover the gate."

The gateway reappeared. With a final punch to the stone, the legendary Magic Thief began to weep.

Slowly, almost in a daze, I rocked back on my heels and draped the Amphora over my neck, exhausted and ill from the draining use of magic and the lingering poison. Was it over?

Some yards away, the Duke of Lofton cradled his nephew to his chest. "How like your father you are, David. But even a half-magic can only collect so much. Let's get you fixed up."

It wasn't quite over.

"Gabriella." The familiar voice, the most beautiful one I knew, carried over the hum of activity between us.

Marcel picked himself up off the floor and started toward me as I, suddenly energized, sprang up to meet him. Then he collided with Young Jonathan. They tumbled to the floor, and I skidded to a stop.

Both apologizing, they helped one another up. Young Jonathan handed Marcel a pistol and took hold of his arm, asking him something. Marcel looked helplessly over his friend's shoulder at me but turned back to the enchanter.

"Sorry about letting Keldan sneak up on us like that." Young Jonathan scuffed the floor with the toe of his boot.

My fingers curled into my palm, though my scar no longer needed hiding. Steeling myself, I glanced at Keldan. He lay crumpled and still, his former master's wand beside him, broken. The fragments slowly collected themselves and gathered to the open cask like iron filings to a magnet. The green haze about the cask turned to a mourning gray as the dark fragments clouded together and dipped into the cask. My throat burned as I looked away, struggling under a strange mixture of sorrow for Keldan and anger at the Call, at whatever had induced Keldan to accept it, and at Keldan himself for all the evil he'd done.

"I should have been paying more attention," Young Jonathan said, dragging my thoughts away from the Called. "By the way, I think you should tell Farro about that grabbing-the-bullet thing," he continued. "It's a bit of a flaw."

"I will. Don't worry," Marcel said.

He looked up at Marcel, his head cocked. "For a non-magic, you handled all this really well. Are you sure you're not an enchanter?"

"I'm sure."

"Half-magic?"

Marcel shook his head and glanced at me. "Just an ordinary non-magic."

"Well, you don't seem ordinary. There's magic in your blood somewhere," he replied. Marcel merely smiled.

Sidestepping a smoldering section of cask, I drew near them.

"Nonetheless," he continued, "it was a pleasure to fight alongside you. If you'll excuse me, I need to get Stephan to the medic." He sniffed and peered at the smoke-obscured ceiling. "I hope someone puts out these fires."

"You know what they say about the one who notices what needs to be done ..." Marcel began with a smile.

Young Jonathan laughed, momentarily abashed. "You're right—he's the one who should do something about it. I'll help after I see to Stephan." They shook hands. Then the enchanter noticed me, favoring me with a pleased expression and a bow before he walked away.

I watched him go and then brushed my loose hair behind my ear and slowly turned to Marcel.

He stared at me, so many expressions chasing across his soot-stained face. "Gabriella."

His voice had a tug to it I felt all the way to my bones. My fingers tightened around a handful of skirt, and I focused somewhere over his right shoulder. *Think. What to say?* "You were right about the Magic Thief being a half-magic."

He nodded.

My gaze skittered over his face and then away to focus over his shoulder again. *Coward.* I toyed with my cuff. "Will your cousin be safe now that—" *Ackman's Called is dead, his plan ruined.* My throat thickened as I rubbed my fingertip. *Was there no other way to free a Called?* "I'm sure the Duke of Lofton will take care of Ackman soon, then your cousin will be safe."

Marcel took a step closer. "Emil will always be in danger so long as he continues with his inventions. But you're right about Ackman. With no Called and his wand broken, he won't be as much of a threat as he was." He paused, then added softly. "I'm sorry about Keldan. I wish we could have done something for him, but I think he knew what he was doing when he attacked Tyndale instead of Lofton."

My lip trembled, but I straightened and met Marcel's gaze. He held out his hand, and I moved to take it, but then my eye caught his ring finger, empty where his traveling ring should have been. Heat flushed my cheeks, and I drew back.

He'd tricked me. With a kiss. A stolen kiss.

Whatever expression crossed my face must have warned him of potential danger, for he stilled, and blushed. "Forgive me, Gabriella. I never should have—"

"Marcel Gustave." There's something endearing about a man who blushes. And who apologizes. And who risks his life for yours.

His eyebrows rose into his shaggy red bangs.

How I loved that plain face. "I'm glad you came back."

He laughed and met me in one stride, drawing me to his chest. I wrapped my arms around him as he kissed my hair. "Always, Gabriella."

"What's going on?"

We jumped apart at the bellow that echoed through the chamber.

Marcel's fingers brushed mine, and I slipped my hand into his. Mavern and Henry plowed into the chamber, dragging an unconscious, bound man between them. They tossed him down with the rest of the sorcerers.

Mavern wiped his hands on his handkerchief and looked around. "We've rounded up the duke's treasures, captured this fool by the wagons, and tied up a lion—that thanks to Henry's excellent bass voice and penchant for lullabies. What's left to do?"

His gaze searched the room and stopped to glower at me. Something in his countenance warned me my rank would offer no protection from the scolding he planned to give me for leaving the safety of the drawing room. The feeling was amplified by Henry's cowed look.

I squared my shoulders. I was a Floraison. He could not scold me like a scullery maid.

Mavern took note of my expression and appeared unimpressed. His gaze skipped on to Marcel. He looked away at no one in particular. "Ah yes. If anyone sees Lord Ellsworth, they might warn him to lie low for a while. Assistant Inspector Chead is back at the house, incensed to say the least, and threatening to hold the Duke of Henly responsible for the attack on himself and his colleague that resulted in Ellsworth's escape. He's determined to have the young baron for information on Farro's disappearance and for refusing to give a satisfactory explanation as to how he got into Farro's house the night of the attempted theft, or some such nonsense."

Marcel stiffened. The pallor of his face matched the bloodless feel of mine. I squeezed his hand.

"Well, what's left to do?" Mavern padded around the chamber, inspecting the sorcerers' bindings and putting out one of the remaining fires.

"You asked what to do," I spoke up, my voice weak from a sudden return of weariness. "There are several men here and in the tunnel who could use your assistance. I hope you brought the emergency kit." I held up the Amphora. "And I'll give you charge of the Thief's cell." I passed off the Amphora to Young Jonathan to give to Mavern.

Mavern blinked back surprise and darted another glance about the room before his gaze landed on Damien's enclosure. He strode to it. With a glance at us,

Henry followed Mavern. Marcel stared after them, the lifeless resignation in his eyes igniting as much frustration as concern. I wanted to shake the man.

"I'm sorry," he said at last, softly.

"For the trouble you've once more caused my family ... or for leaving again?"

A Floraison never gives up, Marcel. Nor should an Ellsworth.

He shook himself and gave me a sidelong glance. "Does the latter bother you?"

I gave him a look and pulled my hand away, but he snatched it back, the life back in his eyes.

"Gabriella, Carrington's not in good shape now, but in a few years, when—"

"There he is." Ryn ran up. With a sigh, I looped my arm through Marcel's.

"Ryn? Whatever are you doing here?" Surprise laced Marcel's voice as he reached to shake the boy's outstretched hand.

Almost quicker than the eye, Ryn caught Marcel's hand and tugged. "Come. Papa needs you."

He dragged us to his father and the duke. The medic in the dusty brown coat moved from them to the other men lying flat on their backs.

The duke gazed up at us, looking older and more careworn than I'd ever seen him. "You two have a funny way of staying safe and allowing me to deal with things." His lips curled in a smile that was tired but no less genuine for that. "But I told you to look after one another, didn't I? I suppose that takes precedence." He cocked his head to peer around us. "Mavern. Henry. You're here at last." His eyes narrowed as the two half-magics dragged Damien, bound and unconscious, beside the injured men and dumped him there.

Still pale from his earlier fight against the poison, Henry stepped up beside us. Marcel gripped his shoulder in a friendly gesture before Henry, with a smile of relief, handed me the Demandez à Voir mirror and the Amphora. I whispered my thanks, and he moved off to help the medic.

"There's plenty for you to do, Mavern." The duke gestured to the overworked medic and the injured on the floor.

The medic spotted us and rose stiffly, returning Marcel's ring to him with a look of gratitude that made my heart swell.

"I only brought a small emergency kit." Mavern frowned as he examined the injured men. "And I've already used some of it." He jerked his chin to Tyndale. "I'd use the rest of it on him and still not fix him up."

"You're not treating him for that reason." The duke fixed his gaze on Marcel, and I knew Marcel wouldn't be leaving with the security of his ring. "David's father will have to do it. It's not the way he wanted his son to return, but I dare say he'll be glad to have him back, nonetheless."

The duke grasped his nephew under the arms and began to lift him. Tyndale's head lolled with the movement. Marcel and Ryn grabbed Tyndale's arms, and, together, they raised him to his feet.

"Ellsworth," the duke said, "would you employ your ring to take my nephew to his parents?"

"Of course." Marcel didn't hesitate to pull off his ring.

"No, you *take* him." He draped Tyndale's arm over Marcel's shoulder and surrendered his weight. "You'll have to explain what happened to my sister and brother-in-law."

"But I can't take a passenger with the ring." Marcel glanced at me, his expression unreadable. But it wasn't hopeless or resigned. "And I have to turn myself over to Assistant Inspector Chead."

The duke pulled a signet ring from his own pocket. "That's a king's ring officially. It will take a wounded man a long way if the king's representative commands it, and assists it."

Marcel held out the ring, and the duke pressed the seal of his ring against Marcel's. A glint of light raced around the traveling ring, a hint of the power of enchantment the duke imbued it with. Beside me, Ryn watched with the stoic face only an urchin used to pain and sorrow can manage.

"What about Ryn?" I asked.

As if there had never been a question as to that, the Duke of Lofton answered, "I need him here to help me clean up things and then show me to his siblings. We will join his father later at my sister's." He tucked the signet ring away. "You must stay with them, too, Ellsworth, incognito, for a time. The Ceurians and the sorcerers won't give up easily."

"What about Chead's threat against the Duke of Henly?" Marcel asked.

"I have a solution for that." Mavern nudged Damien's leg, and the unconscious Thief bore the image of Marcel Ellsworth.

Marcel, after staring at his doppelganger for a moment, held out the traveling ring to the duke.

"You'll have to twist it," he said, "since I don't know where I'm going." He looked to Henry. "Don't start searching for a new employer yet, old friend."

"I won't," Henry said. "I'm still counting on that library you promised me."

"You'll get it." Marcel shifted, adjusting Tyndale's weight, and our eyes met. "Take care of Leah for me." He paused, opened his mouth again, but then shut it.

Say it.

The duke slipped the traveling ring on Tyndale's finger.

"And Gabriella," Marcel said in a rush, "in a couple of years, when Carrington's running smoothly—"

The duke twisted the ring. Marcel and Tyndale disappeared, leaving a lonely shadow on the floor that lingered half a second before realizing it, too, needed to go.

Ryn slipped my wand, my true wand, into my hand. "He was going to give it back."

"I know, Ryn." I slid the wand into its pocket. "He had need of it." Ryn sagged against me, a tired, frightened child, as I wrapped him in a hug. "You should come home with me tonight, while your great-uncle attends to details here."

"But he wanted my help."

"You can help tomorrow." The duke clasped Ryn on the shoulder, and Ryn stared up at him timidly, seeming to search for something in the duke's eyes. "You did well tonight, Ryn. I'm proud of you."

Whatever affection or acceptance Ryn was looking for he must have found, for he rushed into his great-uncle's arms, hugged him, and then stepped back to me.

The Duke of Lofton ruffled Ryn's hair. "Until tomorrow, nephew. And you, Lady Gabriella." With a look of appreciation, he joined the other enchanters.

Ryn's head dipped, then jerked up. He blinked. "Could I have something to eat? I wasn't hungry at dinner."

With a laugh, I took his hand and looked around for a certain person. "I'm sure we can find something in the kitchen." The man's head popped up. Was I the only one who wanted a hot bath to remove the dirt and blood and to soak away the aches? "Henry, will you walk us home?"

With a nod of approval from Mavern, Henry pushed to his feet from beside an enchanter moaning as he woke. "Walk?" he queried. "Sterling's out front. He didn't seem upset about anything when we arrived, only waiting."

"I can't imagine what reason he'd have to be upset," I said innocently. Henry cocked an eyebrow, and I held up my finger. Dried blood smeared the top. "Not anymore," I added with a twist of a smile.

Henry gave me an appraising look. "Marcel?"

I nodded with a pride that made me fear my heart would burst. "The toy wand."

"He always did want to use a wand." His chest rumbled with laughter as he offered me his arm. "Let's be off then. We left Harvey with Sarcodinas—against his will—to keep him out of a magics' fight. We'll pick him up on the way."

As I took Henry's arm, Ryn looked over his shoulder at the spot where two men very much cared for had disappeared. I squeezed his hand.

"Your father will heal," I said. "Soon you'll join him and his family, and you'll all live happily together."

He didn't respond at first, but then he slowly nodded, hope warring with the exhaustion in his eyes. "What about Lord Ellsworth?" he asked as we set out.

My heart skipped a beat. *The plain, bumbling Baron of Carrington.*

"'She caught the thief who stole her heart,'" Henry quoted from a children's story under his breath with a sideways glance at me.

"'And though for a time from the land he fled ...'" I whispered.

Henry smiled. "He'll be fine, Ryn."

With a kiss he'd sealed the vow: for her hand he would return.

I touched a hand to my lips and smiled.

Epilogue

And return he did.

The Magic Thief by Charlotte James

SEVERAL MONTHS LATER, ESTATE OF THE DUKE OF MARAM, BROTH-
ER-IN-LAW OF THE DUKE OF LOFTON
MARCEL ELLSWORTH

"ARE YOU SURE you'd rather not go outside and play?"
Turning from my perusal of the race of droplets
down the window, I resumed pacing around the
Duke of Maram's library. "It's raining, Ryn."

"I don't mind." He looked pointedly at the unfinished
letter on the table and the unopened book on the settee.
"Besides, you look restless. What's a little rain to adven-
turers?"

I looked at the letter and book as well. He had a point.

"You're staying inside and learning strategy, young
man." Mrs. Morcos's glare successfully guided Ryn's attention back to the chessboard between them. It also
kept me from agreeing with him.

"You claimed to be too old to play 'children's games'
with your siblings and grandparents," David's housekeeper and nanny continued, "so you're going to play a game
for mature minds."

"But that's not fair. I was going to *watch* them play."

"Who said life was fair? Hurry up and move." The
acerbity in the kindly old woman's tone proved more interesting than pacing or racing raindrops, inducing me to

perch on the settee to better observe the curious house-keeper.

Ryn made his move, then sat back and studied Mrs. Morcos as she contemplated the board. His expression grew solemn. "Are you mad at Papa for moving us here? You've been avoiding him ever since he recovered enough to leave his room. That's why we're in here, isn't it? Because Papa's with the others?"

My eyes widened, as did Mrs. Morcos's. She dropped her rook, barely catching it before it knocked over her own knight. "Nonsense," she spat, steadying the rocking knight. She took her time straightening each of her pieces. "It's lovely here," she continued in a softer tone. "Everyone's kind and loving and ... kind. I'm glad we're here and that your father's back with his family, back to using his real name, and that you children have a real family now." Her cheeks, which had gone pale, now blossomed like the reddest rose in Gabriella's gardens. She made a hasty move, two actually, and gestured for Ryn to take his turn.

Some grandmothers or women of such an age, have rosy cheeks due to rouge or years of being in the sun, but Mrs. Morcos's wrinkled face colored with all the fervor of a much younger woman's.

I leaned forward. She'd never let any of the half-magics in the family touch her beyond a gloved hand-shake, not even David. She was shy around the enchanters and, among the adults, seemed most comfortable with me, the non-magic.

Was she cursed, or disguised and in hiding? Did David know? Was he recovered enough to do something about it?

One corner of my mouth tilted up. Something told me he did know and would soon be ready to turn his attention to his enigmatic housekeeper.

"When we finish this match, Ryn, you can go play," Mrs. Morcos conceded softly, interrupting my conjectures.

Ryn's eyes lit up, then fastened on me.

"But not in the rain. Lord Ellsworth is not that restless."

The tightness in my chest urged me to argue, but I opted for a compromise. "How about a rousing game of table tennis?"

"Yes!" Allowing himself one triumphant cry, Ryn devoted his energies to finishing the match as quickly as possible, and I attempted to write my letter to my estate manager. I'd been secluded with David's family for months, and I'd grown to love them dearly. David's parents treated me as another son, as did Lofton and his wife. I was a beloved uncle to the children and glad to be so. Yet I was restless. Soon, Lofton said, I would be free to go. I prayed it would be so.

Damien's identity had been exposed after he was thrown into the Ceurian prison, when the disguise spell wore off. Unfortunately, the Ceurians were trying to sort things out in such a way that they could still drag me in to lead them to Emil Farro. It wasn't over for me yet, but many powerful men, enchanters among them, were working on my behalf. Lofton had even started the rumor that I was in hiding with Emil so that Inspector Olan's men wouldn't be constantly looking for me at Silvestris Castle and Carrington, harassing my family and friends there while doing so. So I was trapped here, confined to David's family circle, to prevent shattering the rumor.

I glanced down at my empty ring finger. I didn't need the traveling ring as proof I was loved and worthy anymore, and it was safer locked away in my room. It was too tempting to twist it. *To Henly Manor, wherever Gabriella is*, I wanted to command it. Thanks to Lofton's wife—whose kindness I could never praise enough—I was able to talk with Gabriella through a magical connection between Gabriella's father's Demandez à Voir mirror and the duchess's own mirror. The more I talked with Gabriella and the more I got to know her, the more I wanted to return to her.

"Who are *you* and what happened to you?" Ryn's excited question jolted me from my thoughts, and my mind quickly shuttled delayed messages through my consciousness. A knock on the door, Mrs. Morcos's approval of admittance, a door opening and in stepping ...

My gaze shot to the doorway, to the tall man with bright blue eyes staring at me from a monstrously hairy face. His clothes were that of a common laborer and dirty, though it looked as if he'd tried to brush them off.

"Giles! What on earth happened to you?" I jumped up and greeted my cousin, Prince Giles Bête, with a firm hug and a handshake. At the table, Mrs. Morcos let out a breath, no doubt relieved someone claimed this slim version of a talking bear who had invaded her sanctuary.

I made a quick introduction, and Ryn's eyes lit up, likely anticipating another explorer to go on adventures with around the estate. Giles refused a seat on account of his filthy condition, so we continued to stand.

"I repeat: what on earth happened to you?" I asked, then my stomach knotted. "Wait, haven't you been at Henly—"

Giles nodded quickly, urgently. "There's been a bit of an uproar at Henly."

My heart might as well have vanished, for it stopped beating. Had the sorcerers returned? Was Gabriella okay?

"All your fault, of course."

Catching the teasing glint in Giles's eyes, I reined in my galloping thoughts. "I'd be disappointed if I wasn't involved," I said drily. "Everyone is okay, I take it?"

"Maybe ..." He gave a devilish grin in response to my glare. "Or will be as soon as I get back."

I raised my eyebrows, fighting an equally devilish grin at the thought of Lady Alexandria—for he was surely referring to her—welcoming anyone in his state. What *had* happened during his month's stay there?

His expression sobered, deepening with brotherly affection and empathy. "Another young lady's condition would also be improved by a visit—from you."

Ryn said something about happily putting off our table tennis match if I'd give Gabriella a greeting from him. Mrs. Morcos's smile had a decidedly wistful character to it for half a moment before she hastily faced the chessboard again, her face drawn, as if all hopes and dreams had been sucked out of her.

I understood the feeling. Though warmed by Giles's confidence in Gabriella's affection, the spike of joy he'd brought was short-lived. Lofton would never allow it.

"I spoke with the Duke and Duchess of Lofton when I came in and wheedled three hours of freedom for you," Giles said, earning him the status of favorite cousin. "Well," he amended, "the duchess wheedled it for you, but I suggested it and promised to look after you. You're to stay out of sight to all but the immediate family. The Duke of Henly knows now what you did for Gabriella. He won't be angry to see you. On the contrary, I should think."

My exclamations of shock and gratitude were cut short as Giles hurried on, "Don't think I'm doing this solely for your benefit, you know. ... You ... you know how Alexandria and Gabriella are together quite a bit and ... well ... and ..."

My eyebrows rose again. Giles was as confident as the cold Lady Alexandria and never hesitated in his speech.

"I'd ... uh ... like a moment alone with Lady Alexandria to sort out a misunderstanding." He pushed the words out, his neck reddening.

Giles unsure of himself and blushing like Mrs. Morcos. I had a few hours of freedom to see Gabriella. Life was full of wonders, indeed. And wonderful.

THE GARDENS AT HENLY MANOR
GABRIELLA FLORAISON

"It's not a dream then. Or a doppelganger. You really are here." I gazed up at Marcel, my face surely expressing a level of joy any unengaged woman would be embarrassed to admit to. But the strange restlessness of the past few months was gone, as was the loneliness I'd expected. He'd come back for me, as he'd promised.

Marcel drew me closer to his side as we wandered the gardens, radiant with blooming roses and other summer flowers. "Did you doubt I'd come back?"

"Did you doubt I'd welcome you?"

"I wouldn't dare." He winked at me. "After all, I *did* save your life. By rights, you should be madly in love with me, and I wouldn't impugn your honor by supposing you'd cast me off for another in the few months I've been away."

"But Henry also saved my life," I said archly, stepping away from him purportedly to admire a particularly beautiful rose, creamy white with a sunset pink setting off its edges, like the horizon at dusk. I cocked my head to look back at him. "Am I to be madly in love with both of you?"

"You definitely should not," he growled. Taking my hand, he tugged me back to his side with a look clearly indicating that was where I belonged. I made no argument to that, and we resumed the rose-lined path. "That does present a problem, though," he said in mock seriousness. "I'll have to come up with some other reason you should be rapturously happy to see me. Unless you have one you'd like to offer?"

You are not going to make me say it first, Marcel Ellsworth. Pursing my lips, I raised my chin and looked away, trailing my fingers along the soft moss clinging to the walls of the sunken walk. "What about the reasons you should be happy to return to me? After all, *I* rescued *you*. Are you not madly in love with me?"

We slowed as we neared the raised walkway arching over our path, stopping in the coolness of shadows under the rose-drenched bridge.

"In love with you?" Marcel released my arm. Taking both my hands in his, he stepped back and looked me up and down, the teasing glint in his eyes belying his contemplative mien. "Well, now that you mention it, you *are* the perfect height. I have to agree with Mavern there."

I glared a warning at him, and he grinned. But then the teasing look faded, and he pulled me into his arms, hugging me to him.

"But you are the perfect height," he said softly as I relaxed against him, leaning my head against his chest and wrapping my arms around him. "Neither too tall nor too short." He kissed my hair. "And the perfect age. And beautiful." He looked down at me, a tenderness in his eyes I couldn't mistake for mere friendship, even if I'd wanted to. "Would you be pleased if I told you it was love at first sight?"

"It is highly flattering, I'm told." I hugged him tighter. *If coming from the right man.*

"That's a pity, because it wasn't."

Surprised, I tilted my head back to better search his face. His expression was serious, and a bit concerned at my shock, I suspected.

"Oh, I admit I thought you the most beautiful woman I'd ever seen and perhaps the one I wanted to love," he assured me, salvaging my feminine pride. "But I didn't truly love you until I'd actually gotten to know you, to know your courage and kindness, your virtue and honor, your scars and struggles. Then I was ... hopeless."

He paused as if considering, and though I very much wanted to give him the gift he'd just given me, to tell him how much I loved him, I knew I needed to hear him out first. But I could give him a nudge. "Hopelessly in love, I trust?"

He smiled down at me, a wealth of meaning in his voice. "Very much so."

"I'm glad," I whispered. "No one should be hopeless." I met his gaze. "Unless they're hopelessly in love."

"That's a state I know all about, thanks to you. ... Do you mind?" His gaze intensified, and I knew what he was asking. He didn't need a lengthy speech that would probably only get interrupted anyway, if history were to repeat itself. His expression, given strength by his actions of the past, was as much a declaration of the depth of his affection and desire of sharing a life with me in marriage as any elaborate, bended-knee proposal.

I don't mind at all. I shook my head. Then I realized how that gesture could be misconstrued and started to reassure him, but I hesitated, the seriousness of what I was about to say demanding a pause. But this wasn't a hasty decision for either of us. For months, I'd known and respected the kind of man he was, and our friendship had only deepened as we'd communicated during his absence, making his plain face the handsomest one I knew.

Despite the butterflies in my stomach and even a hint of fear, I raised my gaze to his. "I think it's the perfect state for two."

He gently cupped my face. "For you and me?"

"For you and me."

"Wisdom is definitely one of the Floraison virtues," he said. And then he kissed me, but it wasn't hopeless at all, but full of hope, for our future.

"Gabbie Marie!"

Marcel and I startled and drew apart, but he kept an arm securely around my waist, as if signaling he wasn't disappearing this time. I covered his hand with mine and scowled at the tall, thickly-built man tromping down the pathway toward us.

Of all the impudent servants ...

"That had better be Lord Ellsworth with you."

... Harvey was my favorite.

Acknowledgements

THANK YOU, THANK you, to you and you and you. A paraphrase of a line from "So Long Farewell" from Rodgers and Hammerstein's *The Sound of Music* is running through my head. Both the original "adieu" and my "thank you" are equally applicable, but for the moment, I'll stick to the paraphrase of gratitude. I have all the usual folks to thank—my beloved family and church family for putting up with me and encouraging me and patiently answering my questions about which blurb or cover design or so on. And for asking me when my next book was coming out—I needed the push. There's also my longtime, invaluable critique partners and friends Susan Donetti and Lucy Thompson. I can't begin to thank you for your efforts and patience over the lengthy development of this story. Thanks as well to the members of ACFW Scribes 224—lots of applause to my Ever Afters—Scribes 245, and Scribes 250 for your critiques and encouragement. A special thanks to my beta readers Sabyl Broset, Laurie Lucking, and Katie Cook. The fact that you took the time to read my lengthy manuscript makes me very happy. That you truly enjoyed it and offered valuable feedback makes me very, very happy. Leesa Barnes, my talented friend, I th-thank you for lending your professional expertise to the cause of making Marcel's stuttering more accurate.

And dear reader, here's a spot for you, _____, for giving your time and attention to the story of the bumbling Baron of Carrington and the lovely Lady Gabriella Floraison (soon to be Lady Gabriella Ellsworth).

About the Author

E.J. KITCHENS loves tales of romance, adventure, and happily-ever-afters and strives to write such tales herself. When she's not thinking about dashing heroes or how awesome bacteria are—she is a microbiologist after all—she's enjoying the beautiful outdoors or talking about classic books and black-and-white movies. She lives in Alabama.

To find out about E.J. Kitchens's upcoming releases, visit her website, www.ElizabethJaneKitchens.com, and sign up for her newsletter.

Books by E.J. Kitchens

The Magic Collectors

THE ROSE AND THE WAND

TO CATCH A MAGIC THIEF

Short stories

HOW TO HIDE A PRINCE
(TALES OF EVER AFTER: A FELLOWSHIP
OF FANTASY ANTHOLOGY)

THE SEVENTH CROWN

A SPELL'S END
(ENCIRCLED ANTHOLOGY)

Adventure and romance are only a page away.

Made in the USA
Lexington, KY
09 November 2019